THE DAY COYOTE DANCED

A SUSPENSE NOVEL
OF RELIGION, EMPIRE
AND A SILENT COUP

by

PETER REYNOLDS

The Day Coyote Danced

A Great Divide Book

Borderland North Publishing

https://www.borderlandnorth.com

ISBN 978-0-9629261-6-7
First published 2017 v.1.1.

All characters and events in this book are fictional except for the Goddess, the Black Madonna, and Our Lady of Guadalupe.

Every book has people who have made it better.
I especially want to thank my development editors
Maria Janta, Jane Mickelson, and Nicole Sault.

Organizations, Staff Members

and Principal Characters

EarthRage
Jack Adair   *journalist & founder*
Renato Ocampo-Mendoza   *scholar & fugitive socialist*
Amadeus, Deirdre, The Hoosier   *activists*
El Tigre, Constanza   *safe house leadership*

The Fellowship of the Eighth Dispensation
Dr. Duane Boone III   *televangelist & founder*
Dean Weed   *executive director*
Orville Fuller   *liaison to Krator*

Kelly's Family
Kelly Grazziella   *a firefighter*
Giovanni   *Kelly's friend*
Joe Grazziella   *Kelly's father*

The Krator Corporation
Vaughn MacVain   *attorney & founder*
Tricia Culhane   *special assistant*
Wassily Tweecus   *chief scientist*
Celestine Brittle   *predictive criminality analyst*

888th Special Operations Brigade
General G. Lyle Acre   *commanding officer*
Chad Weed   *civilian contractor*
Acre's adjutant   *psychological warfare officer*

The Council of Seventeen
The Chairman
"Skipper" Van Squint   *the nation's top spin doctor*

Coyote

The Goddess

BOOK I

THE SILENT COUP

1

THE RUBICON POINT

> The Rubicon Point is that moment in a nation's history when the empire absorbs the republic. Once that point is reached, practices and policies developed for the borderland become acceptable in the homeland.

> *The Digital Surveillance State*
> by Renato Ocampo-Mendoza

Jack Adair opened his eyes, straining to focus in the lattice of sun and shade cast by the ragged weave of the wall.

He listened for the soothing sound of the surf—but the beat was too loud, its rhythm dissonant.

Then in the lull between the waves the cadence of the captain's stride and the faster pace of unfamiliar feet.

A firm hand parted the fronds that formed the door, and two men stepped into the shadows, their features masked by the glare of azure sky behind them. One of the men moved forward, blocking the daylight—it was a cheerful, sun-tanned face, the Australian captain of the EarthRage launch.

"You look bloody wasted, mate," the captain told him. "Time to get up. We've got a paying customer here."

The other figure stepped into the circle of light made by the missing thatch in the roof. He was a short, wiry, Mexican man with thick, black hair and the joi de vivre of a tax collector. He seemed out of place on a surfer beach the morning after a party.

"Are you Jack Adair?" the Mexican man asked, with the look of someone who had expected more. "The guerrilla journalist?" he clarified.

The appellation caught Jack Adair by surprise. Digging his toes into the sand like a crab, he managed to stand up, waiting for his mind to catch up with his body. His sun-bleached hair was grainy with sand, his blue eyes red with fatigue. He adjusted his swimsuit as if it were a necktie. "*Mucho gusto,*" he said, proffering his hand.

"How do you do?" the Mexican man replied in English, shaking it firmly. "I am Renato Ocampo-Mendoza. I understand you have the most powerful motor launch on the beach."

Mr. Ocampo was younger than his formal bearing suggested but with an earnest yet somewhat distracted demeanor. He was dressed as if he had come from an art exhibit, in a stylish, long-sleeved shirt and tailored slacks, both of good-quality cloth.

"Mr. Ocampo took the overnight bus from Mexico City," the captain explained.

Jack Adair cupped his hands around his eyes and squinted through the shaggy palms of the palapa to the bright, blue ocean beyond. The Pacific looked as tempting as it did almost every morning, but the rhythm of the waves made the surfer in him nervous.

"There's a hurricane coming," he reminded the captain.

"Yes, but it's heading north by northwest," the captain said. "We can take him out before the weather hits. He has agreed to the charter rate."

Jack Adair wondered if EarthRage was being set up for a drug bust.

"Fernando told me to give you this," the visitor explained. He held out a twenty peso coin, one minted in 2001 for the new millennium. On one side, heralded by the Spanish words for "new fire," the Aztec god of the sun danced the next cycle of earthly years inside of an eight-pointed compass rose.

The guerrilla journalist took the coin and examined it. Then he placed it god-side up against the crystal of his wristwatch, a matte-black chronometer with an analog dial. He aligned the northern point of the compass rose on the coin with the number twelve on his watch dial as Fernando had told him. He read the time indicated by two nearly invisible dots etched on the coin. It matched the time he was expecting. He mentally squared the hour and minutes, then added the two numbers together: 202.

Jack Adair wondered if his visitor had murdered Fernando and pocketed the coin. "Did Fernando give you a reservation number?" he asked, a grave expression on his face.

"Yes: 202," the visitor replied.

Jack Adair casually slipped the coin into the zipper pocket of his swimsuit.

"You'd better get her ready," he told the captain.

"Right," the Aussie said. He nodded at the visitor: "*Hasta luego*, mate."

"We'll need to get our feet wet," the guerrilla journalist informed his visitor. He walked down to the water line, then turned to see if the Mexican man was behind him. Ocampo was still at the palapa, taking off his shoes and socks. Jack Adair waded out into waist-deep water. He plunged his head in the ocean and sloshed it around—when he came up for air, his hangover had drowned.

His visitor was waiting in the splash zone, looking tentatively at the white froth washing around his ankles. Adair came back to the water's edge and stood next to Ocampo, apparently staring out to sea. He waited until a big wave hovered over the sand, then asked his question as it crashed.

"This excursion, where do you want to go?"

His visitor waited until the next wave broke.

"Fernando said you know the best places."

The surf boomed. "Maybe a short excursion…"

"Sure."

He assessed his client. "Do you have any other clothes?"

"You mean beach clothes? Like T-shirts?" The visitor furrowed his brow. "No. All I brought is books."

"Where is your luggage?"

Renato Ocampo-Mendoza gestured toward the palapa. "Over there."

"Then there's no reason to hang around. Let's get your gear."

Jack Adair hefted Ocampo's suitcase, assessing the weight. "Books, you say? It's as heavy as gold bricks," he laughed, putting it back down.

"They're gold to me," his visitor replied.

"I'd love to see them."

Ocampo opened the suitcase. Aside from toiletries and a change of clothes, all of the space was filled with books. Any one of the titles could land the reader on a watch list.

"It's the lending library for the Young Socialist Alliance," Ocampo explained. "You can read these without being traced."

Jack Adair took out several books at random and pretended to thumb through them, making sure they were not hollowed out and filled with cocaine.

"We'll have to wade through the surf to get to the boat," Jack Adair said. "Lucky for you, I have an extensive wardrobe." He reached for the only article of attire in the palapa, a pair

6

of board shorts hanging on a nail. "Put these on. Your clothes go in the suitcase, so they'll stay dry."

Jack Adair perched the suitcase on his shoulder as if it were made of styrofoam, then slogged up the beach toward the next headland. Ocampo, awash in baggy shorts, struggled to keep up.

"It's almost low tide, so we can just make it," Jack Adair announced, wading into the water.

"They can't get wet."

"Don't worry, I won't drop them."

The founder of EarthRage often doubled as the guide on tours to threatened habitats of endangered species. With a practiced eye, he monitored his companion's progress, at one point taking his arm and gently guiding him through the surf. As they rounded the headland, they were protected from the full force of the waves by a spine of dark rocks further out, but the frothy surge reached almost to Ocampo's chest. Beyond the headland, the broad, sandy beach gave way to a crescent-shaped cove with calmer water. Streaks of broken shell glistened in the transparent shallows like mother of pearl. The EarthRage launch, the *Green Wave*, was riding just beyond the breakers, waiting to pick them up.

"May I introduce our deck hand, Memo?" Jack Adair said, handing off the luggage to a muscular man in his forties, his skin tanned dark as leather.

Memo put the suitcase into a waterproof bag like an oversized Ziploc. When the luggage was sealed in, he handed Ocampo a life jacket and a boogie board with a rope attached.

"Here's the plan," Jack Adair told his visitor, helping him to put on the life jacket. "I wade out to the boat, and you ride on the boogie board. You just have to hold on tight. I'll do the rest."

Ocampo nodded agreement. From the beach, it seemed like something that even a hydrophobic urbanite could do. But when put into practice, it meant floating at eye level into an oncoming wall of water. Then just at the point where the wave threatened to drown you, it passed harmlessly below, revealing a file of menacing waves behind it. Beyond the surf, the beach dropped off sharply, to the point that not even Jack Adair could wade. He swam the last ten meters, with Ocampo bobbing behind him, clutching the board as if it were trying to escape.

The Australian captain grabbed Ocampo under the arms and lifted him into the boat like an anchor, while Jack Adair pulled himself over the gunwale. Memo arrived a moment later, towing the floating bag full of books like a raft.

A pair of powerful engines ignited in a puff of acrid smoke.

"Where are we going?" the captain shouted to the founder of EarthRage.

"Let's show him some blue water," Jack Adair shouted back.

He turned to his visitor. "It *is* the fastest boat on the beach," he said proudly. "We can overtake any poacher."

The *Green Wave* turned slowly, then surged forward, heading out to sea. Jack Adair put on dark glasses and made himself comfortable under the shade of a nylon tarp. Renato Ocampo-Mendoza joined him.

"Can we can talk here?" Ocampo asked.

The guerrilla journalist nodded affirmatively. The rush of the wind and the throb of the engines made it impossible for even the captain or the deck hand to overhear their conversation.

"I'm surprised that EarthRage is allowed to operate in the open," Ocampo said.

"The Mexican environmental authorities are glad that we're here—we say what they would like to say but can't."

The visitor nodded agreement. "I subscribe to your newsletter."

"Then you know what we're up against," Jack Adair said. "We keep a parade of foreign dignitaries passing through on our ecotours. It's our life insurance policy."

"Fernando said you are good at balancing on a fast-moving board."

Jack Adair fixed his visitor with an inquisitive stare. "How long have you known Fernando?"

"I've known him since we were in primary school together," Ocampo replied.

"Remember that skinny, little chihuahua he used to own?"

"Ulysses?"

"That's the name!" The guerrilla journalist laughed, remembering how he used to tickle its stomach. "I remember the day he got it—it had been hit by a car in Mexico City, and he nursed it back to health."

Ocampo gave him a quizzical look. "Wasn't it Cuernavaca?"

"You're right. It *was* Cuernavaca" Jack Adair took off his sunglasses, studying Ocampo with intense blue eyes. "Why did Fernando tell you to come?"

"One, to warn EarthRage. And two, he told me that you would help me to disappear."

Jack Adair waited for more.

Renato Ocampo-Mendoza chose his words carefully. "The government of the United States is planning a phony terrorist attack. All dissidents will be rounded up, like they did in Chile under Nixon."

"Ah yes, September 11, 1973." Jack Adair did not look surprised. "When is this event supposed to happen?"

"Next Wednesday."

Jack Adair's jaw hardened. A week was not much time to cash in his chips.

"Did Fernando tell you to tell me this?"

"Yes."

Jack Adair stared at the sea, his eyes focused on infinity. Then he looked at Ocampo to continue.

"Fernando said that the U. S. attorney general will use his emergency powers to privatize all police, military, and espionage functions," Ocampo related. "Then the United States will be hollowed out—its assets looted and moved offshore."

"That's happening already. What's your part in this?"

"I am a doctoral candidate in philosophy at the People's University of Mexico. But I am also the liaison between the socialist community and Journalists Without Beds."

"What about Journalists Without Beds? Do they believe the story?"

"They believe it—they have already dispersed their assets. Fernando himself has left Mexico City. The *gringos* need to close down any independent journalism before the event."

"And what about you? What do you want to do?"

"I want to stay in Mexico."

"You won't blend into a beach town," Jack Adair laughed, putting his sunglasses back on.

"I know. It's a problem."

"How long do you think you'll need to be underground?"

"The Mexican government is pro-Washington right now. But you know Washington—they're so ignorant and heavy-handed they're bound to do something that will alienate their Mexican support. I give them two years at the most."

Jack Adair smiled. Ocampo had no illusions about the leadership of the Free World. And the timetable sounded right.

"They keep this boat under constant surveillance," the guerrilla journalist said. "I bet your mug lights up their screens like Las Vegas on New Years Eve."

Ocampo looked more earnest than before.

"But we can use that to your advantage," Jack Adair said. "Now that you're an experienced boogie boarder!"

He got up and moved forward to confer with the captain.

"Where are we heading?" the captain asked him.

"Acapulco."

"Acapulco! What about the party at De Las Locas tonight?"

"Forget the party—the game has changed. Take the boat to Acapulco after Mr. Ocampo and I go ashore. We'll be getting off after dark. Do you think you can find two more passengers to replace us before first light?"

"No worries."

"A tall one and a short one. Dress the short one in Mr. Ocampo's clothes. And put the other in my poncho and brimmed hat."

"All right."

"When you get to Acapulco, sell the boat for the best price you can get for it."

"Sell it?"

"Yes, for cash. Several people have made offers to buy it—I'll give you their names. Make sure you have the money in your pocket by next Tuesday."

The captain's face turned grave. "Foul weather?"

Jack Adair nodded. "Do you still have a brother living in Bangkok?"

"I do."

"You ought to go visit him. No later than Tuesday."

"All right. Will I see you again?"

Jack Adair put his hand on the captain's shoulder. "Sure. EarthRage isn't going belly up; it just needs to lie low for awhile. Some day it will have an Australian branch!"

"What do I do with the money when I sell the *Green Wave*?"

"I think we're a little behind on your salary," Jack Adair admitted.

"I reckon about six months."

"Pay your salary and Memo's severance. Put whatever is left in a safe place."

"All right," the captain agreed.

"Do you remember the beach where the illegal dumpers shot at you?"

"Bloody right, I do."

"Take us there tonight. We have a brief window between the weather and the change in tide. We'll use the inflatable to make the landing."

The captain looked Jack in the eye. "You be careful, mate."

"I'm always careful," he laughed. "And when I'm not I'm lucky!"

After nightfall, the captain reversed course and returned to a point they had passed earlier. The *Green Wave*'s low-slung profile made it almost invisible to radar, but the boat's sonic signature was well known to the surveillance buoys that the Americans had deployed in Mexican waters. The captain cut the engines, allowing the current to carry them closer to their destination. With thick cloud and no moon, the only light was a strand of street lamps on the coast road.

"The drone detector is showing zero," the captain whispered. "We're good to go."

Even Ocampo could tell that the waves were running higher now, the peaks closer together—evidence of the approaching storm.

Jack Adair turned to Ocampo and explained the plan in a whisper. "You and I are going ashore. Right about there," he said, pointing into the darkness. "But we'll travel in style: we'll be in a rubber boat. Once we land, EarthRage will get you some decent cover."

The drumbeat of surf grew louder, and Jack Adair cocked his head, listening to the rhythm of the waves.

"Let's get ready," he told the deck hand.

In the faint beam of a filtered flashlight, Memo untied the raft and slipped it silently into the ocean. Jack Adair stepped into it and gestured for the waterproof sack containing the suitcase full of books.

Ocampo's feet felt for contact in the darkness below, his eyes searching for a surface in the wan circle of red. The neoprene floor yielded under his weight, and he fell backwards into a nylon net stretched across the bow of the raft. With feigned sangfroid, he sat upright on the taut netting, clutching the guide ropes with both hands.

The raft rose and fell ominously with the storm swell.

"What happens if I fall out?" he whispered.

Jack Adair gave a wry grin. "Don't worry, you're wearing a life vest. It's an incoming tide. The waves will just roll you around like a soccer ball and toss you onto the beach!"

2

THE MISSING MADONNAS

Two Years Later...

On the eightieth floor of Lone Star Christian Tower, Dean Weed emerged from the elevator with a brisk and confident stride. Through floor-to-ceiling windows of tinted glass, the reflective facades of downtown Dallas stared back with empty eyes.

Dean Weed was tall and angular, a silver-haired man in his early sixties with a flawless EKG and the prostate gland of someone ten years younger. He was proud of the fact that he had never touched coffee, tobacco, or alcohol, not even in the army. Now he was the executive director of the Fellowship of the Eighth Dispensation, the most powerful religion in the Free World.

"Mr. Fuller is waiting in your office," his secretary told him.

Orville Fuller was curled like a ferret in one of the upholstered leather chairs. He was a slightly-built man with suspicious eyes and a salesman's too-eager smile.

He was the Fellowship's liaison to the Krator Corporation, the private security firm that managed police and espionage functions in the Free World.

"How nice to see you," Dean Weed said, sitting down opposite. "What brings you to Dallas?"

"A meeting with the Advisory Board. I thought I'd drop by and say hello."

"I appreciate it. How's the weather in Colorado Springs?"

"Hot—too hot."

"When I was a boy, my family used to vacation there. Pike's Peak had snow on it in those days."

Dean Weed was trying not to notice Fuller's unconvincing brown toupee.

"I hear the expanded program in Mexico is going great," Orville Fuller said, nervously patting his hair.

"Yes, indeed, we've established assemblies throughout the northern third of the country," Dean Weed beamed. "And we're expanding the Young Mexico rallies in Mexico City."

"The work of the Lord always inspires me."

Orville Fuller cleared his throat, summoning the strength to approach a painful subject.

Dean Weed encouraged him with a look of bland attention.

"The other day, I talked with the Krator chief of station for Mexico, and he brought me up to date on the terrorist situation there," Fuller said. "There's been a resurgence of support for banned terrorist groups like EarthRage."

"I'm not familiar with that organization."

"It was founded by a renegade American named Jack Adair."

The executive director's face indicated his lack of familiarity with the name.

"He's one of 'America's Worst Traitors,'" Fuller explained, citing a popular television show that demonized critics of the regime.

"Why don't they just arrest him?"

"I asked the chief of station about that, and he said that we don't have his biometrics."

"I thought you said Jack Adair is an American citizen?"

"He is," Fuller replied. "He was born to White American parents in Mexico. And the U.S. embassy there got the DNA sample, fingerprints, and retinal scan as required of all citizens. But the samples in the national database belong to a European man of about the same age."

Dean Weed's face flickered his concern and disapproval. "Does Krator have an explanation?"

"Krator thinks he hired a proxy. Anyway, the chief of station says there's a new group called the Mexican Cultural Heritage Society that has been publicly accusing the Fellowship of stealing art from Catholic churches."

"Is that some leftist front?"

"No, their members include the heads of prominent museums, archaeologists, patrons of the arts—all of them influential people."

Dean Weed listened intently. Up until now, only the Mexican police had shown any interest in the thefts—and that half-heartedly.

"And there's some evidence that Jack Adair's organization, EarthRage, is joining forces with this Mexican Cultural Heritage Society—that could be trouble for us."

"The Mexican police have been very cooperative, and I am sure that they will find no involvement by the Fellowship whatsoever."

"Well, since Troy Oil took over management of the Mexican oil fields, there's been an anti-American backlash in that country."

"Troy Oil was invited in by the Mexican government to protect infrastructure from acts of sabotage by terrorists," Dean Weed announced as if reading from a press release.

"That may be, but the Krator chief of station thinks we need to squash this partnership between EarthRage and the Heritage Society before it gets off the ground."

"So you're saying that we need to take precautions in the light of the changed political situation?"

"That's right."

"I will be talking with Duane later today. I will mention your concerns to him directly."

Dean Weed stood up and laid a fatherly hand on Fuller's shoulder. "Thank you for bringing this to my attention. And let me know immediately if you hear anything more about threats to our programs in Mexico."

Dancing Coyote Ranch

Deirdre was working in the old adobe when she heard the distinctive chug of Amadeus's poorly-patched muffler. Amadeus is the son of a prominent surgeon, but he left medical school after only a year to take a degree in theology. Now he served as associate pastor to a progressive congregation in a racially-mixed neighborhood in Laredo, Texas. Once a week, he drove from Laredo to Dancing Coyote Ranch where he gave Bible lessons to the handicapped children who attended the four-week programs of horseback riding, roping, and round-ups.

Afterwards, Amadeus always stopped by the old adobe to visit with Deirdre, the camp's director. The old adobe is a cubical shed of sun-hardened clay built over a century ago. Without electricity or plumbing, there is no easy way to wire it for surveillance devices, while the walls are so thick that wifi signals cannot penetrate—both Deirdre and Amadeus talk almost freely there.

Amadeus knocked twice on the heavy wooden door: one dot, one dash, cued by the force of the blow.

It was answered by Deirdre's smile and the glint of her sea green eyes.

She was dressed in her work clothes—tight blue jeans, cowboy boots, and a Western-style shirt with pearl snaps down the front, her long red hair tied back with a mock turtle shell comb.

The back wall of the old adobe faces miles of unfenced cattle range uncluttered by trees or buildings. On one side, a single small window looks out on to an exterior wall made of steel plate. The steel panels were cut from discarded shipping containers that Deirdre had found in Corpus Christi. An architect had arranged the panels in a pleasing geometrical design that belies the frugal source of the construction materials. With the wall in place, there is no line-of-sight to the window from anywhere on the ranch.

Amadeus was toting a scuffed, cowhide briefcase that used to belong to a country lawyer. As he methodically undid the straps and buckles Deirdre could imagine him as the doctor he had been slated to become.

"I found more background information on the theft of the Catholic religious art," Amadeus said.

He handed Deirdre a double-spaced manuscript about a dozen pages long.

"What's this?" she asked, pointing to a paragraph on the cover page printed in antique type.

"It's a facsimile of a royal decree from 1559, by Queen Elizabeth the First, ordering destruction of the English artistic heritage. I think it conveys the flavor of the iconoclasts."

Deirdre read it through silently, her quizzical face framed by fine red hair:

> that they [agents of the Crown] shal take away,
> vtterly extinct and destroy all Shrines, coueryng
> [coverings] of Shrines, al Tables, Candlesticks,
> Tryndalles, and rolles of waxe, pictures, payntinges
> [paintings], and all other monumentes of faigned
> myracles [feigned miracles], pylgrimages,
> idolatrie, and superstition, so that there remayn
> no memorie of the same in walls, glasse wyndows,
> or els where, within their Churches and houses....

The Puritans had long been a mystery to Deirdre, and she had once asked Amadeus to explain their religious rationale for witch hunts and iconoclasm. She had forgotten what he had said about their theology but she did remember his wisecrack—"the founders of the New England colonies were the Taliban of their day."

"Funny you should bring this to me now," Deirdre mused. "I was just about to tell you that a truckload of religious icons crossed the border at Laredo."

"A truckload!"

She opened her day pack and retrieved an official document. "You will find this interesting. It's a printout of the customs manifest. It itemizes everything in the truck."

As Amadeus studied it, his expression changed from surprise to interest to concern.

"These are all images of the Virgin Mary." he exclaimed. "The Fellowship of the Eighth Dispensation has got to be involved in this. It has a special hatred of images that portray the divine as female."

"They're identified as reproductions on the manifest, but they could be the ones stolen from Mexican churches."

"Yes, claiming that they're reproductions would be a good way to import them."

"They were imported under a U.S. Custom's SENTRI pass too—talk about proof!" she exclaimed.

19

At the time of 9/11, over four million trucks a year crossed the Mexican border, and it proved impractical to search every vehicle. The United States government developed a plan to give shipping companies access to high-speed traffic lanes where customs checks were at best cursory. It was called SENTRI for "Secure Electronic Network for Travelers' Rapid Inspection." Once installed, it did not take long for shippers of contraband to recognize the advantages of using the fast lane.

"They are either very arrogant or very careless."

"Probably both," she said.

He thumbed through the document looking for an address. "Do we know where the truck was going?"

"Our contact person also gave us this," she said, returning to her desk and handing him the bill of lading.

He read the address out loud: "The Glass Nativity Gallery, Inc., Houston."

"I looked it up on the Web. It's from a well-known dealer in folk art with retail outlets in major U.S. cities. Their corporate headquarters are in Los Angeles. Houston is their distribution center."

"The detail in this is amazing," he said. "These descriptions could be used to identify stolen objects."

"At least they're not burning them," she added hopefully.

He did not look consoled. "Did you have to pay for this document?"

"No, it's a favor from someone we've helped."

"Has 'he' seen it yet?"—both Amadeus and Deirdre refrained from speaking Jack Adair's name out loud.

Yes, she nodded. "I put it in the pipeline as soon as I got it."

Amadeus nodded in satisfaction.

"And how is the 'tour guide' business going?" he asked, forming his fingertips into quotation marks as he spoke.

His question made her think of the Hoosier.

20

* * *

One morning, Deirdre found a man, his wife, and their baby sleeping in the old adobe. His broad face had been contoured by smile lines that had since been eroded by worry. His wife's fearful eyes peered out from under a curtain of dark hair that hung down to her waist like a damp towel. Even the child was quiet, although pink-cheeked and well scrubbed.

"Don't worry Ma'am, we're just leaving," he said.

"Where have you come from?" Deirdre asked.

"Indianapolis."

"And where are you going?"

He seemed at a loss for words.

Deirdre realized they were refugees.

"Have you had breakfast?" she asked rhetorically. "Wait here. I'll get you some."

The man was a union organizer who had worked in an American assembly plant of a Chinese shoe manufacturer. He said that one day after work he had tried to fill a prescription using a health plan number when the clerk informed him that the number did not exist. Then, through a series of embarrassing commercial transactions, he discovered that all of his other identification numbers had disappeared too.

"What did you do?" Deirdre asked.

He mimicked the bored passivity of a corporate functionary: "This call may be recorded for your protection. Press 1 for English. Press 2 for Spanish. If you are filing an 'erroneous termination' form, please press 3.

"You have reached Erroneous Termination. Our customer service representatives are receiving an unprecedented number of calls. Please stay on the line, and your call will be answered in the order in which it was received.

"And they don't tell you that the 'customer service' reps are linked into loops of toll-free numbers that always return to the starting point."

He told her that his driver's license, insurance, and car registration numbers had all vanished. Even his bank accounts were frozen shut, but the regime did not want to convert creditors into allies of the victim, so with appropriate paperwork, money could be freed up for the payment of debts.

Deirdre had heard rumors of the revocation of digital identity, but she had never come across a confirmed case before.

"This tactic isn't new," he told her. "In the 1940s, the United States government circulated secret blacklists of workers who had been accused of being communists. But that took time and money. Now they wipe you out with the flip of a bit."

"How many people have been affected?" she asked.

"Nobody's counting," he shrugged. "But union organizers, anti-war protesters, abortion rights advocates, you name it, have all disappeared from the computers of the Free World. Everyone pretends that we still live in a democracy, but there's been a Silent Coup."

It was the first time that Deirdre had heard that phrase.

"What makes it silent?" she asked.

"Because no one admits that the government is controlled by the Council of Seventeen. The Congress still makes laws, the White House still issues executive orders, just like they teach you in school. But now the Council tells them what to do."

"The Council of Seventeen is never mentioned in the media," Deirdre noted.

He nodded sadly. "It's grounds for revocation of digital identity to even mention the Council's name."

"You can't drive, you can't take a plane. So how did you get here?" she asked.

"A friend drove us, one of my union buddies. We hoped to cross into Mexico."

Laredo is the northern terminus of the Pan-American Highway, and measured by the number of motor vehicles, it is the principal port of entry into Mexico from the United States, with multiple bridges across the river that separates the two countries. The city had more than doubled in size since the 1990s, keeping pace with the shift of American factory jobs to non-union *maquiladoras* south of the border. It drew the digitally dispossessed like a magnet.

But like so many others, the Hoosiers hit a wall when they arrived in Laredo.

During the presidency of George Bush I, the United States government began sealing the Mexican border with a twelve-foot high wall of steel panels. Bush's wall began in the Pacific Ocean 340 feet from shore and marched inland, with occasional breaks, all the way to the mouth of the Colorado River. Then it resurfaced intermittently in the well-traveled corridors of the border towns, only to disappear in the long stretches of sparsely populated desert.

After the Silent Coup, the Krator Corporation built an electronic version of the Berlin Wall almost two thousand miles long, equipped with countless motion detectors and video cameras powered by solar panels. Like that fabled structure that heralded the collapse of the Soviet Union, the new fortifications were designed to keep citizens in, not foreigners out. The guards looked the other way when Mexicans came north, for White Americans were no more willing to pick strawberries in the twenty-first century than their ancestors wanted to pick cotton two hundred years earlier.

As Deirdre watched the man pack their few belongings into a knapsack and the mother strap the baby into a cradle board of nylon and aluminum, she felt a sense of desolation she could not ignore.

"Please stay awhile," she told them. "I'll see what I can do."

She went to talk to Enrique, the new Mexican wrangler she had hired not long before. She sensed that his work permit was phony and that he had recently crossed the border somewhere near Laredo. He visibly flinched when Deirdre hurried up to him with fire in her eyes.

"Don't be alarmed," she told him in Spanish. "I don't care whether you are here legally. But there's an American family that needs to be smuggled into Mexico. I want to contact whoever brought you here."

Enrique told her that he would have to talk to his cousin who worked in Laredo, so she had one of the workers drive him there.

Later that afternoon, Enrique returned with a man in a new red pickup truck with stereo sound that heralded its coming half a mile ahead. The man was a coyote, one of those who earn their living by smuggling people across the U.S.-Mexican border. He was middle-aged with a pencil mustache, alligator cowboy boots, and a stomach that appeared to have never known hunger. There was a hard edge to him like someone who traded in lives.

"Thank you," she nodded to Enrique, indicating it was time for him to get back to work.

"Please, over here," Deirdre told the coyote, leading him into the windbreak of cedar trees. "It's more private."

"It used to be that Americans drove across the bridge and Mexicans waded the river," the coyote told her, pleased with the irony of the new reality.

"Yes, well, now you'll have customers coming and going."

Deirdre could tell by his expression that he understood the economic implications of the changing situation.

"I do not know what Enrique told you," he said. "I am not in the tour guide business myself. But I have a friend. Perhaps my friend can help you."

"Do you know what your friend charges for his services?"

"My friend prepares an estimate based on the number of people who need a tour guide. How many are in the party?"

"Two adults and a baby."

"There is a surcharge for babies because they may cry and disturb the other tourists."

"I understand."

"What is the family's name?"

Deirdre thought about it a moment, then made one up. "Hoosier," she said. "The Hoosier family."

"And when would they like to go on the tour."

"Today if possible."

"Often my friend has vacancies at the last minute. If you would like, I can ask him."

"Please. And the cost too."

"Clearly. And they'll be leaving from here?" he asked.

"I think it would be better if they met your friend on the road. There is a culvert a mile before the gate."

"I saw it."

The coyote's face was that of predator taking measure of its prey, his amber eyes as still and unrevealing as a subterranean pool. "Also, my friend wants half of the tour money in advance," he said, "with the balance paid on completion of the tour."

"No! No money until they're safely on the other side," Deirdre insisted, fixing him with fierce green eyes.

"All right," he said with a hint of collegiality.

"How long does the tour take?"

"My friend does not like to spend more than half a day."

"After you ask your friend, how do we find out about the cost and the time?"

"He will leave a note in the mailbox by the road with all the information you need."

"I appreciate you coming all the way out here to help my guests with their arrangements. If they like the tour, I will inform my other guests as well."

After that, a steady stream of the digitally disadvantaged came to the ranch seeking shelter, and Deirdre was no more able to send the later arrivals away than that first family she had found in the old adobe. But faced with increasing demands on her time, her administrative instincts took over. She negotiated a volume contract with the coyote that guaranteed him a minimal number of customers per month, ensuring substantial savings to the refugees in her care. Then she secretly met with sympathetic people in the ranch's donor churches, letting them know that a channel into Mexico had been established.

* * *

Deirdre remembered when she first told Amadeus what she was doing. It was before she had built the wall out of scrap metal, and it was still possible to look out the window and watch the wranglers putting new campers through their paces.

"The Underground Railroad!" Amadeus exclaimed, referring to the secret network established before the Civil War to help slaves escape from plantations in the South. "Many of the principals were Protestant clergy who made their churches into safe houses on the road north into the free states. But the Underground Railroad was illegal," he reminded her. "It was a violation of federal law to move run-away slaves across state lines."

"The ranch is owned by a charitable corporation I don't control."

"That doesn't matter. The police can seize the ranch without even charging the owner with a crime."

"So you think I'm putting the ranch at risk?"

"The ranch has powerful backers. I am more concerned about your personal safety."

"I've set it up so the travelers stay at the ranch a day or two as tourists, then move to I don't know where. The coyotes actually handle the crossings. The money goes directly from the travelers to the coyote; but they let me know when they reach the other side, so I learn if anything goes amiss."

"That's a good way to keep it. You're probably below Krator's radar."

"I'm glad you don't disapprove. I was afraid you were going tell me that it's my Christian duty to obey the law."

"Well, in any case, agnostics have a special dispensation," he said with a grin. "But Christianity distinguishes between *just* and *unjust* laws."

"Yes, people in our donor churches have been very supportive of this."

"There *is* a moral dimension—prudence, but it sounds like you've already considered the possible effects. So you're comfortable with your decision?"

"'Comfortable!' she laughed. "No, but it's still better than being ground down on a daily basis by doing nothing."

Amadeus nodded. "The beauty of the present system is that since there's no security in obeying the law, people might as well do the right thing!"

***

In the corrals a group of handicapped children about seven years old were learning to ride horses.

"Look at those faces," Amadeus said, stopping to watch.

"I love it when they're riding for the first time," Deirdre said. "All their lives they've struggled to keep up, and suddenly they're as fast as the wind. I know we're making progress when they forget they can't run."

"Originally, the ranch was just for polio victims, wasn't it?"

"Yes. It was founded in 1950 by a church in Houston, just before the first polio vaccines hit the news. The founders were concerned that they had built a fifth wheel. But it turns out"—her face hardened—"there's no shortage of land mines."

27

Two adult staff members lifted the waiting child into the saddle and adjusted the reins and stirrups. Then a wrangler led the horse around the corral in a circle, talking to the child. After a few circuits, he stationed the horse at the end of a row of horses with riders, where it stood patiently waiting for orders, apparently unaware that its small burden had just grown to a cowhand ten feet tall impatient to lasso longhorns.

* * *

Deirdre and Amadeus reached the parking area where he had left his car.

"Are you still planning to be in Laredo Thursday morning?" he asked her.

The mid-day sun brought out the mahogany-brown of his hair and the glint of his opalescent eyes.

"Yes. I could stop by for coffee."

"I would love it," he said with a smile.

She gave his hand an affectionate squeeze.

* * *

Deirdre returned to the old adobe and retrieved Amadeus's manuscript on iconoclasm. She rolled the pages into a cylinder, stuffing them into a section of PVC pipe that had been painted the color of desert sand. She sealed the ends with fitted caps of the same material. When loaded with documents, the container looked and felt like a pipe bomb.

In the cool semi-darkness of the stable Deirdre's horse eyed her with anticipation, expecting its evening ride. The air was heavy with the smell of horse sweat, straw, and manure.

Deirdre hefted the bulky Western saddle onto its back and tightened the cinch.

Then she put the plastic cylinder in the empty scabbard where the rifle used to go and headed down the trail that intersected the highway about a mile west of the ranch house. When she reached the draw that ran under the road, she casually tossed the pipe onto the ground without breaking stride. Out of the corner of her eye, she watched with satisfaction as it rolled to a stop near the base of the road sign, invisible to anyone who did not know it was there.

3

DIRECT ACTION

Jack Adair sipped his coffee in a terrace restaurant on the main plaza in a provincial town in the highlands of Mexico. The table overlooked the main entrance to the Catholic church, a squat, white-washed structure dating from the early Spanish colonial period with two bell towers rebuilt in the late 18th century. Next to the parish house, a narrow staircase led underground to a partially excavated Aztec temple. The archaeological exhibit did not open until ten, so there was no guard on the church grounds. Morning Mass was still in progress.

The founder of EarthRage is over six feet tall, with a broad forehead, reddish, sun-streaked hair, and Irish eyes of beguiling blue. Wearing sandals, baggy shorts, and a T-shirt decorated with brands of tequila, he passed unnoticed as another tourist.

A short man with a tall coffee approached the table. He was dressed like a tourist, his eyes hidden by dark glasses.

"May I join you?" the young man asked in American English with a Mexican accent.

Jack Adair recognized the coordinator of the local EarthRage chapter. "Pull up a chair."

"Most people come to see the Aztec ruins," the young man said.

"I'm mainly interested in the statue of the Virgin," Jack Adair replied, watching the entrance of the church as he spoke, giving only an occasional glance at his companion. "They say that the Virgin is on display for only the rest of this week; then it will be removed for restoration. They say that it could be two years before church is open to the public again."

"That's true. But last week no one visited the church but the prepaid tour groups," the chapter coordinator said, a hint of discouragement in his voice.

"What about today? Are there other tourists here to see the statue?"

"So far, you're the only one."

Jack Adair smiled. "Well, maybe today we'll get lucky."

A pair of clean-cut teenage boys walked briskly across the plaza and through the open door of the church. A moment later, a young woman carrying a tote bag with a corporate logo climbed the front steps, looked nervously around, and disappeared inside.

The two men were young and agile enough to climb a rope, and the woman could be their accomplice, hiding their tools in her bag.

The founder of EarthRage glanced at the chapter coordinator who replied with an affirming nod.

Jack Adair hurried from the cafe and walked casually towards the church, cradling an expensive camera in his arms.

An elderly fruit juice vendor, a fixture on the plaza, wheeled his cart to the foot of the church steps, chocked the wheels, and unfolded the hinged counter as he had done every morning for thirty years.

A knot of regular customers gathered around the juice cart.

"*Jugo de naranja*," Jack Adair said with a friendly nod, as if he bought orange juice there every morning.

The vendor took an orange from the top of a pyramid of fruit, deftly halved it with a worn knife, and squeezed it with a treadle-powered juicer into a paper cup. The fresh orange juice had a rich and aromatic smell, more sweet than acidic.

The few elderly worshippers filed out of the church.

A workman dressed in coveralls and carrying a long, plastic tool box climbed the stone stairs to the church entrance. He put the tool box down so it blocked the doorway and spread the accordion shelves so they formed a barrier. Then, he took out a bulky extension cord and reinforced the blockade with intimidating orange coils.

Jack Adair waited, leisurely sipping his juice while contemplating the bustle of the plaza. One of the EarthRage bodyguards, dressed in a gray suit and tie like a banker, stopped at the juice cart.

"A beautiful morning," the well-dressed bodyguard told the vendor in a voice loud enough for Jack to hear. "I'm even two minutes early today."

Two minutes to zero hour—a theft was in progress inside the church.

The bodyguard sat down on the low retaining wall where several elderly people were enjoying the sun. From a plastic medicine bottle, he poured an incapacitating dose of pepper extract into the juice. A moment later, he stood up and climbed the half-dozen steps to the church entrance.

The make-believe repairman was still blocking the doorway. "They're fixing some hot wires inside. The church'll be closed for maybe twenty minutes."

The bodyguard dressed as a banker launched the juice into the phony repairman's face. As the man's hands went to his eyes, the chapter coordinator pinned his arms behind him and forced him face down on to the stone walkway.

Jack Adair leaped over the barrier and disappeared into the nave.

A young rock climber in a harness belt was hanging from the beams above the main altar while another stood below him, anchoring the rope.

Jack Adair turned on his strobe, aimed his telephoto, and triggered the video. The church's dim interior glowed with bright, white light, highlighting the statue of the Madonna in the hands of the suspended thief.

An EarthRage operative bounded up the center aisle to the altar, vaulted the rail, and tackled the thief who was holding the rope. The airborne accomplice clutched the stolen statue to his torso, then tripped the release and careened down the rope to the altar dais, colliding with the melee at the bottom, while Jack Adair captured it all on video.

The girl with the tote bag was standing in the side aisle watching the events unfold, apparently too terrified to run. The EarthRage lookout raced down the stairway from the choir loft and blocked her escape.

Then, as the climber attempted to flee with the statue, two armed policemen who lived in the parish, accompanied by the pastor and sacristan, emerged from the sacristy and confronted the thieves.

Lone Star Christian Tower

The Fellowship's director of communications poked his head into Dean Weed's office, a grim expression on his face.

"There's a problem in Mexico," Gus announced. "Two young men were photographed stealing art from a Catholic church."

The two executives strode downstairs side by side, resolute and dour.

In the communications command center, a wall of screens was tuned to the American franchises of One World News, but Gus pointed to a single television in the bottom, left-hand corner.

"This is a video clip of the two thieves caught red-handed," Gus said. "Fortunately, we got advance warning that it was coming, and One World News killed the story in the Free World. We're looking at EuroNet, the eastern European channel":

> "Today the Mexican police arrested three thieves in the act of stealing a seventeenth-century Madonna from a Catholic church near Mexico City. This is the first time that police have arrested anyone in the wave of thefts of antique artwork that has plagued this Latin American country for over a year.
>
> "Authorities estimate that more than two dozen Madonnas, nearly all of them irreplaceable, original works of art from the sixteenth to eighteenth centuries, have disappeared without a trace. The Mexican Cultural Heritage Society claims to have evidence that many of these pieces were shipped to the United States."
>
> The camera lingered on a young man who was suspended from climbing ropes high above the altar of the church in Mexico, his eyes filled with humiliation and fear.

"Fortunately, there is nothing to connect this incident to the Fellowship," Dean Weed commented.

"There's no mention of the Fellowship *yet*," Gus replied, "but that will change. A Heritage Society press release says that the two chimney sweeps are members of the Fellowship. The girl may be too."

"Is that true?"

"Yes."

The executive director grimaced.

One of Gus's assistants handed Dean Weed a video phone. "Your secretary. She says it's urgent."

Dean Weed walked to the far end of the room and sat down in one of the empty cubicles.

"You have an urgent call from Orville Fuller. I'm putting him through."

"There's a problem," Orville Fuller said in slow motion. "In Mexico."

He hesitated after each phrase as if it were too painful to proceed. "The police have arrested... three members of the Fellowship... in a burglary... of a Catholic church."

"Mexican or American members?"

"Mexican."

"Anything that links them directly to the Fellowship, besides their membership?"

"The two young men are both organizers in the rallies of Young Mexico."

"That's unfortunate."

"And the press has a picture of them wearing Fellowship T-shirts," Fuller added.

"Anyone who goes to a rally can buy a T-shirt."

There was a pause. "Let me read you this: it's from the press release from the terrorists:

> 'Last year, the Fellowship's founder, Dr. Duane Boone III, told a gathering of the church's missionaries that 'pulling the props out from under the local witch doctors is critical to our success.'"

Dean Weed looked displeased.

"One of the thieves was filmed hanging above the altar with a statue in his hands," Fuller added.

"I saw it."

"Then you know that the video is playing right now on Mexican television. It's on some European and Asian channels too."

"Yes, but it's been blacked out in the homeland. We'll issue a statement in Spanish condemning the theft and excommunicating the thieves, so the fallout in Mexico will be limited too. There's nothing to be concerned about."

"Well, there are things to be concerned about," Fuller countered. "One news report mentioned that a truckload of stolen statues crossed the United States border a few weeks ago. Is that true?"

"I have no direct knowledge of that."

Orville Fuller's ingratiating smile had vanished. "Well, I hope it's not true, because idols used in pagan worship should have been burned."

Dean Weed's voice conveyed a flicker of annoyance at Fuller's inflexible attitude. "I am sure no member of the Fellowship was involved in saving pagan idols."

"I hope not. Those two brave, young men were risking their lives to do the Lord's work. But criminals used them for profiteering. If the idols had been burned as required, we wouldn't have to worry about this. I plan to raise this issue with Duane personally."

"You'll find he's completely supportive of the burning of idols," Dean Weed assured him.

Mexico City

Renato Ocampo-Mendoza paused at the corner to scan for police, then walked with a confdent stride towards the Monument to the Revolution: four massive, multistory arches arranged as the sides of a cube and topped by a dome of gleaming copper. He was dressed in casual but conservative clothes, like a clerk in a government bureau; yet the student backpack slung over one shoulder gave him the air of a person bridging two worlds.

For the past two years Ocampo had avoided public places for fear of the Policía Contra-Terrorista. But a week ago, mercenaries hired by the Troy Oil Company occupied the Mexican oil fields. After the invasion the president of Mexico went on television to announce "the need to renew our sovereignty by rekindling the spirit that animated our revolution"—and Ocampo marched down the Paseo de La Reforma with a hundred thousand others to reaffirm Mexican independence.

He turned onto the Avenida de La República, edged by a row of flowering trees. It was almost deserted and free of police—yet he felt the presence of unseen eyes.

A drunk approached him, asking for directions to the bus stop on Avenida Insurgentes. Ocampo told him how to get there.

"God will repay you," the drunk said. The choice of phrase indicated that the rendezvous would take place as scheduled.

As Ocampo reached the corner, a silver-gray sedan pulled up to the curb. Sitting in front on the passenger side was a sandy-haired American in his thirties with a calm, inexpressive face—El Tigre, the EarthRage chief of security. Dressed in khakis and a designer shirt, he could stroll unnoticed past the glittery commercial facades of the Polanco district, but his nickname, El Tigre ("the Tiger"), reflected his reputation in the resistance movement.

He gave the Philosopher a nod and gestured to the back seat of the car. The Mexican driver pretended not to see him. Ocampo climbed in, and El Tigre gave instructions to the driver in the sign language used by the deaf. Then he turned to Ocampo.

"Lie down on the seat, face down. It's for your own safety. Take a nap if you like. I'll tell you when it's OK to get up."

For a long time, the car lurched through stop-and-go traffic, then merged onto a high-speed highway. An hour later, it turned off onto local streets.

"You can get up now," El Tigre said.

They were driving down a private road that ran between two uniform ranks of maguey plants, each plant a radial cluster of leathery, blue-gray leaves, each leaf as long and pointed as a broadsword. The road terminated at a fortress-like wall of pink cement, more than twice the height of a man and punctuated by a single arch. As the sedan pulled up, a guard emerged from a kiosk to record the license of the car and to identify the passengers.

"*Buenos días*," the guard said with a hint of familiarity, thrusting a touchpad through the window to El Tigre. Inside the kiosk, a second security guard fingered a pump shotgun.

El Tigre's fingerprint identified him as the registered guest of an owner of one of the units. The guard glanced at it perfunctorily, then gestured for the Philosopher to put his thumb on the touchpad too.

"He's an old friend of the family," El Tigre said in Spanish, speaking in a tone that indicated that they would settle up later.

The guard nodded and waved them through.

The driver drove directly to one of the houses, hidden by a pink, stucco wall and entered through an imposing gateway large enough for a moving van. He stopped on the cobblestone pavement in front of a massive, hand-carved door, then gestured for Ocampo to get out.

"*Hasta luego*," El Tigre said, as the car disappeared around the bend of the wall.

* * *

The door to the house opened on its own. Only when it closed behind him did Ocampo see the petite woman in a dark blouse and pants. Her face was older than her figure, like a thirty-something who had done hard drugs or a fifty-something with an unhappy marriage and a health club membership.

She led him through an expensively furnished living room to a separate wing that served as the guest quarters. The bed in the guest bedroom was large enough to sleep an extended family and the walk-in closet deep enough to lie down in. She slid back the wall paneling to reveal a steel door with a biometric touchpad that responded to her hand. Inside was a windowless executive suite, sparsely furnished with a small conference table with straight-back chairs at one end and several computer workstations at the other. Against one wall was a settee in basic beige. Above it, a poster proclaimed: "Regime change begins at home."

Suddenly, Jack Adair, the founder of EarthRage, was standing behind him, smiling broadly, his bright eyes partially eclipsed by the habitual squint of a surfer. He was casually dressed in a T-shirt, shorts, and flip-flops as if he had just come from the beach.

"Welcome to Tranquility Base," he said in Spanish, enveloping Renato in a bear hug. Then he turned to the woman who had led them through the house. "May I introduce Constanza, our managing editor. She keeps EarthRage purring like a Porsche."

"How do you do?" Renato said, studying her in the light. She was as weathered as a piñon pine, with sad, compelling eyes.

"And this is the safe room," Jack said with an enthusiastic sweep of his arm as if talking to a prospective buyer.

"Good set-up," Renato nodded approvingly. "Absentee *gringo* owner, live-in 'housekeeper,' 'family' visits occasionally."

"If EarthRage has an editorial office, this is as close as it gets," Jack explained. "The house used to belong to a drug lord, and it had several unusual amenities that attracted my attention"—he nodded towards the sliding steel door. "Make yourself comfortable."

Renato sat down on the beige settee, his student backpack at his feet.

"We can talk freely here," Jack said, closing the door. "You said you had some good news."

"Yes. The Mexican Cultural Heritage Society was so impressed by the success of the recent EarthRage action that the board of directors would like to meet with you personally to discuss further collaboration."

Jack gave a satisfied smile. "Until now their president would only talk with us through a go-between."

"Well now they can't wait to meet you."

"We can thank Troy Oil for lubing the gears," he chuckled.

"Seizing the refineries was the stupidest thing the *yanquis* could have done," Renato agreed. "Every child, if he knows nothing else about Mexican history, knows how President Cárdenas stared down Standard Oil and nationalized the oil fields. Now, the *yanquis* have rubbed our faces in the dirt."

"I remember when we first met on the beach, you told me that the new regime in Washington would alienate its Mexican supporters within two years—you were right!"

Renato remembered as if it were yesterday the beach and the boat, the approaching storm, and the terrifying, surf-tossed landing. But after he and Jack had vanished into the vast anonymity of Mexico, the subsequent weeks and months were now a blur of throw-away cell phones, fake accounts on taxi apps, nameless benefactors that they would never see again...

He realized that Jack was talking to him. "We'll be more comfortable outside. There's a wet bar, swimming pool, and comfortable chairs."

On the sun-dappled patio, azure water sparkled in a lap pool of blue-and-white tiles imported from Tuscany. Bougainvillea reached skyward from ceramic pots inlaid with turquoise, providing a canopy of welcoming shade.

Renato's eyes shifted nervously. "Can we talk out here?"

"Yes. The previous owner had trellises installed that scramble radio waves and confuse drones. It's American gear made for use in Afghanistan." He looked as proud as if he had built it himself.

"The reason I invited you here today is to tell you how much EarthRage has benefitted from your insight—and how much I've personally enjoyed working with you over the past two years."

"Equally," Renato replied.

"So, I wonder if you'd be interested in participating in the EarthRage leadership officially—as a member of the editorial staff?"

"I am honored, but I have too much to write as it is—my thesis and my book."

"You won't need to write anything. The managing editor does that. What EarthRage needs is someone who can analyze events and spell out their logical implications. Isn't that a philosopher's job?"

"Yes, it is."

"Well, events have been running on fast-forward lately. There's more history happening than there's time to put it in, much less time to think about it."

"Everyone's noticed that."

"It would be a great help to have someone who can analyze the big picture. Especially since EarthRage is expanding its mission. The environment remains a priority. But since the Americans have high-jacked the news media, we are going to focus on stories that highlight Yankee crimes in Latin America. I'd like to have you on board to help EarthRage navigate these dangerous waters. We need someone who understands Mexican politics, American imperialism, and religious propaganda—you're a natural!"

"You know I'm not a journalist. I don't write in the popular style, and I hate deadlines."

"We don't need another journalist," the founder of EarthRage emphasized. "We need a logical mind on the bridge. What do you say?"

Renato was flattered—no one wanted philosophers anymore.

"Would I have to participate in direct actions?" he asked.

"No. Our chapters do that. The editorial staff is strictly literary."

"And what about fact-finding? Do I need to do my own interviews and leg-work?"

"No, EarthRage couriers connect our principal action areas, even inside the United States. We can get you any information you need as fast as you need it."

The Philosopher looked like he might be persuaded.

"But before I make a decision, I want to meet the other editorial staff."

"You already have."

"I've only met you and Constanza."

"You met everyone in editorial," Jack told him.

"There are only two of you!"

"Well, there is a video production unit and a media coordinator who helps select story material but only two people who write copy and approve final content. Constanza and I file all the stories that go out under the EarthRage label."

"Constanza. May I ask about her?"

"Go ahead."

"Is she a deaf mute?"

"Not exactly. Constanza is a journalist who was tortured because of a story she was writing."

"Where was that?"

"Chiapas. Now she no longer speaks. She talks in the sign language used by deaf people. She gives lessons in it to the bodyguards and me. The staff training was El Tigre's idea. He says that there might be times when keeping silent is a matter of life and death."

"And what was she writing about?" Renato asked.

"She wrote a story about a proposed hydroelectric dam, saying that it would give little benefit to the people who lived there. The electrical power was going to be sold to other countries, while the dam itself was a ploy to log the old-growth timber that the lake would flood."

"Why didn't they just kill her?"

"They used her to show recruits how to torture a woman. There were two squads and each member took a turn."

"Who did this?" Ocampo asked.

"Well, the torturers were Policía Contra-Terrorista, but their officers were trained at Fort Benning, Georgia. Also, American advisors from the 888th were there too."

Renato's expression signaled his unfamiliarity with that unit.

"The 888th Special Operations Brigade is an American paramilitary unit that operates secretly in Central America," Jack explained. "The cover story is that they are American advisors reporting to the local military. But we've learned that they're one of the no-name brigades."

"What is a 'no-name brigade?'"

"They are paramilitary units recruited from the Fellowship of the Eighth Dispensation. On the organizational charts of the American military they are denoted by numbers; but they have secret names known only to their members, such as Last Judgment, Divine Wrath, and Chariots of Fire, names whose existence is denied to outsiders. They report to the Council of Seventeen, not to the Pentagon."

"So now *yanqui* militarism is married to religion."

"Yes, and it's a marriage made in hell."

The 888th

The EarthRage chief of security, the well-groomed American known as El Tigre, parked a green SUV in the underground garage of a shopping mall and rolled down the window. He gestured to the parking attendant, a wizened old man in a ball cap who was stooped from work in the fields.

"Señor?" the man asked, approaching the open window.

43

El Tigre slipped some bank notes into the man's hand. "I am expecting a friend," he said. "Maybe you could direct traffic to another lane?"

The attendant replied with a toothless grin.

A few minutes later, a small, bow-legged man appeared at the end of the parking lane, apparently perplexed as to where to go next. He had emerged from the department store, rather than arriving by car as El Tigre had suggested. He spied the green SUV with the strand of green tape tied to the antenna and moved cautiously towards it. His face was tanned almost black by the sun, but the skin of his forehead was fairer, suggesting that it was usually protected by a broad-brimmed hat such as a farmer or cowboy might wear.

El Tigre wondered if he was one of the many small farmers who had been put out of business by NAFTA.

They exchanged passwords, and the man clambered into the front seat. He was a representative of Guloggers, the volunteer espionage organization that tracked prisoners in the American gulag.

"El Tigre finally meets El Gavilán," the EarthRage chief of security said, as they cordially shook hands.

The Mexican man smiled, for his nom de guerre means "the hawk" in Spanish.

"I feel like we've known each other a long time, even though it has only been by messenger," the man said with feeling.

"Likewise," El Tigre said.

"Can we talk here?"

"Yes."

"It is so good to be able to speak freely."

El Tigre was pleased. "It is something I like to provide for my guests."

El Gavilán studied the face of the EarthRage chief of security, noting that faint look of impatience that Americans get when normal human socializing goes on too long.

"And, I know you are eager to hear about why I wanted to see you," El Gavilán said.

He took out a paper road map of northern Mexico, ceremoniously opened it, and propped it on the dashboard, pausing until El Tigre moved closer to see it. Then he pointed to an insert for the city of Matamoros, located in the northeast corner of the country, where the Rio Grande reaches the Gulf of Mexico. He pointed to an airfield on the outskirts of the city.

"This is listed as a training facility for the Mexican air force," El Gavilán said. "But it is really the headquarters for a no-name brigade."

El Tigre gave his companion a penetrating stare. "A no-name brigade? What makes you so sure?"

El Gavilán counted off bulleted items using his fingers: "All take-offs and landings logged. Daily flights to and from Dallas and Twentynine Palms, California. And regular flights to and from known U.S. rendition bases."

He paused to rummage in his pocket. "And one of the soldiers lost this." He held up a sterling silver lapel pin inscribed with the number 888.

El Tigre took the pin, feeling its weight, then turned it over in his hand to read the engraved motto.

He gave the Gulogger a satisfied smile.

Boone's Prize Bible

Dean Weed emerged from the elevator on the eightieth floor of Lone Star Christian Tower and hurried toward the office of Duane Boone III. The foyer to the televangelist's suite was hung with original paintings by Frederic Remington, and a gold-colored carpet marked the way to his office as clearly as a yellow brick road. In the inner office of the Fellowship's founder, a spiral staircase climbed to a private observation lounge on the roof. It was built to the televangelist's own design, inspired by a Boeing 747. Boone likes to compose his sermons early Sunday morning with the lights of Dallas spread out before him.

"He's in the Sky Lounge," Boone's secretary told the executive director in a sympathetic voice. "But he's given orders not to be disturbed."

"Is he having one of those… 'infusions of the spirit?'" Weed asked.

"Infusion" was Boone's own term for those occasions when the Spirit spoke to the prophet directly; the word "channeling" was deemed too New Age to be used by the fellowship's members.

The secretary's thin lips fused in a conspiratorial smile.

Dean Weed turned toward the glass-fronted safe where the prize Bible was stored—a Bible that had been presented to Boone by the Lone Star Christian Network in honor of his achievement as the nation's top-grossing televangelist. It had once belonged to Silas Garvey, the nineteenth-century American theologian who is now remembered as one of the founding fathers of dispensational theology. Garvey assigned passages in Scripture to one of seven dispensations, marking each page with his own annotations; and it was Garvey who self-published an edition of the Bible containing his own footnotes and appendix in 1908.

Network executives had purchased Garvey's personal Bible and had it rebound in deer skin with a dedication embossed on the cover in gold leaf:

Dr. Duane Boone III, Christian, Leader, and Prophet

Secured by alarms and biometric locks, only Boone could remove the Bible from its safe, and he did so only when prompted by what he called "the fast, hot breath of the Spirit." On those occasions the televangelist took the book with him like a lucky charm, transporting it to and from his ranch in a glass-fronted display case installed in his office RV.

Dean Weed peered through the highly reflective glass into the dim interior of the safe—Boone's prize Bible was gone.

* * *

Dean Weed remembered all too well the last time that Boone had removed his Bible from its place of honor.

Boone had summoned his executive director to his office, opened a manila folder, and pushed a sheaf of pages across the teak wood desk.

It was a manuscript entitled *The Book of Voo*, a title that Dean Weed had never seen before.

"It lists all the passages in Scripture that need revision, while giving their replacements," Boone said in the calm and genial demeanor that he usually presented to donors, without a hint that he had been awake all night transcribing messages from the Spirit.

Dean Weed suppressed the impulse to put the manuscript back in the envelope. "You're saying that the Bible is in need of revision?" he asked, hoping that he had misheard.

"Not all of it, of course. Just the verses I've indicated."

Boone opened the Bible to show where he had crossed out entire verses and written page numbers from the *Book of Voo* in assertive script on the margins of the pages, dominating Garvey's cramped and fastidious annotations.

Dean Weed gulped when he saw that Boone's revisions included some of Scripture's most famous passages.

"And what do you plan to do with this document?"

"I will present it at next Friday's telethon."

The executive director moved his chair closer and looked the televangelist right in the eye. "Duane, this is an amazing theological achievement. But I am worried that it will be over the head of the rank and file. And the controversy it creates will compromise the Rapture of the First White Kernel."

Boone opened his mouth to reply, noticed Weed's determined face, and paused a moment as if uncertain what to say next. Then he asked what the executive director would suggest.

"I suggest that you circulate it first among your panel of theological advisors—under a pledge of complete secrecy."

"How can I suppress a revelation from the Spirit?"

"Just for awhile, until the top echelon of the Fellowship has had time to assimilate this… this revelation." Dean Weed said. "Everything has its season."

Boone looked as if he might object, then put the manuscript back in its folder. "I will do as you suggest for now. But I plan to incorporate the *Book of Voo* a into a new edition of the Bible with my own notes and appendices. It will become the new standard for all of Christendom."

Lone Star Christian Tower

The Fellowship's director of communications was waiting in Dean Weed's office, the worry lines on his face more prominent than ever.

"The story about the stolen Madonnas," Gus confided. "It's been hard to contain. One World News knocks it down in one place and it pops up somewhere else."

"Why do you think that is?"

"I think our enemies think the Fellowship is vulnerable."

"Is that just a hunch?" Dean Weed asked.

"More than a hunch. Only last week Dr. Boone predicted a sudden convergence of three events that would shape the Fellowship's destiny."

Dean Weed reflected that in the span of a single day there had been a warning about EarthRage from Krator, blowback from Troy Oil's occupation of the oil fields, and a news story about the stolen Madonnas that had gone viral—three convergent events that could affect the Fellowship's destiny.

Dean Weed's placid manner tightened to a stance of executive concern. "Did Duane say what they were?"

"No, but they were weighing on him."

"Well, let me know if anything else happens—as soon as it happens."

Tranquility Base

El Tigre settled into the beige sofa with black metal arms, the only concession to comfort in the EarthRage editorial offices. He looked impassively at Renato's face as if memorizing the features, then turned to Jack Adair.

"For the past six months I've been working with Guloggers—the group that tracks the prison population of the American gulag," El Tigre told them. "I can tell you that it's a model of how a resistance espionage organization can work. Guloggers has been tracking rendition flights to and from the United States. And today I learned that the 888th Special Operations Brigade is back in Mexico—it's operating from a Mexican air force base in Matamoros."

"Matamoros—'Moor killer,'" Jack translated. "What a name! It's almost too good to be true."

"I've seen the raw data; it's very impressive."

"Is the 888th behind the stolen Madonnas too?"

"They wouldn't steal statues—they'd burn down the church with the congregation inside."

Jack Adair played with his forelock as he did when he was nervous.

"We crossed paths in Afghanistan," El Tigre continued. "The 888th ran the interrogation centers in my sector. Technically, they are contractors, outside the military chain of command, and the spooks cover for them. They're untouchables."

"What do you think they are doing in Mexico?"

"Murdering journalists for starters."

"Do you think you can find out more about them?"

"I have an agreement with Guloggers—we work quid pro quo. We give *them* something, they give *us* something."

"What did we give them in exchange for the 888th?" Jack asked.

"They haven't asked for anything yet, but I suggested that maybe we could assist them in public relations. They run a good espionage operation but have limited access to the media. EarthRage could help them with that."

"What kind of access do you think they'll need?"

"We didn't discuss that, but I think that one of these days they'll want to make something instantly available to the worldwide media, maybe take credit for a caper they pulled off. EarthRage could do that for them."

"That would be easy for us," Jack agreed. "What does editorial have to do regarding this?"

"Right now, nothing. Just file it as a possibility."

Lone Star Christian Tower

Alone in his office, Dean Weed looked out over the city. It was a sunny day in Dallas, but occasional gusts of wind rippled the six flags on the roof of the Stockman Hotel. It reminded him of that day two months ago when he went horseback riding with Duane.

He had been summoned to the Boone family ranch by Duane's wife Tammy Jo. A chronic dieter prone to vomiting, she was as thin as a famine victim; her bleached, blond hair had the texture of steel wool. When he arrived, she was standing in the Grecian portico of the monumental ranch house tapping her foot nervously.

"I can't get Duane away from the TV," she told the executive director. "All he does is watch 'Divine Wind' over and over. You know, that show about the Japanese kamikazes? I told him you were coming by to go riding," she added slyly.

The executive director found the nation's top televangelist slumped in front of the television, his powerful physique dwarfed by the cathedral ceiling of the knotty-pine great room of the ranch house. He barely looked up from the screen, mesmerized by wave after wave of suicide bombers hurtling at American warships, the pilots apparently oblivious of their imminent deaths.

Dean Weed was repulsed by the spectacle—he associated suicide attacks with Arabs.

"Remember we're going horseback riding this morning?" he told Boone.

"Come on, Honey Bear," Tammy Jo urged her husband, taking his arm.

"A great day for a ride," Dean Weed said with unconvincing cheer, donning the Stetson hat that the houseboy handed him.

The televangelist arose slowly from the sofa and followed the executive director out of the house, with Tammy Jo riding herd like a trail boss. Outside, Boone surveyed the bright blue dome of sky as if looking for Japanese bombers, then ordered Calvin the groom to saddle the horses. The two men waited silently in the glare of the summer sun. Dean Weed's face glistened with sweat, but the televangelist's face was pale and dry as if air-conditioned by God.

Boone mounted his chestnut on automatic pilot and took off down the equestrian trail that circled the ranch. Dean Weed followed him a horse length behind. As they neared the low rise where a wind turbine rotated lazily, the blades suddenly picked up speed. Then a sudden gust lifted Boone off the saddle. He pressed his feet against the stirrups to steady himself, an heroic figure framed against the Texas sky.

Later that day, Duane Boone III confided to the executive director that he had felt the presence of the Holy Spirit on that grassy knoll. His clinical depression had vanished, and now his eyes were wide with enthusiasm.

"It was God himself who lifted me out of the saddle, like Paul on the road to Damascus," he said in an excited voice. "At first, I thought it was the wind that lifted me up, but then I felt the infusion of the Word, and saw my whole life spread out below me like a map—my biblical exegesis, my television ministry, my oratory, my foundation of the Fellowship, my benefactors, my political connections. And I knew that God was preparing me for the greatest task of all—rebuilding the temple in Jerusalem!"

Boone leaned across the table until his face was only inches from the executive director's. "You understand what that means?" the televangelist asked, fixing Dean Weed with one of his famous exegetical stares.

"What?"

"The faster the temple in Jerusalem gets built, the sooner Bible-believing Christians get raptured out!"

Since that day, Boone was a changed man, waiting for the moment when God would send his sign: the rapturing of a witness purified by fire that would herald the beginning of the Eighth Dispensation.

BOOK II

THE RAPTURE

4

THE MISSING FIREFIGHTER

The California Wine County

Still panting hard, her tank top and running shorts wet with sweat from her run through the vineyards, Kelly stopped and listened.

She brushed back the wisps of blond hair that had fallen across her face, her hazel eyes fixed on the range of blue hills that formed the eastern horizon.

"Listen like a deer," her grandfather had taught her. "Nose to the wind and perfectly still."

A breeze rustled the live oaks and whispered through the straw-yellow grass. Then dust devils danced down the rows of vines—the breath of a distant desert.

Her telephone's tinny jingle sounded the alarm:

> Attention: wildfire advisory. The National Weather Service has issued a red flag warning for northern California, predicting a conjunction of high temperature, low humidity, and strong, dry winds, gusting to forty miles per hour.

By the time Kelly reached her two-room cottage under the redwoods, the blinds were clattering against the window frames. The picture of her grandparents was lying flat, knocked over by the wind. In the right lower margin of the photo, her grandfather's precise, authoritative script noted the place and year: "Indian Springs, Almaden County, 1968."

It had been taken on the lawn of the farmhouse where the winery now stood. Her grandparents were standing arm in arm like newlyweds, the steep slope of the west ridge forming a backdrop behind them. The glass in the picture frame had broken, and a single crack bisected the slope behind them, roughly following the track of the fire road. Kelly closed the window and carefully replaced the picture in its stand.

She tossed her tank top and running shorts in a long arc into the hamper, then turned on the shower, mentally rehearsing a list of to-dos for the long days and sleepless nights ahead.

In her sun-filled bedroom, on a comforter printed with pink flowers and framed by a white dust ruffle, her uniform of forest-green cargo pants and gray-green shirt was laid out on the bed like a scarecrow, her sturdy boots standing at attention by the door.

A blue and gold shield on the shoulder of Kelly's shirt proclaimed her place of work: the California Department of Disaster Response. The agency, abbreviated CDDR and pronounced Cedar, manages a statewide network of fire stations and emergency vehicles, with command of disasters of any kind.

Older now in somber shades of gray and green, Kelly went into the kitchen and set the timer for the security lights, advancing the count to eight p.m., the hour transitional to dusk. A bright red number eight stared back at her from the readout. Her grandfather had died in August a year ago, in another summer of record-setting heat.

Kelly jumped into the red command vehicle parked in her driveway and radioed the fire station.

"Tell Jim I'm coming in. But first I'm checking out the weather from the west ridge."

As her vehicle climbed the steep slope, she could see the full length of Deep Creek valley, from the massive, earth-fill dam all the way to the river. Over the centuries, Deep Creek had eroded into a narrow, wedge-shaped plain about fifteen miles long that widened in a southeasterly direction between two high, converging ridges. The valley floor and the lower hillsides were bright green with wine grape vines, abruptly yielding to brown about half way up the slopes, where the dry scrub known as chaparral took over. The house trailers where the Mexican farm workers lived were crammed into the margins of the roads, while the live oaks and redwoods had been logged to make room for more vines.

Kelly had last driven this route with her grandfather. In the photograph, he was a vigorous, muscular man tanned from a life in the vineyards, but she remembered him more as the pale, frail figure who had asked to see the valley from West Ridge Road. She drove him to the overlook where the road levels out, and he gazed silently at the land where he had spent his life. Then he turned to her as if trying to etch her face in memory. In a breathless voice as dry as chaparral, he told her:

"Kelly, never be afraid to pass through the fire—it's your element."

She studied him, half mystified, half in wonder, unsure of what he meant, but from his eyes she surmised that his mind had moved on—her questions would have to wait until tomorrow. But cancer is a disease of false summers and sudden squalls—a few days later he was gone.

Kelly parked the red SUV at the overlook. Directly below, a peristyle of Greek columns honored the Italian-Swiss farmers who settled the area at the end of the nineteenth century. On a pedestal in the center, circled by bas-reliefs of fruit trees and hop vines, a pioneer couple forged in bronze looked down the valley towards the town of Oscuridad, as if choosing wineries for a tasting tour.

Far below the monument, on the valley floor, the white, stucco walls and rust red roofs of Indian Springs Winery gleamed in the morning sun. A long driveway, edged with deciduous oaks planted by Kelly's grandfather, ran from the highway to the door of the tasting room, where the porch of the farm house used to be. Behind it, the three-story, windowless wall of the winery thrust above the treetops.

* * *

In the Indian Springs tasting room, Giovanni was setting up for the first customers of the day. Monday mornings were usually slow, and the full-time servers worked only in the afternoon. He stacked the glassware from the dishwasher and lined up the bottles in the preferred order of serving.

He went into the barrel room to get more wine for tasting. Inside, it was as cool and dim as a grotto, the air redolent with the fruity smell of fermentation. The owner, the winemaker, and the vineyard manager were seated at a small table, engaged in a solemn discussion about the effects of the heat on the zinfandel grapes.

"The zins are so close to physiological ripeness now," the vineyard manager was saying, "that we're going to have to pick no matter how hot it is."

"I know we shouldn't even be thinking of picking when it's so warm," the owner, Charles Clydesdale, added. "But it's not cooling down at night like it used to do."

"This proves my point," the vineyard manager said. "We need varieties that've been genetically engineered for increased heat tolerance."

Clydesdale's eyes narrowed in a frown.

The winemaker answered for him. "Well, last season ended unusually cool. Thanks to those forty-year old vines,

60

the higher prices we'll get for last year's vintage will carry us through the next season, no matter what happens over the next few days."

Giovanni appeared with a case of two-year-old zinfandel perched on his shoulder.

Clydesdale fixed him with a managerial stare. "If the weather breaks we'll be picking at dawn tomorrow."

"We're ready to go," Giovanni replied in a confident voice.

In the tasting room, a burly, broad-shouldered man was waiting at the counter. Graying at the temples but with a young and exuberant face, the visitor carried himself with palpable strength, as if ready to lift the refrigerator and walk off with it.

"Nice place," the man said, looking around at the white stucco walls and the earthenware vases of sunflowers.

"We just built the tasting room two years ago," Giovanni replied in the cordial, upbeat voice of a veteran of the hospitality wars, checking to see that the "CLOSED" sign was still displayed on the door.

"It's nice and cool in here," the man enthused. He picked up one of the price sheets and began devouring its contents. "You specialize in zinfandels! I love zinfandels!"

"I'm sorry, but the tasting room doesn't open 'til ten. But if you have an e-mail address, I'll put you on the mailing list. You'll receive advance notice of tastings and sales."

The visitor took out an expensive phone and wired his contact information to the winery's database. Giovanni read it aloud from the screen with widening eyes: "'Producer of Disaster Coverage, One World News, Los Angeles.' I hope you're not here to cover a disaster?"

The burly man laughed. "Just the opposite. Digital detox. My wife and I are staying in the spa down the road. Four days of rub-downs and no phones!"

Giovanni nodded. "A good choice for a get-away. Nothing ever happens in Oscuridad."

* * *

61

On the fire road above, Kelly's heavy SUV shuddered in a gust of wind, and a utility pole fell across her field of vision, the electrical wires snapping in a shower of sparks. She heard the thump of the pole hitting the ground and the crackle of twigs being smashed into splinters. A moment later she detected the smell of burning leaves.

She activated the incident report button in her vehicle, which relayed the location, the time, and the weather conditions to the fire command center in Sacramento.

"Sparking electrical wires in dry brush," she told the voice memo. "I'm taking a look."

Kelly put on her helmet and gloves, then grabbed a trenching tool and fire extinguisher. With the extinguisher in one hand, the tool in the other, she started down the slope in the direction of the monument. What Kelly remembered as a natural gully with a gradual descent, easily traversed, had been filled at the top with dirt and gravel when the road was widened earlier in the year. Because of the foliage, Kelly did not see the drop-off at the end of the fill. Suddenly she was sliding uncontrollably on the steep slope, the extinguisher caught in a tangle of brush somewhere on the slope behind her. She half fell, half slid down the gully towards the parking lot below, the sharp branches jabbing her legs.

The broken chaparral twigs were dusted with pollen, and the falling sparks made a dozen little pinpoints of heat with embers almost too small to see. The southeast wind, with delicate puffs, fanned them into gossamers of faint blue smoke. The first gust fanned them into tongues of yellow flame. A stronger gust blew the burning twigs into the chamise bush on the steep slope above the parking lot. Caressed by the breeze, they took off with a low roar, the wind behind them urging them on. In a matter of seconds, the bush exploded into flame, with yellow tentacles straining to reach the road above.

She felt it on her face before she saw it: a wall of flame was coming up the slope to meet her. Her first impulse was to turn and run. She spun around, using the trenching tool like a ski pole to try to get some leverage, but the mixture of clay and gravel crumbled under her feet, sliding her further down the slope. Dropping the tool, she tried to haul herself back up by using the bushes as rungs, but the brittle stems broke off in her hands. She turned again to face the fire—horrified to find it moving sideways as well as up, as if trying to flank her with a pincer movement.

She dropped face-down on the ground, her feet toward the fire, her nose pressed into the dirt, her head buried in her helmet, her cheeks shielded by the heavy gloves—and prayed.

* * *

When Giovanni emerged from the barrel room at Indian Springs Winery, wind gusts were rattling the fiberglass panels on the machine shed. Only an hour earlier it had been oppressively still. As he walked across the loading dock, he heard the sound of sirens off in the distance, in the direction of the station that housed the fire-fighting vehicles for the California Department of Disaster Response. That would be Kelly's unit, he reflected. He stopped and waited, trying to discern where they were heading.

As Giovanni stood listening, the sirens became gradually louder, then fell almost silent. He surmised that the engines had turned into a side canyon, which muted the sound, and were heading up the west ridge, perhaps to the fire road that ran above Indian Springs. He looked up, fixing on the distant dome of the monument which poked above a knoll. With a jolt, he registered the splash of yellow flame behind it moving soundlessly up the ridge in advance of any smoke.

Giovanni ran into the barrel room. "There's a wildfire burning on the ridge above the winery!"

Now there were sirens converging from all directions, as the red flag warning brought out the volunteer engine companies and municipal fire departments from nearby towns. Everyone in the winery ran outside to watch.

"It looks like it started just above the monument," the winemaker said.

"It's a good thing the wind is from behind us," Clydesdale said. "It will carry it away from the wineries."

A reconnaissance airplane passed overhead, sending digital photos and weather data to the fire command center, a hundred miles away in Sacramento. There strategists hunched over computer screens, studying digitized topographic maps of the Deep Creek area. The computer projections showed the fire racing up the steep part of the ridge at a speed of almost three meters per second, then slowly fanning out into the canyons on the opposite side. From there, with a strong wind behind it, the fire could get into miles of roadless, mountainous terrain where it would be hard to fight. The California Department of Disaster Response ordered teams of smoke jumpers air-dropped west of the fire to keep it from moving into the next valley, then dispatched air tankers to drop retardant on the ridge to slow its progress. Kelly's unit was ordered to hold the road as the eastern fire line, while engine companies were sent to retard the fire's progress on the southern and northern flanks.

A helicopter toting a thousand-gallon water bucket flew over the winery, low enough to read the registration number.

Every few minutes, a tanker plane approached parallel to the ridge, then dropped so low that it seemed to be flying through the flames. Bouncing from the turbulence, each plane disgorged a stream of reddish retardant, then veered upward and headed back to base for another load, passing noisily over Indian Springs. After each drop, the fire retreated momentarily in a cloud of blue smoke, then lunged forward at a different angle.

As they watched, the cloud of smoke shifted, and the crowd suddenly fell silent.

"My God," Giovanni said, speaking for everyone.

On the road above the monument, they could see a bright red vehicle burning, its tires now four columns of black, carboniferous smoke.

* * *

By the time the first firefighters arrived on the fire road, the hillside was a dune of black ash, and the advancing edge of the blaze was burning the top of the ridge, well beyond the reach of the hoses. Kelly's bright red vehicle was now a blackened, smoldering shell—and there was no sign of the driver.

One of the engines headed down the spur road to the monument to investigate the source of the blaze. The bronze statue of the pioneers was darkened by soot but otherwise undamaged.

When a CDDR official arrived to take command of Kelly's unit, the firefighters were standing on the road discussing her mysterious disappearance. The commander ordered them to suppress any hot spots on the slope above, while he formed the bus-load of convicts into a search party. With so many serving in the Middle East, three quarters of Kelly's strike team consisted of convicts from the county jail.

In a ravine above the monument, the searchers found an unused fire extinguisher and a clump of unburned bush that looked as if it had been sprayed with fire retardant. An investigator was already on the scene determining the origin of the fire. He was a big, broad-shouldered man, with an unhurried demeanor and a country drawl. Looking more like a lumberjack than a detective, he walked through the burned-over area with the delicacy of a deer stalker.

The fire had parted as it rushed up the gully, burning the slopes on both sides but leaving an island of unburned bush in the center that was dusted with a thick layer of ash. In the middle of this island of green was the imprint of a human being.

It was an ash-free shadow of exposed clay and crushed leaves where the missing firefighter had pressed herself to the ground. The fire had passed on either side of Kelly Grazziella as if an angel had stood guard with a hose.

"What the hell is that?" the commander asked, amazed by the imprint in the ashes.

"When I first saw it I thought it was a cardboard cut-out of a human figure that someone put there," the inspector confided. "I thought the sheriff's crime-scene investigators had got here ahead of me. I've never seen anything like it before."

"But she's alive?" the commander asked.

The investigator shrugged, his face hopeful.

"Then where'd she go?"

The investigator pointed to some nearly invisible scuff marks on the ground. "Here's where she slid down the slope. And here's where she ran or fell. You can see the broken branches where she tried to haul herself back up." He gestured for the photographer and the technician to get to work preserving the evidence.

The water from the hoses on the road became a rivulet that ran down the gully and pooled in a depression above the unburned area. "The water has washed out any traces of footprints up above," the investigator said. "But she did not go down to the monument." The only footprints in the ash below were their own. "She must have walked out on the fire road."

"Then why didn't the initial response team see her?" the commander asked.

"Because she went in the other direction, out the watershed."

"What do we do now?"

"I'll ask the sheriff to check the roads and wineries. And we could use a chopper too."

A deputy sheriff drove into the yard of Indian Springs Winery and told the assembly that the road that ran past the winery would be closed to all but residents until further notice. Tourists were being turned back at the toll road exits.

"Listen up," she announced, reading from her phone. "Has anyone seen a missing firefighter? White female, 25 years old, 5 feet 9 inches, hazel eyes, blond hair. Wearing a CDDR uniform. Name: Kelly Grazziella."

Giovanni looked stricken. "Kelly Grazziella?" he asked.

"That's the name," the deputy said. "Have you seen her?"

"Not for a few days. What do you mean 'missing'?"

"She went missing during the fire. Her vehicle was found burned."

Giovanni's throat turned to ash. The deputy's voice seemed fragmented and remote: "Notify the sheriff's office... the 911 number...the search...any facts... "

"You'd better close up," Clydesdale told him.

Without the tourists, the tasting room at Indian Springs Winery was so quiet that Giovanni could hear the spring water as it trickled through the groove in the concrete floor. Rays of golden sunlight brightened the white walls with an almost celestial glow.

Only last summer, he and Kelly had met again for the first time since high school. It was a warm Friday night, and all the restaurants in Oscuridad had knots of tourists waiting for tables. Usually Giovanni parked diagonally on the square, but that night he had to park in the lot behind the mall. As he crossed the creek on the footbridge, he ran into Kelly coming in the other direction. As he stepped aside to let her pass, they recognized each other.

"Kelly Grazziella!" he said. He was fourteen years old when Kelly first attracted his gaze, and far too shy to approach any girl, especially a pretty one two years older than himself.

Seeing her again years later, Giovanni learned that his youthful passion, instead of attenuating with the passage of time, had simply lain fallow in some little-visited region of desire. He had to make a conscious effort to avert his gaze from her athletic body with her strong, shapely limbs; supple wrists; and smooth, golden skin.

"I'm on my way to Zack & Zeke's" she said, not meeting his eyes.

"I'll walk you there."

They stopped to look at the collection of Mexican *santos* and Madonnas displayed in the window of The Glass Nativity art gallery.

"Look! A Black Madonna!" Kelly said, pointing to a carved wooden statue about eighteen inches high with intricately painted robes of black and gold, the gilt medallions shimmering with the lights from the shops across the square. The faces of the mother and her infant were painted black.

"My mother prays to the Black Madonna almost every day," Giovanni confided, studying Kelly's reaction in the glass.

"My grandparents were Catholic," she replied, noticing that Giovanni was looking at the reflection of her face in the window while pretending to study the statues. "When I was in Switzerland, I visited the town where my family comes from. I'll never forget it. By luck, I arrived there on the feast of the Black Madonna. I walked in the candle-light procession around the church square—it was so beautiful."

"In Europe, do they say why the Black Madonna is black?" Giovanni asked.

"There are various theories about it. A popular one is that her face has been blackened by centuries of candle smoke, but I don't believe it—the other statues have candles too, and they're not black."

Giovanni looked thoughtful. "I asked my mother once why the Black Madonna is black, and she told me that Our

Lady had passed through the fire—but I didn't know what fire she meant. What do you think?"

"Many of the shrines in Europe predate Christianity and are built near springs and grottoes sacred to the Goddess. A mother goddess of black earth transformed by fire—that feels right to me."

In the tasting room, Giovanni closed his eyes—the pain of Kelly's disappearance made him wish that the Black Madonna were as real to him as she was to his mother. He wished she would appear to him now and tell him that Kelly was safe. He looked apprehensively around the room, but there were no apparitions.

Giovanni walked to the barrel room and peered through the transparent panel in the door. The cool, concrete cavern was a refuge in hot weather, and Charles Clydesdale was seated at a small table paying bills. He was a massive man, muscular but not overweight, with a serious, heavily lined face and temples touched with gray.

Giovanni recalled that Kelly resented the Clydesdales, blaming them for tearing down her grandparents' home in order to build the new winery at Indian Springs, as she blamed her father for selling the farm that had been in the family since the end of the nineteenth century. Her great grandfather on her father's side, a landless peasant born in Switzerland, had purchased the land from a Forty Niner who claimed to be the first White settler in Deep Creek valley.

Once when Giovanni and Kelly were talking at Zack & Zeke's, leaning into each other's faces to hear above the din, the Clydesdales had entered the saloon, and Giovanni offered to introduce her to them. "You'll like them," he told Kelly. "They've preserved the old oaks that mark the driveway to the tasting room."

"I don't want to talk about Indian Springs again," she replied. "It makes me too sad"—and Giovanni changed the subject.

***

When Giovanni entered the barrel room, Charles Clydesdale looked up from the antique secretary where he was writing and rotated in his chair to face him.

"I usually handle the tasting room on Mondays," Giovanni told him, "but it's closed today, so I have a favor to ask."

"Yes," his boss said tentatively, trying to anticipate what was coming.

"I'd like a half day off so I can help look for Kelly Grazziella, the missing firefighter."

"Do you know her?"

"We've known each other since high school."

"Really. But isn't finding her something better left to professionals?"

"Maybe, but the professionals have struck out. That was her vehicle we could see burning on the fire road. She must be somewhere right around here."

"The road is closed to the public. They won't let you up there."

"I know, but I can walk up the hill behind the winery."

Clydesdale looked thoughtful. "OK," he said, "but you need to be back this afternoon. I'm still hoping to do the picking tomorrow."

"I'll be back in time."

"It's a lot steeper than it looks," Clydesdale warned.

Giovanni went to the machine shed where they stored the wide-brim hats that were loaned to visitors during tours of the vineyard. He grabbed one from a hook and put it on his head, testing the fit with his little finger. He tucked a curved grape picker's knife into his belt. Then he retrieved a bottle of mineral water from the cooler. He tried sticking the plastic bottle in the waistband of his pants, but it was too bulky, so he looked around for something that could serve as a rucksack. Spying one of the red tablecloths, he improvised a sling by rolling it into a tube and tying it over one shoulder with the

70

water bottle inside. Glancing at his own reflection in the glass, he was startled by an Italian-Swiss peasant from centuries past.

* * *

On the road above the winery, the CDDR commander shielded his eyes against the blowing grit and yelled into the wind to the leader of the sheriff's search-and-rescue effort. "You say there's no sign of her?"

"None!" the deputy shouted back. "We've been to all the wineries on the west side."

"We need to consider the possibility that she was caught by the fire after she left the gully," the arson investigator said, his hardhat pulled down against the rain of blowing ash. "Perhaps she went upslope."

The commander looked skeptical. "Do you think we should search upslope?"

"We need to check all possibilities."

The helicopter lifted into the wind and systematically traversed each contour from one end to the other, raising dust storms of ash that marked its progress. The helicopter found nothing and returned to its parking spot near the burned-out vehicle.

"Amnesia is not uncommon in cases of trauma," the arson investigator told the CDDR officials. "The person may walk away from the scene, not knowing who they are or what happened to them."

"Amnesia? So you think that's what happened to Grazziella?" the commander asked.

"It's consistent with the evidence."

"Now what?"

"Wait. Amnesia victims usually come to the attention of the police when they're reported wandering around."

The radio barked a status report from headquarters. The Deep Creek fire was now contained on the southern and western flanks. Any shift in the wind would either move the blaze toward the reservoir lake or force it onto burned-over areas, where it would die from lack of fuel. Kelly's unit was ordered to pull out.

* * *

In the ravine where Kelly Grazziella disappeared, crime scene technicians from the sheriff's department were preparing to move a casting of her impression that had been poured shortly after its discovery. It was made of a plastic-like substance that hardened almost instantly when sprayed, forming a protective layer of waterproof film on one side while preserving every detail of the ground on the other. Much of the ash had already blown away, leaving the impression of Kelly's body as a bas-relief formed of black plastic.

A television crew from One World News arrived and filmed the process from behind a line of yellow police tape. As the cameras rolled, four technicians, wearing gloves and watched by uniformed deputies, gingerly lifted the black plastic casting of the body's impression by each of its corners and deposited it gently on a bed of foam that been taped to the floor of a van.

* * *

The strong gusts of wind had ceased, replaced by a smoky, debilitating heat refracting a blood-red sun. Giovanni, his shirt glued to his back from perspiration, his pants streaked with dirt from crawling between clumps of nearly impenetrable brush, reached the grounds of the Italian-Swiss Monument and collapsed in the meager shadow of a coyote bush. He took off his hat to mop his brow and drank the last of the mineral water. Surveying the monument grounds, he saw that a dog handler from the county search-and-rescue team was at work, watched by two bored deputies waiting in the thin arc of shade cast by the ornamental dome.

For the second time that day, the dog handler was walking back and forth across the monument grounds with a pair of beagles, hoping for a scent of the missing firefighter. He had started below the peristyle and made a series of passes from one end of the property to the other. Now he was in the home stretch, searching the gully between the monument and the fire road.

When the team reached the unburned bushes where Kelly had disappeared, the dogs suddenly stopped and began sniffing eagerly, moving in larger circles while trying to pick up the scent, then pulled in opposite directions.

"They can't get a clear fix," the handler complained out loud, nudging the beagles towards the van. "The search is negative. There's nothing here."

"Let's get outta here," one deputy signaled the other.

Giovanni remained hidden a few minutes more until the vehicles were gone. When he emerged, the area was deathly still. The wind had stopped, and the hazy, mid-day sun intensified the desolation of the blackened slope above. For the first time in hours, the sky was empty of aircraft, the sirens silent. As he walked across the parking lot to the gully, he could hear each footstep on the gravel.

Giovanni headed for the small unburned patch of bush that intrigued the dogs. He slipped under the yellow police tape and climbed to where he had seen the dog handler standing. He remained motionless for several minutes, trying to imagine what had happened. Remembering the strong east wind that had rattled the tiles at the winery earlier that day, he surmised that the fire had started near the fallen telephone pole, rushed up the gully, and jumped the fire road, trapping Kelly's vehicle in the process. Where would she have gone? He visualized her in a crisp CDDR uniform, standing near her truck, with fair skin, athletic body, and shoulder-length blond hair whipping in the wind, and doing...doing what?

He studied the scene systematically: the fire road winding along the ridge parallel to the valley, the short spur road that connected it to the parking lot for the Italian-Swiss monument, and the burned-over slope, rising to the ridge line to the west. From the winery, he had seen the helicopter searches and surmised that the police would have found Kelly had she been injured or tried to walk out on the road. She must be someplace close by—perhaps even hiding out, immobilized by fear or disorientation.

Giovanni walked up to the fire road: it glared back at him in the noonday sun, silent and empty, blurred by the drifting smoke.

There was a sad, black smudge where Kelly's vehicle had burned.

He felt that she was alive and trying to speak to him.

5

THE FIRST WHITE KERNEL

Dean Weed's secretary formed a defensive line in the doorway to his office. Behind her, the Fellowship's director of communications bobbed like a quarterback looking for a wide receiver.

"Can I show you some more TV coverage?" Gus asked rhetorically, ignoring the meeting that was underway.

"Mexico again?" Dean Weed asked.

"You'd better see for yourself."

The executive director apologized to his conferees and followed Gus one floor down to the communications command center. The blinds were closed against the Dallas skyline, and television screens were stacked three high along one wall, all of them tuned to One World News.

"It's from a wildfire in California," Gus explained, whipping a remote from his pocket.

On the video, police technicians poured a black plastic compound into the depression in the leaves where Kelly Grazziella's body had lain, carried the imprint up the ravine, and carefully loaded it into the back of a van.

The anchor narrated:

A firefighter with the California Department of Disaster Response disappeared in the line of duty today and experts are mystified. There are no remains of a body, only a depression in the ashes where she sought shelter from the flames.

"It looks like she was lifted bodily into the air," one firefighter was quoted as saying.

Gus flipped from one station to another.

The imprint of the missing firefighter's body was on every television screen in the country, and talk show hosts were whipping the nation into a frenzy of speculation, fueled by pundits who had been abducted by extraterrestrials.

"When did this air?" Dean Weed asked.

"A few minutes ago. It's a breaking story. We're going to get questions about this. Believe me, this is hot."

In Gus's awed and hopeful voice, Dean Weed heard the apocalyptic yearning of the Fellowship's more than thirty million members—and he knew he had to head it off.

"We can't do anything until we show this to Duane. And he's addressing an off-site retreat in Provo, Utah," Dean Weed explained.

"Yes, 'The Challenge of Islam to Western Civilization.' He'll be finished soon."

Gus displayed the feed from Provo. There was a wide shot of the audience—a sea of White, expressionless faces, with a scattering of impeccably dressed Asians, some earnest Hispanics with neckties, and a handful of Blacks the color of cafe au lait. Then a close-up of the founder of the Fellowship, the nation's top-grossing televangelist, Dr. Duane Boone III, moving like a dancer in a silk suit of shark-skin gray, his deep voice rolling like thunder, his microphone slashing like a patriarch's staff:

> Evil cannot be coddled, evil cannot be appeased, evil cannot be bought off. Evil must be confronted with a sword!

76

The time is at hand for the final, cosmic battle on the plains of Armageddon. There the armies of the godless will converge on the remnant of the righteous—and be vanquished by the hand of the Lord!

It is not just the fate of one small, beleaguered, freedom-loving nation, not just the survival of the Free World—but the future of the human race will be decided by the fate of Jerusalem

"Only another eight minutes," Gus said confidently, looking at his watch.

* * *

Dean Weed left a message with Boone's road manager, then walked down to the break room in order to stretch his legs. Two Christian Network employees were eating take-out meals, their eyes glued to a television suspended from the ceiling.

"It's amazing—she's completely disappeared and there are not even tracks," one of the employees said to the other.

"It was a miracle—she was snatched to heaven by the hand of God," the second affirmed.

The executive director felt his stomach tighten like a noose—he couldn't keep the Rapture of the First White Kernel bottled up forever. Now it was about to go viral.

* * *

Dean Weed returned to his office, knowing that he could not do anything until he had a chance to assess the televangelist's reaction to the image of the missing firefighter. A biographer in WikiFree had written that Duane Boone III suffered from bipolar disorder, but the televangelist denied that diagnosis and took no medication, though his mood swings were common knowledge to his staff and to the press. During his manic moods, Boone often had what he called "infusions of the Spirit" that put Dean Weed in the awkward position of countermanding God. The executive director wondered which of Boone's two personalities would return his call—the enthusiastic televangelist rushing down the hall barking orders to his retinue, Gus sprinting beside him talking on the phone? Or would it be Duane the sullen prophet afflicted with depression, boarded up against the world, moving slowly as if through a viscous fluid?

Dean Weed's secretary poked her head through the door.

"Dr. Boone needs to speak with you immediately on video phone three!" He could tell by her voice that it was Boone the televangelist calling.

"We need to get ready for an announcement—a major announcement," Boone said with palpable excitement. "I told Gus to reserve the Stockman Hotel main ballroom for my presentation and the Dallas Bankers football stadium for the Christian Cadette Corps. We need to kick this thing off big-time!"

"But which day?" Dean Weed asked in a worried voice.

The Fellowship taught that there was a period of time between the initial disappearance of the First White Kernel and the transformation of the transported into a fully glorified state, but there was disagreement among the theologians as to the number of earth days in one turn of the prophetic clock. One school maintained that the prefiguration of the rapture occurred three days from the First White Kernel's initial disappearance, another school that two cycles of three days each were needed. Boone tended toward the 3 + 3 interpretation, but the Fellowship had never made an official pronouncement on the subject.

"If that firefighter's not found by eleven minutes after eleven Central Daylight Time on Thursday morning, then I will take it as a sign," the televangelist announced.

Dean Weed gulped—they had only until Thursday morning to talk him out of it.

"I want to get the ball rolling today so we're ready when God gives the nod."

"I agree," Dean Weed said. "But there's another thing we need to do first."

"Yes?"

"The announcement will be much more effective if there is no public speculation and argument about the time of occurrence. Since it's possible that the rapture event is three *plus* three days away, I suggest you initiate a worldwide clampdown on discussion of this topic until the date is finalized."

"A good idea. Do it."

Dean Weed called the director of communications. Gus's stock will soar with the countdown to the rapture, but he could rein him in for now. "Duane wants me to tell you that he's initiated a clampdown on press releases and communiqués about the impending rapture until further notice. For maximal impact, he doesn't want any leaks."

"I understand," the director of communications said, more relieved than disappointed.

"Tammy Jo Boone is on line 2," Dean Weed's secretary informed him. "She says it's urgent."

In the early years of the movement, when their children were small, there were Weeds in the back yard of the Boone family home almost every day. But now the wife of the organization's founder only called when there were sensitive issues pertaining to the Fellowship.

"Have you seen the story on One World News about the missing firefighter?" Tammy Jo asked in her rural, east Texas drawl. "Disappearing during a fire without a trace, just an imprint of her body..." She lowered her voice. "I'm worried that Duane will use her disappearance to publicly announce the Rapture of the First White Kernel."

"That's my concern too. In fact, I just spoke with him, and he's already asked Gus to reserve the Stockman Hotel and the football stadium."

"O my God! This time we might not be so lucky," Tammy Jo said ominously. "Once Duane makes the announcement, the cat will be out of the bag, and there will be no getting it back in," she warned.

Dean Weed had hoped this day would never come, and now it had appeared out of nowhere. "What do you suggest?" he asked her.

"Find that firefighter—before Duane makes a fool of himself!"

"I'll talk to Vaughn MacVain," he assured her.

"Good. And the less he knows the better."

Colorado Springs

Deep in his bomb-proof office thirteen stories below ground, Vaughn MacVain, the founder of the Krator Corporation, was reviewing a list of high-priority dissidents that had been targeted for assassination. His steel-gray eyes were narrowed in concentration; his face was pale and expressionless. But to those who knew him the taut curl of his thin lips conveyed his pleasure in the work.

MacVain was startled by the ringing of the red telephone. It was a stand-alone device, like a museum piece from the Cold War but isolated from general telecom traffic and reserved for members of the Council of Seventeen—the secret committee that ruled the Free World. With the exception of the corpulent accountant known as the Chairman, MacVain was that body's most powerful member.

The red telephone rang a second time.

"I'm glad I found you in," Dean Weed said without introduction. "There's a crisis situation developing. Do you have a TV there? Take a look at the breaking firefighter story."

MacVain clicked a few icons, and news video hung in the air in front of his desk.

A dignified, fair-haired woman in a dark blue business suit reprised the day's events:

"The California Department of Disaster Response reports that there are twenty-nine wildfires burning in the state at this time, at least two of them threatening structures. With a red flag warning in force, control of the wildfires will depend on a change in weather conditions. Today's blaze in the Deep Creek valley, in the heart of the Almaden County wine-making district, has been seventy-five percent contained."

The reporter's image dissolved to the uncanny outline of Kelly Grazziella's body in the bed of white ash. The lens lingered as if to heighten the sense of the occult.

"The disappearance of firefighter Kelly Grazziella remains a mystery. Crime scene investigators from the Almaden County Sheriff's Department and arson investigators from the California Department of Disaster Response have found no evidence of a crime and no physical remains."

An earnest sheriff's deputy told the audience that they were investigating the possibility that the missing firefighter had been given a ride out of the area by a Good Samaritan.

A female spokesperson in the gray and green uniform of a CDDR firefighter told the audience that they were working on the assumption that Kelly Grazziella had suffered a memory loss as a result of trauma and had wandered away from the fire under her own power.

MacVain turned off the news channel and picked up the red telephone. "I saw it—so what?"

"Almost certainly, the rank and file are going to see this as the prefiguration of the rapture."

The founder of Krator looked mystified. "Refresh my memory."

"Remember when the Fellowship announced the doctrine of the Rapture of the First White Kernel—someone purified by fire who will herald the countdown to the end time?"

"Oh, yes," MacVain said, sure that he had never heard of it before.

"This missing firefighter fills the bill. Already, employees of the Lone Star Christian Network are talking about her rapture."

Vaughn MacVain firmly believed in religion—but only as the thin edge of the wedge in Latin America. He found theology incomprehensible and struggled to make the connection. "I still don't see the downside," he admitted.

Dean Weed wondered how much to tell him about the hidden history of the nation's most prominent religion. "Duane once came within a hair's breath of a debacle like the Millerites. At that time, in 1843, tens of thousands of people assembled with great fanfare throughout the eastern United States to embrace the second coming of Jesus who, to put it plainly, never showed up. Years ago, Duane prophesied the date on which the battle of Armageddon would begin, and it was only technical difficulties that prevented him from announcing it on the air."

The executive director did not say that he had arranged the technical difficulties himself, nor that he and Boone's wife, Tammy Jo, had since trained the producers at the Lone Star Christian Network to kill the audio if the televangelist ever again tried to give the exact time and date of prophesied events.

Dean Weed spelled it out for Krator's founding father: "There's concern that if Duane proclaims this missing firefighter to be the Rapture of the First White Kernel, and then she turns up again, well, it would discredit the entire prophetic Christian movement. It could mean the end of the Fellowship."

MacVain did not have to be told that Krator without the Fellowship would be Intel without Microsoft.

"How can Krator help?" he asked.

"Find that missing firefighter—either dead or alive. And before 11:11 central time on Thursday morning."

"I'll initiate a red alert."

* * *

Vaughn MacVain beeped his special assistant, Tricia Culhane, in her office down the hall. "We need to talk," MacVain told her. "*Before* it hits the fan!"

Tricia Culhane was a sturdy, energetic woman in her late thirties with reddish, close-cropped hair who held a law degree from Midwestern University and a masters in administration from Hardwood Business School. Her friendly, Midwestern manner hid a life-long fascination with power. As a public prosecutor, she had impressed MacVain with her ability to bend the law without breaking it, and on his recommendation she had been appointed as legal counsel to a little-known federal agency that later became Krator's covert operations division. When the Krator Corporation abolished the United States Department of Justice, MacVain appointed Culhane to the company's highest position held by a woman.

No one had planned Culhane's job description, but after a spate of assassination attempts, the Council of Seventeen forbade physical meetings of the full committee in order to ensure that all the leaders of the Free World were never together in the same room. Instead, each member of the Council sent an emissary, who subsequently became known as that member's special assistant. What began as a temporary security measure had evolved into a safeguard against coups and conspiracies, so that face-to-face meetings among Council members nowadays rarely occur, while physical meetings of the entire Council no longer take place. All of the special assistants are women, and all of them are lawyers.

Tricia Culhane hurried down the hall and through the automatic, roll-down doors. Even though the founder of Krator works deep underground, MacVain's outer office is furnished like a corporate law firm, with thick carpets and wainscot walls. On one wall, where the picture window would ordinarily be, a high-definition video screen provides a live, panoramic view of the New York City skyline as seen from the top floor of a fictional high-rise office building at the corner of Wall and Broad Streets.

A year earlier MacVain had commissioned a cyberarchitect to build him a replica of the palace of the doges in Venice. Once this magnificent Renaissance edifice was constructed, MacVain had virtual reality projectors installed in his physical office so he could work in the palace on a regular basis. From that time on, the senior attorney proceeded directly from the parking garage to the simulation, pausing only long enough to retrieve a cup of liquid yogurt and nod to administrative staff. Once the antique double doors of the Doge's Palace clicked shut, people rarely saw him except in cyberspace.

The fact that MacVain had summoned Tricia Culhane to a live meeting in physical space signaled the gravity of the subject matter.

"He's in the Doge's Palace," MacVain's secretary told her. "Go right in."

On the wall adjacent to the doorway was a brass plate that said simply: "Office of the Senior Attorney." MacVain disdained the usual titles of chairman, president, and CEO, preferring a more discrete designation that better conveyed his law degree from Hardwood University.

As the special assistant approached the entrance to the senior attorney's lair, a smart camera recognized her face, and the massive, ornate doors stripped from an ancient church in Italy yawned open to admit her.

Tricia Culhane sat down in the Renaissance side chair, a real antique purchased for authenticity. It had once belonged to a Borgia pope.

"A firefighter went missing during a wildfire in California today, and everyone's in a dither about it," MacVain told her. "Dean Weed wants Krator to find her ASAP."

"Is he afraid she might be the Rapture of the First White Kernel?"

The senior attorney sometimes found the breadth of her knowledge disconcerting. "Yes, that's the reason."

"A red alert?" she inquired.

"A red alert is appropriate. We should convene a task force too. And I have someone I want on it."

Tricia Culhane waited for the name—hoping it would be Celestine Brittle.

MacVain slid a printout in her direction. The photo showed an attractive woman in her twenties, with shoulder-length blond hair and an angular face that made her look English.

"Her name is Celestine Brittle," MacVain said. "She's a research analyst at the Predictive Criminality Center in Laredo, Texas. We need a pre-indite done by someone of her caliber."

Laredo, Texas

On the day that the wildfire hit the news, Celestine Brittle had taken compensation time from work; she was at home reading a monograph on the number of the beast. Celestine had graduated Phi Beta Kappa with a major in mathematics, and she recognized numbers the way most people remember faces. Some numbers were as much a part of her as slippers to a ballerina, while others she found cold, threatening, or boring. When Celestine thought of 666, she saw the repeating patterns on a serpent. It was a number endlessly flexible and intertwining, mysterious, and a little frightening. She subscribed to several list servers on the Internet that did nothing else but explicate the Book of Revelation's hidden prophetic messages and decrypt its numerical symbolism. When she watched the late-night news, she interpreted the stories in the light of biblical prophecy about the reign of the beast.

Although a proclaimed Christian, Celestine secretly preferred Saint Paul to Jesus. The Son of God she regarded as overly tolerant of sinners and lacking in evangelical zeal. She usually skipped the Gospels to concentrate on the Acts of the Apostles and the Pauline epistles. But her favorite book was Revelation, with its obscure but vivid imagery about the final battle between the forces of good and the forces of evil.

Celestine had grown up in the Fellowship of the Eighth Dispensation, and both her father and uncle were early supporters of Duane Boone III. They had organized the first assembly of the Fellowship in Midland, Texas, and it was only natural that Celestine Brittle became a member of the Fellowship church in Laredo when she was transferred to the Krator facility there.

Laredo was the mother church of the Fellowship, first founded as a drive-in revival camp; and for many years Duane Boone III himself had presided there as pastor. Shortly after the attack on the World Trade Center, Boone resigned the pastorship in Laredo to spend more time in the Fellowship's national office in Dallas, but Celestine had met him one Sunday when he returned to preach a sermon to his former congregation.

It was a sunny spring day, and Celestine had paused after the service to admire the flowers blooming in the patio next to the church when Boone came up to her and shook her hand warmly.

The televangelist was a tall, broad-shouldered Texan with a smile as wide as his hat brim. "I knew your father well. I knew he had a daughter, but I had no idea she was such a pretty and charming young woman."

Celestine blushed.

"May I present my wife, Tammy Jo?"

Celestine turned to a slight, anorexic woman of indeterminate age and predatory features. Her bleached blond hair had the texture of Brillo. "Why how do you do?" Tammy Jo said sweetly, with a firm hand and a practiced smile. "Your father was one of the founding members of the Fellowship in Midland. Are you enjoying your stay in Laredo?"

"Very much," Celestine dissimulated.

"You make us wish we were staying longer, so we could get to know you better," she said.

Boone took Celestine by the arm and turned her gently so she faced the chairman of the search committee. "The search committee needs some young blood. Would you be interested?" he asked her.

She was relieved that she was no longer the topic of discussion and too surprised to do anything but nod in the affirmative.

"I'm counting on you to get us a good pastor," he said with a smile, patting her hand before moving on.

The new pastor had all of Boone's rigidity and intolerance but none of his charm and charisma. Celestine found herself spending less time at the Fellowship church and more in private devotion. She spent hours each day reading books on theology. Although she never talked about religion at work, she had installed a copy of the New Testament on her phone, from which she silently read a passage every day before lunch.

About a year earlier, she had begun exchanging e-mails with a clergyman at a Protestant church in Laredo who had been referred by someone she knew in Dallas. He was not a fundamentalist, but she was immediately attracted to his Internet handle—Amadeus. In his physical life, he hosted a weekly interfaith Bible study group that ministered to busy professional people. It convened during lunchtime in a restaurant in North Laredo. In their first e-mail exchange, he had questions about the various schools of interpretation pertaining to Revelation, and Celestine referred him to several books. A month later he e-mailed back with some questions on the readings, and their subsequent e-mail correspondence blossomed into a relationship that touched on all the big questions in religious thought, with a candor and mutual respect that thrilled her.

On the door of her refrigerator she posted a printout of an e-mail from Amadeus, the last sentence underlined in yellow marking pencil:

> You'll recall that in the story of David and Goliath, the boy David was brought before King Saul. Before sending him forth to slay the giant, the king dressed him in his own armor—but David could barely walk in that heavy metal suit. Instead, David left the armor behind and went forth to meet Goliath carrying only his slingshot. <u>You have real giants to slay, but your fundamentalist premises are far too heavy</u>.

Celestine was interrupted by the ringing of the land line telephone. She rarely used it, and no one but her supervisor knew she was at home.

"Celestine Brittle?" a woman asked.

"Who is calling please?"

"I am Tricia Culhane, special assistant to senior attorney MacVain at Krator headquarters. Is this Celestine Brittle?"

"Yes," Celestine answered nervously.

"Sorry to disturb you at home, but I need to talk to you right away on a secure phone."

"I'll log on," Celestine said.

Celestine's laptop computer scrutinized her retina, voice, and fingerprints, then established a secure communications link, converting anything that went over the line to an incomprehensible stream of bits readable only to Krator employees with Krator computers.

Special assistant Tricia Culhane looked to be in her late thirties, business-like, somewhat plain in her looks but with a round and cheerful face under a bob of reddish brown hair. She was wearing a warm-up suit and appeared to be calling from her home office. Behind her on the side table was a television screen almost completely hidden by a stack of library books. Celestine had never seen library books in someone's home before. Publishers now required public libraries to charge a reading fee and to keep accurate records of who read what, so books no longer circulated.

"You may have heard about the firefighter, Kelly Grazziella, who disappeared in California today during a wildfire? Krator is forming a task force to assist in the search, and you have been selected to participate. Until further notice, you are on special assignment, reporting to me. Your supervisor has already been notified."

"Oh!" was all that Celestine was able to say, and that with audible surprise and excitement.

"All task force members are being asked to participate in a virtual conference tomorrow morning. You will need to be in the virtual conference center at your facility at six-thirty tomorrow morning, local time, for preparation and familiarization. Understand?"

"Six-thirty tomorrow."

"Also, to begin its work, the task force will need a pre-indictment profile of the missing firefighter. I want you to prepare a pre-indite right away."

"Is it all right to write it from home."

"That's fine, but do it as quickly as possible. When you finish, send it directly to me. And *don't* copy your supervisor or coworkers on anything while working for me."

"Your eyes only. I understand. May I ask a question?"

"Certainly."

"Is the missing firefighter a predicted criminal?"

"Not yet, but find out if she had any reason to disappear. I'll see you tomorrow morning."

The Pre-indite

When Celestine Brittle dragged the Social Security number of Kelly Grazziella into the primary search field, it displayed a page of clickable buttons accessing her photographs, DNA profile, fingerprints, voice print, driving record, employment records, medical records, tax returns, credit rating, insurance policies, e-mails, phone bills, web page visits, retail purchases, online friends, family members, business associates, and a list of all trips she had taken out of the country. The only thing missing from the file was her police record—because she had none.

Using the GPS coordinates automatically relayed from the sheriff's patrol car when the missing person report was radioed in, Celestine downloaded the Defense Department's satellite photos. A moment later a Grecian monument with a copper dome was clearly visible on her computer screen. Although there were no previous police reports involving the site of the Italian-Swiss Monument, that fact did not deter her investigation. When Celestine Brittle thought of Californians, she thought of Mexicans—and Mexicans were either heavily involved in the drug trade or living in the United States illegally.

As a child, Celestine had once played with the little boy of a Mexican neighbor, but her uncle took her aside. "They pretend to be good Americans," he told her darkly, "but they take their orders from the pope in Rome." At the time, she had no idea what a pope was—but it was clear from her uncle's tone of voice that Rome would be better off without one.

At the Sunday Fellowship services, her minister preached that Catholics were slaves to a demonic religion that worshipped statues and promoted alcoholic beverages. Unless they renounced their idolatry and were born again through baptism by total submersion, they would be damned to hell for all eternity—children and infants too. Celestine Brittle did not like to think of tens of millions of Mexicans burning in eternal torment, but she consoled herself with the thought that they had brought it on themselves through their own obstinate refusal to be baptized a second time.

Also, her supervisor had told her, lowering her voice as if in confidence, that one should assume that any structure in the California countryside is cover for a Mexican drug ring unless conclusively proved to be otherwise.

And California—who knew what went on there? It was common knowledge in her church that even the White people in that state practiced unnatural sex. At work Celestine sometimes peeked at the police reports that Krator staff circulated for their own amusement, reports containing lurid descriptions of what agents found entwined together in bed during some of their predawn raids. Every sort of pornography and vice was freely available in California. Liquor was sold in grocery stores, and there was not a dry district in the entire state. As for the Wine Country, the Fellowship taught that it was a slippery slope from a Sunday sip of the sacrament to the selling of psychedelics.

From the Institute for Genetic Assessment and Profiling, Celestine learned that Kelly Grazziella was descended from an Italian-Swiss family that had settled in Almaden County in the nineteenth century. Checking the national real estate titles database, she learned that the Grazziella family had once owned all the land from the valley floor to the ridge line but had sold it off in the 1990s, in two parcels, one to a family named Clydesdale and the other to a real estate development company named Ridgeline Castles, L.L.C. The new owners had no police record.

Celestine accessed the database on entries and exits from the United States. The records were updated in real-time by passport control at every port of entry in the country, as well as periodically enhanced with names, dates, and destinations purchased from the airline reservation services. They were cross-referenced to visas processed by Immigration. She dragged the target's passport number into the search field and waited expectantly. The result was disappointing. Grazziella had been out of the country only once, as a summer language student in Spain during her junior year in college; and while there, she had visited only one other country—Switzerland.

Grazziella's cellular telephone, the best way of tracking suspects, had ceased responding about the time of the fire. Since then, there had been no telecommunications anywhere in the world that could be linked to the target.

When Celestine clicked on the California Department of Motor Vehicles icon, Grazziella's photograph popped onto the screen. Celestine thought the target must be stunning in real life to look so attractive on her driver's license—she did not know that for an extra fee drivers in California could get digital enhancement of their photos by beauticians at Hollywood studios.

The target's medical records were the most revealing. Grazziella had given up a baby for adoption at the start of her sophomore year at Davis University. The father was listed as "unknown." To ensure privacy, the names of the adoptive parents were sealed by the family court in Sacramento, California.

Celestine noted that the baby born out of wedlock would bump Grazziella's predictive criminality score into the range of African-Americans, but otherwise the firefighter was not good pre-indictment material. There were no targeted words in her e-mail, and her correspondents did not appear on any of Krator's watch lists. There were no political or pornography sites in her web page preferences. She had the same credit card account since college and had never missed a payment. She maintained good grades in school, had won championships in track and field, was president of the rock-climbing club in college, and had been promoted to acting strike team leader at the California Department of Disaster Response.

There was nothing to suggest that Grazziella had intentionally fled the scene of the fire.

Celestine wrote up the pre-indictment profile, including a list of Grazziella's friends and associates for agents to interview, and sent it by e-mail to Tricia Culhane.

L-RetroBan

In his office thirteen stories below ground at the apex of an inverted pyramid, the founder of the Krator Corporation was reviewing a secret report on the memory suppression drug, L-RetroBan. The report was a thick, perfect-bound document full of charts and graphs; even the executive summary was written in chem-speak.

Vaughn MacVain put down the document and phoned his special assistant. "Have you read the final report on L-RetroBan yet?" the senior attorney asked.

"You bet," Tricia Culhane acknowledged.

"Refresh my memory."

"Well, as you know, about ten years ago, the drug was touted as the humane alternative to the body in a car trunk. And it was extensively field tested on Latin American military officers. But apparently, the amnesia is less permanent than was thought. The latest research shows spontaneous memory recovery after trauma, like a bad fall or a house fire. The suppressed memory over-rides the memory of the most recent trauma," Tricia Culhane explained.

"You mean, like a guy suddenly remembers that he put the second bullet into Kennedy but forgets that he just slipped in the shower?"

"Yes, exactly. Not only that, but the suppressed memory comes back with vivid enhancement of the original scene, with improved recall, like a heightened state of consciousness. People think they're back in the original situation and can remember things they did not even know they knew."

The senior attorney looked grim. "That could play havoc with witnesses suffering irreversible memory loss."

"It has already compromised several operations."

"What do we need to do in reference to this report?" he asked.

"Each department is supposed to prepare a risk assessment chart that lists the potential risk for each operation in which L-RetroBan was used, and to propose a remedy, with a budget estimate of what it will cost to implement."

"None of this applies to the Office of the Senior Attorney," he said in a dismissive tone.

"That's right. It's only for departments with covert operations."

"Thank you," he said, hanging up.

MacVain felt a twinge of gastritis. Not even his special assistant knew about the Tall Blondes project, now threatened with exposure by the shifting sands of L-RetroBan. He found some consolation in the fact that not even the chemists knew the exact odds of memory recovery, and all were agreed that the rate was very low.

MacVain telephoned his personal security officer in the siege bunker below his office. Designed to protect the senior attorney from any breach of the security perimeters, it also served as the office of Cole Kincaid, the point person for MacVain's own black bag projects.

"Have there been any hits on the tripwires for the Nathan Whyte Laboratory?" MacVain wanted to know.

"No, sir, not in months."

"We might get some activity there, so let me know right away."

"Yes, sir."

"Also, has there been anything involving Tall Blondes in Mexico?" MacVain asked.

"Just that journalist I told you about," saying the word "journalist" as if it were synonymous with child molester. "The one that wrote that article on American medical experiments in Mexico."

"The Latin American bureau chief for *Left America*?"

"That's the one."

"What is the status of that?"

"I'm expecting closure any time now."

"Let me know as soon as it's been successfully concluded."

The senior attorney clicked the icon for the Tall Blondes project and scrolled through the database. As he suspected, there had been no contact or follow-up with the experimental subjects in the six years since the research had been completed. At the time of the experiment, they had all been college students in Davis, California, but now they could be anywhere.

MacVain buzzed his secretary, a middle-aged Mormon woman who mothered him. "Charlene! My stomach is bothering me again. Do we have any bicarbonate?"

The Adoption Agency

Tricia Culhane called Vaughn MacVain on their dedicated phone line.

"Are you sitting down?" she asked him. "Krator Sacramento unsealed the records of the adoption of Kelly Grazziella's baby. What they found is unexpected—and a little disturbing."

95

The senior attorney's stomach rumbled. Now that L-RetroBan was compromised, anything could happen—and now it had.

"When they investigated the adoption agency all they found were bogus digital identities," Tricia Culhane told him. "Apprehension and Detention can't find a single warm body to tie to the place.

"You're telling me that after Kelly Grazziella was knocked up in her freshman year she gave her baby up to a phony adoption agency?"

"That's right," Tricia Culhane confirmed.

MacVain turned to the computer and ran a search of the task force Wildfire database: "Wassily Tweecus, Chad Weed, Nathan Whyte Laboratory."

The cursor spun for a millisecond that seemed to MacVain like an hour, then beeped and displayed: "no items found"

Thank God, he thought—Tall Blondes is still secure.

"A baby sale racket?" he asked.

"They don't know."

"What about her baby? Is that phony too?"

"No, she had a real baby. Student health center records show that Grazziella tested positive for pregnancy, and a hospital in Sacramento confirms that a birth took place. The mother's DNA is the same as Grazziella's. They have a doctor and a nurse who remember her too."

"So what happened to the baby?"

"It was handed over to a representative of the adoption agency as soon as it was born—and the trail goes cold."

MacVain searched the Davis University database, confirming that he had removed from the college's computers all records that proved Wassily Tweecus had done bioweapons research while a professor at the medical school, as well as any references anywhere to the quality control phase of Tall Blondes, as he now referred to the experiments. He also double-checked the paper trail put in place by the phony adoption agency to ensure there was nothing that could lead investigators back to the Nathan Whyte Laboratory.

"Who's the father?" he asked.

"That's a mystery too. The Wildfire task force talked to every one of Grazziella's college friends and roommates, and not a single good candidate for the father has emerged."

"Are there are other mothers in the same boat?"

"The Wildfire task force is checking the hospitals in Sacramento. So far, there are two other mothers besides Grazziella who gave up babies to the same agency."

"There are still too many unanswered questions," MacVain snapped. "Let's keep this from the press, even from One World News, until we have a coherent story. There's enough speculation as it is."

"First a missing firefighter, now a missing adoption agency!" Tricia Culhane laughed before hanging up.

The senior attorney brooded over the new situation. The information conveyed by his special assistant had only one logical explanation—that the missing firefighter had been one of Wassily Tweecus's experimental subjects. He could not imagine a worse conjunction of circumstances—unless, of course, the firefighter started to remember.

MacVain activated the telephone log and replayed a recent conversation with the Krator chief scientist to see if there was anything he had missed. Tweecus's shrill voice pierced the cloistered silence, indignant and annoyed, as if he had been asked to explain why he had changed the batteries in his flashlight:

> Only three American women were involved— they were needed to assure the quality of the product shipped to Mexico.

"Jesus!" MacVain snarled, "You couldn't have gone to Mexico and tested the goddamned product there?"

97

"Nine months in Mexico? We had to use local women so I could monitor them personally without disrupting everything else. Besides, the women only knew about the adoption agency. They know nothing about the lab."

"How can you be so sure?"

"I gave them the L-RetroBan myself."

MacVain telephoned Tweecus.

"Is there any chance that the missing firefighter was ever a subject at the Nathan Whyte Lab?" MacVain asked him.

"It's impossible for anyone to say if anyone was ever an experimental subject," the chief scientist said in his haughty, high-pitched voice. "Chad Weed was the only person who knew the subjects' identities, but he never knew the nature of the experiments. I knew about the experiments but not the subjects' names. It was all done with code numbers."

"You are sure there are no records linking the names of the women in the adoption agency to the subjects of the experiments?"

"We've been over this a dozen times already," the scientist whined. "You destroyed the computerized records yourself."

"All right," MacVain muttered, hanging up.

The senior attorney sat glowering in the cavernous marble hall of the doge's audience chamber, convinced that the chief scientist knew more than he was telling. Until he read the report on L-RetroBan, MacVain had complete confidence in the firewall he had built around the Nathan Whyte Laboratory. Yesterday, he had thought that only three people now alive besides himself—Chad Weed, Wassily Tweecus, and G. Lyle Acre—knew what had been done there. But now that the wonder drug was compromised, it was just a matter of time before the experimental subjects remembered too.

Chad Weed—he winced at the thought of that name. During MacVain's first week as attorney general of the United States, the man who later became the chairman of the Council of Seventeen had approached him with what had seemed a simple request, asking him to give the son of an old friend a chance to start a new life. MacVain, then eager to please, had fabricated a fatal cerebral hemorrhage on the eve of Chad Weed's arrest, then replaced the photos and biometrics in Weed's criminal records with those of a deceased young man of the same age. Only later did he learn that Chad Weed was Dean Weed's ne'er-do-well son.

Then a whole train of similar requests followed in its wake. First, editing Chad Weed's academic history to remove the two previous colleges and any trace of attendance at Davis University. Then adding the phony bachelor's degree from Duchess University, his father's alma mater. Finally, sanitizing the psychiatric records, removing the drug treatment centers, and obliterating that doctor's diagnosis that the kid was a clinical sociopath. He should have drawn the line there. But no, he gave Dean's son a new identity in a foreign country too. Now Krator did not even have a recent photo of the elusive trouble-maker—and no idea where to find him.

The senior attorney pushed himself away from his desk with an angry thrust.

He was still furious about the congressional legislation that privatized federal police agencies but had exempted local law enforcement from the consolidation, as had originally been planned. It offended his sense of order that every county and town in the United States had its own police department investigating murders and burglaries, instead of a single national force as in other civilized countries. Krator could give them federal grants, invoke federal statutes, and plead national security, but it was still not the same as controlling the salary of the cop on the beat. He fumed at the workarounds he was so often forced to use so that members of the ungrateful public could sleep more securely in their beds.

And that firefighter—she came out of nowhere. If she were an experimental subject, and if she remembered anything in her "heightened state of consciousness," she would certainly remember her abductor Chad Weed, his boss Wassily Tweecus, and the Nathan Whyte Laboratory.

MacVain stood up and paced like caged leopard.

Suppose the terrorist media got hold of Grazziella's story before Krator could bottle it up? Then Tall Blondes would be on every news screen outside of the Free World.

He rang his secretary. "We need to set up a physical meeting tonight," he told her. "With General G. Lyle Acre, 888th Special Operations Brigade."

"Here, in your office?"

"No, tell him to meet me at the landing strip—he'll know what I mean. And try to set it up for nine tonight. If he balks, tell him I want to introduce him to a tall blonde."

The senior attorney telephoned Cole Kincaid, his personal security officer, in the siege bunker two floors below his office.

"How would you like to go hunting tonight?" the senior attorney asked.

"Tonight?"

"Varmint hunting. Some coyotes have been nosing around the ranch. I want to teach them a lesson they'll never forget."

"Sure. I'd love to go," the security officer responded, flattered to be asked.

"Come by the airstrip at nine o'clock. I'll be in my Hummer."

"Sure. I'll bring my .223 with the night scope."

"At the airstrip. Nine o'clock."

Finally, Vaughn MacVain rang Tricia Culhane. "I meant to ask you. How is that research analyst working out on Wildfire?"

"Brittle? Well, I've only talked to her once. But she's smart and prepares a good pre-indite."

"So we could use her on some other project in the future?"

"So far so good."

* * *

Celestine Brittle's computer signaled another incoming call from Colorado Springs. She was expecting Tricia Culhane, but it was a middle-aged woman with a dour face—MacVain's secretary.

"Senior Attorney MacVain will be with you in a moment," the woman said.

As Celestine watched the telecommunications screen, she was startled by a man's voice—a dry, no-nonsense voice devoid of recognizable feeling. MacVain was calling in audio-only mode.

"I hope you are enjoying the added level of responsibility of task force Wildfire?" he asked flatly.

"Very much. It is highly challenging."

"Sometimes I think we do not challenge our young staff enough here at Krator, which is why we sought you out. We're impressed with the work you've done so far, and we would like to give you some first-hand experience working with people in headquarters."

"Thank you."

"I would like you to prepare two pre-indites that are not, strictly speaking, part of the red alert. They are for my eyes only. Do not post them in the Wildfire database and do not copy them, or even mention them, to Tricia Culhane either."

"I understand—your eyes only."

"The subjects of the pre-indite are the other two women who gave up babies to the adoption agency. Their current addresses are essential."

"The phony adoption agency that Grazziella used?"

"Exactly."

"When do you need them by?"

"Right away, say within an hour?"

"That might not be enough time."

"Two hours."

"Yes. Do I send them to your personal e-mail?"

"That's perfect. Let my secretary know as soon as they're ready. Also, I have a meeting Friday morning in Laredo, and I would like you to attend."

Celestine suppressed her surprise and steeled herself to sound as professional as possible. "Certainly. I appreciate the opportunity."

"My secretary will provide you with the details and set up a time. I look forward to meeting you in person."

The secretary reappeared on the video screen and told Celestine that the meeting would be in the senior attorney's executive jet at the Laredo airport. She also informed Celestine of a dress code: no pants suits or slacks, only suits with skirts or conservative dresses.

Tall Blondes

Vaughn MacVain parked his Humvee in the tall grass and listened for the drone of the airplane. Built by the Forest Service to provide emergency access to the back country, the airfield was nothing more than a strip of bare ground bulldozed through the middle of a meadow, with a wind sock hanging from a pole. It was sometimes used by cattle herders in summer and by deer hunters in autumn. On a bluff high above, the tops of the conifers glowed with the pink of the setting sun. The airstrip was almost dark.

The senior attorney left the headlights of his Hummer turned on, the beams aligned perpendicular to the runway, with several battery-powered lanterns marking the other end of the airstrip. He looked at his Rolex. In the distance he heard a plane. He cocked an ear as it drew closer. Suddenly, it burst into view above the bluff and made a wide circle around the airstrip. It was a thick-bodied plane with two engines, designed for short take-off and landing. It was a military aircraft, fitted with weapons mounts but without any military insignia. Painted a mottled black and gray, only its running lights showed against the clouds as it circled in the eastern sky. A moment later, it dropped rapidly, then bounced down the airstrip, coming to a stop in front of the Hummer.

When MacVain turned off the headlights, the plane turned off its running lights, and suddenly both vehicles vanished into the shadow cast by the cliff above. With light from only a single lantern, the conifers were black against the rosy sky.

MacVain got out of the Hummer and stood impatiently in the tall grass waiting for his visitor. The senior attorney was almost unrecognizable in bespoke blue jeans, a hand-stitched denim shirt, and a bolo tie fastened with a chunk of turquoise sunk in a mound of hammered sterling silver.

A moment later, the hatch opened and a tall, gray-haired man in camouflage fatigues emerged from the plane and clambered down the wing. It was G. Lyle Acre, commander of the 888th Special Operations Brigade. From its secret base in Matamoros, Mexico, on the Gulf Coast just across the Texas border, the brigade performed covert operations inside the United States, as well as military and police tasks that the government of Mexico was unable or unwilling to do.

"Good to see you," Acre said, shaking the senior attorney's hand. "How long has it been?"

"Two years at least. You're looking younger."

"It's the exercise," the general admitted, patting his stomach like a drum so the senior attorney could hear its tautness.

"Let's talk in the car," MacVain said, getting back in the driver's seat. No light went on when the door opened. He closed the bullet-proof blinds on the windows and turned up the lights on the dashboard.

"How are the boys and the little lady?" Acre continued.

"The boys are undergraduates at Hardwood. And the little lady has a horse ranch now, about fifty miles from here, that takes up most of her time."

"Hardwood. I'll be damned—smart, just like their old man."

MacVain was flattered.

"Is it just the two of us?" Acre asked.

"My security officer will be arriving later. But he doesn't need to meet you."

"My guy will talk to your guy," Acre said, "but you didn't ask me here for the sunset."

The senior attorney cleared his throat. "The Nathan Whyte Lab is about to go public."

Acre gave him a knowing look. "Because of L-RetroBan?"

"Yes."

"You remember what I said—that when there are time-tested methods then you ought to use them? And leave the experiments to the scientists?"

"You were right," MacVain admitted.

"The Mexican side does not have L-RetroBan exposure problems."

"The problem is what to do about it now," MacVain said sharply.

"How much exposure are we talking about?"

MacVain took out a legal pad and wrote out two sentences, turning it so Acre could read it: "Three American coeds were impregnated and their babies autopsied. I think one of them is the missing firefighter."

"Damn!" the general snorted.

"Krator personnel on the red alert team already know about the 'adoption agency,' but they don't know about the laboratory," MacVain said.

"At least we know the names of the people who are suffering memory disorders, don't we?" Acre asked.

"I've brought you three pre-indites. Maybe none of them remember anything, but we can't be sure they never will. There is another problem too." He took the yellow pad and wrote: "Chad Weed was Tweecus's lab assistant."

Acre snorted in disbelief. "You used who?"

"That was Tweecus's brainstorm. Nobody knew he was a psychopath until later."

"This keeps getting worse. Anything else?" the general asked, not disguising his disgust.

The senior attorney paused, considering how best to spell out the details of murdering three witnesses without saying anything that might look suspicious if it were printed out as a transcript. "A serial killer is stalking the missing firefighter. That's why she fled the scene of the fire in the first place."

"Logical," the general agreed. "Who's the killer?"

"It's someone who's known her since high school, who's obsessively followed her career. A local boy."

"I bet he's an illegal Mexican," Acre suggested.

MacVain realized the general was right. Otherwise, there would be too many loose ends.

The senior attorney underlined the name "Chad Weed" on the pad, then turned it so the general could read it. "And what do we do about this one?" MacVain asked.

Acre tapped Chad Weed's name with his index finger, then formed it into a gun and fired at three imaginary targets.

MacVain wished that he had thought of it. Using Chad Weed as the killer—such economy! If Kelly Grazziella was one of the guinea pigs and if she started to remember then she could put Chad Weed behind bars. The other two women could too. Weed already has the motive and the means, and Krator could give him the opportunity.

But Chad Weed was a wild card. "After the kid helps us out he'll be even harder to control," the senior attorney worried aloud.

"We'll see that he gets the proper medical attention," General Acre assured him.

"But what will his father say?" MacVain asked.

"After he disappeared, the old man never inquired about him *once*," Acre noted. "Just tell Dean the kid came out of retirement and offer to hush it up."

The senior attorney smiled to himself at the elegance of the plan: Weed kills the three women, an illegal Mexican takes the fall, and Special Ops silences Weed forever! MacVain liked working with Acre—the man could connect the dots.

"How do you see this playing out?" Acre asked.

Once again, Vaughn MacVain sketched a neutral scene with his words. "There are two possible scenarios, so Krator is planning for both. One possibility, the firefighter is found murdered by the 'psycho' who's been stalking her. Another possibility, she's found alive by local law enforcement first— then Krator takes custody and ... well, we'll cross that bridge when we come to it. But in any case, I hope to see all of them die natural deaths."

MacVain fished in his pocket for the flash memory containing Chad Weed's real biometrics. "The kid might be hard to find," the senior attorney noted.

"Hell, we know where he is," the general said. "We hid him, remember?"

MacVain put the storage device back in his pocket.

"The kid has got to be operating as a Krator investigator on this," Acre demanded. "It will make the job easier. And working out of Colorado Springs, with seniority."

MacVain was amused by the thought of Chad Weed as a law enforcement officer, much less one with seniority. "Sure, whatever you think he needs. Krator will give Special Ops access to the red alert surveillance data. We'll keep the channel in place until it's not needed anymore."

The general nodded agreement. "Is your security officer heading up the red alert task force?" he asked.

"No, my special assistant," MacVain admitted.

"That might complicate things. Lawyers get hung up on legal technicalities. I'd rest easier with a security guy in charge."

"It's safe. My special assistant has never heard of Tall Blondes."

"Special Ops needs confidence in the rest of the team if it's going to carry the ball. Why don't you put your security officer in charge of the red alert task force?"

"It would look funny. My special assistant usually handles the high-profile projects, and I appointed her before we learned about this problem."

"Well, make him co-chair, for Chrissakes."

Vaughn MacVain looked hesitant.

The general gave him a condescending smile, as if to ask him who was in charge—the senior attorney or his special assistant.

"I'll put my personal security officer, Cole Kincaid, on the Wildfire task force as security advisor," MacVain agreed.

"Good, we'll deal with him exclusively."

A pair of headlights popped over the edge of the bluff and began zig-zagging down the slope toward the airstrip.

"That's him now," MacVain said. "Where's your guy?"

"He's in the plane."

The general opened the car door and patted MacVain on the arm. "I'll see you, when? Another two years?" he laughed, disappearing into the darkness.

MacVain's security officer, Cole Kincaid, pulled up in his Jeep, the .223 slung from the gun rack behind him.

The senior attorney opened the door of the Humvee and gestured for Kincaid to get in.

The wan light of the dashboard showed a man in his early forties, with a featureless face and unreadable eyes. Kincaid was surprised by the airplane: he had been looking forward to shooting coyotes.

MacVain waited until the door closed itself quietly before breaking the silence. "I am appointing you security advisor to task force Wildfire, reporting directly to me while nominally reporting to Tricia Culhane."

"It is an honor, sir. Thank you very much."

MacVain was touched by Kincaid's sincerity—perhaps the man had been kept too long in the basement bunker. The senior attorney resolved to invite him to a virtual meeting.

"Here are your instructions. You will be covert point person to 888th Special Operations. The missing firefighter is being stalked by a serial killer. Make sure that Special Ops receives all surveillance on Kelly Grazziella and her stalker. And make sure surveillance and data access continues even after task force Wildfire is dissolved, until I say otherwise."

The senior attorney asked his security officer to repeat the instructions, then nodded in satisfaction.

"You and Special Ops can work out the details," MacVain said, pointing towards the airplane.

A moment later, MacVain's Humvee roared down the runway and disappeared into the switchbacks that climbed the deserted bluff.

The Search

In Oscuridad, the wind had died, and the smell of burned vegetation settled over Deep Creek valley. The western sky was Halloween orange. Giovanni was getting ready to go home when two plainclothes policemen appeared in the doorway of the barrel room, flashing their Krator badges.

"What's this about?" the winery owner asked them.

"Just routine. We're talking to anyone who might have information about the missing firefighter. Who am I talking to?"

"Charles Clydesdale. I am the owner of Indian Springs Winery. This is Giovanni, supervisor of plant operations."

The officer gave them each his business card. He was a senior investigator from Krator headquarters in Colorado Springs. When Krator was given the management contract for all police and espionage functions in the Free World, federal agencies such as the FBI and the DEA were disbanded, while their personnel were rehired by the company as independent contractors. Most were re-assigned to district offices as agents and senior agents, but a few became investigators, reporting directly to Krator attorneys in Colorado. Investigators were the new elite police, focused exclusively on high-profile targets, with command of red alerts.

"She disappeared right above this winery," the investigator noted. "I thought you maybe had seen or heard something."

"We first heard about it when the deputy sheriff told us she was missing," Clydesdale replied.

"Is that your story too?" he asked, looking at Giovanni.

"Yes."

The senior investigator continued to stare at Giovanni. "I understand you're an old friend of Kelly Grazziella. Is that true?"

"Yes."

"Is there a place where we could talk in private?" It was not a question.

"Use my office," Clydesdale told them.

The senior investigator sat in Clydesdale's swivel chair and rotated it several times, as if testing the bearings, then gestured to Giovanni to take the straight-back chair next to the desk. The silent partner remained standing between Giovanni and the door.

"I didn't know that Krator investigated missing persons," Giovanni said.

"Normally we don't. How long have you known Kelly Grazziella?"

"Since high school."

"Do you have any idea where she might be?"

"No."

"Did she have any favorite getaway spots?"

"Not that I know of."

"When did you last see her?"

"This past weekend, at Zack & Zeke's."

"Is that a restaurant?"

"A bar, a local hangout."

"What did she talk about?"

"The hot weather mostly. The early crush."

"Did she mention going away anywhere? To see a relative, maybe?"

"No."

"Does she belong to any political organizations?"

"No."

"Have you ever heard her criticize GMOs?"

"No, never."

"Does she belong to any religious group?"

"I don't think so."

"Is Kelly your girlfriend?"

"No."

"Was Kelly ever your girlfriend?"

"No."

"Does she have a steady boyfriend?"

"Not that I know of."

"Did she break up with anyone recently?"

"I don't think so."

"Where were you when the fire broke out?"

"In the barrel room, and then I heard the sirens when I went out to the loading dock."

"Can anyone vouch for that?"

"Mr. Clydesdale, the vineyard manager…"

The detective held out his hand to indicate that he had heard enough. "Did you see any strangers around this morning?"

"Yes, a customer came by the tasting room."

"When was that?"

"A little after nine. I hadn't opened the tasting room yet."

"Do you have that person's name?"

"I can get it. It's in the guest register."

The senior investigator nodded to his partner to get it. "Did you see anyone around here this morning wearing a broad-brimmed hat and a red sash?"

Giovanni was embarrassed. "That was me," he said finally.

"Operations supervisor. Is it part of your job to walk in the vineyard?"

"Yes. I'm in charge of the crush."

"You said you were in the barrel room."

"I thought you meant at the time of the fire."

The detective did not respond. "Do you know where Kelly Grazziella went to college?"

"Davis University."

"Did you ever visit her there?"

"No, we did not keep in touch during those years."

"Ever meet any of her college friends?"

"No."

"She never talked with you about her experiences in Davis?"

"No."

"Thank you for your time. If you think of anything, anything at all about Grazziella, even if seems trivial, give me a call. You've got my card."

* * *

As Giovanni parked in the crowded lot behind Zack & Zeke's, he remembered the last time he saw Kelly. She was standing where the long Victorian bar made a right-angle bend under the big window on the square, and her skin was even softer in the long light of a summer evening. She had to stand with her face close to his so they could hear above the din. He had ordered her a glass of zinfandel. She scrutinized the inky liquid as the barman poured it, anticipating the taste. She looked at Giovanni and smiled slightly as she picked it up.

He noticed the delicate grip of her strong, smooth fingers as they closed around the stem. He watched her twirl the glass like a connoisseur, inhale it deeply, and raise it to her lips in a slow arc that seemed to take forever. She looked at his face before swallowing, then toasted him with her eyes. It was like seeing wine drunk for the first time. He wanted to drink in her quick smile, her fine blond hair, and sensitive face.

Inside Zack & Zeke's, all the regulars were clustered around the television watching a recap of the Deep Creek fire. The winemaker from Indian Springs Winery was standing alone at the far end of the hand-carved bar drinking a frozen margarita, apparently lost in thought. He nodded to Giovanni to join him.

"In this weather a frozen margarita looks real good," Giovanni said.

"The problem is the climate change," the winemaker reflected. "When I was a kid, these hills had oak and redwood on them. Even the chaparral was more scrub oak than chamise."

One of the employees from Indian Springs Winery sidled up to the bar accompanied by the sullen cowgirl he hung out with. "Don't tell me you guys are still talking shop. Let's shoot pool—we need a fourth for doubles," the man said to Giovanni.

"Count me out. I'm beat."

"We almost got into an argument today," the winemaker confided to Giovanni after the couple left. "He told me that predictive criminality was just what the country needed. He said 'Unless you're guilty you got nothing to worry about.' He didn't seem to notice the contradiction there."

Giovanni thought of his interrogation by the Krator agent and shuddered.

The bartender reached across the bar between them, whisking the brass rail with a rag. "I heard Indian Springs is going to have maybe the first August crush ever," he said.

"In this heat, we have no choice," the winemaker replied.

"From what I hear, a lot of growers are worse off than you. The past weekend would make you believe in global warming if you didn't already."

"It pisses me off that the United States government refuses to ratify the international treaty," the winemaker commented. "Washington thinks every place should look like Texas."

"It's not the government of the United States anymore," the bartender said. "It's been taken over by a secret coalition of militarists, Zionists, and criminal bankers."

"You'd better be careful," Giovanni warned him.

"Don't worry, if you say the obvious out loud, they just label you a conspiracy theorist!"

6

TASK FORCE WILDFIRE

> In popular speech, indisputable evidence is often referred to as "finding a smoking gun," so legal scholars playfully referred to the new model of criminality as *sine armis fumus*, or "smoke without a gun." The public, unschooled in the fine points of jurisprudence, called the new legislation the "no-fault arrest law."
>
> *The Digital Surveillance State*
> by Renato Ocampo-Mendoza

In the long light of early morning, the drab, beige office blocks of the Predictive Criminality Center rose like megaliths out of the featureless plain.

Celestine Brittle's new boots of polished black leather made assertive clicks on the marble floor of the elevator lobby, a floor inlaid with the image that appears on the back of the dollar bill: a steep-sided pyramid topped by an all-seeing eye.

Above the bank of elevators, inscribed in green jade, is the motto "Novus Ordo Seclorum"—"the new order of the world."

"You're early today," the burly guard said with a smile.

"Yes, an early meeting," Celestine replied. "By the way, how was your son's birthday party this weekend?"

The man beamed. "He loved it!"

"He's seven years old now, right?" she asked, stepping into the opening doors.

"Yes, a big guy!" the guard beamed again, pleased that she had remembered.

The virtual conference studio was on the top floor of Building A, not far from the director's office. It consisted of several conference rooms with electrically active mesh embedded in the walls to prevent the escape of electronic signals. Each room had a small oblong table with several executive chairs on one side and a curved, floor-to-ceiling screen on the other. A bank of cameras hung from the ceiling like a low chandelier.

"Please sit between the yellow lines," the virtuality coordinator told Celestine when she arrived promptly at 6:30 Tuesday morning.

There was only one other person in the room, a laconic man with thinning hair who seemed uncomfortable around people. His color-coded badge identified him as a second-level manager from data processing. When Celestine sat down next to him, he buried himself in his tablet.

The virtuality coordinator asked them both to introduce themselves so she could test the equipment. The room lights dimmed, and Celestine was startled to find herself seated at one end of a long, polished conference table opposite an animated facsimile of herself. At first it was unnerving to see her slightest gestures and facial expressions emulated by her own clone in virtual reality a fraction of a second later. Then the image of the data processing manager popped up next to her at the conference table. Celestine had heard of goggle-free virtual reality but had never experienced it before.

"It's a spin-off of retinal security screening," the virtuality coordinator explained. "The projection system tracks the retina of each participant in the meeting from multiple angles simultaneously. Then the software sews these 3-D video images seamlessly together, and presents to each person the imagery appropriate to their retinal view. So you have the illusion of being in a real meeting."

"It is very convincing," Celestine said.

"You both look great. Take a look at yourselves and make sure your hair is combed and whatever. Like a real meeting, you will not see your own images once the meeting starts."

While she waited, Celestine kept thinking about the treatise she had read the night before on the number of the beast. The author argued that the number 666 connected the mathematics of the ancient Near East with the radical monotheistic theology of the Hebrews, succinctly expressing their relationship in a single number, though the author was vague about what the exact relationship might be. She wondered if the square root of 666 might be relevant—then dismissed the string of decimals as too ponderous and ugly.

Suddenly, there was a buzz of white noise, followed by a hubbub of voices as the virtual images of about a dozen participants popped up around the table. Celestine recognized the red-haired woman with the round face she had talked with the night before.

"Thank you all for attending," the red-haired woman said, as the white noise dropped to zero. "I am Tricia Culhane, special assistant to senior attorney Vaughn MacVain. I will be serving as head of task force Wildfire. Now, senior attorney MacVain will tell us why we are here."

Celestine was thrilled to meet the secretive leader of the Krator Corporation, but when he suddenly appeared at the head of the conference table he was less imposing than she had imagined: an intense man in his late forties with expressionless eyes and an energetic manner. He might be short in stature, but it was impossible to tell from his virtual image, which bobbed without reference to physical landmarks. MacVain paced back and forth as he talked, making eye contact with every person in the meeting as if addressing a jury:

> Task force Wildfire is an elite team, and each of you has been selected for your commitment as much as for your professional skill. All of you have dedicated your lives to impartial public service, but in your personal lives you come from the tradition of Reformed Christianity that recognizes the dangers posed to the political traditions of the American republic by subversive, godless elements.

> At our academy in Quantico, you all learned the history of Krator. That our mandate grew out of DEA, the Drug Enforcement Administration, founded by President Nixon in 1973; and that the DEA was a lineal descendant of the Bureau of Narcotics, which in turn was a lineal descendant of the Bureau of Prohibition—the agency created in 1927 with the mission to enforce the national laws against alcohol. At Quantico, you also learned that Franklin D. Roosevelt and his nest of communists and Muslims tried to impose a socialist regime on the United States—with its concomitant moral decay.

> The fact that we are here today proves that his effort has failed, but our enemies never sleep. Just yesterday, a firefighter mysteriously disappeared during a wildfire in California. If she is not found

by Thursday morning, terrorist sympathizers will use her disappearance to discredit the Fellowship of the Eighth Dispensation. She must be found immediately, either dead or alive!

If she is already dead, it is essential that we retrieve a recognizable body that can be seen by everyone to be Kelly Grazziella. And if she is found alive, Krator will take pride in returning her to a grateful nation.

This is your challenge, ladies and gentlemen. Good hunting and good luck.

The senior attorney disappeared as suddenly as he had come, leaving the participants focused on an empty spot in virtual space.

"I'd like the members of task force Wildfire to meet one another," Tricia Culhane said. "Anyone not present at this meeting is not a member of the task force. Most of you already know each other, but for the benefit of the others, we'll go around the table, so everyone can give their name and title."

She began the introductions with the most important person at the meeting, "Skipper" Van Squint, owner of One World News Corporation in Los Angeles. He was in his forties, sun-tanned and jogger-thin, wearing a pink button-down shirt and a navy blazer. His pleasant, business-like demeanor belied his role as the Goebbels of global capitalism.

Seated next to the spin doctor was Cato Magruder, the deputy bureau chief of Apprehension and Detention. He was a fierce, athletic man with dark eyes, a hairless head, and a prominent black mustache. MacVain judged Magruder to be a smart, streetwise cop, good at managing complex logistics while ignoring judicial restraint, so he often gave him high-profile assignments without bothering to inform Magruder's boss, the nominal head of the agency.

Also present was the bureau chief cf Domestic Surveillance, Krator's top spy, who was accompanied by his subordinate, the director of the Remote Surveillance Center at Cheyenne Mountain, Wyoming. Both were poised, gray-haired men, with the measured movements of seasoned bureaucrats.

As the discussion was about to start, the bureau chief of Firearms, Alcohol, Tobacco, Narcotics, and Irreverent and Pornographic Literature finally arrived. The last-named executive had come to the virtual meeting directly from a house where a cache of weapons had been found, and he was still wearing a black bullet-proof vest with "FATNIPL" in prominent yellow letters.

"Are bullet-proof vests mandatory for this committee?" the director of the Cheyenne Mountain facility asked Tricia Culhane with apparent seriousness.

"Not yet," she said.

Culhane turned to Celestine's co-worker, the data processing manager, and asked that he brief the group on the computer resources that would be available to members of the task force.

He told them that a dedicated Wildfire database had been put in place to display all police reports and sightings relayed from the Remote Surveillance Center in Cheyenne Mountain, as well as any information submitted by the public and local law-enforcement agencies. It would also give access to a telemetric camera that had been set up at the crime scene in case Grazziella returned there.

When talking about technology, the technician's voice betrayed a human range of emotion. "It's a cool device," he said enthusiastically. "The telemetric camera has infrared and motion detectors. The data's transmitted by satellite so we're usually getting the pictures in almost real time. The bullhorn icon on your desktop can be set to beep when the camera activates. But the main problem is too much data," he added.

"There's a lot of junk, like pigeons and animals tripping the sensors, and we don't have the manpower…"

The director of Cheyenne Mountain cut the techie off. "Yesterday morning, we put a FANTOM trace on Grazziella."

FANTOM is an acronym for "Field-Available Notification, Tracking, and On-line Monitoring," which notifies authorities of any telecommunications activity anywhere in the world that involves the suspect, whether a simple phone call or the purchase of a pack of gum.

"Any response?" Tricia Culhane asked him.

"Not yet."

Tricia Culhane looked at Celestine Brittle. "If she calls anyone, who is that likely to be?"

"Her father. She lives alone, and her brother is serving in Pakistan."

"We'll put her dad on the intercept list," Domestic Surveillance said.

Tricia Culhane asked Celestine to summarize her recommendations to the field based on her pre-indictment profile of Grazziella.

"She's a homebody," Celestine said. "With the exception of a summer language institute in Spain while in college, she has lived in only two places, both in northern California: the town of Oscuridad, where she was born and raised, and Davis, where she went to college. She has a strong tie to the land, especially to the Deep Creek valley where her family once owned a farm. Today, she lives and works within five miles of where she was born. It may be significant that the place where she disappeared was on land that had once belonged to her family."

Cato Magruder, MacVain's favorite street-wise cop, stared at Celestine Brittle until she began to feel uncomfortable.

Although in his forties, he was hairless except for a prominent handlebar mustache, with his skin stretched tight over his skull, as if someone had performed cosmetic surgery.

She later learned he had been burned by a Molotov cocktail in an assassination attempt in California.

He asked Celestine why Grazziella was up on that fire road when the fire broke out.

"The dispatcher at the California Department of Disaster Response said that Kelly told her she wanted to take a look at the weather from the West Ridge Road," Celestine explained. "But her exact motivations are not known."

"She was away from her unit during a red flag warning," Magruder scowled.

"It was her day off," Celestine replied.

Tricia Culhane cut in: "CDDR told Krator that the fire would have been a lot worse if Grazziella hadn't been on the scene to report it, so they're not complaining."

Cato Magruder fingered his mustache and narrowed his eyes. "No boyfriend?" he asked suggestively.

"No one special is indicated in the police reports," Celestine answered.

He nodded knowingly. "California. You don't suppose she's 'one of those'?"

Everyone was looking at Celestine. "There's no indication of unusual sexual preferences," she said. "In fact, Grazziella had a baby out of wedlock."

Magruder looked relieved. "The public is already behind this thing," he commented. "A firefighter. A survivor. Maybe a hero. If there's anything in the closet, we need to find it *before* the terrorists do."

"I'll second that," Tricia Culhane said.

"What about liaison with state and local law-enforcement agencies?" the bureau chief of Domestic Surveillance asked.

"We'll take all the help we can get. The priority is to find her as soon as possible," the special assistant emphasized. "For now, we're keeping the public informed on the progress of the search."

Skipper Van Squint looked at Magruder with a bland expression. "*Is* there any progress?"

The policeman did not respond but looked at Tricia Culhane.

"Almaden County Sheriff is dispatching their CSI team first thing this morning to sift the site a second time," she said. "There should be a report later today."

"Those local yokels will step on their, er, hands," Cato Magruder complained.

"They have jurisdiction," Tricia Culhane reminded him. "But Krator crime scene investigators will be present in an advisory capacity."

She turned to Celestine and told her to copy task force members with any significant new data as soon it was reported to the Wildfire database, as well as to update reports and recommendations that went out to the field. "And re-check Grazziella's time in Davis and see if you can turn up any leads."

"I will."

"Any questions or points of clarification?" Tricia Culhane asked.

"What about that TV producer of disaster coverage who was at the winery yesterday morning?" the official from Domestic Surveillance inquired. "Was One World News tipped about an impending fire?"

"The TV producer said he was on vacation," Magruder replied. "His story checks out. And there's no evidence of arson."

"That's it for now," the special assistant announced. "I'll call you all back here as soon as there is anything that requires a group decision. And remember, if a sighting is confirmed, we'll convene as a virtual command center immediately. Until then, good hunting and good luck."

* * *

All of the virtual images vanished except for Tricia's, who was seated at the opposite end of the long rosewood conference table, her reflection visible in its lacquered surface.

"Celestine, I asked you to stay behind because I want to talk with you one-on-one."

Tricia Culhane assumed the manner of an older sister. "This is your first task force, and there are a few security procedures you need to know. While working on Wildfire, do your work in the room reserved for the task force by the director of your facility. Use the safe for physical documents when you leave the room for any reason. You should be seeing your room assignment on your screen."

The room number popped into view, hanging in virtual space above the virtual table. It was on the top floor of building A—just down the hall from the room they were in. Celestine wrote it down.

"I have a question," Celestine said. "If I need more information than what I can find in the online sources, I usually follow-up by telephone with outside sources and experts. Is that permitted while working on Wildfire?"

"Yes."

Celestine nodded and waited for more instruction, then realized that Tricia just wanted to talk. Celestine took the opportunity to express her appreciation.

"This special assignment took me completely by surprise," Celestine said with enthusiasm. "It is really an honor."

"I'm sorry I ruined your evening. I hope you didn't have anything important scheduled."

"No, Laredo does not have a lot of distractions," she added, betraying her dissatisfaction.

"Yeah, Colorado Springs is not very good for a single girl either," Tricia said. "What do you do in Laredo for fun?"

She hesitated a moment. "I am active in my church. I work out in my health club."

"Except for skiing in Canada, there's nothing to do here either. If I didn't work all the time, I'd go crazy."

"Do you travel a lot?"

"I wish I did. Since I've been special assistant I spend almost all of my time in virtual meetings. Except for yesterday, I hadn't seen my boss outside his virtual office in almost a month. By the way, has senior attorney MacVain contacted you?"

"Yes. He invited me to a meeting on his plane Friday morning."

"Did he say what the meeting is about?" the special assistant inquired.

"No, he didn't."

Tricia Culhane gave a knowing smile, then faded from view like the Cheshire cat.

* * *

A portfolio under her arm, Celestine walked with an authoritative gait to room A-25, the office assigned to the Wildfire task force. She was dressed for her new assignment in a tailored navy-blue suit that complemented her tall figure and shoulder-length blond hair. Prominent on her lapel was a new white security badge that granted her unrestricted access to building A. She was excited to have met Tricia Culhane, a woman who could check out library books, and on Friday she would be meeting with Vaughn MacVaine. Celestine felt confident and pretty.

The assigned room had spacious windows with a commanding view of the endless plain and cloud-dappled sky to the east. There were two computer work stations set up in opposite corners, each with a thermos of coffee and a pitcher of water. The ergonomic chairs were upholstered in attractive fabric.

A secretary came running up to her. "Are you Celestine Brittle?" the woman asked.

"I am. How do you do?"

"I am very sorry," the secretary said in a thick drawl, "but the conference room is needed by the director for a meeting, so the Wildfire task force office has been re-assigned. It's now in B-49."

"Where's that?"

She itemized the floors with her fingers: "Level G is the garage. Level T is the transit corridor. Level B is below that."

"A third-level basement!" Celestine could not conceal her disappointment.

"I'm sorry, honey," the woman said, taking her by the elbow and gently guiding her toward the elevator. "But I don't make the room assignments. I just point to the doors."

In the elevator there was no button for Level B. While she was studying the panel, the door closed on its own and the car headed down. Celestine was annoyed with herself. In the span of only thirty seconds her elation had dissipated, replaced by a peevish frustration. In the solitude of the elevator, she said a short prayer to calm herself, asking God for humility and the grace to accept things as they are. By the time the door opened on the garage level lobby, she had regained her composure.

She asked the guard in the kiosk about Level B. She noticed his eyes reading her white security badge, and it made her feel important. "Level B is only accessible from the freight elevator," he told her, pointing all the way across the garage to another elevator she had never noticed before. She felt her importance drop another notch.

There were no cars parked near the freight elevator, and the only sound was that of her own footsteps echoing off the concrete buttresses. She pressed her left palm against the touch panel adjacent to the elevator. The security check seemed to take forever to process.

The touchpads at the Laredo center were part of a new experimental security system that read the nucleotide sequence of the DNA in the cells in a person's hand, measuring resonance fields that react to bursts of an electronic probe too faint to be felt, then verifying the chemical fingerprint against the sequences on file. Its inventors claimed it was the only completely fool-proof means of identification, as only identical twins had completely identical DNA, but it took a long time to make its computations, even with integrated circuits designed for the purpose.

Celestine could tell by the acceleration that the ride to Level B was longer than a single floor. When she finally emerged from the elevator, she was at the intersection of three concrete utility corridors hung with pipes and conduit. The utility network apparently interconnected all the buildings in the facility, like the transit corridors on the level above. Each utility corridor converged on a distant point like a railroad track.

To confuse terrorists and spies, there were no names, titles, or directional signs anywhere in the facility, but on Level B even the room numbers were deliberately assigned without numerical order so no one could navigate without a map. Celestine decided to search systematically, beginning with the corridor on her left. Every fifty feet or so, the concrete walls were punctuated by unmarked steel doors that appeared to access utility bays, but there were no doors that appeared to lead to offices. The corridor hummed with the pervasive drone of machinery. By the time she was halfway down its length, the subliminal noise had grown to an unpleasantly loud roar. Then, on her right she saw it: B-49. It was a double door with a small glass window in each section, the kind of door that swings open in both directions such as one sees in hospital wards. She half expected a gurney to emerge pushed by an orderly.

There was no security touchpad, and the double doors opened with a push, revealing a large utility space converted to a makeshift office. It was sparsely furnished with government-issue desks and chairs. Dim fluorescent fixtures hung from gray acoustic ceiling tiles. The machine noise was somewhat reduced, but it was still too loud. She could not imagine spending much time in this dreary place.

The desktops were bare, and the shelves devoid of personal effects. Level B reminded Celestine of the genre of science fiction movies in which the protagonist wakes from a coma to find a deserted world. But in Hollywood, even after an alien invasion, there are a few eccentric characters left to move the plot along. Level B appeared to lack even those.

As she was trying to decide whether to call the director's secretary on the eighth floor to complain, one of the desktop telephones rang. At this time yesterday, Celestine would have let it ring because it was not for her, but in the span of less than twenty-four hours her routine had been turned upside down. Now she served on a high-level task force, had spoken with Vaughn MacVain, and had been issued a white badge with unrestricted access to the building where she worked. Celestine picked up the phone.

"Can I talk to Celestine Brittle?" a man asked in an earnest voice.

"Speaking."

"I'm glad I reached you. I tried to call you on the eighth floor. I'm Nate, assistant facility manager. I wasn't here when the director's office asked for a temporary office for two people, and my assistant assigned B-49 because she thought it was for a performance review or something. She didn't realize it was for a senior research analyst reporting to Colorado Springs." He waited, as if expecting to be reprimanded.

"I do have some concerns about security," Celestine said with appropriate gravity.

"Rightly so," he replied, as if thinking along the same lines himself. "Room B-169 is more appropriate for you. It is a much better office. It's more comfortable. It's quieter. You'll have your own access code. There's a window too."

127

The sales pitch made her wonder what was wrong with it, but Nate anticipated her next question. "It's the deputy chief scientist's office adjacent to the lab."

"Is it far?"

"Well, there's a long way and a short way."

"I've walked a long way already."

"The short way is through the lab, but I'll have to key in a pass first."

"That's fine."

"Aren't there supposed to be two of you?"

"Yes, but I don't know my colleague's schedule." If the taciturn data-processing manager never showed up to share the office, that was fine with her.

"OK. Go back outside to the corridor and continue walking away from the elevators. When you get to B-121, touch the touch panel, then go through the lab in a straight line. When you get to the spiral staircase on the far end of the lab, B-169 is on the landing. You can't miss it."

Celestine repeated the instructions and got the man's extension number.

"Give me five minutes to set up the code," Nate said.

When Celestine was buzzed through the door of B-121, the laboratory did not look like anything she could ever have imagined. It was a subterranean space larger than a football field and over three stories high—and completely empty. The only contents of the vast enclosure were light fixtures and a wide variety of stand pipes and circuit boxes with nothing connected to them. The machine noise was subliminal and far away. At the far end of the laboratory was a steel staircase that rose through a series of landings and disappeared into a hole in the ceiling. Although Nate had called the staircase a spiral, Celestine knew enough mathematics to recognize a helix when she saw one: the stairs wound around a cylinder not a cone. The first landing opened onto a foyer with offices.

"He's right," Celestine mused, 'You can't miss it.'" She walked across the sea of concrete, the sound of her shoes echoing loudly.

As if thumbing its nose at security regulations, B-169 had a prominent brass plate next to the door that said "Deputy Chief Scientist." There was a window that overlooked the cavernous lab space, and the office was pleasantly lit with recessed lighting. There was a desk and credenza in Scandinavian style, with thick carpeting on the floor. The fixtures smelled new, and there was not so much as a paper clip stuck in the crack of a desk drawer. On the desktop was a transparent packet of office supplies that appeared to contain everything she was likely to need. Embedded in one wall was a built-in safe with a touchpad on its door. It clicked open when she pressed her thumb against it. Celestine settled into one of the comfortable executive chairs and turned on the computer. She took comfort in the familiar login screen.

Celestine picked up the telephone on the first ring.

"Hello, Nate," she said.

"How do you like it?"

"Much better than the other one. But I was not expecting to be here all alone." Celestine found working on Level B a little spooky. Perhaps the manager from data processing would not be such a bad roommate after all.

"It's perfectly safe," he added. "The security cameras are working already. I can see you now."

Celestine found that less re-assuring than he. "Is there a camera inside this office?"

"No. You can close the blinds for privacy. The deputy chief scientist's office is the only place in the subterranean labs without built-in surveillance. You'll be the first scientist to use it."

Celestine realized that Nate thought she was doing research related to the mission of the laboratory and that she had been sent on ahead to evaluate it. No wonder he put her in the office of the deputy chief scientist.

"So where am I?"

"You are situated directly below the main building but thirteen floors below ground."

"Thirteen floors!"

"That's counting garage and transit levels. There is another lab above you, but it's double height."

"This lab is bigger than anything I've seen before."

"And it's not the biggest either," he said proudly. "It's the smallest. The floors get smaller as you go down, like an inverted pyramid." He seemed pleased to have someone he could talk with about the design.

Celestine wanted to ask what all the laboratory space was for, but decided it was probably classified. "Well, I'd better get to work," she said. "Thank you for all your help."

"You're the first researcher to arrive," Nate added, "so if there is anything about the facility that you think needs attention—just let me know personally. We want everything shipshape when Wassily Tweecus arrives later today."

"*The* Wassily Tweecus?" she asked. The scientist was a legend at the academy: a former professor of genetics at Hardwood and a recipient of the President's Medal of Freedom.

"Yes, the 'Gene Gnome of Krator.'"

"What is he doing here?"

"A personal walk-through of the new laboratories for remote sensing of DNA."

Celestine had learned about that too. Known as the civil genetics program, the plan was to use each person's unique DNA molecule as a unique identification number. Since a person's DNA is usually identical in each of the billions of cells in the body, and remains constant from conception to death, there is no possibility of tampering or falsification. At the moment of conception or as soon as possible thereafter, a non-invasive biometric probe converts the individual's unique pattern of DNA into a unique identification number and deposits it in a centralized database, where it can be linked to any subsequent information about the individual acquired in the course of a lifetime.

As Celestine was taught at Quantico, the Tweecus process is the ultimate tracking and identification technology, exemplifying what Krator called the "PACT" criteria—Precise, Affordable, Comprehensive, and Tamper-proof.

So that's what the underground laboratories are for, Celestine thought to herself. Civil genetics is going into mass production.

* * *

Alone on Level B, Celestine found it hard to concentrate on work. She opened the thick packet of stationery supplies and carefully arranged them in the desk drawers, even though she rarely did any work on paper. Also, for some reason, she kept thinking of prime numbers. A prime is a number greater than one that is evenly divisible only by itself and one. The primes form an infinite series, and she expanded the series in her mind: 2, 3, 5, 7, 11, 13, 17...

Enough of this, she thought. Tricia Culhane had asked her to re-examine Grazziella's life in Davis, California, and it was time to get to work.

Information collected under the red alert was automatically copied to the Wildfire database, and Celestine was amazed at how much data a red alert could generate: thousands of tips phoned in by the public and thousands of follow-ups by district agents, as well as numerous false positives from hundreds of Krator observation points, each one of which preferred to err on the side of diligence.

Since yesterday afternoon, Krator agents had interviewed dozens of Grazziella's college friends and acquaintances, including her team mates in track and field, but there were still no leads worth following up, and nothing that Celestine could add to the advisories.

Agents had also reviewed the video footage from all of the surveillance cameras within a fifty-mile radius of Oscuridad, but there were no clues to the whereabouts of the missing firefighter.

The baby born out of wedlock remained the only dark corner in Grazziella's life. The records had been sealed by the family court to protect the privacy of the adoptive parents, and Krator was getting a court order to unseal the files. Maybe something would come of that.

Special Evidence

When Vaughn MacVain arrived for work he ignored his cup of yogurt.

"Authorize a Krator badge for a new senior investigator," he told his secretary. "The name of the agent is Chad Weed. Do it immediately and get it from Special Evidence, not from Personnel. And hold my calls. I'll be downstairs for a few minutes, meeting with Cole Kincaid."

MacVain's secretary, Charlene Remington, was too shocked to do anything but nod affirmatively. The senior attorney had never skipped his yogurt before or shown any interest in meeting personally with his personal security officer.

As MacVain walked towards the entrance to the bunker, he glowered at the deficiencies in the emergency escape route, mentally composing the blistering memo he planned to send to the Krator physical architect as soon as the Grazziella case was behind him. Instead of a personal stairway that opened into his office, he had to walk down the corridor used by administrative personnel and past the staff restrooms to get to the emergency elevator. He would not want to traverse this route if seconds mattered.

The elevator stopped in a small containment area blocked by a heavy steel door with a small, bullet-proof window the size of a face. Cole Kincaid was looking back at him. Whatever information passed through the security control room was seen by MacVain's personal security officer—and by him alone.

The door slid open with a hiss.

MacVain pulled one of the metal stools towards him and looked his security officer in the eye. "Did you give the 888th access to the red alert database like we discussed?"

"Yes, sir. It's all set. They'll receive all surveillance data and police reports on Grazziella."

"How about that material from Special Evidence I requested?" the senior attorney asked.

"It just came," Kincaid replied, holding up the cardboard envelope that had been delivered by courier a few minutes earlier.

The senior attorney took out a pair of disposable gloves from his suit coat pocket and pulled them on. He took the envelope from Cole Kincaid, opened the flap, and looked inside. It was filled with printouts of stories from newspaper web sites. He took out a thick handful of papers and examined them. All the printouts looked original, but discolored and spotted as if they had been stored for years in a cardboard carton in a damp garage. Almost all were from the *Oscuridad Tribune*—and all were about Kelly Grazziella: her sports achievements, her graduation from high school, her track and field trophies in Davis, and her graduation from college.

"This psychopath has been stalking Kelly Grazziella for years," MacVain explained. "He may have killed that brave firefighter already."

Cole Kincaid's eyes hardened at the injustice of it.

MacVain held a page up to the light. "To make this completely convincing, get a hold of some recent Internet articles on her disappearance too. Some crisp new printouts will visually convey the timeline to a jury."

Cole Kincaid made a note of it.

"And you charged this to L-RetroBan clean-up and not to Wildfire?" the senior attorney asked.

"I am charging all requisitions to the new account number you gave me."

"Good," MacVain said, suddenly remembering that he had not yet had his yogurt.

* * *

For the second time in two days, Tricia Culhane was called to the Doge's Palace. She made herself as comfortable as she could in the Renaissance side chair, facing the senior attorney across an uncluttered physical desktop decorated with a single photographic print of MacVain's wife and two children. It was mounted in a fifties-style frame of blond wood.

"There was a meeting of the Council of Seventeen a little while ago," he told her. "There was a lot of discussion about this missing firefighter. And the impact of her rapture on the situation in the Middle East. Someone actually suggested that the battle of Armageddon was what the country needed—it would drum up support for Israel. I pointed out that the last thing we want in the Middle East is the final battle."

"It's a good thing you were there."

"Even so, the Council decided to send some of the no-name brigades to Jerusalem just in case Boone turns out to be right about Armageddon." He gave her a look of amused tolerance.

MacVain's off-hand remark suggested to Tricia that the impending rapture might be a diversion hiding something bigger.

"Now subversive elements are saying that the United States staged the disappearance of the firefighter in order to initiate the end time and occupy the Holy Land," MacVain

134

continued, apparently reading her thoughts. "They have no understanding of geopolitics."

"The best way to squash these rumors is to find her," Tricia Culhane said.

"The Council agrees with you. They want a tight rein on the Wildfire investigation, with a task force member providing daily reports to them. Since there's this extra work, I've asked Cole Kincaid to join task force Wildfire as an extra pair of hands. He could do the report to the Council."

Tricia Culhane was caught completely off-guard. "It's too late in the day for someone to be brought up to speed—we only have until Thursday morning, and by then the search for the firefighter's moot." Her voice betrayed a trace of hurt.

The senior attorney had hoped to avoid an emotional scene. "I see Kincaid as handling some of the paperwork—surveillance requisitions, stuff like that."

"What about the report to the Council?"

"If you have the time to do it, I don't have a problem with it."

Culhane looked mollified. "I have the time," she said.

The New Security Advisor

When Rose Underwood poked her nose into Tricia Culhane's office, she found her boss sitting with her chin in her hands, an angry scowl on her face. A plump brunette, married with two children, Rose had been hired when the special assistant was still a rookie prosecutor in Illinois and had stayed at Tricia Culhane's side during her climb up the Krator ladder.

"What's wrong?" Rose asked, in a voice redolent with years of motherhood. She thought that all personnel problems were like skinned knees when you got down to the nitty-gritty.

"Cole Kincaid," Tricia Culhane replied.

"The administrative staff can't stand him either," Rose agreed.

"Security advisor to the task force—that's a project management responsibility, it's not just technical. Kincaid has no project management skills whatsoever."

"Locked in the basement, it's no wonder," Rose sympathized.

"The worst part is that Vaughn appointed him without even asking me first."

Rose looked concerned. "Did you know that Kincaid received a courier package this morning addressed to him with the title 'Security Advisor, Task Force Wildfire'?"

Tricia Culhane's brow furrowed in anger. "So he's been charging stuff to the Wildfire account without even asking me! Do you know what was in that package?"

"It had to be signed for personally, so I pointed the messenger to Charlene. But I'll see what I can find out."

Rose Underwood came back a few minutes later and poked her head through the partially open door of the office. "Got a private minute?" she asked.

Tricia Culhane gestured for the assistant to close the door behind her.

"About that courier envelope that Cole got this morning," Rose said.

Tricia Culhane perked up.

"It wasn't charged to your task force. It was charged to an account number that was created yesterday afternoon. It's for the cost of assessing the risk of L-RetroBan exposure and for any associated clean-up costs."

Tricia Culhane was stunned. MacVain himself told her that his department did not have any covert operations that required L-RetroBan disclosure.

"What's L-RetroBan? An insecticide?" Rose asked.

"A toxic chemical with unpredictable side effects."

* * *

136

Tricia Culhane turned off her telephone and let her shoes fall to the floor—she thought better in stocking feet.

Everything about the Grazziella case could be explained by natural laws except for the phony adoption agency. That had Krator's fingerprints all over it—and it was exactly the sort of scheme that Vaughn MacVain would put in place himself.

The firefighter was blond and blue-eyed, just as the senior attorney liked; but she was more a rock climber than a long-distance runner, whereas Vaughn MacVain wanted them willowy. Still, the firefighter's features reminded Tricia Culhane of the mysterious file on MacVain's desktop, "Tall Blondes." It was a name so secret that it was a felony to know it without a clearance, but now it was her little secret too.

One day, about a year ago, MacVain invited Tricia Culhane for a tour of his new virtual office—the facsimile of the palace of the doges in Venice built at his request by Krator's cyberarchitect. The senior attorney was an enthusiast of art history and could not resist showing it off to his colleagues.

When anyone was in the physical office with the senior attorney, the virtual office could only be activated in visitor mode, without access to the file system or computer controls—a security feature built-in by the engineers to ensure that no one was holding a gun to the senior attorney's head. Whenever the physical door to the office was opened, any decrypted files disappeared instantly, ensuring that nothing was ever left exposed on a virtual desktop for a janitor to see. But Krator security planners did not give sufficient weight to human vanity.

On the virtual tour of the Doge's Palace, MacVain described the provenance of each piece of furniture and stopped at each painting so Tricia Culhane could admire it. She ooed and ahhed appropriately.

"But how do you get into your private office?" she wondered aloud.

"It's easy," he told her proudly. "My office," he commanded, and the public halls vanished, replaced by MacVain's new palatial office positioned in physical space in reference to his Empire desk and the Renaissance side chair.

"Wow! Very impressive," Tricia Culhane said with genuine enthusiasm. As she watched, an animated scene of fifteenth-century Venice unfolded through the narrow, grilled window on the wall next to her. "It's so realistic, you think you're back in those times," she said, looking out.

The senior attorney smiled a genuine smile.

"Where's your work space?" she wondered.

He touched a button on his desk and spoke "My eyes only" to the virtuality computer. The machine responded with a warning beep. "It won't open because you're here," he explained. "It's a shame you can't see all the new features I've had added to personal mode."

"What happens when I leave?" she asked.

"It will activate like it's supposed to. Try opening the door and closing it."

Tricia Culhane got up and went to the door, then opened and closed it.

MacVain asked the virtual office to activate—again it beeped its refusal.

"See, it knows you're still here. It's very smart."

"What happens if I leave by the window?" Tricia Culhane laughed.

"Go ahead, see what happens."

She went over to the narrow virtual window and blocked the fifteenth-century street scene with her head.

"My eyes only," MacVain commanded.

Suddenly MacVain's workspace appeared in front of them, cluttered with stacks of digital documents. Tricia Culhane's practiced eyes noted the name of the file that was lying open in front of Vaughn's chair. It was a code name that the special assistant had never seen before: "Tall Blondes."

As she jumped back from the window, the file system disappeared instantly, leaving a polished, uncluttered desktop with a framed picture of MacVain's wife and two children.

"Gosh, sorry," Tricia Culhane said sheepishly.

"There's a glitch in the software," MacVain growled. "I will speak to systems operations about this."

* * *

That night, Tricia Culhane could not sleep, thinking about the code name Tall Blondes. She wondered if it had anything to do with the procession of tall blondes that paraded through Krator's high-security task groups and committees.

When the special assistant arrived at work the next morning, she confirmed that "Tall Blondes" did not appear anywhere in the Krator databases, so it was not a code name for a project that could be traced by means of its other participants. It was more likely one of MacVain's personal file names, and she knew that he was attracted to women that matched that description. He liked to assign obscure female employees to task forces in Colorado Springs, and almost always they were women as blond as Norwegian models and a foot taller than himself.

One of Culhane's responsibilities was to approve a pool of potential task force members, and this provided the perfect cover for her own inquiry into the mysterious name. What better way to investigate something than with a rigorous process of due diligence?

In her capacity as MacVain's special assistant, Tricia Culhane called the director of data-processing and requested on-going access to all the internal audits involving personnel being cleared for the red alert pool, as well as the log of communications that had passed back and forth. As with all secure computer facilities, the Krator data-processing department maintained a log of all file transfers and telecommunications in the organization. Special software, invisible to ordinary users, kept a complete record of who accessed which file when and who sent what to whom.

Thousands of digital phone calls, e-mails, and file transfers had been involved in the vetting of the personnel pool for red alert task forces, but Tricia Culhane soon found what she was looking for—special treatment for tall blondes. All of the female candidates that had been proposed matched this physical description, and all had been surveilled at the request of MacVain's personal security officer, Cole Kincaid.

Tricia Culhane began her inquiry into Tall Blondes with the candidate at the top of the list, a predictive criminality analyst in Laredo, Texas, a woman named Celestine Brittle.

She telephoned the office of Domestic Surveillance in Laredo. "I am calling on behalf of Senior Attorney Vaughn MacVain," the special assistant told a startled surveillance specialist, who could see her title and clearance level displayed on his screen. "I understand that you are surveilling a subject named Celestine Brittle."

"Yes."

"I want to ensure that the requisition submitted by Cole Kincaid is correct. Could you confirm the location of the surveillance?"

"It's in her bedroom, in the mirror of a vanity."

"And the distribution?"

"Vaughn MacVain and his personal security officer only."

"Thank you for being on top of this."

Tricia Culhane had no access to the content of the surveillance—the data were encrypted at the camera and e-mailed directly to MacVain's and Kincaid's accounts—but she had a good idea of what was in the files. MacVain was using routine surveillance requisitions to take photos of women in their bedrooms and bathrooms. Then he would move them within striking distance by special assignment to task forces and committees.

From Personnel, the special assistant learned that Brittle was a fundamentalist Christian who had taken a vow of chastity until marriage. Who better to track the senior attorney's prurient interest than an unimpeachable young woman of chaste sensibilities? Tricia Culhane had thought of telephoning Brittle on a pretext, but dismissed the idea as too dangerous. She decided to follow a slower but safer course: cultivate a personal relationship with Brittle after MacVain recruited her to one of his committees.

White Rabbit

At lunchtime, as Celestine Brittle was climbing the spiral staircase to the elevator landing, she nearly collided with an energetic, slightly-built man with a pink face and a mane of white hair. He was wearing a white lab coat and a founder's badge, which indicated a long association with Krator. He reminded her of the White Rabbit in *Alice's Adventures in Wonderland*.

"Oh my goodness!" he exclaimed, suddenly aware that someone else was in the laboratory.

Celestine was taller than the scientist and wearing her official-looking navy blue suit with the prominent white badge. Initially he seemed intimidated by her.

"It will be good when they get the elevators to the mezzanine working," Celestine said to reassure him. She wondered if he was Wassily Tweecus, the scientist she had learned about in the academy at Quantico.

"I hate elevators," he replied "I always take the stairs. Do you work here?" He had cultivated an English accent when he had studied at Oxford University, but Midwestern vowels kept slipping through.

"I am working on Level B."

"How do you like it?" he asked.

"Very comfortable."

141

"Frankly, I had higher hopes for the lab," he said frowning. "I told them I wanted it above ground with windows to the outside, but that was nixed for security reasons. But I did insist on a small museum to ensure that all laboratory personnel have a grasp of our tradition of scientific excellence, as well as knowledge of the great discoveries I have made."

"I didn't know there was a museum."

He scowled. "It's been declared off limits for security reasons."

"That's a shame, but at least the labs have plenty of space," she said, gesturing at the vast emptiness behind him.

"Yes, in three months, this space will be full of people."

"Will you be working here too?" she asked.

"Oh no, I work in facility 289," he said, as if he expected her to know that already. "I don't do much bench work myself anymore." He looked at her for the first time. "So you're part of the initial build-out team from Bethesda?"

"I'm on assignment to Colorado Springs, but I work here in Laredo."

"Really, I didn't know we had any geneticists in Laredo."

"I'm in predictive criminality," Celestine told him.

"Oh," he gasped, his face falling. "But that is the whole idea, isn't it?" in a tone of mock collegiality—"marrying the two?" Without waiting for an answer, the White Rabbit turned and disappeared around the curve of the staircase.

When Celestine returned from lunch, the telephone was ringing in the deputy chief scientist's office.

"Hello, Nate," she said as she picked it up.

"Do you know who you were talking with on the stairs?"

"The man in the white coat?"

"Yes."

"I bet it was the father of civil genetics—Wassily Tweecus."

"Yes!" Nate confirmed in a thrilled voice. "You met the Gnome of Krator!"

The Task Force Reconvenes

Tuesday afternoon Tricia Culhane called a special session of task force Wildfire to discuss a .22 caliber shell casing that the sheriff's CSI team had found that morning in a culvert on the fire road, just above the gully where Grazziella had disappeared.

Tricia Culhane began the meeting by introducing the group's new security advisor, Cole Kincaid. "Cole is well known to all of us on senior attorney MacVain's staff as the invisible man in the basement bunker. We all hope that he will continue in this capacity while serving on task force Wildfire."

She turned to Cato Magruder, the mustachioed cop with the bald pate. "I've asked the deputy chief of Apprehension and Detention to summarize the recent findings."

"We got the CSI report a few minutes ago," Magruder announced in his chronically angry voice. "The shell is from a batch of ammo bought in Oscuridad several years ago by…." Magruder paused, studying with a quizzical expression the name of the purchaser —an East Indian name with an excess of vowels. "By, er—by a convenience store owner with a registered hand gun," he continued. "A year ago, the man reported a .22 pistol and a box of ammo stolen from his store. His pre-indite looks clean. The crime lab can't determine how long ago the shell was fired, or exactly where, due to the circumstances of where it was found. In a culvert. It might've been carried there by runoff from the fire hoses on the hill above it."

"But no more than a year ago?" someone interrupted.

The policeman shrugged. "We asked the owner if he had ever been on the fire road, and he said no. He claims he never lent the weapon to anyone either."

"Is the bureau interpreting this as possible evidence of foul play?" the director of Domestic Surveillance asked Magruder.

"No, just the opposite. It might have been planted there just to mislead us."

"What do you mean?" Tricia Culhane asked.

"The bureau doesn't believe in miracles. If Grazziella wasn't burned in the fire, and she wasn't taken up to heaven, then she must have left in a vehicle. If she was abducted, why eject the shell casing and leave it behind? But if she left under her own power with the help of a confederate—well, then it makes a kind of sense."

"You're saying she staged her own disappearance?" Tricia Culhane asked.

"I'm saying we need to consider that. Read the pre-indite—she doesn't have any enemies."

Everyone looked at Celestine, who nodded in agreement. "No law suits, no unpaid debts, no drugs, no public controversies, and no ex-spouse."

"So what's that leave?" Cato Magruder snorted. "I'll tell you. One of her college track team members said she belonged to a witch's cult—lesbians, group sex, dancing naked during full moons…"

"There was nothing in that police report about sex, nudity, or full moons," Celestine said pointedly. "Only that she once belonged to a drumming circle founded by a woman linked to Goddess worship."

"Same thing," Magruder sneered. "Maybe she's trying to embarrass the Fellowship."

"I thought that the bureau had already determined that there were no other vehicles on that fire road yesterday morning except for Grazziella's vehicle," the official from Domestic Surveillance asked.

"That's right," Magruder replied. "We talked to all the wineries on the west side of the valley and checked with the drivers of all delivery trucks that serve that area. No one reported a vehicle."

"A question," Van Squint interjected. "If someone picked up Grazziella in a vehicle, wouldn't it be detected by the vehicle surveillance system?"

"Ordinarily, it would," the bureau chief of Domestic Surveillance answered. "But there are no detector towers on the fire roads in that area."

"And no one noticed Grazziella's vehicle until it was found burned," Tricia Culhane added.

"That's why we're thinking she faked her disappearance," Cato Magruder emphasized. "Once we admit the possibility of a confederate who drove her away in another vehicle, we can see this case from another angle."

"If Grazziella planted that shell casing, she either has a stolen gun or a confederate with a stolen gun," Domestic Surveillance noted.

"We cannot discount either possibility at this time," Magruder said.

"CSI thinks that the shell casing washed down the culvert with the fire hose runoff," Tricia Culhane reminded him. "The evidence for staging is highly speculative."

Cato Magruder gave the special assistant a severe look. "If she's a Goddess worshipper, she's sympathetic to banned environmentalist groups with a history of eco-terrorism. She has a motive to damage the Fellowship. We need to start from there."

Tricia Culhane looked at the senior research analyst. "Celestine, where would Kelly go if she went to ground?"

"Home," Celestine replied.

"I think so too," the special assistant said, turning to Magruder and fixing him with a stare. "The Bureau of Apprehension and Detention will re-check every home that Grazziella's ever had: the family farm, her student housing in Davis, her cottage—whatever. I don't want any dancing naked by the light of the moon until we've exhausted the other possibilities."

Everyone laughed except Cato Magruder, who looked furious but said nothing.

"Is this .22 shell for public release?" asked Skipper Van Squint, the nation's top spin doctor.

"Senior attorney MacVain wants any evidence kept on a need-to-know basis to prevent further fruitless speculation by the media," Tricia Culhane announced to the group. "For now, we let the public enjoy a good mystery and hammer home the message that Krator is doing all it can to find the missing firefighter. If by tomorrow night it looks like she won't be found, we'll revisit the issue at that time."

* * *

After the meeting adjourned, Culhane spoke privately with Celestine Brittle. "Celestine, please re-check the phony adoption agency in Davis. Maybe there's something there we missed."

"Virtually everything about it was fabricated," Celestine reminded her. "The names on the legal documents, the address, even the hospital administrator who liaisoned with the agency."

"But the mothers are real. Check into their backgrounds and see if there's anything that connects them to Grazziella. And I want their heights and weights, as well as whole-body pictures of what they looked like before they became pregnant."

"Whole body?"

"Yes, like from a distance, so I can see their figures. And don't post your findings on the Wildfire database—I want to evaluate them first."

The Missing Data

Celestine read through the pre-indictment profiles of the two women that she had written for Vaughn MacVain. Like Kelly, both were in their twenties and had been living in Davis at the time they became pregnant, although they apparently did not know one another or have any contact with Kelly's alma mater. Both women had been active and healthy at the time they gave birth, but their subsequent medical records showed a history of psychological problems. One was diagnosed with clinical depression and had been put on medication. The other was diagnosed with post-traumatic stress syndrome and had tried a wide variety of therapies, from psychological counseling to shamanistic healers, though the medical plan had refused payment on the latter.

The Krator office in Sacramento had interviewed both women on Monday evening. They denied any knowledge of Kelly Grazziella, but both stated that they had become pregnant after a party but did not remember the details of the encounter or the name of the boy they had been with. In both cases, the hospital recommended the adoption agency.

The investigative officer was an agent named Profumo, who had spent most of his career working undercover for the U.S. Drug Enforcement Agency in the Sacramento area, then was transferred to the Krator office there when all of the federal police forces were privatized.

He was at his desk when Celestine telephoned.

"Profumo speaking," he growled. He had the gravelly voice of a chronic smoker and the demeanor of a pit bull. When she told him she was a research analyst on the Wildfire task force, he turned from sullen to cooperative.

"Yeah, I interviewed those two women. What about 'em?"

"I am trying to obtain pictures of them at the time they became pregnant—photos that show their full figures, not just the face."

"We've got nothin' like that here—I'd have to talk to them again," Profumo informed her, clearly unhappy with the prospect.

"Can that be easily done?" Celestine asked.

"I can tell you what they look like. They're both still an eyeful— tall, blond, blue eyes—just what the serial rapist was looking for."

"What serial rapist?"

"I filed a report about it in the Wildfire database."

She knew that there was no mention of this subject in the Wildfire database.

"I don't remember reading that in your police report," she said.

"Who knows what you read?"

"Well, I would like to hear it in your own words."

"Like I said in my report, a serial rapist and date-rape drugs—it's the only thing that makes sense of the three pregnancies."

Celestine was stunned. "Can you e-mail me your police report with that information?"

"Sure."

"Is there anything else you can tell me about Grazziella or the adoption agency that's not in the report I have here?" she asked.

"I never heard of Grazziella until the day before yesterday," he told her. "Maybe she was at the Davis University campus when I was there, but I don't remember the name. I never saw her before either, until Monday when her picture was on TV."

"You worked at the Davis University campus?"

"Yeah, I worked there undercover in narcotics for years."

"Is there any connection that you know of between the two other women and Kelly Grazziella?"

"Like I said in my report, they're connected by the M.O. of the serial rapist."

"Thank you for your help," Celestine told him. "If I have any more questions, I may call you again."

"Why not? We gotta help our firefighters."

Celestine Brittle called the manager of data processing. "How do I get archived case files?" she asked him.

"Is this a request pertinent to the Wildfire task force?"

"Yes."

"I can do it for you. What are the files?"

"Any criminal investigation at Davis University during the dates of Grazziella's tenure there."

Ten minutes later, she had a view of the requested records. She searched on Kelly's name—it did not appear. She searched on Profumo's name—then read with increasing interest the case history displayed on the screen.

During Kelly Grazziella's first year at the university, Agent Profumo was working undercover in the medical school, tracing periodic thefts of pharmaceuticals. While undercover, the agent worked as a clerk in the shipping room, which enabled him to track any packages that came or went, as well as to go anywhere in the medical center without arousing suspicion. As the result of his work, a suspect had been arrested but, apparently, never tried. The perpetrator was a pre-medical student named Chad Weed who worked part time as a research assistant at the Nathan Whyte Laboratory, an off-campus facility that the university managed under contract for a defense firm. Weed had used his position there to generate fraudulent orders to pharmaceutical supply for a date-rape drug whose name had been subsequently classified. The judicial record had been expunged at the request of a judge.

Every year, Krator prosecuted hundreds of narcotics cases similar to this—sad accounts of ruined lives and trusts betrayed, energized by relentless dependency, quick thrills, and the glitter of easy money. There did not seem to be anything about the Chad Weed case that would reverberate years later.

A moment later, Profumo's own report arrived by e-mail. Just as he said, the three women who had given their babies to the phony adoption agency appeared to have been victims of a serial rapist.

She wondered if the rapist had been Chad Weed.

As she read further, Celestine had a feeling of vertigo. For four years, she had been using Krator databases to predict the criminality of people—and now she wondered how many records had been altered before she was put on the case.

7

OF PURITANS AND
PROPHECY

The Fellowship's founder fused the moral self-
righteousness of Southern fundamentalism
with a fictive theory of history.

The Hidden History of the Eighth Dispensation
by Amadeus

It was still dark when Giovanni drove down Deep Creek Road
toward Indian Springs Winery. The car audio played a song
in honor of Kelly Grazziella. It was a traditional tune called
"Gospel Ship," recorded in the mid-twentieth century by a
folk musician accompanying herself on acoustic guitar, her
high-pitched voice lifting her up to Jesus in the clouds.

In the first light of dawn, the vineyard was a dark island in
a glittering sea of metallic gray. Indian Springs Winery pruned
its vines to grow like bushes, and when they leafed they formed

a miniature orchard, with dense green foliage hiding clusters of purple grapes. At all the neighboring wineries, the vines were trained on wires stretched between steel turrets. The trellises made the grape clusters more accessible and easier to pick, but even in summer the vineyards bristled with steel, and in the winter after the leaves had dropped, the fields looked as inviting as orthodontia.

When Giovanni arrived at the vineyard, the eastern sky was lemon yellow, and the pickers were already moving single file toward their starting positions on the uphill side. The vineyard manager and the winemaker were somewhere among the grapes taking final readings of the sugar. Clydesdale drove up a moment later, an anxious look on his face.

"Is anything wrong?" Giovanni asked.

"No, everything's all set. It's picking so early in the season that has me worried. It doesn't seem right."

Giovanni nodded sympathetically. It was the first crush he had ever supervised—and he was nervous too.

As he watched the pickers begin their work, Giovanni reflected that after only two years at the winery, he had become Clydesdale's right-hand man, handling everything in plant operations except the growing of grapes and the making of wine.

Giovanni had moved into winery work from the thermal energy plant at Almaden Peak. After high school, there were no longer any mill jobs, as the old-growth redwood had all been logged, so Giovanni enlisted in the navy on the expectation of seeing the world. Instead, they trained him as a pipe fitter and stationed him at a shipyard on San Francisco Bay, a two-hour drive from where he was born. When his enlistment was up, the power company hired him to maintain pipes at its thermal energy plant, a never-ending job, as the hot, volcanic, mineral-laden waters, pressurized deep within the earth, ate pipes and valves like candy. Giovanni loved the pressures of steam and the flow of hydraulics, but he disliked the remoteness of the facility. It was above tree line on the eastern, sun-scorched face of Almaden Peak. As barren as the moon, it reeked of sulfur and was an hour's drive to the nearest town. Giovanni wanted to be down in the valley and closer to his girlfriend.

Giovanni's mother asked the Black Madonna to ask Jesus to get him a job closer to home. Each day, she put fresh flowers in a vase in front of a small framed picture of Our Lady and lit a votive candle. Then she closed the door to her bedroom and fell to her knees. When she emerged an hour later she was usually confident and calm. Giovanni had learned that when his mother felt strongly about anything, the Mother of God almost invariably felt that way too, so he did not argue when she suggested one day that he apply for the job of hospitality manager at Indian Springs Winery. Even though his knowledge of wine was largely based on pull-tab cartons of bargain reds, he realized it would be easier to put in a job application and be turned down than to wage a war of attrition with his mother about why he could not do it.

When Giovanni finally went by the winery for the first time, on a clear day after a winter rain, he found the owner in the tasting room, wearing rubber boots and pushing water out the door with a squeegee. Indian Springs had recently built a new winery of white stucco in the style of a Mexican hacienda, constructed around an interior courtyard tastefully strewn with antique ox carts. The architect had designed the tasting room with a nod to both Permaculture and Imperial Rome, channeling some of the spring water through a notch in the concrete floor, so that visitors could enjoy the ambience of free-flowing natural waters on even the hottest days of summer. Visually, the design was a triumph, winning the architect critical notice in a major periodical, but he had not reckoned with the seasonality of flow. In summer, a thin trickle transected the tasting room with a pleasant bubbling sound as it had been designed to do. But in the rainy season, water spread across the floor, discoloring the pavement with a scrofulous black algae and making it so slippery that walking was dangerous.

"Looks like you've got some seepage," Giovanni volunteered.

Clydesdale shot him an angry glance. "It's not seepage. It's the valve on the pipe from Indian Springs."

"So Indian Springs flows through here?"

"Yes. We've had three different valves installed," the owner complained, "but none of them properly regulates the flow. In the winter it floods the tasting room."

"Are you saying you try to regulate flow with a valve and an overflow pipe?"

"Yes."

"Oh, I wouldn't recommend that," Giovanni said, shaking his head gravely. "In the winter you'll get seepage."

Clydesdale looked at Giovanni as if he might throw him out: "What would you recommend then?"

"The water on the floor is not from a defective valve," Giovanni explained. "In winter the whole hillside becomes a seep. You need a waterproof retaining wall on the uphill side, with drains behind it to channel the flow off to the sides."

The owner looked Giovanni up and down for the first time. "What are you here for?" he asked finally.

"The job of hospitality manager that you advertised," Giovanni said tentatively.

"Have you managerial experience?"

"No."

"Have you serving experience, pouring or as a waiter?"

"No."

"Have you any experience in meeting and greeting the public? In the hotel business or retail?"

"No."

"What is it that you do then?"

"I'm a pipe fitter at the Almaden plant, where I do maintenance."

"Oh," Clydesdale said. "We have a position available in plant operations too. Would you accept a combined position in operations and hospitality, until you learn the hospitality end of the business?"

Giovanni looked at him in disbelief. "I should tell you I've never done any hospitality."

Clydesdale seemed unconcerned. "I'd rather teach a pipe fitter how to pour," he shrugged, "than try to teach a wine snob plant operations."

* * *

Everyone watched anxiously as the first load of grapes was towed down the hill to the crusher. The bin was hinged on one side, and when the tractor pulled it into position, a mechanical hand slowly tipped it over, emptying a ton of fruit into the hopper. A conveyor belt exited the crusher, dumping the stems and leaves into an over-sized trash can on wheels, while the juice and skins flowed into the stainless steel tanks where the alcoholic fermentation takes place. In the past, these tanks were housed indoors and fitted with complex refrigeration systems, but at Indian Springs Winery, they were partially buried in the side of the hill and heavily insulated with foam. The arrangement allowed the wine to be stored at a constant temperature for a fraction of the energy cost. On the first day of the crush it was much cooler in Oscuridad than it had been the day before, and it was clear to everyone at the winery that the picking would be completed before any spontaneous fermentation of the grapes could take place.

The winemaker filled a wine glass with the juice of the first crush. He smelled it deeply, then held it to the light to check its color and consistency. With a professional flourish that masked his apprehension he sloshed the liquid around in his mouth, searching for the flavors that he hoped to taste in the wine over subsequent months and years. As the owner, the vineyard manager, and the operations supervisor watched with growing anticipation, the vintner imagined the taste of the wine at each stage of its production cycle: the taste after fermentation in the stainless steel tanks, the taste after barrel aging and blending; and the taste of the mature wine when poured from the bottle after years in the cellar.

Like other graduates of the viticulture program at Davis University, the winemaker had been taught all the latest theories and statistics, but at the end of his first season at a winery he knew that the textbooks could only carry him so far. When he took that first taste of the sugary juice of the first crush of the season, he was flying by the seat of his pants. Only experience could tell him what flavors were implicit in the grapes—what strain of yeast would coax them out, what length of time in oak would mature them, what fractions of other varietals added to the mix would make them explode on the pallet. There was science to be sure, but wine making was an art, and every season was its own.

The winemaker spat out the grape juice on the ground and took a second sip, swirling the liquid in the glass as he tasted it. He spat that out too.

Clydesdale edged closer. "Well?" he finally asked.

The winemaker acted as if he did not hear him.

Giovanni and the vineyard manager huddled closer, quiet with anticipation.

"Not great," the winemaker said finally. "But not as terrible as we expected."

Guadalupe

Renato Ocampo-Mendoza emerged from the metro station and spied a late-model sport sedan with tinted windows. He peered cautiously into the interior through the windshield, recognized the driver as El Tigre, and got in.

"Where are we going?" Ocampo asked in English.

The EarthRage chief of security ignored the question. Without turning his head, El Tigre's eyes shifted constantly from the rear view mirror to the side mirrors and back again. He maneuvered the car through the heavy traffic, quickly merging from one lane to the next so as to be almost impossible to follow.

El Tigre nosed the car on to the Paseo de la Reforma.

"Krator usually tracks targets electronically," El Tigre volunteered, as if reading the Philosopher's thoughts. "But you never know."

"Won't they be able to track us by satellite?"

"They could—it depends on how important you are."

Ocampo wondered if working with Jack Adair made him important enough. "Do you mind if I ask you some questions?"

"For that book you're writing?"

"Yes."

"Wait until we get past the embassy."

Always a formidable presence, the United States embassy had been reinforced with vehicle-proof barriers and an electric fence. At night the entire facade was illuminated by floodlights like a stadium while infrared cameras probed the shadows looking for protestors and terrorists. In spite of the enhanced security, every morning, new graffiti had to be erased from the perimeter wall.

El Tigre turned into a neighborhood of streets named for the world's strategic rivers. He skillfully navigated from the Tigris to the Tiber, then slowed as if preparing to park. The driver of a white sport utility nodded as he drove past; it was followed by a second car. Only at that moment did Ocampo realize that El Tigre had been leading other vehicles. The chief of security relaxed and became more expansive. "What do you want to know?" he asked, edging the sport sedan back into traffic.

"You served in the Middle East, right?"

"Yeah—Iraq, Iran, Pakistan, the Emirates, Afghanistan—the whole nine yards."

"I'd like to understand the reasons why you left the army. Was there any single event that was responsible?"

El Tigre looked thoughtful. "No, the entire war—it was a big lie to begin with. How much time do you have?"

"As long as it takes."

"Before we went in, we were told we would be hailed as liberators. Liberation my ass! You couldn't drive down the street without an armored escort—that's the literal truth. Then we were told that the army had to pacify the country but with the same number of troops needed for a liberation. When that didn't work, they said that the U.S. Army was led by cowardly commanders. Then they said the troops were hooked on heroine. Finally, they said the invasion was all the Army's idea.

"My outfit had thirty percent casualties, but Washington thought it was a Rambo movie." He looked thoughtful. "I wanted to make the army my career—my father, he was a major."

They stopped for a red light, and El Tigre took his eyes from the road for the first time and looked directly at Ocampo. "But for me the turning point was when they created the no-name brigades. I signed on to serve my country, not fight a religious crusade."

"Do you know any people who joined them?"

"A lot."

"But you weren't interested in joining?"

He gave the Philosopher a severe look. "The religion's just a smoke screen. They think the United States Army is a 'nigger army.' My paternal grandfather was wounded during the Tet Offensive. My great grandfather, on my mother's side, died on Bataan. Don't ever say 'nigger army' to me." His eyes hardened at the recollection of an incident. "They only said it once."

158

When the light changed he shot out of the intersection to get ahead of several cars.

"And then when they made membership in the Fellowship a leg-up for promotion I knew it was time to quit."

"How did you meet Jack?" Ocampo asked.

"I went looking for him. When I was in Pakistan, I met a journalist working on assignment for EarthRage. He had hiked into the war zone to do a story on the effect of the fighting on the mountain sheep—if you can believe it. He had a camera, a water purification kit, and a bag full of candy bars for gifts. I thought he was a goner, but two weeks later I ran into him again in Karachi. He had his story.

"So I asked him what EarthRage was. He said it was founded by Jack Adair. 'Who's that?' I asked. He said he was an American journalist who still cared about the Bill of Rights. So I had to meet the guy."

"Did Jack offer you a job as a bodyguard?"

El Tigre laughed. "No. Back then, he was running EarthRage from a palapa on the beach: he told me he didn't need any bodyguards."

They both laughed.

El Tigre doubled back in the direction they had come. "Now it's my turn to ask you a question," he said firmly, his voice shifting into professional register. "Why is a Marxist so interested in protecting Catholic Madonnas?"

Ocampo furrowed his brow and lapsed into a moment of uncharacteristic silence. Then he turned to face his interrogator. "Did you know that the war for Mexican independence began when the Catholic priest Miguel Hidalgo rang the church bell in the town of Dolores in September of 1810 and shouted to the assembled people: 'Death to the Spaniards! Long live the Virgin of Guadalupe!'?"

El Tigre looked shocked. "No," he answered.

"Did you know that Hidalgo, as leader of an army of liberation composed of eighty thousand Indians and poor people, marched on Mexico City?"

"No."

"And that the army marched under the banner of Our Lady of Guadalupe, with her image on the soldiers' hats?"

"No, I didn't know any of that," El Tigre admitted.

"And in your country too," the Philosopher continued. "When Caesar Chavez led his first march of striking farmworkers in Delano, California, they marched behind a banner of the Virgin of Guadalupe. So when I think of the image of the Virgin, I don't see Catholic art—I see an expression of the revolutionary spirit of the people of Mexico!"

El Tigre looked at him in astonishment. "We'll talk some more," he said. "But right now you have to catch the Tranquility Base express." He stopped the car and pointed to a courier company van parked on the cross street. "That van there is one of ours. Get in the passenger side and lie down in back—you know the drill."

Rapture

In the safe room, Jack Adair tapped one of the computers to wake it up. A video clip from One World News-in-Spanish filled the screen, announcing itself as "Mysterious Disappearance of Firefighter."

"Here's what I wanted to show you," Jack said. "This story is all over the television in the United States. I think it's important."

As they watched it together, the Philosopher became increasingly uncomfortable. He thought all *gringos* were crazy but had made an exception of Jack Adair—now he wondered if the guerrilla journalist was going wacko too.

"Are they really implying that the missing firefighter was lifted bodily into the air?" Ocampo asked him, thinking perhaps it was a bad translation from the English.

"That's exactly what they are implying," Jack assured him. "They are implying that she's the Rapture of the First White Kernel."

The philosophy student looked at him with consternation.

Jack retrieved a document from a stack of papers on one of the workstations. "This is background reading," he said, handing it to the doctoral candidate.

Renato read aloud in English: "'On Puritans and Prophecy' by Amadeus. Who's Amadeus?"

"Some years ago, before travel to Europe required exit visas from the United States, I met an American clergyman at a conference in Berlin," Jack recounted. "Amadeus belonged to no radical groups, had no friends on the watch list, and did not participate in the resistance, yet he listened attentively to everything I said about Washington's worldwide war on the environment, asking intelligent and provocative questions, and leaving no doubt as to which side he was on.

"It was Amadeus, in a Berlin hotel lobby, who first pointed out to me the connection between the theology of fallen nature and the need to transform wilderness into profit. I've not seen him since, but we keep in touch by private courier."

"Amadeus? Is that a nom de plume?"

"Yes. When we were in Germany, getting ready to leave for the airport, he suggested that we continue our conversation at a distance. 'Not by your real name,' I warned him. 'You will need a nom de guerre.'"

"'Better a *nom de Dieu*,' he said. 'How about Amadeus?' So that's how he got his Internet handle."

"Amadeus is Latin for 'beloved of God,'" Renato pointed out.

Jack looked surprised—he thought it was an allusion to Mozart.

"Look up 'incremental rapture' in the index," Jack told him.

Renato found the page and buried his nose in the manuscript, then read a passage aloud, as he often did when reading English:

> A scriptural polymath who could inundate critics with blizzards of citations, Duane Boone III first rose to prominence not as a televangelist but as the iconoclastic divinity student who first promulgated the doctrine of the incremental rapture.
>
> Where the theologian Silas Garvey and his followers had envisioned a universal and instantaneous moment of transport, a rapture when all born-again Christians disappeared from earth at once, Boone suggested that the process would begin slowly, with a few scattered transportations, then gradually increase to a crescendo of disappearances. He likened the rapture to microwave popcorn. As the bag starts to puff out, there are only a few scattered pops at first, soon followed by a steady tattoo of pops, culminating in a nearly universal whoosh of pops that stretches the bag to the limit.

"The incremental rapture is a key doctrine of the Fellowship of the Eighth Dispensation," Jack replied. "The other is the idea of the eighth dispensation itself."

Renato looked it up: "'dispensation defined; dispensations, number of; dispensation, theology of'—here it is—'eighth dispensation, innovation of.'"

He read the section aloud:

> One evening during his two-hour, prime-time slot, Boone announced that the incremental rapture does not occur between the sanctification church of the sixth dispensation and the millennial kingdom of the seventh dispensation as

everyone had thought. Rather, there is an eighth dispensation that must be established on earth before the rapture can begin. The start of the eighth dispensation is signaled by a prefiguration of the rapture: the assumption into heaven of someone somewhere whom God has chosen as an involuntary herald of the new age. Boone called it the Rapture of the First White Kernel.

Like his previous innovations, the new synthesis had an unorthodox edge that made the theologians nervous. Not only was an eighth dispensation a serious departure from dispensational orthodoxy in its own right, but Boone maintained that the first person raptured out did not even have to be a Christian. The First White Kernel could be anyone purified by fire.

Slowly, the Philosopher put down the manuscript, a concerned look on his face. "Is this what we're seeing with this missing firefighter story? The Rapture of the First White Kernel?"

Jack nodded affirmatively. "I heard from Amadeus today, and he confirms that the firefighter fits the theory. Amadeus says that the Rapture of the First White Kernel begins the age of the eighth dispensation, when all the armies of the godless converge on the plain of Armageddon. There they are defeated by a Christian army aided by higher powers. Then the Christian remnant rebuilds the Jewish temple in Jerusalem, with hegemony from the Nile to the Euphrates."

"My God!" Renato exclaimed. "Is this a countdown to a world war?"

"Amadeus thinks that conclusion follows logically from the theology."

Renato reflected that he was having a conversation in a former drug dealer's bunker with a renegade American about a religious zealot who thought that a firefighter had been lifted into heaven as a signal to begin the final battle between good and evil in order to rebuild the temple in Jerusalem—and somehow none of it was implausible, given the temper of the times.

"But how can anyone be sure if she is the First White Kernel or not?" Renato asked with evident concern.

"One can't tell from appearances—the Fellowship has to proclaim it."

"Ah! Does Amadeus think she is?"

"He doesn't know," Jack explained. "It's possible that the Council of Seventeen has staged the disappearance of the firefighter to justify a major war in the Middle East, or maybe the Fellowship's enemies have staged it in order to embarrass them."

"How's that work?"

"Suppose Boone proclaims her the First White Kernel—and then she shows up again safe and sound?"

"Ah!" the Philosopher exclaimed. Dispensational theology was starting to interest him.

"If you don't mind, I would like to borrow this article by Amadeus and read it through carefully. Then I might be able to make a more informed interpretation of the current situation."

Jack gave him a pleased grin. "If you do decide to join editorial, what editorial position would you like?"

"Editor-at-large," Renato replied without hesitation. "But I need to think about it. Do you have any more articles by Amadeus?" he asked.

"Yes, a whole stack of them."

"I'll read them all."

8

TALL BLONDES

Jack Adair surveyed the block-long street. Faded row houses faced the ancient flagstone pavement, each façade protected by a head-high wall topped with loops of razor wire. There had been no place to run.

Two shrouded bodies lay crumpled in the gutter, a good ten meters from where the car had hit them. Two paramedics and two traffic policemen were busy with their phones, but the row houses appeared to be deserted.

Jack Adair introduced himself to one of the policemen who had answered the call. The guerrilla journalist was neatly dressed in cotton pants and a sport shirt, like an engineer on the way to work. He showed the policeman the press badge from One World News that he always carried with him. It had been made without a photograph so as not to trigger the face-recognition software that the Americans had installed in the world's telecommunication system.

"We received a tip that one of our reporters was hit by a car—a Canadian man, named Dunkirk," he explained. "Latin American bureau chief for *Left America*."

At a nod from the officer, one of the paramedics bent over and lifted the shroud to reveal the body of a thin man in his early forties, his red hair turning to gray at the temples. It was the person that Jack Adair feared it would be, a journalist whom he had met for the first time in the formative days of EarthRage, then had met again only last week. In life, his colleague had a face filled with energy and emotion, but now it was unlined and expressionless, more like a mannequin than a man.

"Is that your reporter?" the policeman asked.

"That's Dunkirk, all right. How did it happen?"

"Hit-and-run," the policeman replied.

Jack Adair turned away from the policeman and surveyed the second cadaver.

A slim, pale hand extended from under the sheet, as if reaching for a lifeline.

"Who's the second victim?" Jack Adair asked.

The paramedic delicately lifted the shroud in a manner befitting a lady. In life, she was a tall, slim blonde, perhaps in her late twenties, with a good figure and a stylish wardrobe. In death, her left profile was framed by a nimbus of darkened blood, spilled from where her skull had fractured on the curbstone.

Jack Adair suppressed a shudder. "I don't know her," he told the officer. "I never saw her before. Who is she?"

The policeman shrugged you-tell-me, then photographed Jack Adair's badge—his digital tablet scanning the phony name into the crime report. But before the policeman could photograph Jack Adair's face, an EarthRage body guard yanked the guerrilla journalist away by the arm.

"You're needed at headquarters right away!" the bodyguard said in a loud voice, one hand cupped over his earpiece.

"Stick around," the policeman said. "The investigators will want to talk with you."

"The judicial police are on the way," the bodyguard whispered.

"First I need to call the story in," Jack Adair told the policeman.

As the guerrilla journalist headed back toward the taxi, a balding, middle-aged man with tortoise shell eyeglasses emerged from one of the houses and stopped in front of him.

"They were on the sidewalk, and the car headed straight for them and accelerated," the man said in a confidential voice. "There is no way it could have been an accident."

"Thank you," Jack Adair said. "Thank you for telling me."

"Why do you think they were killed?"

"Because they tried to tell the truth."

Around the corner, the taxicab was waiting, its engine idling. Jack Adair dove into the back seat while his bodyguard jumped into the front. As the taxi pulled away, a second police car, its lights flashing, roared down the thoroughfare and turned into the narrow street.

The taxi sped past nondescript rows of functional housing, then turned off the boulevard and into an underground parking garage adjacent to an American-style supermarket. It traversed a half-empty parking area until it reached an even more deserted section where two exit ramps converged. A silver-gray sedan was parked facing outward, as if primed for a quick getaway. Two serious-looking men were visible through the windshield, the only clear glass in the vehicle, and behind them a vague silhouette of a third person. Above the car, the lens of the video surveillance camera had been shattered.

"Take five," Jack Adair told his driver and his bodyguard. "I want to talk to El Tigre alone."

"Tough break," El Tigre said, slipping into the cab next to Jack Adair. "But he took off on his own, before the escort knew what was happening."

"This is a double message," Jack said, the tautness of his voice conveying his anger. "One, Krator is telling journalists that they can't write certain stories. Two, they're saying EarthRage can't protect them if they do."

"I've already initiated some changes in operating procedure."

The guerrilla journalist nodded his approval, then gestured at the sedan parked nearby. "The man in the back seat—is that Dunkirk's bodyguard?"

"Yes, he's a little shaken."

"I want to hear it from him."

Dunkirk's bodyguard took El Tigre's place in the taxi. A sturdy American of Mexican ancestry, he was one of the disillusioned ex-servicemen from the Third Afghan War that El Tigre favored for these assignments.

"Tell me how Dunkirk slipped away," Jack Adair asked the man.

"I was with him at his apartment all morning," the bodyguard said. "Mostly he worked at his computer. I'd been with him for three days, morning shift. No problems. Friendly guy. This morning he told me he was expecting an important call from a source and might have to leave on sudden notice."

"He used that word, 'a source'?" Jack Adair asked.

"Yes."

"The phone rings and I listen in like I'm supposed to do. It's a woman, and she says: 'Calle de los Niños.' 'When?' Dunkirk asks. 'Right away,' she says. 'OK,' Dunkirk says, then hangs up."

"That's it? The entire call?"

"Yes."

"What did the caller sound like?"

"A woman, an American woman."

"She spoke in English?"

"Yes."

"But the street name was in Spanish?"

"Yes."

"Go on."

"I ask Dunkirk if that's the source he's waiting for. He says it is. 'Let's go,' he says—suddenly he's in a big hurry.

"So we head downstairs to the parking garage. Dunkirk says it's a short way and he asks me to drive. I don't think anything is wrong yet. I ask him where we're going and he says he'll show me. We get in the car and I start it up. 'Oh!' he says, all excited. 'I forgot my notebook,' and he jumps out of the car and runs back into the building. So I turn off the engine and run after him. I head upstairs to the apartment, but it's locked and he's not there. Then I realize he's ditched me. So I call Control."

"And what did Control do?"

"They called El Tigre."

"Then what?"

"El Tigre asks if I have the address where he went. I tell him it's Calle de los Niños. El Tigre orders me to wait at the apartment in case he turns up."

Jack Adair looked sympathetic. "We can't protect someone who doesn't want to be protected," he said. He nodded to indicate that the interview was over.

As the bodyguard left, the chief of security slipped back into the taxi.

"There's still something I don't understand," Jack said, looking El Tigre in the eye. "He wasn't killed on the Calle de los Niños—so how'd you find him?"

"We had a man outside the apartment building too. When he saw Dunkirk get into a taxi without the guard, he called Control and followed him."

Jack's eyes brightened. "Good work!" he said in English.

"When Dunkirk got where he was going, the tail called Control with the address, then parked the car as fast as he could," El Tigre continued. "But by the time he got to the alley, Dunkirk was already dead. The woman too. I called you as soon as I heard about it."

"I'm glad you did—I was able to see for myself."

Jesus! El Tigre thought. The founder of EarthRage was as suicidal as Dunkirk—but so far, he had been luckier. "I'm trying to keep you alive," the chief of security said sharply.

"I'm still here, so you must be doing your job."

"Did you find out anything?" El Tigre asked.

"I talked to an eyewitness—it was definitely murder. They were on the sidewalk, and the car accelerated and aimed right for them."

The chief of security did not look surprised. "Who was the woman?" he asked.

"A tall blonde, but no one I recognized."

"Probably the American woman from the phone call. I'll see what I can find out."

"Where is Calle de los Niños? I never heard of it."

"The 'Street of the Children' is probably a code word," El Tigre said, translating the name into English as he spoke. "A pre-arranged meeting site, or maybe a reference to a story or a source."

"Dunkirk told me that he was working on an important story that would 'blow wide open' the American presence in Mexico—and now this," Jack reflected.

"Well, the fact that he got a death threat on a cell phone registered in someone else's name means they've been on to him for some time."

"So why do you think he ditched his bodyguard?"

El Tigre paused before answering, as if he had not considered the question before. "Maybe he was trying protect the blonde's identity," he suggested.

"EarthRage is taking this hit personally," Jack said angrily. "We owe it to the deceased."

iGAP

"Brittany Weer is returning your call," Vaughn MacVain's secretary told him. "I'm putting her through."

A natural blonde with voluptuous curves, Brittany was the only child of America's most prominent general. She had grown up in the Deep South among successful, powerful men who had nurtured in her the unbounded ambition usually reserved for their sons. Her placid face and ingratiating manner belied her Machiavellian talents.

Brittany Weer was the director of the Institute for Genetic Assessment and Profiling, more commonly known as iGAP. She had begun her career as a publicist at the Charleston Banking Group, then had advanced rapidly through Washington bureaucratic circles to become the youngest publicist to ever head a scientific research agency.

"Vaughn, how nice to talk with you again," she said in a mellifluous voice.

"How's the new pied-à-terre on the Chesapeake?"

"Ten thousand square feet and right on the water!"

"Do you spend your weekends there now?"

She paused. "No, actually, it's been almost a year since we built it but we haven't had a chance to use it yet. But Thanksgiving for sure," she added as if trying to convince herself.

"What can Krator do for you?"

"We're putting together an international conference on the Muslim population bomb in Europe. We predict an unprecedented growth rate from fifty million Euro-Muslims today to a projected 150 million within nine years."

"That is quite an increase," the senior attorney said politely.

"We're not going to save the French a third time, but we think the Swiss and the Germans can be made to see reason," she said. "If not, then America is going to have go it alone."

"We need to stay the course," the senior attorney agreed. He favored draconian measures in demography as in the streets.

"In order to better inform the European media of the Muslim menace," the director continued, "the conference will be held in Davos, Switzerland, with free accommodations for journalists and their spouses. Also, a number of prominent left-wing scientists will be presenting research findings that are supportive of our policy."

"How did you get their participation?"

"We're paying them."

MacVain was pleased that the energy invested in her was bearing fruit. "And what is Krator's role in this?"

"I am hoping that you can recommend independent experts who would be willing to serve as session chairs at the conference."

"Surely iGAP has plenty of experts on the Muslim population problem?" MacVain asked.

"Yes, it does, but scientists are too concerned with facts."

"Isn't managed expertise more Skipper's department?" the senior attorney wondered.

"I am told that Mr. Van Squint does not know about our proactive measures for countering the Muslim threat."

"He doesn't need to know," MacVain agreed.

"What we need in Davos are experts who share your strategic vision of the problem and what is being done to solve it, experts who can steer the discussion away from sensitive areas while still eliciting the support of European scientists whose cooperation is needed."

"That is very delicate."

"Yes, it is."

"Have you talked to Titania Troy about this?" he asked.

"Yes. Titania participated in the initial planning meeting. We both agree that since the conference has implications for policy, Krator should play a proactive role in nominating the session chairs."

The senior attorney could not agree more. "Why don't you fly out to the Springs today and we'll discuss it one-on-one?"

"Vaughn, I'd love to."

* * *

Cole Kincaid, MacVain's personal security officer, telephoned the senior attorney from his lair in the basement bunker. "Sir, you asked me to tell you as soon as we had closure on that journalist in Mexico, the Canadian from *Left America*."

MacVain gave him his full attention.

"I just got confirmation that he was killed in a hit-and-run accident in Mexico City."

The senior attorney's thin lips gave a twitch of satisfaction.

"What's more, we got lucky," Kincaid continued. "A former employee of the Institute for Genetic Assessment and Profiling was killed in the same accident, someone that internal security has had under surveillance for some time. She was suspected of selling classified information to the press. As of now, there are no more security issues that could impact Tall Blondes in Mexico."

"Excellent," MacVain said, allowing himself the trace of a smile. "You can close the file on those two traitors."

* * *

In the lobby of the Flyers' Club, an exclusive hilltop retreat open only to members and their guests, the sudden appearance of Vaughn MacVain startled the imperious maître d'hôtel. It was unusual for the senior attorney to emerge from his underground headquarters before dark, even rarer to take lunch at the club.

"Senior attorney MacVain. An honor to serve you again, sir," the maître d' announced.

"Adolfo. How have you been?"

"Very well, sir. Will you be taking lunch in the Lindbergh Room?"

"No, the Rickenbacker Room."

The maître d'hotel realized that the senior attorney was lunching alone with Titania Troy, the well-known collector of primitive art and heiress to the Troy oil fortune. He also understood that the senior attorney—a short, sturdy, balding man—wanted to arrive after Titania Troy had been seated so they would not both be standing up at the same time: her long legs and svelte proportions would make him feel uncomfortable.

"The rest of your party has already been seated," the maître d' assured him, leading the senior attorney down a corridor hung with framed, black-and-white photographs of the great names in American aviation, each print numbered and signed by a famous photographer.

Titania Troy looked up with a brittle smile. She was in her late forties, with the face of a younger woman and the physique of a marathon runner. Her dark, wine-colored suit made her appear even thinner.

"Vaughn! How wonderful to see you again," she gushed, offering a bronzed cheek to be kissed.

"Titania, you are looking so young."

"Why Vaughn," she purred. "I can see how you twisted those jurors around your little finger. But don't stop! —I love it."

The senior attorney had argued before the Supreme Court but saw no reason to inform Titania that he had never presented a case before a jury. He sat down in the captain's chair opposite, thinking back to the night in Washington when they met for the first time at the reception for the new chief justice. As then, she was wearing a gold chain from which dangled a single large teardrop diamond, a legendary jewel that had once belonged to the Romanovs.

"And your tan looks natural," he told her without artifice.

"Thank you. It *is* natural. I was in Ixtapa last week to check on the progress of my new beach house."

"I thought you had one there already?"

"I did, but I had it torn down. I need something to showcase my collection of Spanish colonial religious art. The old place did not have the appropriate ambience."

"Ambience is critical when art is concerned," the senior attorney agreed.

Titania took out a phone and displayed the architect's drawings. "It's right on the beach, and it is designed to take advantage of the setting. It combines world class security with world class views, while recreating traditional colonial architecture. From the outside, it looks like a sixteenth-century monastery, but inside it is completely up to date."

The senior attorney made admiring noises.

"When it's completed next year, I want you to be the first to see it," she said, knowing that MacVain had never been to Mexico and had no desire to go there.

"I would be delighted," he replied.

"But Mexico wasn't all chips and salsa. I also visited our little project to ensure that the grant from iGAP is being properly administered," she said, referring to the Institute for Genetic Assessment and Profiling by its insider shorthand.

MacVain waited with interest, but Titania insisted on playing the tease.

"Is it?" he asked finally.

"It is going very well. The prototype team has achieved the initial goal for the first year."

When Titania talked about money, her face assumed the same merciless remoteness as her grandfather's. "And I had a sit-down talk with the head of Ridgeline Castles' Mexican subsidiary. He tells me that the sales team has been hard at work—he had some numbers to back it up too. *All* 5,000 'condos' have already been sold!"

"That is *very* good," MacVain replied.

"And not only that—he begged for more! He says he can sell whatever quantities we can give him."

"So there is nothing standing in the way of the ramp-up we discussed?"

"All it needs is the grant payment," she said, glancing coyly at the senior attorney. "My staff has already prepared the follow-on grant proposal."

"I would like to take a look at it before you submit it," MacVain told her. "Perhaps the office of the senior attorney could send a letter of support."

"By all means," Titania said with a self-satisfied smile.

"Did Ridgeline Castles say whether Dean's people have been helpful during the prototype phase?" the senior attorney asked.

"He said that Dean Weed was a tremendous help—they could not have met the sales quota otherwise."

"And at the rate we suggested?" the senior attorney persisted.

"Yes. Each buyer has agreed to the initial down payment plus ten percent of their gross income for each unit for twenty-one years, plus all mandated repair and maintenance."

"That's great," MacVain said, mentally estimating the net profit and dividing the result by the percentage of shares he was authorized to buy in the Mexican subsidiary.

"In the ramp-up phase, a million units will be produced the first year," Titania reminded him. "And it goes up exponentially, as Malthus predicted."

A poker-faced MacVain mentally multiplied his previous result by one million—he felt giddy with anticipation. "That's a lot of 'condos,'" he acknowledged in a blasé voice.

"This would be a good time to exercise your options," Titania suggested, reading the senior attorney's mind.

On the Tarmac at Freedom Field

Brittany Weer, the iron magnolia who directed the Institute for Genetic Assessment and Profiling, stood patiently at the bottom of the boarding ramp while MacVain's ground security officer x-rayed her attaché case.

"Do you have a purse, Ma'am?" the officer asked. "Any other carry on?"

"No, just the attaché case."

She walked up the ramp with a self-confident stride befitting the only daughter of the nation's highest-ranking military officer. She was wearing a form-fitting dress of cobalt blue with cleavage that promised more.

The senior attorney was standing in the entrance to his airborne office, seemingly unconscious of his height, and gazing at her with undisguised desire.

Brittany smiled, put down her attaché case, and kissed him on the cheek.

"We'd better attend to business first," he told her, "or we might not get to it."

He waited until she was comfortably seated before sitting down at his Regency writing desk.

Brittany put the attaché case on her lap and handed him a digital storage device. "Here is a complete list of the current donor candidates," she informed him. "And this," taking out a stack of paper bound by a metal clamp, "is an executive summary of each candidate coded by their Krator pre-indite numbers. There's a thumbnail photo next to each one."

She knew that lawyers liked hard copy.

The senior attorney examined the list of candidates and nodded with satisfaction. All were tall blondes.

Then he put the papers aside and met Brittany's attentive eyes. "Is there anything else we need to discuss?"

The director of iGAP snapped the case shut and bent forward to put it on the floor—giving the senior attorney an unobstructed view of the cleft between her breasts.

* * *

Two hours later, Brittany Weer combed her hair in the mirror, then followed Vaughn MacVain down the aisle of the airplane to the rear hatch, which he opened manually with a flourish. She gave him a passionate kiss.

"Don't forget the samples," he said, handing her an insulated container, the kind used for shipping frozen medical specimens.

"How could I ever forget them?" she said with large eyes.

MacVain's ground security officer was standing on the tarmac near the executive jet, pretending not to notice the curvaceous blonde who sashayed down the gangway and blew the senior attorney a kiss. She was carrying an attaché case in one hand and an insulated container in the other.

* * *

"The Chairman tried to reach you while you were in conference," MacVain's communications officer informed him. "I told him that the signal was breaking up."

"I'll take the call now. Where is he?"

"He's at his home in the Caymans."

MacVain remembered the floating, man-made island with its indoor air-conditioned beach. He had a vivid memory of the Chairman in swimming trunks as broad as a bed sheet easing into a jumbo jacuzzi, the displaced water spilling over the sides of the tub, then racing across the artificial lagoon like a small tsunami.

"The Chairman—on audio-only," the officer announced.

"I have some good news," MacVain said without introduction.

The Chairman of the Council of Seventeen snorted in response.

"Titania tells me that all of the 'condos' in the first run of subscriptions have been completely sold out," MacVain told

178

him. "What's more, 3Kids wants as much product as we can give them."

"So I can assure the Council that the ramp-up will proceed as scheduled?"

"Titania assures me that the planning for the ramp-up is going well and is on schedule."

"I don't need to tell you how important this project is," the Chairman said with feeling. "The White man is a minority on his own continent. The White House has more Blacks than public housing."

"Tall Blondes will turn the tide," MacVain assured him.

9

THE GOOD SAMARITAN

Orville Fuller, the Fellowship's liaison to Krator, walked into Dean Weed's office and flopped down in one of the leather arm chairs.

Once again Fuller was somber and preoccupied. Until recently, he had always been reflexively cheerful.

"There's a problem with the missing firefighter," he said.

"The firefighter?"

"Krator has issued a red alert, but there is still no sign of her. Some are saying that we are witnessing the last days of the late great planet Earth."

Dean Weed had expected Fuller to be thrilled by the imminence of the end time. "What's the matter?" he asked.

"Some unseemly details about Grazziella's life are coming to light," he confided. "First of all, she had a child out of wedlock while in college. She was apparently 'well known' to members of a fraternity there, and the father has never come forward."

"At least she didn't have an abortion," Dean Weed said.

"That is the one thing in her favor."

Dean Weed was beginning to hope that Grazziella was too morally depraved to be a suitable rapture vehicle.

"But there's more." Fuller's lips opened and closed silently like a beached fish. "She is a Goddess worshipper," he said finally, uttering the word "Goddess" as if it were an incurable disease.

"Not one of those red-diaper dykes that scream profanity at World Trade meetings?" Dean Weed asked.

"The same. One of her teammates in Davis reported"—he took out a notebook and read from it—"that Kelly Grazziella participated in a drumming circle during her senior year in college. After returning to her home town of Oscuridad, she danced during full moons for at least a year." Fuller paused, as if summoning the strength to go on. He put the notebook back in his pocket. "She can't be the First White Kernel— God would never allow it!"

"Does Duane know about Grazziella's paganism?" the executive director asked.

"Not yet. I thought I should discuss it with you first."

"I appreciate that. The Exclusive Assembly needs to be informed before we tell him."

Fuller leaned forward assertively. "I think paganism should disqualify her immediately."

"The Exclusive Assembly needs to affirm the correct scriptural interpretation on this," Dean Weed agreed.

"Scripture is very clear on this point," Fuller said, narrowing his eyes. "Only born-again Christians can be taken directly to heaven by God. If Grazziella has been transported anywhere, it's a trick of the Evil One designed to mislead the faithful."

"I'll remind the members of the Exclusive Assembly of that."

* * *

181

When Fuller departed, Dean Weed settled back into his ample executive chair, thinking through the implications of the new information.

He remembered when Boone first announced the doctrine of the First White Kernel. Weed was on the board of the Lone Star Christian Network, and immediately there were murmurings to pull Boone's show and demand his resignation. But Dean Weed had kept his head about him, urging the board to stay calm until the poll results were in. When the e-mail and toll-free-number statistics were tabulated, viewer opinion was overwhelmingly in favor of the eighth dispensation and the rapturing-out of a witness arbitrarily chosen by God.

In that moment of crisis, Dean Weed read a viewer's e-mail aloud to the assembled board of directors: "Who the hell are we to tell God who He can rapture?"

When they heard this, the directors of the Lone Star Christian Network looked at each other with glances of recognition and approval. The anonymous viewer had succinctly positioned Boone's radical innovation within a concept of God of which John Calvin himself would approve. The Network president looked relieved as the topic of discussion shifted to how best to present these new ideas to the public.

Boone's ratings with the viewership became higher than ever, and a short time later Dean Weed left the Network to become executive director of the Fellowship of the Eighth Dispensation, the number two man in the organization, reporting directly to Duane Boone III.

* * *

Dean Weed dialed Vaughn MacVain.

The senior attorney picked up the red telephone on the first ring. "I'm glad I found you in," Dean Weed said pleasantly.

"About the missing firefighter, we're expecting a breakthrough in this case at any moment," MacVain said.

"That's good news. Everyone at the Fellowship realizes how hard Krator staff have been working on the Grazziella case, but I'm not calling about that."

There was a puzzled silence at MacVain's end.

"I need to know about this so-called Goddess worship."

"Those tree-hugger dykes that scream profanity at world trade meetings?" Vaughn MacVain asked.

"That's right," the executive director said. "The problem is that Duane is sometimes so infused with Christian forgiveness that he would let anyone into heaven. Duane needs to be informed about the moral depravity of these people. He needs to know the facts about Goddess worship—witchcraft, satanism, lesbianism, nudity, human sacrifice!"

"All that's in our standard information packet," MacVain informed him.

"That's perfect! That's exactly what we need."

"I'll have one e-mailed right away."

* * *

Dean Weed stopped by Boone's office to inform him of Grazziella's pagan proclivities, secretly hoping that it would prompt him to cancel the rapture. But the televangelist cut him off.

"You don't know what you are asking," Boone said, his face conveying the implacable conviction of his manic mode. "You're asking God to change His mind."

He looked Dean Weed in the eye. "I am only His vessel, filled with His Word."

* * *

Dean Weed found the director of communications conferring with two of his staff members.

He pulled Gus aside, and they sat down in the producer's chairs next to a console thick with switches.

"I hear you're getting mixed signals from Duane's office," Dean Weed said.

"Darn right," Gus replied. "The theologians can't agree if the prefiguration of the rapture is three days after the disappearance of the First White Kernel or three days after three days."

Exasperated, Gus pointed to a pair of clocks on the wall of the studio that were visible through the glass booth. "Look at that," he complained. "I've had *two* prophetic clocks installed—one that counts down to Thursday morning, the other to Sunday morning—and I have no idea which one is right, or maybe both of them. Do you realize how much it costs to book a pro-football stadium twice?"

"I know how you feel," Dean Weed replied. "The regional leadership has been giving me an earful of exactly the same problem."

"And I don't even know whether she's the Rapture of the First White Kernel or not. If she's not, how do we explain the fanfare?"

"The Fellowship needs to have three scenarios ready to go to air," Dean Weed told him. "One in case the firefighter is found alive, another if the firefighter is found dead, and a third for her not being found at all."

"When is Dr. Boone going to make a decision on this?" Gus asked, exasperated.

"Well, he's been conferring with theologians for two days, but they can't agree among themselves on the time. If she does not turn up by tomorrow morning at 11:11, I am pretty sure Duane will go with the rapture."

"There's going to be a real credibility issue here if tomorrow goes by without some official announcement by the Fellowship." Gus said. "What do I tell the media?"

"I wish I could give you a definitive answer, Gus, but we need to hang in there a little bit longer. The Exclusive Assembly will weigh in on this issue later today."

＊＊＊

Dean Weed hastened to the teleconference room for a virtual meeting with the regional elders of the Fellowship. They were all middle-aged White men with shiny shirts and shinier faces. A few had haircuts like Lyell Lovett, the rest crew cuts or toupees.

Everyone had heard rumors of the impending Rapture of the First White Kernel, and all knew that 11:11 Central Daylight Time on Thursday marked a significant point in the countdown of the prophetic clock. They were desperate for an official interpretation to give to their congregations, and Dean Weed was happy to provide one.

He opened the meeting with a prayer, then gave a short speech:

> It is important to understand that the countdown of the prophetic clock only applies *if* Kelly Grazziella is the Rapture of the First White Kernel. If she is not, then the clock is not turned on.

> And how do we know if she is the First White Kernel or not? Only God determines that moment, but in His wisdom and beneficence, he gave us Holy Writ to guide us here on earth. Even as we are meeting here, Dr. Boone is alone with his Bible, praying for the wisdom to make a true interpretation guided by the Spirit. We know that if we come to God with open hearts and make sincere appeal to His guidance, He will not disappoint us. So I ask that each one of you, like all of us here at Lone Star Christian Tower, wait for the moment of inspiration with prayer and patience.

185

I ask that each of you go back to your assemblies and join in public group prayer to ensure that the souls of all members of the Fellowship are united with Dr. Boone at this historic moment. And we pray that the brave firefighter Kelly Grazziella be found alive and safe.

These two prayers—a prayer for the gift of wisdom in the interpretation of Scripture and a prayer for the safe return of the firefighter—should both have equal place in our hearts. It is God who will make the choice.

And it is especially important that at 11:11 on Thursday morning, the public sees the faithful of the Fellowship praying that God's will be done.

Later that afternoon, Dean Weed met with the Exclusive Assembly of the Fellowship in the teak-paneled board room adjacent to his personal office suite on the eightieth floor. Normally, Boone would preside over meetings of the board, but the televangelist had excused himself to reflect on the announcement of the Rapture of the First White Kernel.

Before the meeting, Dean Weed had talked with every member of the Exclusive Assembly and provided each of them with the lurid information packet on Goddess worship compiled by Krator's disinformation division, taking the time to personally point out the practices most relevant to Grazziella.

"She dances during the full moon, swaying to the beat of jungle drums. Without deodorant," Dean Weed informed each member. "And she had a child born out of wedlock, without any known father."

* * *

After the meeting, Dean Weed met in physical space with the president of the Exclusive Assembly, a stout, pink-faced man who owned the largest chain of car dealerships south

186

of the Mason-Dixon line. When the car magnate learned that Boone was disposed to declare Kelly's rapture, he shook his head in dismay. "Even a Catholic would be better than a Goddess worshiper. I don't know what to do about this," he admitted.

"We need to find her as soon as possible," Dean Weed said. "I was thinking that a reward might get the public motivated."

"That's a great idea. I bet $100,000 would get some results."

"It can't look like it came from the Fellowship—Duane would be furious."

"Let's put it out through Parents That Lost Children—that's an appropriate organization and non-denominational," the president of the assembly suggested.

"Will you talk to them today?"

"I'd be happy to."

"The executive director's office is prepared to give whatever amount is needed for this. Just tell Parents That Lost Children to provide us with a secret Chinese bank account number."

"I'm sure they'll oblige us!"

"Also, there needs to be a national hotline/website that is linked to the Fellowship's communications command center, so we have a record of all calls and hits," Dean Weed said.

"You know, it would help things a lot if the missing firefighter converted to the Fellowship just before her rapture."

"Good idea. I'll ask Krator to do it."

As the president of the Exclusive Assembly stood up to go, he looked the executive director in the eye. "Dean, whatever you need to do to prevent the rapture of a Goddess worshipper, the assembly will back you up."

"Thank you, I may need that vote of confidence."

* * *

Dean Weed telephoned Vaughn MacVain. "How difficult would it be to document the baptism of Kelly Grazziella?" he asked the senior attorney.

"I didn't know she was baptized."

"I don't think she ever was. But we need to ensure that if Duane goes through with this announcement, only a born-again Christian is transported directly into heaven. The rapture of a pagan tree hugger implies divine approval of environmentalists."

"My God, we don't want that!" the senior attorney agreed, realizing the nature of the request. "But I don't think Krator has ever done a baptism before. One of those infant things?"

"Total immersion."

MacVain was wondering if it could be done in the corporate swimming pool, and should he enlist Cato Magruder to throw her in?

"What exactly do we need to do for that?" the senior attorney asked.

"Provide her with a baptismal certificate."

"Is that all?"

"Yes."

When was she baptized?"

"Shortly before the fire."

"Krator will get it to you right away."

Intercept

Giovanni rolled to a stop in front of the home of Kelly's father. During the high-tech stock boom of the 1990s, many of the old families in Oscuridad sold off uneconomic parcels of ranch land to dot-com millionaires from Silicon Valley eager to start their own boutique wineries. With cash in hand, many families upgraded to starter mansions on lots the size of postage stamps. The subdivisions had looked beautiful when new, but they were built of such inferior materials that after only two decades most of the houses were in need of major repair.

Like all the other houses on Brandywine Way, the Grazziella home was an over-sized replica of a prairie farmhouse from the Dust Bowl era. On closer inspection, the clapboard siding was made of prefabricated concrete panels with a repeating pattern of wood grain embossed at the factory. The Grazziellas had covered the now badly pitted walls with lush climbing vines of pale pink roses.

An elderly man was sitting on the wrap-around porch drinking tea from an ice-filled glass. He had thinning hair and a runner's physique, and was dressed in faded dungarees, a plaid shirt, and up-to-date running shoes

"I'm very glad to meet you again, Mr. Grazziella," Giovanni said, shaking his hand warmly.

"People call me Joe."

Kelly's father is a man of quick dislikes and quick decisions, and he had decided that he liked Giovanni. "Kelly is usually close-mouthed about the men she meets, but she's talked about you. She says you're the most intuitive man she's ever met."

Giovanni was surprised and a little embarrassed. He turned to examine the riot of flowers that covered the front wall of the house. Up close, the Cecil Bruner roses were intertwined with wisteria, two strong strands growing together, creating a chaotic tangle of life.

"Kelly planted these when I first moved here. Because of my balance she won't let me climb the ladder for pruning—so I make up for it by fertilizing and watering," her father said with a smile. Giovanni brightened, and Kelly's father offered him iced tea. They went into the house together to get it.

The living room had been designed for a mansion several times larger, but the subdivider's architect had scaled it down to fit in a faux prairie farmhouse. To create the illusion of spaciousness, there was a vaulted ceiling, a wall-sized mirror, and overly tall windows that looked into the house next door. In recesses near the ceiling, the builders had installed a row of back-lit niches suitable for displaying a lifetime of collectibles. But the house was sparsely furnished, with little bric-a-brac, and that forlorn and dusty.

"Kelly's mother passed away five years ago," her father explained, sensing Giovanni's reaction to the austerity of the room. "So I just gave a lot of the stuff to the kids or sold it—I didn't want it getting broken and being wasted. Besides that's the way her mother would've wanted it."

"Is Kelly your only daughter?"

"A son and an angel," he said. His choice of noun was the only thing that betrayed his anxiety about his daughter. "Her brother is serving in the Middle East and can't get leave."

The kitchen had been inspired by an issue of *Home Gourmet* from twenty years before, with synthetic marble counter tops and cabinets of lustrous, hand-crafted hardwood. To save on construction costs, the subdivider had used wood that had been insufficiently dried, and over the years the cabinets had shrunk and warped to the extent that none of the doors still closed. It irritated Giovanni to see it.

"What could we do?" Kelly's father asked with a shrug of his shoulders, following Giovanni's gaze. "Since they canceled the medical insurance, we needed to sell the farm property to pay medical bills—my father had cancer, Kelly's mother too. The only houses available in Oscuridad were these," he said, gesturing with a broad sweep of his hand. "Kelly hated it when we sold the old place. The clapboards were made of wood."

"You sold all the land?"

"Yes, half to the Clydesdales, half to a developer. Except for the quarter acre where Kelly has her cabin."

On the kitchen table was a big stack of flyers. They were professionally designed with a photograph of Kelly that captured her warm smile and the mischievous eyes she shared

190

with her father. The copy shop in Oscuridad had donated them.

"Have the police found anything yet?" Giovanni asked.

"Nothing. The deputy in Missing Persons at the Almaden County Sheriff's department does a good job of keeping me up to date."

"I don't think Kelly would have just walked away with a fire in progress," Giovanni reflected.

"Oh no, she wouldn't do that. But if she's suffering some sort of memory loss, it's possible she went back to the mountaintop."

Joe Grazziella was startled by his own inadvertent admission.

"I didn't think to tell the police at the time because I thought they would find her near the fire," he explained. "But after her freshman year in college she hiked up a mountain in the High Sierra and spent several nights on the peak doing, well, a vision quest, like the Indians used to do."

"I didn't know she was religious," Giovanni said.

"She's not religious, but she talks with the Goddess."

"Do you know which mountain it is?"

"No, she said it is a sacred place where no one can find her—that's all I know. But I know she's alive," her father added.

"She is," Giovanni agreed. "I can feel it."

* * *

In the subterranean bunker at Krator Headquarters, Cole Kincaid was at the small refrigerator getting another Dr Pepper when the klaxon sounded. He raced back to the screen and listened to the conversation between Giovanni and the missing firefighter's father with growing excitement. Then he called Vaughn MacVain.

"One of Grazziella's friends just talked to her father. I think you should hear it."

The senior attorney listened to it immediately:

> I didn't think to tell the police at the time because I thought they would find her near the fire. But after her freshman year in college she hiked up a mountain in the High Sierra and spent several nights on the peak doing, well, a vision quest, like the Indians used to do.

"We've got her," the senior attorney said in a monotonic voice. "She's on some goddamn mountaintop in the Sierra Nevada."

* * *

In the deputy chief scientist's office on subterranean Level B Celestine Brittle heard the chime for incoming data and clicked on a streaming audio file. Although it made her feel like a peeping tom, she listened intently to the conversation between Giovanni and Kelly's father. When it finished, she played the religious part again:

> She's not religious, but she talks with the Goddess.

Celestine Brittle was disturbed to learn that the missing firefighter was not a half-pagan like the Roman Catholics but a pagan pagan.

As Celestine was praying for the salvation of Kelly's immortal soul, she received a call from Tricia Culhane.

"I got your e-mail about a controversial finding," the special assistant opened. "What's up?"

"I spoke with Agent Profumo of the Sacramento office about the two other women who had given up their babies to the phony adoption agency, like you asked me to," Celestine explained. "He told me that the two women still live in Davis, and he interviewed them Monday night as part of the red alert. He said that they are linked to Kelly Grazziella by the same M.O. as a serial rapist who was active at the same time that Kelly was a student at Davis University. The rapist used

192

a date-rape drug stolen from a university laboratory. Profumo sent me a copy of his original report that he submitted to the Wildfire database."

Celestine hesitated, wondering if her investigation was taking her out of bounds.

"Continue," the special assistant said reassuringly.

"Well, the original police report discusses the date-rape drugs and a serial rapist, but there is no information about any of this on the report that is posted on the Wildfire database. This means that Profumo's police report had been edited before it was posted."

There was a long pause at the special assistant's end. "You did right to consult me before doing anything with this information. Don't post it on Wildfire. Just sit on it for now."

"I will."

"Did Profumo say anything else?"

"He said that at the time that Kelly was a student he was working under cover at the university, investigating the theft of the date-rape drugs. He arrested a student named Chad Weed for the theft."

"Did Profumo say whether he thought Chad Weed might have been involved with the two other women, perhaps as the date rapist?"

"No, but I'll ask him."

"Thank you for informing me of this, but remember— don't post it," Tricia Culhane said firmly.

"I won't. Also, one more thing. I asked Profumo to get me photographs of the two women at the time of their pregnancies like you want, but he was not sure if it would be possible. But he did say they were both young and attractive, quote, 'tall, blond, blue eyes—just what the serial rapist was looking for.'"

O my God, Tricia Culhane thought—tall blondes again. She began thinking through some of the possible reasons why MacVain might be interested in covering up a rape case.

"Do you want me to pursue the photographs of the two women through other sources?" Celestine asked.

"No, I have enough information."

* * *

Tricia Culhane called the data processing manager assigned to task force Wildfire.

"A police report from Krator Sacramento was changed in the Wildfire database. Are you familiar with that?" she asked him in her most authoritative voice.

"Yes," the data-processing manager said anxiously.

"On whose authority was data removed from the database?"

"On the authority of Cole Kincaid, security advisor to the task force."

"Why was I not consulted?"

"Kincaid has the root password. He can change anything in the database he wants, or ask me to do it."

"Do you know how he got the root password?"

"Senior attorney MacVain asked me to give it to him."

"That clears it up," she said in a frigid voice.

The Good Samaritan

Giovanni had just finished delivering the flyers to wineries on the west side of the valley when he received a call from Kelly's father.

"Hear that racket?" Joe Grazziella asked.

Giovanni could hear what sounded like a shower turned on full.

"The house is surrounded by Christians with candles— praying," he complained. "I'm going crazy."

"When did this start?"

"They started arriving this evening. Around seven o'clock, the crowd mushroomed. Now TV crews and the police are

194

here too. The neighbors can't get their car out of the garage and are blaming me for it. I have a question for you."

"Sure."

"Earlier today, when I mentioned that Kelly had a sacred mountain in the Sierra. Did you tell that to anybody?"

"No, I wouldn't do that."

"I didn't think you would. But Krator came by here asking about it. I think it would be better if we talked somewhere else from now on."

* * *

The tasting room was just closing by the time Giovanni reached the last winery on the tour map. It was nestled in the foothills where the southern end of the fire road begins, a good ten miles from the Italian-Swiss Monument. The west ridge is lower here, wearing a mantle of dry grass that shimmered a rich gold in the late afternoon sun.

Giovanni introduced himself as the plant operations supervisor at Indian Springs Winery.

"Indian Springs? Isn't that where the fire started?" the server asked.

"Right above our vineyard. The helicopters and transport planes were going over the winery all day. We had to close the tasting room."

"We never even opened. When the fire broke out, they told me to go home. And boy, after this heat wave I really needed a day off!"

"Tell me about it—we had our first crush yesterday."

"How can I help you?"

"The family of Kelly Grazziella is asking local businesses to put up a flyer, in case anyone knows of her whereabouts." Giovanni handed one to the server.

"I'd like to help, but the boss doesn't want me to put up announcements without clearing them first," the man said.

"You could tell him that all the other wineries are supporting our firefighters," Giovanni suggested.

The server promised to talk to his boss. "Have they got any idea what happened to her?" he asked.

"No, the police think that Kelly walked out on the fire road, in a state of shock and amnesia, and was picked up by somebody, a Good Samaritan. Did you see any cars coming down West Ridge Road about the time of the fire?"

"As I told the deputy, at that hour on a Monday morning, nobody uses that road. But I was only here a little while, until they closed the toll road," he shrugged.

Then he noticed the expression of sadness and disappointment on Giovanni's face. "I don't know if this helps, but you know the Vitus Veritas Winery?"

"Sure, 'Almaden-Only Grapes'—everyone knows their jingle."

"It's a good jingle all right, but, well—you won't tell anyone where you heard this?" he asked in a low voice.

"I want to find Kelly. That's all I'm interested in."

He looked Giovanni in the eye as if sealing a contract. "Vitus Veritas buys a lot of grapes from the central valley."

Giovanni was stunned—it was illegal to put the name "Almaden County" on a wine label when the grapes were grown somewhere else.

"During the crush, trucks come through here in the middle of the night, make a drop in the Vitus Veritas vineyards on the fire road, then go out the north end by the dam, so no one will see them leaving empty," the server told Giovanni.

"You're sure about that?"

"I've seen them unloading grapes there myself."

"Do you know when Vitus Veritas had their first crush?" Giovanni asked.

"The day of the fire—the earliest crush in Deep Creek valley ever."

Coyote I

Alone in the deputy chief scientist's office, her work done for the day, Celestine was once again thinking of prime numbers. She opened the desk drawer and took out paper and pencil. She began writing the series of prime numbers: 2, 3, 5, 7, 11, 13, 17...

She paused, recalling the numbers of the rooms that she had seen earlier that day: 25, 49, 121, 169. She wrote the numbers down in the order in which she had seen them.

Staring at the page, she sensed a deep connection between the two series of numbers, but it continued to elude her, like a word on the tip of one's tongue.

Suddenly the alarm for the camera at the crime site beeped, and Celestine almost jumped out of her chair. She had been so caught up in her speculation that she had not noticed that night had already fallen—there were no windows, so she knew the time only from the clock. She turned back to her computer to see a live picture from Oscuridad painting itself on the screen.

After dark, the crime scene camera took its pictures in the infrared range, and it was a moment before Celestine's eyes adjusted to the mottled shades of greenish gray. At the right edge of the photo was a large dog with a bushy tail like a German shepherd. It was trotting parallel to the film plane, heading towards the Italian-Swiss Monument, its nose to the ground. The camera took a series of shots, making a jerky animation. When the animal reached the middle of the camera's field of view, it stopped and looked straight into the lens. Its snout was too pointed and its body too rangy for a German shepherd. Celestine realized it was a coyote. She waited, but there were no pictures for the next twenty-five seconds, suggesting that the animal remained frozen in that position, as if studying the camera. The next few pictures showed it moving diagonally away to the left at a rapid trot. When almost off frame, the animal stopped and looked back, like a dog encouraging its master to join in the hunt. It held that posture for another nine seconds, then disappeared into the darkness.

Celestine wished she could follow the animal to see where it went.

10

MEDUSA

Tlatelolco

In Mexico City, in the place still known by its Aztec name of Tlatelolco, Jack Adair stepped out of a taxicab and into a crowd of young people from the nearby polytechnical school. He made his way through the milling throng to the steel pedestrian bridge that crosses the noisy thoroughfare.

He stopped to survey the scene behind him, noting the dark, hand-hewn stones that form the walls of an ancient temple complex. The temples had been built before the Spanish conquest, and archaeologists found the remains of people that had been sacrificed to the Aztec gods. Centuries later, in 1968, the Mexican government had murdered protesting students there on the eve of the Olympic Games. Above the site of the massacre, a multistory building faced in white marble rises like a tombstone.

Ahead of him, in a weathered concrete apartment tower, Jack Adair could see the signal for "all-clear" displayed in one of the windows. Two of El Tigre's men led the guerrilla journalist past murals commemorating the Mexican revolution to an apartment that had been made into an improvised meeting room. The meeting had been organized by Lazarus, the coordinator of the EarthRage chapter in Monterrey, an industrial city a thousand kilometers north of Mexico's capital.

The EarthRage chapter in Monterrey supports a number of direct-action and fact-finding teams. It also maintains a pool of couriers on both sides of the border, as well as safe houses in Laredo, Texas, and El Centro, California. Most of its members are Mexican, although the movement includes many expatriate Americans.

When Jack Adair arrived a minute before the scheduled start time, all the other participants were already there, sitting like yogis on sofa cushions arranged in a semicircle on the floor. In addition to Lazarus there were representatives from other EarthRage chapters. One group, Southern Zone, is responsible for all direct actions in Chiapas and Yucatán, including movement across Mexico's borders with Belize and Guatemala. Southern Zone was represented at the meeting by a young woman of Mayan descent, barely five feet tall but with the compact energy of a high-voltage battery. She had made her reputation by staring down the bulldozers sent by a mining company to drive local farmers off their land.

Lazarus introduced Jack Adair to a journalist who had been born in Mexico City but raised in the United States. The man had done well as a business reporter, but he lost his digital identity for revealing that the Charleston Banking Group had engaged in securities fraud. Now was helping EarthRage to protect journalists from reprisals in both countries.

"Two bizarre events have come to light in the past two weeks," Lazarus opened. "And I want to show some video taken by the Hoosier's group."

"What's the Hoosier's group?" the Mayan woman asked.

"A direct-action and fact-finding unit, one of the best," Lazarus replied.

"They are all expat Americans and mad as hell," Jack Adair added. He told how the Hoosier, his wife, and their year-old baby girl had been smuggled across the border at Laredo. When the Hoosier arrived in Monterrey, EarthRage taught him the art of avoiding the Policía Contra-Terrorista and enough Spanish to run a meeting. With his organizational abilities and corn-fed bonhomie, the Hoosier was soon on a first-name basis with hundreds of expatriate Americans living in the area, contacts which he used to form one of the largest and most effective EarthRage networks.

"Does everyone here know about the MEDUSA story?" Lazarus asked. "The NGO?"

"No," Jack Adair answered. "So start with a short overview."

"OK, well, a year ago, we investigated a claim that a clinic in Monterrey was sterilizing Mexican women under the guise of free birth control," the coordinator from Monterrey explained. "They found that the clinic receives regular shipments of frozen biomedical materials from the United States, but the clinic claims they are free contraceptives, and EarthRage can't prove they're not. That's where things stood until last week."

He plugged a flash drive into his laptop. "Now we have this video."

Maria

A hand-held camera moved through a congested sprawl of tiny shacks made of packing crates and rusted metal. Barefooted children played in drainage ditches, while women bathed their babies in dishpans on the ground. Exposed electrical wires, strung without conduit, snaked through eaves and around corners, terminating in bare light fixtures hanging from improvised utility poles. Trash burned in an unattended fire. The camera stopped at one of the houses, made of broken pieces of wallboard scavenged from a demolished building. A female narrator asked if Maria was at home.

Maria peeked furtively from the shadows. She was in her early twenties, with a good figure and a care-worn face, dressed in tight blue jeans and an open-midriff blouse, a Chinese knock-off of an Italian design that had once been fashionable in New York.

"Maria," the narrator said. "These are the people I said I would like you to meet. Are you willing to tell them what you told me?"

Yes, Maria nodded. She gestured for them to come inside.

The house was barely large enough for two people to lie down side by side, but it had been divided by an improvised curtain into a bedroom and living area. Plastic utility boxes turned upside down were the only furniture. One box served as a stand for a cactus garden—a dozen different species each in its own fast-food throw-away carton. Behind the garden was a framed picture of the Virgin.

Maria sat down on one of the plastic boxes, the woman narrator on the other.

"Just tell me what you told me the other day," the narrator said gently. "You told me how you suddenly started remembering things."

Maria nodded, a painful look in her eyes. There was a long moment of silence, as if she did not know how to begin. When the words finally came, they did not stop.

"For a long time, a part of my memory was missing. I could remember everything up to a point, a point when I was nineteen years old. My family told me that a few years ago I had gone away for nine months without telling them first, until eventually they thought I was dead. But I did not remember that at all. I would not have done that without telling them first, so I thought they made it up.

"Then a few weeks ago, I was hit by a bus. It wasn't serious—I sprained my ankle and got cuts on my elbows

202

and hands. My back was covered with bruises. But the bus stopped and people crowded around. My sister was with me. Though I don't remember the bus hitting me, my sister told me about it. Then on the way home, I started remembering what happened several years ago. But it was so vivid, like a dream, only more real than a dream. I thought I was really there. I saw it like it was just happening.

"I remembered that at that time I went to the clinic that gives away contraceptives, and they gave me some. They asked me to come back in a week for a free medical exam. So I did.

"After I had the free exam, a nurse asked me if I needed a job. Yes, of course, I said. My father is in the United States, and since the wall was built, he is no longer able to visit or send money. My mother died six months ago. My older brother is in Mexico City. My younger brother and sister live here—she gestured to the space behind the curtain.

"The nurse at the clinic offered me a job for nine months. She said that I would live at the hospital, and all food and lodging would be provided. There was a good salary too. But I told her that I did not want to go away for so long a time because my family needed me here. She said she hoped I would reconsider. Then I remember she said there was one more test she wanted to do. She produced a syringe, and the next thing I knew I was in a hospital ward that was more like a prison. There were over fifty girls there, all from small towns, and all of them were pregnant—including me!"

"But you have no memory of becoming pregnant?" the narrator asked.

"No, none of us did."

"Where was the hospital?"

"I don't know," Maria said. "No one ever got outside."

"Were there guards?"

"There were, but you never saw them, unless there was a disciplinary problem. Usually we saw only nurses."

"Tell me about the nurses."

203

"They were Brazilian and couldn't speak Spanish. The supervisors spoke Spanish but only talked about medical topics."

"Did anyone try to escape?"

"No. It is hard to climb a wall when you're pregnant!"

The audience suppressed smiles.

"We were well treated. The worst part was being cut off from my family. There were no telephones."

"Did they pay you the salary they promised?"

"Yes, I remember that."

"What happened to your baby?" the narrator asked. Maria looked grief-stricken. "I don't know. Even now, I don't remember giving birth. I only know that I can't have any more children." She looked away.

"Thank you, Maria." the narrator said. "Thank you for sharing your story with us."

* * *

"When I first heard about this," the business journalist commented, "I thought 'My God, Monterrey wants us to do a tabloid story.' But now, after seeing this video…" He looked angry.

"That's what the Hoosier's group initially thought too, until a second woman appeared telling the same tale," Lazarus noted. "The two women do not know each other, but they are both pointing fingers at MEDUSA Also, a doctor has confirmed that Maria has given birth and has been sterilized."

"Is the Fellowship of the Eighth Dispensation behind the sterilization?" the woman from Southern Group asked.

"No," Lazarus replied. "They advocate chastity and adoption, not forced sterilization."

"What ties MEDUSA to the United States?" the former business journalist asked.

"It receives small but regular shipments of frozen medical supplies from California, and some of the clinical staff are *gringos*."

"MEDUSA's headquartered in Switzerland," Jack Adair added.

"Is there any evidence that Maria has been anywhere except to a home for unwed mothers?" the business reporter asked. "Maybe that's what MEDUSA does—identify pregnant women and send them to a home for nine months?"

"Right now, we can't dismiss that possibility," the Monterrey coordinator admitted.

"Sterilizing Mexicans is something U.S. racists *would* do—they did it to the American Indians," Jack Adair interjected. "What's your take on the story?" he asked Lazarus.

"I agree with the Hoosier that we need to follow up. The more we find out about MEDUSA, the more it sounds like an EarthRage story."

"We're stretched real thin on the Central American Corridor story," Southern Group's representative cautioned.

"Well, part of the Monterrey chapter's mission is the cross-border traffic," Lazarus pointed out. "And if they get supplies from California..."

Everyone looked at Jack Adair.

"I think the MEDUSA story will repay any efforts we put into it in the long run, even if the pieces of the jigsaw don't make a recognizable picture right now." Jack scanned the circle of faces to see if there were any objections.

"Maybe Monterrey could provide us with regular updates on their progress," the former business reporter suggested.

Jack Adair made eye contact with Lazarus. "Copy everyone in this group with any breaking news on MEDUSA. If anyone still thinks it's a waste of time, then put it on the agenda, and we'll talk about it again."

Orwell Revisited

Renato Ocampo-Mendoza made his way to the busy plaza in Coyoacán, an historical section of Mexico City popular with tourists. He walked briskly under the trees, past the dancers and souvenir hawkers, past the beggars and buskers and women with strollers to the two larger-than-life coyotes that cavort in the perpetual rain of the fountain.

As the Philosopher stopped to gaze upon the emblematic statues, a man with tousled gray hair approached the fountain. He had the assertive manner of a tout and was holding a packet of restaurant flyers. He handed one of them to Ocampo.

"It's your kind of place," the tout assured him.

Ocampo noted the name of the restaurant —Quinta Luz—and the hand-drawn map on the back. "Thanks, I'll give it a try," he said.

"Be sure to keep the flyer, and you'll get a free meal."

The Quinta Luz was located only a few blocks from the bustling plaza, but it was miles from the normal tourist track. There was no sign of the restaurant from the street, only a tall adobe wall that had been reinforced decades ago with a layer of cement. In places where earthquakes had cracked the concrete, the original bricks were crumbling out of the fissures and making cones of yellow-brown dust on the ground below like miniature ant hills. A single narrow doorway, guarded by a stern maitre d'hotel, gave a glimpse of an interior courtyard.

"Mr. Villa is expecting me," Renato Ocampo-Mendoza told the maitre d'. The man immediately turned on his heel and led Ocampo through the garden and into a spacious, colonial-style home. In contrast to the perimeter wall, it was clean and well-maintained, with many of the original furnishings and an air of warm familiarity. There were no tourists, only Mexicans, and the clientele looked as if they dined there every day.

At the entrance to a private dining room the maitre d' handed him off to one of El Tigre's men. The sentry appeared to recognize the Philosopher but demanded the flyer that he had been given at the fountain.

Jack Adair was seated at the only table in the room, wearing a white linen bib and an enormous black mustache reminiscent of Pancho Villa.

"Mr. Villa! What a pleasure!" Renato laughed.

"I have always been attracted to the man," Jack admitted, slipping the mustache into his pocket. "A guerrilla leader who led America's most prominent general on a two-year wild-goose chase through the deserts of northern Mexico. If World War I had not intervened, the *gringos* might still be chasing him!"

The waiter came and took their orders. He did not appear to recognize the guerrilla journalist, with or without the mustache.

They ordered from the *menú*, the fixed-price, three-course meal served in the afternoon.

"How did you get so good at disguises?" Renato asked.

"I come from a theatrical family," Jack said. He had the good looks and dramatic manner of a movie star. "I thought I told you that story?"

"Just bits and pieces, and under less pleasant circumstances. I would enjoy hearing it once more."

* * *

Jack's maternal grandfather had grown up in Los Angeles and performed in several plays under the stage name of Dirk Devon. In 1949 Devon got a leading role in a Hollywood film that was being made by a prominent director. But the FBI secretly fingered Jack's grandfather as a possible communist sympathizer, so the studio dropped him from the cast and added his name to the black list. Dirk Devon never worked in movies again. Instead, he became a yacht broker, selling the powerful new motor launches to wealthy members of the Hollywood community. There were trips with movie stars to

Catalina Island, and Devon was there when the world's most prominent pop singer serenaded the assembled yachts from the fantail of his own. Affluent if not rich, in the 1960s Devon moved his family to Puerta Vallarta to enjoy the nights of the iguana.

Dirk Devon's daughter became the well-known stage actress Greta Del Loro. She had grown up in two cultures, moving effortlessly between Spanish and English, and from one lover to another, while performing in summer theater. When she met Sean Adair, the dashing skipper of a charter yacht out of San Diego, she dropped out of dramatic arts to experience monogamy.

Their only son, Jack, combined the expressive face and good looks of the thespian side of the family with the self-confident agility of the seafaring Adairs. He spent most of his childhood in the Caribbean, including three years at an English-language preparatory school in Jamaica staffed by expatriate British. Over Christmas break, he helped with his parents' yacht business, while he spent the hot, slow summers at the beach, where he claimed to have majored in surfing, margaritas, and girls.

After prep school, Jack cofounded a successful dive concession in Ixtapa, the luxury resort on the west coast of Mexico, but the daily drudgery of commerce convinced him that business was not for him. He sold his share two years later and crewed for awhile on the ecotours that plied between the sea turtle beaches of southern Mexico and the gray whale calving grounds in Baja California. It was on one of these trips, when they passed close to an Asian fishing boat, that he photographed the crew lopping the fins from sharks caught on long-lines and throwing the writhing animals back into the sea. At port in Acapulco, Jack Adair distributed the digital video on the Internet and wrote a story to document it. His career as a guerrilla journalist was born.

"But enough about me," Jack said. "I wanted to talk to you about your book. I really like the title: *The Digital Surveillance State*. It sums it up."

The Philosopher looked pleased.

"Can I speak freely here?" Renato asked.

Jack gestured caution. "*Comme ci, comme ça*. The police are not welcome here. But don't say anything you wouldn't want in your dossier. The last time we talked about it, you were trying to figure out when the United States crossed the Rubicon Point."

"I see Iran-Contra as the seminal event," Renato said. "The CIA swapping arms for the American hostages in Iran, then selling drugs to secretly buy arms for the Contras in Nicaragua after Congress banned any aid to them."

Jack's eyes narrowed. "It's a clear case of the imperial bureaucracy defying the orders of Congress, yet not one person went to jail for it—well, except for a citizen jailed for protesting it without a permit."

"In my book I've been using the date of Reagan's inauguration, January, 1980, as the birthdate of the run-away surveillance state."

"Maybe the date of Reagan's *second* term is even more appropriate," Jack suggested.

Renato gave a smile of recognition. "Ah, 1984! Orwell would be pleased. When that book was written, the original title was *1948*. But the publisher made him change it because it would become outdated too quickly."

"So Orwell was writing about the present, not the future," Jack mused.

"Do you know where he got the idea of a totalitarian state based on mass media and manufactured news?"

"No," Jack admitted.

"From working at the war-time BBC."

"That makes sense. In his book, television was invented to spy on the viewers. But in real life that would have to wait for the smart phone."

"For Orwell, the totalitarian state was invented by government—he never imagined it as an arm of big business."

"Now business and government have fused to the point that you can't tell the two apart," Jack said. "Big Brother is Big Data."

They both sat in moody silence as the waiter collected the empty plates.

"Any more thoughts about a place on the masthead?" Jack asked.

"I'm *not* a journalist," Renato emphasized. "I wouldn't have to file stories to deadlines, would I?"

"I meet the deadlines," Jack said firmly. "We need a philosopher."

"That's very encouraging. What would be my duties?"

"You would tell us when we are doing the right thing—and when we're not."

Renato's eyes widened, his rationalist equivalent to effusiveness. "I'd be pleased to accept the position we discussed," he said.

"Great!" Jack grinned, reaching across the table to shake his hand. "Welcome aboard!"

"What is my first assignment?"

"Project MEDUSA."

"Project 'Jellyfish'?" Renato translated. "What does that mean?"

"Hell if I know. The new editor-at-large is going to tell us!"

Stolen Madonnas

Celestine was scrolling idly through the Wildfire database when she received a call from Tricia Culhane.

"Task force Wildfire has slowed to a crawl, so I am giving you a second assignment, a short project, one you can do today," the special assistant told her.

"Will I need to work in the high-security office again?" Celestine asked, reluctant to return to the cave.

"No, work at home if you want. It's not a task force assignment. I explained it in an e-mail."

Celestine logged on and read the e-mail from Tricia Culhane:

> The media in Mexico have made allegations that the Fellowship and Krator have been involved in thefts of art from Catholic churches.
>
> I want you to investigate these claims and tell me if anything incriminating can be found through digital sources. I need a report before end-of-day today. I am attaching some documentation to get you started.

Attached was a list of the stolen art compiled by the Mexican authorities. The majority were statues of the Virgin Mary, plus a number of paintings of similar subjects, almost all beginning with the name "*La Virgen*."

Celestine used the list of names as a search string in the U.S. Customs database. Almost immediately, she found that a truckload of Mexican religious art had recently crossed the border at Laredo. It was bound for The Glass Nativity Gallery in Houston, Texas, and had come across the border on a SENTRI pass, meaning the cargo would not have been inspected. The pass had been issued by the ranking Krator officer in Los Angeles, where the art gallery was headquartered. The Glass Nativity Gallery was a well-known reseller of folk art, with outlets in major American cities.

Using the search tools for worldwide banking transactions, Celestine learned that The Glass Nativity Gallery had purchased the art from a reputable dealer in Mexico, in San Miguel de Allende, who in turn had purchased it from a reputable art broker in Cuernavaca. There the digital trail went cold.

As Celestine reflected on what she found, she realized that a folk art dealer was the ideal partner in crime, since any valuable work of art could be shipped out of Mexico in the guise of a low-cost reproduction, then diverted into the black market after it reached the United States. If one assumed that the stolen art was on the truck that went to The Glass Nativity Gallery distribution center in Houston, then at some point, perhaps before it even arrived there, the real art would be replaced by the reproductions listed on the manifest. The process was almost fool-proof too. All one needed was an accomplice to make the switch, while the shipper and receiver would both claim that the cargo consisted of reproductions, not originals.

According to financial sources, The Glass Nativity Gallery was founded by a woman named Titania Troy, but when Celestine tried to learn more about her on the Krator databases, she was denied access due to "insufficient clearance," the first time that had ever happened when searching on a person's name.

Celestine telephoned her colleague Ziggy in the Krator tax investigation section, the only department that could view corporate income tax records and release the data to other analysts. He was a chubby man in his forties who was verbally energized by columns of numbers. They sometimes talked over lunch in the employee cafeteria.

She told him she was working on special assignment from Colorado Springs and had hit a snag when requesting information about someone whose name had turned up in the course of a search.

"Who's the target?"

"A woman named Titania Troy."

"Titania Troy!" Ziggy echoed in a surprised voice. "No way. She's an untouchable."

Celestine had never heard the term before. "What's that?"

He adopted an avuncular tone of voice that made her realize how menial her previous assignments had been. "Some people's records cannot be accessed through the Krator databases. Maybe they are involved in classified projects or have important government positions or are related to important people. It's a security measure against stalkers and assassins," he explained. "Have you ever heard of Eliott Ness?"

"No," Celestine admitted.

"Doesn't matter. But here, in tax investigation, we call people like Titania Troy 'the untouchables.'"

"Don't untouchables have digital identities?" she asked. She still wanted to believe in the impartiality of universal surveillance, as she had been taught at the academy in Quantico.

"Think of it this way," Ziggy explained. "If you are really important, you don't need a digital identity because everybody already knows who you are. If you are an unemployed nobody, you don't need one because nobody cares. Only working stiffs like you and me have digital identities or worry about losing them."

"That sums it up," Celestine said glumly.

Celestine found a biography of Titania Troy in WikiFree, but she had to use her Krator credentials to access the overseas web site. The woman was the daughter of the Krator chief counsel and an heir to the Troy Oil fortune. Titania kept her maiden name for professional purposes, but she had been married twice, and her first husband was the more interesting of the two—Nathan Whyte. It was the same name as the laboratory in Davis, California.

Nathan Whyte, now deceased, was much older than Titania. He held a doctorate in molecular genetics from Hardwood University, and he had been assistant secretary of defense for research and development in the Pentagon before Celestine was even born. In cooperation with Wassily Tweecus, he founded a research facility with the goal of producing a race of geniuses by altering fetal DNA.

Celestine was tempted to do a search on the Nathan Whyte Laboratory, but because of Tweecus's involvement, she suspected it was a classified facility. It was a felony for a Krator employee to investigate a classified project without a clear mandate for doing so, and certainly there would be tripwires in the Krator databases to alert the counter-espionage division. Reluctantly, she decided not to pursue it.

Celestine Brittle called Tricia Culhane. "I have the information on the stolen art that you requested. Do you want some background first?"

"Yes, fill me in. I don't usually do Mexico."

"Well, the Fellowship is heavily involved in Mexico through its missionary activity, just as the Mexican media claim. As for its role in art theft, there is nothing linking it directly except for the recent arrest of two low-level Fellowship members (and the girlfriend of one of them) caught stealing a statue of the Virgin Mary from a Catholic church. As for the claim that a truckload of Mexican religious art crossed the border recently—well it did. I checked the U.S. customs registry, and the truck had a SENTRI pass."

"A SENTRI pass! Who authorized that?"

"It was approved by the head of Krator Los Angeles on behalf of The Glass Nativity Gallery, Incorporated—it is a well-known chain of American galleries headquartered in L.A. specializing in primitive and ethnic art."

"Is the art stolen?"

"On the manifest, the art is listed as reproductions. An art appraiser would have to examine it."

"Not our department."

"The art was bought from a reputable dealer in San Miguel de Allende who bought it from a reputable broker in Cuernavaca. There the digital trail goes cold. It would have to be followed up on foot."

"That's a job for the Mexican police," Tricia Culhane noted.

"I thought it would be a good idea to find out more about The Glass Nativity Gallery, so I ran an ownership search. The Glass Nativity Gallery is a California corporation whose majority stock holder is an investment company that is a subsidiary of a closely held corporation owned by an attorney who is legal counsel to a firm in the Cayman Islands owned by Titania Troy."

"*The* Titania Troy?" the special assistant asked.

"Her grandfather founded Troy Oil, and her father is Krator chief counsel."

There was a long pause. "What do you conclude from your findings?"

"Titania was one of the original founders of the gallery, selling her interest only eighteen months ago, about six months before that the thefts started in Mexico," Celestine noted. "But there is nothing that explicitly links the art thefts to either the Fellowship or to Krator. I only learned about The Glass Nativity Gallery because of the SENTRI pass record. But SENTRI pass records are unavailable to the Mexican authorities. Even if someone got the name of the gallery, Titania Troy no longer has any legal connection to it at all."

"It sounds like there is nothing to worry about except a highly improbable disclosure of a coincidental link," Tricia Culhane concluded.

"Legally, there is no connection," Celestine agreed. "But because of her father's position and her grandfather's reputation, if anyone on the Mexican side learned of the

Titania Troy connection it would send up a red flag to investigators."

"What did you think they would find if they looked?" Tricia Culhane inquired in a blasé voice.

"A Mexican investigator would assume that The Glass Nativity Gallery knows that the art is stolen and that it was shipped out of Mexico disguised as reproductions," Celestine told her. "The Mexican investigator would assume that the sales chain was put in place just to launder the theft. From this point of view, the prices paid at each level are way too low, since they assume folk art reproductions, not stolen originals. So a Mexican investigator would look for additional payments from The Glass Nativity Gallery to the Mexican sellers."

Tricia Culhane was glad that Celestine was working for Krator and not for the Mexican government. "Would this hypothetical Mexican investigator find any kickbacks?"

"I didn't look in Mexico," Celestine explained. "I assumed the sellers would want to be paid where large transactions in dollars are normal. So I looked in the United States. I figure the easiest way for an art dealer to pay for stolen art disguised as reproductions is to buy some legitimate art at inflated prices from the same source at a later time. Both parties benefit because the money is clean. Titania's lawyer in the Cayman Islands is an art collector and art appraiser. He collects unknown Mexican artists, and last year he spent seventeen million dollars at an art auction in New York hosted by the art brokerage in Cuernavaca that provided the so-called reproductions to The Glass Nativity Gallery."

"That's very good digging in so short a time," Tricia Culhane told Celestine with evident appreciation. "But from a prosecutor's perspective, all we have is an art collector gambling on the long-term appreciation of some presently undervalued Mexican artists."

"That's right. There's no evidence of any wrong-doing at all—unless, of course, the art on the truck turns out to be stolen."

"Do you know where that art is now?"

"It's already been delivered to The Glass Nativity Gallery's distribution center in Houston."

"Then there's nothing to worry about. Good work. Write up what you told me and get it to me by five o'clock mountain time today."

* * *

Tricia Culhane called Vaughn MacVain.

"I've checked into the allegations made by the Mexican media on the stolen Catholic art," she told him. "There's no involvement of the Fellowship that can be documented through digital sources, but..." she paused.

"But what?"

"If the Mexican art that crossed the border recently was the art stolen from the churches, then it makes denials of Krator involvement unbelievable. The art came across the border on a SENTRI pass issued to The Glass Nativity Gallery."

"The Glass Nativity Gallery? That sounds familiar."

"The company's founder is Titania Troy, heiress of the Troy Oil fortune."

"Damn."

"I'll take that as a compliment," she said.

"What tipped you?"

"An art auction where her lawyer pays seventeen million for undiscovered Mexican artists."

"I never approved that," he said. "But since you've learned the how, you need to understand the why. It is not in the interest of the Free World to have ignorant fanatics burning art—it makes us look like barbarians. It would be better for everyone if it were safe in museums."

217

"So we ought to think of it as seventeen million spent for the edification of future generations?" Tricia Culhane quipped.

"That's a good way to think of it. Backgrounder number two: These arrangements were made before Troy Oil took over the management of the Mexican oilfields. It has leases pending in Central and South America. If it becomes known that their heiress and namesake is shipping Catholic art out of Mexico, even if they're reproductions, the oil deals will get caught up in the current hysteria."

"I understand your concerns," Tricia Culhane said. "Is there anything more you want me to do on this?"

"No. From what you told me, there's nothing to worry about."

* * *

MacVain telephoned Krator's command center in Mexico City. The chief of station was a dignified, well-spoken man from an old-line Boston family whom MacVain had met at Hardwood College. He shared the senior attorney's contempt for the Fellowship's missionaries while agreeing that they were a necessary evil in the battle for Mexican hearts and minds.

"What has been the public response to the Heritage Society's publicity campaign about the Madonnas?" MacVain asked.

The chief of station hesitated. "Highly favorable—from the president on down."

There was a long pause that indicated MacVain was not pleased with these developments. "Talk to the Fellowship's head in Mexico," he growled. "No more art collecting until I give the green light."

218

Second Thoughts

Celestine Brittle was sipping a chocolate pecan milk shake topped with whipped cream, ruminating on the case of the stolen Madonnas. She thought of the hypothetical Mexican investigator again, but this time as the person to fool. She reflected how easy it was, using Krator's bank transaction tools and databases, to follow the path from the art broker in Cuernavaca to the art dealer in San Miguel de Allende to The Glass Nativity Gallery in Los Angeles to Titania Troy's lawyer in the Cayman Islands to an auction house in New York— where the lawyer of the heiress blew seventeen million dollars on unknown artists, a transaction that hovered over the sales chain with all the subtlety of the Goodyear Blimp. Celestine, now increasingly suspicious, suspected that the auction was there to be seen, and anyone who tried to follow that money would be lost forever in the labyrinthine transactions of off-shore tax shelters and Cayman Islands front companies, crisscrossing paths that lead nowhere.

She began to wonder if the real art had ever left Mexico at all. Otherwise, why install a series of road signs pointing to the United States? That sales chain was only needed if the stolen art was not going anywhere. If The Glass Nativity Gallery never received the stolen art, that would explain the unusually detailed manifest that accompanied the truck: it was almost as if the list was supposed to be found—to confirm that the stolen art was shipped to the United States disguised as reproductions.

If the art never left Mexico, then the thefts were child's play. A single, low-level official of the Fellowship could persuade a handful of people to steal from Catholic churches, take possession of the stolen art on the pretext of destroying it, and sell it to unscrupulous collectors with the help of a confederate in the art world. Two people funneling millions. At the same time, no thief would accept payment by check or credit card, and no recipient of stolen paintings would insure

219

them under their right names, so there would be no way to track a crime of this nature through the Krator databases. The Mexican police would have to catch someone in the act of exchanging a stolen Madonna for a gold bar.

Celestine's pessimistic conclusion fed her growing disaffection with her work. The worldwide databases of the Predictive Criminality Center were fine for constructing criminal personas around people like Kelly Grazziella who had never committed a crime, but they were almost useless for bringing any reasonably competent criminal to justice.

* * *

Celestine's brooding was interrupted by the ringing of the telephone.

It was Agent Profumo in California, the narcotics cop who had arrested Chad Weed, the pre-med student who was selling date-rape drugs to his fraternity brothers at Davis University.

"You asked about those two other women in the Chad Weed case—both of them are dead."

"Dead!" Celestine gasped.

"Yeah, within the past twenty-four hours. One committed suicide—drug overdose. The other had a fatal cerebral hemorrhage."

Celestine cleared her throat, attempting to regain her composure. "I have a question," she stumbled.

"Yeah?"

"The Chad Weed case—was there anything special about it?"

"I remember his frat-rat smirk."

"The case involved the Nathan Whyte Laboratory, right?"

"Yeah. Weed thought that his boss at the laboratory would get him off, but Tweecus wouldn't help him."

"Tweecus, like Wassily Tweecus?"

"How many can there be?"

"Why wouldn't Tweecus help?"

"He was furious that Weed forged his name on the phony drug requisitions. And he was furious at all the publicity."

"What publicity?"

"The case got mentioned in the student blog a lot. Some columnist called Weed the White Rabbit, and the name stuck."

Celestine felt her heart beat faster. "Why 'White Rabbit'?"

"The columnist wrote a funny song about him, to the tune of the old Jefferson Airplane drug anthem and posted it on social media. It went something like this: 'One pill makes you horny, one pill makes you fall, and the last pill that he gives you, you won't remember him at all—White Rabbit...'"

The agent sang it, and he had a good voice.

"What happened to Weed? He was arrested, right?"

"Yeah, but it took awhile. His old man is a big shot in the Fellowship of the Eighth Dispensation."

"Really? Was he found guilty?"

"He was never tried."

"Why not?"

"They say he died of a cerebral hemorrhage the day he was remanded into custody."

"How tragic," Celestine said—grasping at convention as words failed her.

Profumo snorted. "How would you like him for your doctor?"

Calle de Los Niños

Federal Espresso is a coffee house in Mexico's Federal District owned by an American expatriate who had lost his digital identity and rebuilt his life south of the border. He hated the government of the Free World and helped out EarthRage whenever he could. When two grim bodyguards walked into his café and stood menacingly on each side of the doorway, the owner thought that the Policía Contra-Terrorista had come to arrest him. Then he saw Jack Adair and broke into a broad smile.

"Well, I'll be!" the owner said, warmly shaking the guerrilla journalist's hand.

"These guys are with *me*," Jack Adair told him, nodding towards the sentries at the door.

The stocky, bald-headed owner locked the front door and hung up the "CLOSED" sign, to the surprise of the few customers at outside tables.

"The usual," Jack Adair told the owner.

One bodyguard sat down at a small table facing the street and unbuttoned his coat; the other sat next to Jack Adair with his eyes on the back alley.

A portable television set hanging above the espresso bar was tuned to One World News in Spanish.

"Do you want me to turn off the TV?" the proprietor asked.

"That's OK. Leave it on. I'm waiting for someone."

On screen, a dapper Mexican journalist was interviewing an American economist from the Free World Commission on Free Trade. The academic's eyes seemed cavernous in the harsh lighting, and his hands were clasped together in front of him, making them appear over-sized and grasping.

> "The United States is too rich to produce its own biological products," the economist was saying. "At present, over ninety percent of all meat and vegetables are imported, a development which has greatly benefitted Mexico in particular."

> "And you see all biological production following this trend?" the journalist asked.

> "The integration of biological production with free trade is a necessary and inevitable step for future economic development—not just in the United States but worldwide."

222

"And does human reproduction fall under that mandate too?"

"Human reproduction is the least rationalized sector of the economy. In that sense, it is the sector in most need of an unsentimental, cost-based analysis."

"Does that include genetic engineering of human embryos, as some technologists have suggested?"

"Economics is not about techniques but about the freedom to choose. We do not advocate, we do not legislate—we let the free market determine the most efficient solution for human reproduction."

"Thank you, Doctor, for joining us.

Until tomorrow, this is Taylor Jimenez, your host for 'Future Markets Today.'"

When El Tigre appeared in the doorway, Jack was lost in thought, his double mocha still untouched.

"Coffee on the house," the owner announced to the new arrival.

"I'll have what he's having," El Tigre said, sitting down next to Jack, then spreading out a paper map of Matamoros, a city in northeastern Mexico not far from where the Rio Grande reaches the sea.

"You were right," El Tigre said. "The Calle de los Niños *is* in Matamoros, but it's not on any of the standard Internet map sites. In fact, even after we knew where it was, we still couldn't find it on the Web. The map sites just show a blank spot labeled 'undeveloped.'" He moved the paper map to where both could see it, then tapped on a cluster of small streets on the outskirts of the city. "Calle de los Niños is a cul de sac in a complex of concrete buildings behind a new maternity hospital."

Jack wondered if this was the finding that had killed the bureau chief of *Left America*.

223

"Dunkirk had a hand-drawn sketch map of this area in his personal effects, but I didn't understand what it meant until I sent it to the Hoosier," El Tigre explained. "Dunkirk may have known about the hospital. He may even have been there—his expense log lists a restaurant about a mile away."

"But no other indication of the story he was writing?"

"There are encrypted files on his computer that match the dates of his flights to Matamoros, so there probably is a story—we just can't read it."

Jack looked frustrated. "So close, yet so far away," he said. "Who was the woman that was killed with him?"

El Tigre shrugged. "We called all of the female names in Dunkirk's contacts, and none of them sound like the woman on the recording. He may have kept his sources somewhere else, maybe encrypted with his notes."

"I'll be talking with the Philosopher. Maybe he can make some sense of it all."

MEDUSA I

On the floor of the safe room in Tranquility Base, the Philosopher created a flow chart with scraps of paper and pieces of string that summarized the findings of the EarthRage team in Monterrey.

"To understand capitalists and fascists, you have to be able to think like a capitalist and a fascist," Renato explained. "This chart shows the relationships of the various functions identified with MEDUSA. By the way, what do the letters stand for?" he asked.

"Medicine Universal South America." Jack answered. "It's the Latin American subsidiary of a Swiss NGO specializing in population problems."

"Fascists have used that proverbial Swiss neutrality before," the Philosopher noted.

He walked them through the chart with his index finger. "The way I see it, poor women are recruited through the MEDUSA contraception clinics in Monterrey, like the woman in the video. They sign a nine-month 'contract,' with or without their consent, for some hypothetical job. The real job is getting pregnant and giving birth. They are made pregnant and taken to a home for unwed mothers. If they don't work out, they are sterilized like Maria and sent home. If they go along, they are used again."

"How do you explain the memory loss of the two women?" Jack asked.

"I can't. There must be some drug or something we don't know about," Renato replied. "When the baby is born, it is taken from its mother and sent by ambulance to a maternity hospital, where it is adopted; or maybe the mother gives birth in the maternity hospital and her baby is taken from her there."

Jack went to the whiteboard. "The missing link here is the fathers. Are the women just unwed mothers or have they been artificially inseminated like cattle?" he wondered.

"Implanted embryos," Constanza wrote. "Incubators."

Jack exhaled audibly. "You know, I hadn't even thought of that."

"It makes sense," Renato said. "The *gringas* don't want to have babies any more, and their birth rate has gone through the floor. Capitalist economists have argued that it is uneconomical for the Free World to produce babies when it can be done cheaper in the Third World."

"Off-shored reproduction!" Jack affirmed.

"Clearly," Renato nodded.

"Is money changing hands?" Constanza wrote.

"It must be—or they wouldn't be doing it. But EarthRage doesn't have that kind of access," Jack said.

"Origin of the embryos?" Constanza wrote.

"You're right. There has to be a lab to put sperm and eggs together," Renato said, taking a moment to add a scrap of paper to his flow chart.

Constanza summarized the points, writing on the whiteboard:

> money trail?
>
> sperm & egg sources?
>
> embryo lab?
>
> adoption agency?
>
> who adopts?
>
> who controls?

Jack read the list out loud. "The big questions are still to be answered. Too bad we don't have a source on the inside." He looked at Constanza: "Please send the list to Monterrey."

"There's a related consideration," Renato said. "If I were a capitalist, I would be concerned about the inefficiency of having one baby at a time. It would be far more economical to have each mother produce twins or triplets—getting doubled or tripled production for an incremental increase in cost."

"So we ought to be looking for multiple births?" Jack asked.

"It would be a good way to identify the adoption agencies at the other end—find out who is offering triplets," Renato observed.

"If the babies are made from Yankee embryos, then the babies will be *rubio* [blond]—not Mexican."

Constanza wrote on the whiteboard: "Not Mexican parents—Mexican *wombs*!"

Jack nodded agreement. "Well, documenting that ought to be straightforward," he said. "We compare the babies to their mothers."

"That's the easiest proof—and the most convincing," Renato agreed.

Jack gave Constanza one of his perfect-wave grins. "Tell the Monterrey group to take some photos of mothers and their babies to see if they look alike."

Coyote II

Sometime after midnight Celestine awoke, frightened by a dream. She dreamed she was watching the infra-red surveillance camera installed next to the Italian-Swiss Monument on the fire road where Kelly Grazziella had disappeared. Once again, she saw the coyote she had seen on Tuesday night, but this time, it being a dream, she was able to follow it and see where it went.

The coyote led her to a city square lined with uniform row houses, such as they have in East Coast cities. Celestine noticed that the houses were numbered in an odd way. Whereas ordinary house numbers increase arithmetically, the numbers of the row houses succeeded to the next prime number: 2, 3, 5, 7, 11, 13, and so on. The coyote stopped at house number 17, which was called Summit House. A stairway connected the sidewalk to the front door; it reminded her of the helical staircase in the underground laboratory in Laredo.

Summit House was an imposing residence, with three floors below ground and four above. The ground floor was numbered 49, the second floor 121, and the third floor 169, the same number as the deputy chief scientist's office in Laredo.

Celestine climbed the front stairs to the landing, where there was a tall, thin, blond woman in a leopard-skin coat. The woman had three tow-headed girls, all of them exactly the same size and dressed alike in archaic gingham dresses. As Celestine came closer, she saw that the girls were identical triplets with the cold, gray eyes and angry scowl of senior attorney Vaughn MacVain. On each of their foreheads was the number six.

Celestine turned away in horror and fled down the stairs, the coyote racing ahead of her.

11

A VISITATION OF THE GODDESS

Kelly Grazziella heard a roar like a speeding train passing through a narrow tunnel, a noise so deafening that her gloved hands instinctively covered her ears. Then she felt the heat through her fire-resistant clothes. Closing her eyes as tight as she could, she pressed her face into the hard clay and flattened her body as low as possible to access the puddle of breathable air trapped at ground level.

When she felt the heat on both sides of her body, Kelly thought it would be only seconds before the flames enveloped her completely, but her mind was at rest, a place of perfect silence. Standing calmly in a receiving line, she said good-bye to all the people that she loved: her mother who died in the nursing home, her father in the empty house, her brother serving overseas, her deceased grandparents, her best friend from high school, her favorite roommate from college—she stopped when she reached the baby she had given up for adoption. Even though she never saw it and never named it (the nurse in obstetrics had advised against it) the newborn's presence enveloped her like a numinous cloud.

It was almost as if the heat of the flames had melted the walls encircling the events of seven years ago, and now they unfolded again with the clarity of a cinema screen, bringing to consciousness the hours she assumed had been lost forever. How ironic, she thought, that at the moment of her death, her memory was restored and her understanding complete.

She remembered the young man who took her to his room, a pleasant but nameless person who tried to touch her breasts before the door was even closed, but her stomach rebelled at the prospect. Leaving the boy standing in the doorway, she ran down the hall to the bathroom and vomited up the boilermaker—she had never even heard of that drink before and was ashamed that she had gulped it down like a beer. Now her brow was sweating and her stomach was turning somersaults. She went back to the room to ask the young man to drive her home, but he had disappeared, perhaps downstairs to the bar. On the stairway, she encountered two young men pooling their money for another liquor run. One of them she had seen around the fraternity before.

"Hi, Kelly," he said.

She was surprised he knew her name, but fraternity boys compared notes. "If you're going out, maybe you could drop me off at my dorm?" she asked him.

"Sure," he said. He had intense brown eyes that were hard to read.

She followed him out to a sleek German sports car painted in metallic silver with a royal blue interior and gray upholstered seats. "What a beautiful car," she told him. "You must have a really good summer job."

He smiled politely at her joke. The seats were real leather, not imitation. "And there's no transponder," he pointed out, referring to the electronic signaling equipment that was built into vehicles at the factory and keyed to the license plate, enabling the police to track any car at will. "A graduation gift, a little early."

"You're a senior!" she exclaimed. Four years older than Kelly, he seemed the epitome of maturity and sophistication: taller than most, with a medium build, sandy-brown hair, and a handsome face that was hard to pin down. His expressions seemed to mirror her own.

"I'm pre-med."

Medicine, the police, and the military were now the only careers with any economic security. Almost every college student claimed to be heading for medical school, but few of them ever reached it.

"Have you chosen a medical school?"

"I got early acceptance to Duchess."

"Wow, that's impressive." He must be brilliant too.

"I've been working at one of the medical research laboratories here as a research assistant. Doctor Wassily Tweecus, the geneticist, wrote a letter of recommendation for me. Have you heard of him?"

"No."

"He's real famous in scientific circles."

"What does he do?"

"He uses the resonant properties of DNA to remotely identify the nucleotide sequence. Do you know about genetics?"

"A little. I know what a nucleotide sequence is."

"The tricky part is determining it remotely in vivo, without using a blood sample."

"He's done that?"

"Remote sequencing, yes. The next step is to do it with what they call intrauterine preparations."

"You mean babies in the womb?"

"Yes."

"What is the benefit of that?"

"It enables doctors to diagnose genetic diseases before the baby is born."

"Then what? Abortion is unconstitutional."

His face flexed in uncertainty, as if Kelly had raised an issue he had never thought about before. "Well, someday, there will be gene correction therapies that will replace the flawed gene in utero."

"That should keep doctors busy for a good long time."

He looked at her to try to determine if she was being sarcastic. She was a pretty girl with hazel eyes and perfect curves. "Do you want to see the laboratory?"

"At this hour?"

"There's a night watchman, and I have a pass."

Kelly was not much interested in medicine, but her stomach was feeling better, and she wanted to talk with the young man longer.

"After hours, you have to call ahead," he explained, picking up the cell phone. "I'm bringing a visitor by the lab. Kelly Grazziella. With two 'Z's."

"I don't even know your name," she said to him.

He smiled perfunctorily. "Chad Weed." She was surprised when he headed the car away from the medical center. "It's an off-campus facility, in a professional building," he explained. "It's not far."

A few minutes later, they pulled into the nearly empty parking lot of a two-story office building in an industrial park adjacent to the campus. Newly planted shade trees, genetically-engineered to grow non-shedding leaves and cloned to the same size and shape, cast circular shadows on the lawn. The front lobby was dark, but the parking lot in back was as brightly lit as a stadium.

"After hours, you have to enter by the back door," he told her, parking close to it.

There was no sign of life, and Kelly felt anxious as she stepped out of the car. Maybe, she thought, this was not such a good idea after all. But the young man had already placed his hand on the touchpad lock and was holding the door open for her. Inside was a small foyer with a uniformed guard sitting behind a counter, watching a bank of unchanging video images. Kelly felt reassured by his presence. The guard asked her to step in front of the retinal scanner, handed her a digital form to fill out, and then issued a visitor badge with the name of the facility, the Nathan Whyte Laboratory.

"This way," Chad Weed said, heading down the hall with the practiced courtesy of a maître d'.

A pink-faced man in a white laboratory coat looked up from behind a spacious mahogany desk. His corona of graying hair resembled a do-it-yourself halo. He blanked the computer screen he had been studying. "I thought we had a visitor scheduled for eight tonight," he said with a hint of irritation.

"Better late than never, Professor Tweecus. Kelly Grazziella here is anxious to see the laboratory."

The wall behind the scientist's desk was covered with framed diplomas and awards.

"Are you a student at the University?" he asked her in an avuncular tone of voice.

"Yes, I'm a freshman."

"What are you studying?"

"I have not declared a major yet."

"But the college of letters and sciences?"

"Yes."

"Have you considered the biosciences or pre-med?"

"No," Kelly said hesitantly. "I don't want to be a doctor."

Wassily Tweecus did not want any pre-meds or biology majors in the quality assurance phase—they might get suspicious. "You have plenty of time to make a career choice later," he said reassuringly. "Chad, why don't you get us some soft drinks from the machine while I show the young lady around the lab?"

"Is diet soda pop OK?" Chad asked her.

The laboratory looked like an over-sized gynecological examination room with what appeared to be miniature satellite dishes mounted in the ceiling above the reclining chair. A row of complicated computerized equipment filled one wall.

"We are perfecting a technique to identify mutations in DNA remotely, by detecting tiny field alterations along the length of the DNA molecule. Now, we are using this procedure on fetal DNA as well, so the genetic health of babies can be assessed without any disturbance to the mother and child whatsoever. This will enable physicians to detect genetic anomalies and diseases while there is still time to treat them."

"What's the chair for?"

"We are at the stage of using human volunteers—pregnant women whose fetuses are at risk for genetic diseases. They have agreed to help us test it, in the hope that the Tweecus technique will provide a higher level of detection than more conventional tests."

He pointed to the various pieces of equipment and briefly explained what each one did. Kelly had the feeling he was playing for time. Chad returned with cans of soft drinks, one for each them, then poured the soda with a flourish into disposable cups.

"Bottoms up!" Chad said cheerily, touching the rim of his cup to hers, then taking a deep swallow. Kelly thought the Sprite had an unusually metallic taste, but perhaps that was the after-effect of the boilermaker. Then a few minutes later, her legs began to wobble and go numb.

"I think the young lady is feeling faint," Tweecus said calmly. He and Chad Weed took Kelly under the arms, dragged her over to the chair, and maneuvered her into it. She was fully conscious but unable to speak or cry out. She tried to grasp the edge of the chair, but her arms no longer obeyed her command.

234

"Easy does it," Chad said, positioning her on the recliner with her arms at her sides as if he had done this many times before.

"And you're sure it's the right time of the month?"

"Her fitness app says it is."

"You can go now," Tweecus said. A minute later, Kelly heard a car start and drive away.

"We don't want any involuntary noises," Tweecus explained, taping Kelly's mouth shut with surgical tape. He unfastened her shoes and took them off, then loosened her belt and opened the buttons. He pulled her slacks and panties off in a single motion, leaving the bottom half of her body completely exposed. She desperately wanted to cover herself, but her hands were powerless to act.

To Kelly's surprise, another scientist appeared out of nowhere, a stout, middle-aged man with short, bristly, gray hair and a distracted manner. He was lost in his own thoughts and appeared to not notice the young woman splayed before him. Tweecus was checking numerical values from a computer printout and did not look up.

"Are you using PG-9?" the second scientist asked. "The one you used on the other two?"

"Yes."

"Did you have a chance to read that investment prospectus I left in your mailbox?" the second scientist asked.

"For the land developer in Almaden County?"

"Yes, Ridgeline Castles."

"It looks interesting."

"It's sure-fire. They buy worthless hilltops and turn them into fortified condo clusters."

"There's a big demand for that," Tweecus acknowledged.

"The company is controlled by Titania Troy—that's good enough for me."

"Really? I'll take a closer look at it."

The second scientist looked at his watch. "I revised the ramp-up projections in the light of the calibration series. Do you think you'll have time to review the figures before you go home tonight?"

Tweecus looked up from his instruments. "PG-9 is a little finicky, and we need to be more careful with the full-term subjects," he replied sharply. "I'll let you know as soon as I'm finished here."

"OK, I'll be in my office."

"This won't hurt a bit," Tweecus told Kelly, spreading her legs apart and positioning her feet in the stirrups. He washed her private parts and swabbed them with disinfectant. He inserted a single gloved finger in her vagina and moved it around inside her, as if testing for size and shape. Her body smelled like cleaning fluid.

He disappeared momentarily behind the door of the refrigerator, then returned carrying what looked like a flexible soda straw attached to a small electronic device with adjustment knobs.

"It's similar to the devices used for the artificial insemination of cattle and horses, but it's been modified for human use," he told her, as if addressing a seminar. He positioned the tube at the entrance to her vagina, then inserted it with a single push until it disappeared. She tried to protest the sudden invasion, but with the tape across her mouth she produced only muffled grunts.

"That wasn't so bad, was it?" he asked without expecting an answer. "In awhile, you won't remember anything. Not even coming here and leaving."

He filled a syringe from a vial and injected it into her arm. She could read the name on the bottle: L-RetroBan.

"Initially, you'll notice an enhancement of sensory acuity—vision will be clearer, faint sounds more audible. There's nothing to be alarmed about. It's perfectly normal and will abate in about an hour. It will be succeeded by retroactive amnesia, and you will remember nothing of this evening."

Tweecus sat down next to Kelly and began to write in a bound notebook.

He was irritated that his secret research deserved the Nobel Prize for Medicine but he had only the President's Medal of Freedom to show for it. He could not count on Krator for the honors that were due him— MacVain cared only about deniability. He had resolved to keep some private proof of his accomplishments in the event of competing claims.

Kelly noticed the pale-green cover of Tweecus's notebook. He had labeled it in his own hand with a calligraphy almost Asian in its precision and clarity:

> Project Name: Tall Blondes
>
> Preparation: Implantation of embryo Lot PG-9
>
> Experimental Subject: Kelly Grazziella
>
> Project Phase: Quality assurance, stateside, full-term
>
> Principle Investigator: Wassily Tweecus, M.D., Ph.D.

When Tweecus finished entering the data from the experimental procedure, he pulled a wheeled, stainless steel cart closer to him. The cart had several open shelves holding medical supplies needed for the experiment. The sturdy frame of the cart was dented in one place, as if it had once collided with another. Tweecus rotated the cart to reveal a small drawer at the opposite end. Inside were two experimental log books of the same size and color as the one in his hand. He added Kelly's notebook to the stack and closed the drawer again.

* * *

Suddenly, Kelly was lying in a gully, dressed in her firefighter's uniform. She uncovered her ears, opened her eyes, slowly raised her head, and cautiously looked around, surveying herself and the landscape. She was safe in a circle of unburned branches, her clothes untouched by the fire, though a layer of powdered ash covered her body.

She needed to get away before Tweecus returned. She struggled to her feet and headed up the gully, pulling herself through the unburned bush, bracing each foot on the roots of the chaparral so as to not leave any tracks. She was convinced that Chad Weed was at the bottom of the ravine trying to pick up her trail. When she reached the road, she saw a fire department vehicle ablaze. The wind was pushing the flame up the ridge, so she headed down the road as quickly as possible, running as if possessed.

On the hillside above, the shrubs cracked like rifles when ignited, sending flaming brands high into the air.

A farm truck was stopped a short distance away.

"You're in danger," she shouted to the two men inside the truck, waving her arms.

The driver opened the door and leaned out as if to hear her better.

He shouted something back in Spanish.

With every momentary shift in the wind, red hot cinders dropped out of the sky and lay smoking on the road.

A cluster of burning chamise bounced down the slope towards them, then veered away and rolled across the road like a tumbleweed, coming to stop behind the truck.

Kelly was afraid that the column of flame would create its own vortex and spin in their direction. She had a fleeting and totally inappropriate glimpse of the Prado in Madrid, and the words burst out of her involuntarily. *"¡Regrese! ¡Regrese!"* she shouted to the driver, telling him to turn around, unaware of her yellow hardhat and green uniform.

At that moment, the driver realized that it was the firefighter's vehicle burning on the road—and that she had no way of escaping. "Get in," he shouted in Spanish, gesturing wildly with his hands.

Kelly squeezed into the front seat and pointed urgently to the road to the Italian-Swiss monument. The driver jammed the gears into reverse, while Kelly hung out the window and guided them back to the spur road. The truck backed in and turned around, then headed out the way it had come, following the winding contours towards the junction with the highway in Deep Creek Valley.

Kelly kept looking furtively behind her.

"What's the matter?" the second trucker asked her.

"There's a man who's trying to kill me," she answered, in a voice so calm as to be believable.

He studied the rear view mirror. "There's no one behind us."

"He's driving a silver BMW with a blue interior."

The truck driver thought BMW drivers were capable of anything. "Don't worry," he said in a reassuring voice. "You're safe with us."

"Why is he chasing you?" the second trucker asked.

Kelly blushed and turned her head away. She put her face in her hands.

The two truckers held a conference in Spanish.

"Do you think she's been, you know?" the driver asked, gesturing sexually with his hands.

The second trucker nodded affirmatively.

The memory of the laboratory was now so vivid, her anger and humiliation so intense, that Kelly could not put it out of her mind. Her conscious self had never come to terms with the experience, and she was convinced it had happened only minutes ago. It played itself over and over like a news clip of a terrible disaster.

She realized that the driver had been talking to her, asking for directions to highway 101 without them being seen.

On Valley Road, firefighting vehicles were streaming north, and a helicopter buzzed low overhead, but Kelly barely noticed them. She was afraid that Chad Weed was still behind them in his BMW.

"There's a police car up ahead," the driver noted.

"Turn off!" the second trucker said. "If they ask for our green cards, we're dead!"

The driver pulled into a farmer's loading dock and put the vehicle in neutral.

"We could let her out here," the driver suggested.

"No!" Kelly pleaded.

"You're a firefighter—the police will drive you home."

She was convinced that the police were in cahoots with Chad Weed and that they would return her to the Nathan Whyte Laboratory. "No police!" she said emphatically.

"We can't just leave her on the roadside," the second trucker said. "She's obviously freaked out. And she won't talk to the police."

He studied Kelly, who was staring straight ahead, too embarrassed to meet his eyes. "Do you live around here?" the driver asked her. "We could take you home."

"That's the first place he'd look for me," she replied, seeing Chad Weed's sinister eyes.

"How about we take you to a friend's?"

"I need to return to my dormitory," she insisted.

"Where's that?"

"At Davis University in Davis."

Her fearful face told them she was serious.

"Davis is on Interstate 80, just west of Sacramento," the driver told the other trucker.

"We're already two hours late. What will the boss say?"

"We just tell him we got rerouted by the fire department in Oscuridad." The driver looked at Kelly to verify his story. "We take 80 to Sacramento, then return to Modesto from there."

Kelly was suddenly aware of her uniform and bright yellow hardhat. "I'm too conspicuous in this," she told them in a terrified voice.

The driver reached behind the sun visor and gave Kelly a baseball cap with a "Modesto Wines" logo.

She took off her helmet and tried on the cap, tucking her hair under it and pulling the brim low over her eyes.

"You look like a trucker," the driver announced, and both men laughed.

* * *

When they reached Davis, the truck dropped Kelly off near the entrance to the university campus. On the highway, she had not seen the BMW once, and the flashbacks were decreasing in intensity.

"I don't know how to thank you," Kelly said.

"No problem."

"But don't tell anybody you picked me up. The man in the BMW works for a secret government laboratory, and he'll be able to trace this truck."

"Don't worry. We don't want anyone asking for our green cards," the driver said.

"Are you sure you'll be able to get home all right?" the second trucker asked.

"Yes, there are friends of mine here."

He reached up to the rear view mirror and unwound a ribbon that held a medallion of Our Lady of Guadalupe. "Take this," he said, handing it to her through the open window.

Kelly's eyes filled with tears. She took the medallion and ceremoniously draped it around her neck. "Thank you so much," she said, pulling the surprised man's head towards her and giving him a kiss on the cheek.

The driver put the truck into gear, exploiting a break in the column of cars. Kelly watched until it disappeared under the overpass, then set out for her dormitory, taking the most direct route through a rural part of the campus. When her path was blocked by a security fence, she found a spot where dog-walkers had bent back the wire.

Although she was sure she had gone to the right place, her dormitory had completely disappeared, replaced by some new building. It was this experience that confirmed the growing suspicion that her memory was seriously impaired. She could not even remember what she had done yesterday or even what she had for breakfast, yet the experiences of the laboratory, the pregnancy, and the childbirth were all so vivid and overwhelming that it was impossible to think of anything else. She needed to commune with the Goddess.

Kelly was relieved to find that her favorite outdoor equipment store, Final Ascent, was still where she remembered it, and that it still rented rucksacks and sleeping bags at nominal prices. The owner knew that no American could rough it in the wilderness without first buying an armful of stuff.

"I'll rent the rainfly and foam pad too," Kelly said.

"We also rent portable camp stoves," the clerk told her. "It's impossible to get back-country fire permits now."

Kelly winced at the irony of it. "I hate to cook," she explained, not wanting to tell him that she planned to fast. "Let me have one of those two-liter water bottles too."

"We don't rent those."

"That's OK, I'll buy it." She added a pair of heavy socks, sun screen, light-weight shorts, and a T-shirt to the other items on the counter.

"You should try these energy bars," he told her, pointing toward a standing display. "They were developed for downed flyers and can sustain life for days, provided you have water."

She took a handful and added them to the stack on the counter.

"Is there a place where I can fill this water bottle?" Kelly asked.

"I'll do it for you," the clerk said, disappearing for a moment into the staff section behind a partition.

Outside, lines of fire-fighting vehicles from all over California rumbled past the store on their way to the mountains. As she watched, she wondered if her own unit had been reassigned to the Sierra.

The clerk returned with the bottle full of water that was cold to the touch.

He noticed the hardhat under her arm. "Do you need any rock-climbing gear today? Pitons? Carabiners?"

"No thank you," she replied, anxious to be underway.

The point-of-sale software took Kelly's picture and compared it to the photos that it had on file.

"Boy!" the clerk exclaimed. "This account was set up before the University of California was sold to private investors! And you're Kelly Grazziella."

As he tallied her purchases, Kelly saw Tweecus bending over some piece of equipment, the fluorescent lights turning his white coat a sickly green. She heard the scientist reading aloud from the digital read-outs.

"I'll need your phone," the store clerk reminded her.

Kelly had no idea where it was. Then she realized that she could not buy anything—cash transactions were against the law.

"I'm sorry, but I must have lost it."

The clerk studied her for a moment, a sympathetic expression on his face.

"Are you with one of the fire crews?" he asked.

"Yes, I am."

He rested his hands on the countertop and leaned towards her in confidence. "You're one of our oldest customers: we can make an exception for you."

Kelly understood that he was alluding to the vigorous underground economy based on Chinese money. She rummaged in the cargo pocket of her pants where she carried cash for emergencies and retrieved a handful of yuan. He took it from her discretely.

"This will cover the purchases, and I'll waive the security deposit," the clerk said, handing two of the notes back to her. "Just remember to bring the gear back when the fire's over— and don't tell anyone I did this."

In front of her was a display rack of life-like fishing lures, each sealed in its own plastic packet. There were rubber earthworms, crickets, and hellgrammites. To her horror, as she looked at them, they seemed to turn into little pink creatures in the shape of salamanders, with gill slits, stumpy limbs, and round heads.

Terrified, Kelly stuffed her purchases into the rucksack and rushed out of the store into the heat. The first thing she saw was a silver BMW turning the corner. Chad Weed must have seen her: he was going around the block.

Then she noticed a fire-fighting support vehicle from CDDR, carrying supplies to some staging area in the Sierra. It was a flat-bed truck, and stacks of sealed cartons blocked any view of the cab. It was stopped in the line of traffic, awaiting its turn to get on the tollway. Kelly darted between the cars and hoisted herself on to the bed of the truck just as it pulled away.

* * *

Kelly felt at home in the Sierra Nevada. She liked the glint of quartzite in the bright summer sun, the cobbles rounded by runoff, and the rockfalls of ice-fractured granite. She loved the cirque lakes scooped by glaciers and the cascades of clear, cold water pouring from the undercuts of late-season snowfields. She loved the moist meadows filled with flowers. She marveled that conifers could split apart boulders and find holdfasts in spillways of scree.

The mountain that Kelly thought sacred to the Goddess was not the highest in the High Sierra. East of Davis the High Sierra is not very high. The uplift of bedrock reaches its highest altitude further south, where the eastern face of the Sierra Nevada forms a wall of granite. By the time the mountain range reaches the latitude of San Francisco, it is about half its maximal height and transitional to the volcanic peaks and cinder cones that dominate the Pacific Northwest.

The highest mountains were magnets for people, and it was not possible to spend more than a few hours on a prominent peak in summer without a visit from solemn-looking rock climbers prospecting for the next ascent, groups of children on an outing, and knots of tourists from a campground far below. But the summits were ringed by peaks almost as high that few people ever visited. What Kelly called the Goddess's peak was the third highest in a line of three. Near the summit, on the north face, there was a protected shelf of rock that over-looked a pristine lake shaped like a crescent moon.

It was almost dark by the time she had hiked to the last relatively flat ground on the path to the summit. The meadow was still mushy from melting snow, and it was a poor spot to bed down. Her sleeping bag would get soggy, so she resolved to go on. She wished she had brought a flashlight, but the meadow held the last stand of trees before timberline, and above this point the sky opened up—not a panoply of stars but bright city lights bouncing off drifting clouds of smoke. There was no trail beyond the meadow, but the spring runoff had etched the only possible route to the top, a track of alluvial gravel that zigzagged among boulders too high to climb over. It was a route that could be felt in the dark.

The steep track ended at a cliff face, and Kelly remembered she had to skirt to the right, then climb up the next boulder blocking the path. She bumped the obstacle with her knee before she saw it, then had to grope the abrasive face of the stone to locate the footholds she had used before. She remembered that once past the boulder, she would have to ascend a chimney formed by a wedge of rock that had separated from the cliff. It was pitch black, and in places too narrow to climb wearing a rucksack, but she was afraid to remove it lest she lose it in the dark. She supported the pack with one shoulder strap and pulled it behind her like a duffle. With every upward hoist of her body in the narrow space, she felt the rough stone through her clothes, and was glad she had not changed into shorts. As she neared the end of the vertical tunnel, she could see above her a circle of stars as if through a telescope.

* * *

"I've decided to retire," the Goddess told Kelly the first morning she was there. "I used to have honor. I used to be Mother Earth. But now everything I do is explained away as chance."

The Goddess had large, sensitive eyes, a kind face, and an enchanted forest of pubic hair. She smelled like spring blossoms with nuances of over-ripe fruit and a hint of musk.

"I know how you feel," Kelly said. "I wanted my first pregnancy to be an act of love. But now I've gone through nine months of discomfort, with people believing the worst about me; and at the end of it all, I don't even have the company of a child or the respect due a mother."

"I give them life, joy, pleasure, and intimacy—but are they grateful?" the Goddess asked rhetorically.

"They seem to hate you," Kelly sympathized.

"They do. I'm a threat to their solitary grandeur."

"Why did they implant that embryo in me?"

"Until the microscope was invented, they claimed that a miniature baby was formed in the semen and that a woman was just a flower pot where the fetus grew for nine months. Now they are trying to make their fantasy a reality."

"It was a man-made embryo?"

"Not man-made—man-damaged. They strip away the beauty, the love, and the ecstasy from my creations until there is nothing left but the microscopic coupling of molecules in a dish—then they say they invented it. Biology has become an extractive industry like mining and logging."

Kelly nodded in agreement. "But in my case, wasn't the embryo doctored in some way?"

"Yes, they used an electromagnetic probe to alter the sequence of DNA nucleotides, in effect mutating the genes." The Goddess looked thoughtful, as if wondering whether to say more. "You were part of an experiment to create life without earth. They love that sky god bullshit."

Kelly looked surprised. "So there isn't any sky god?"

"Of course not. All of nature is my dominion. The sun provides energy. Lightning fixes nitrogen. But to their way of thinking, the living room was created by the furnace in the basement."

"But even as atheists, they refuse to let it go."

"I know. They make movies about blitzkrieg and put lightning bolts on their shoulder patches. But they're not really attracted to the sky—they're displaying their hatred of earth."

"Are there no male divinities?"

"Well, I do have my male helpers: the god of wine, the god of volcanism, and so forth. They are really demiurges, but you know how men are!"

Kelly was too sad to smile.

"You are wondering if I take other shapes," the Goddess said, reading her thoughts. "I will always come to *you* as a mother, but I have an infinity of aspects—virgin, crone, lover, one for every place and time. When I descend into the underworld, I disappear from earth entirely."

"What happens when you do that?" Kelly asked anxiously.

"The earth becomes a desolate, forbidding place. Women become barren, the water too polluted to drink. I dance over the corpses in my necklace of skulls."

Kelly and the Goddess sat together in silence for a long time, watching thunderheads form over neighboring peaks. A kaleidoscope of shadows danced across the bright granite face of the escarpment.

"I know why you came here," the Goddess said gently. "If a supplicant asks for wisdom, I will grant it."

"Yes," Kelly said, in a barely audible voice. She knew some terrible revelation was coming. The soft arms of the Goddess enveloped her and held her close.

"You asked about the health of your baby," the Goddess said, brushing the hair from Kelly's eyes. "The mutations they induced were designed to kill the child a few weeks after birth. Had you kept the baby it would have died."

"What about the poor adoptive parents?"

"There were no adoptive parents. The baby was returned to the laboratory, where it was maintained until it died. Then its brain was extracted for chemical analysis and its body preserved for display in a private museum."

"I see," Kelly said with a manufactured calmness, clenching her fists even tighter.

Then a warm summer breeze from the central valley moved up the western slope of the Sierra, rippling the conifers and smoothing Kelly's fine hair with the intimacy of a mother's touch.

Kelly began to shiver and sob uncontrollably.

12

"The Rapture Is Go!"

> The American Revolution ended the age-old partnership between religion and the state. But the Silent Coup began as a grass-roots conversion to prophetic history—and it transformed the American empire at the apex of its power.
>
> *The Hidden History of the Eighth Dispensation*
> by Amadeus

The nation's top-grossing televangelist nudged Tammy Jo awake. "It is very clear to me now," Duane told her, sitting up in bed, his eyes wide with enthusiasm. "For years, I was in error. I thought that the Rapture of the First White Kernel required one full turn of the prophetic clock after the Lord gives us his sign," he said excitedly. "But a full turn is *not* three days *plus* three days as I thought—it is three *times* three, and not a twenty-four hour day but only one-third of a day. And one third of a revolution is eight hours, so nine times one third is three days. You know what that means?"

"The prophetic moment is today?"

"Yes!" he affirmed, disappearing into the walk-in closet as if cosmic thoughts had vanished from his mind.

"Tammy Jo," he shouted. "Where is my prime-time suit?"

* * *

Dean Weed was dreaming of a hacienda in Old Mexico, a Spanish guitar playing softly in the background, a young woman's voice whispering in his ear.

"Señor Weed," the voice whispered again.

It was his middle-aged housekeeper, handing him the cordless phone. "You have a call from Tammy Jo Boone. She says it's urgent."

"What time is it?"

"Almost five."

The housekeeper set the indirect lighting to summer sunrise, then slipped out of the bedroom on soundless feet, the door closing behind her with a barely audible click. A faint, pink glow began illuminating the valences.

The executive director sat up in bed and popped a breath mint into his mouth. "Good morning, Tammy Jo," he said pleasantly.

"Get your ass down here!" Tammy Jo Boone barked in her nasal, East Texas twang. "Duane is announcing the rapture this morning."

When Dean Weed arrived at the Lone Star Christian Tower, the rising sun was refracted by the mirrored walls of the adjacent high-rise buildings into a kaleidoscope of burnished coppers, reds, and yellows. He felt a wave of numinous anticipation.

Then he saw that Boone's hand-bound Bible was missing from the display case.

The televangelist was in the Sky Lounge, while Tammy Jo was at the base of the winding staircase, looking anxiously upward.

"You can't go up there," Tammy Jo told Dean Weed, "but you can use the cordless."

"Honey Bear," she spoke into the phone. "Dean is here to talk with you." She clicked the speaker phone option and set the volume to low.

"I can't talk with anyone now. I am preparing for my announcement."

"Ask him if he is going to announce the rapture at 11:11 today," Dean Weed told Tammy Jo.

"Honey Bear, Dean wants to know if you are going to announce the rapture at eleven after eleven today."

"The Lord will tell me what to say when the prophetic moment comes."

"Did you hear that?" Tammy Jo asked Dean Weed.

The executive director nodded affirmatively, his face expressionless, his gut taut with anxiety. "Ask him what the exact time of the prophetic moment is."

"Honey Bear, Dean wants to know the exact time of the prophetic moment."

"It is not eleven after eleven like we thought, but it's close to that—the Lord will tell me when the moment arrives. Tell Dean that I have to concentrate now."

Tammy Jo looked at the executive director to indicate the uselessness of pursuing it further. "That's the best I can do," she told him.

"Does Gus know about this?"

She shook her head no. "I thought it would be better if you talked to Duane first."

Dean Weed called the home number of the director of communications and got him out of bed. "Hello, Gus. This is Dean calling."

"Oh my God!" Gus exclaimed. "It's today, isn't it? I'll be right there!"

"Call me when you get here."

Dean Weed looked at his watch: it was an hour earlier in Colorado Springs, but Krator needed to know right away. When he dialed Vaughn MacVain on the red telephone, the call was automatically routed to MacVain's apartment at Krator headquarters. The senior attorney was already up, preparing to go to a meeting in Atlanta.

"Vaughn, I just spoke with Duane, and he is planning on announcing the rapture today. Not exactly at 11:11 Central Daylight Time as we planned, but the time is 'close to that,' as he put it."

"We could've used more time," MacVain said glumly.

"And what about the missing firefighter? Is there any evidence she's alive?" Dean Weed asked, his voice betraying uncharacteristic irritation.

"No, but there's no evidence she's dead either."

* * *

On arriving at his airplane at Freedom Field, Vaughn MacVain told his communications officer to set up a conference call with Cole Kincaid, his personal security officer, and with Cato Magruder, the deputy bureau chief of Apprehension and Detention. MacVain went directly to the war room and repositioned his chair so that a real-time display of the Grazziella search zone filled the wall behind him. When he sat down at the chart table, the peaks of the High Sierra were dwarfed by his presence.

A moment later, Cole Kincaid and Cato Magruder popped into the virtual space in front of him.

"Good morning, gentlemen," the senior attorney opened in a cordial but firm tone of voice. "I wanted to meet with you alone because there are security issues that cannot be entrusted to a routine red alert. What I am about to tell you is not to be communicated to anyone else, not even to each other.

"The Fellowship is going ahead with the rapture, so I've ordered a Krator-only search and rescue on the Grazziella case. And I am appointing Cato Magruder as the new covert leader of task force Wildfire. Kincaid, from now on, you will take orders directly from Magruder. If there is a conflict between Tricia Culhane's order and Magruder's order, you will follow Magruder's."

"Understood," Kincaid said.

"Magruder, your job will be to take Grazziella into custody, whether she is found dead or alive. If there is no new evidence, then play along with Culhane's authority. But once there is hard evidence that the firefighter has been found, whether dead *or* alive, task force Wildfire is automatically dissolved and you take over. As soon as you confirm the evidence, notify Dean Weed and Skipper Van Squint immediately. Also, I've sent you detailed plans to cover both a live Grazziella and a dead one. Make sure both plans are on standby so Krator is ready no matter what happens."

* * *

In her comfortable condominium in Colorado Springs, Tricia Culhane was awakened by "The Ride of the Valkyries." It took her a moment to realize that it was her cell phone playing the new ring tone she had installed, replacing the synthetic chimes that it had come with. She looked at the clock on the night stand—it was not yet six in the morning. She took a few deep breaths to make herself acoustically presentable. She fumbled for the phone. She rehearsed her salutation.

"Hello."

It was Vaughn MacVain. "The Fellowship's going ahead with this goddamned rapture," the senior attorney announced. "At eleven a.m. *today*. Dallas time. And that changes everything.

From this point on, we need to change the ground rules of the search and rescue."

Tricia Culhane took out a pen and legal pad.

"The Council and I agreed that we don't want local law enforcement getting anywhere near Grazziella once the announcement begins," MacVain said. "So after 9:45 a.m. mountain time, it is Krator-only search and rescue, with no notification of other agencies. If local law enforcement makes initial contact with her, we take immediate control and black out contact with the press under the anti-terrorism statutes."

"Can I have that in writing?" Tricia Culhane asked.

"Yes. I'm sending you an e-mail. Copy everyone on the task force too."

Tricia Culhane read it back to him. "Starting 9:45 a.m. mountain time, Krator-only search and rescue. Other agencies out of the loop. Krator takes control if another agency makes initial contact with the target. Black-out any contact between the firefighter and the media."

"Correct."

"I will act on it as soon as I receive your written directive."

"Also, I'm going to ask Cato Magruder to take command of the search if and when there's any new evidence that Grazziella is dead or alive."

"But what happens with task force Wildfire at that point?" she asked, a plaintive tone in her voice.

"The task force is still needed as a coordinating body."

Tricia Culhane tightened her grip on the phone as if it were a cudgel.

"Realistically, what're the chances of finding her alive?" she asked pointedly.

"Realistically? She's already dead or we would have gotten something substantial by now. And let's hope she stays dead. From this point on, we don't want any miraculous resurrections."

"What about interfacing with the Fellowship?" she asked. "Do I keep them informed of new developments?"

"No. Magruder will do it."

* * *

In his executive washroom in Lone Star Christian Tower, Dean Weed splashed some water on his face and was shocked by his own reflection. His eyes were deep in shadow, baggy with age and fatigue. He felt he had aged ten years in the last few hours. The uncertainty of prophecy was taking its toll. Yesterday afternoon, the search looked hopeful—testimony by Grazziella's father that she had a secret hide-away in the mountains. Ground crews fanning out through the woods. Helicopters buzzing mountaintops. Drones surveilling campgrounds. Even Vaughn MacVain was convinced that they had Grazziella in their sights. And now nothing. A red alert with egg on its face.

Dean Weed returned to his office and settled into his commodious swivel chair. In spite of Krator's failure, his own efforts at containment had been successful. By graphically depicting the downside of failed prophecy before the Council of Seventeen, he persuaded the members to extend the Fellowship's blackout to all the news media in the Free World. While religious talk radio continued to beat the drum for the rapture of Kelly Grazziella, in all of North America there had been not a single story, on either the Internet or the airwaves, that indicated any interest in the missing firefighter by the Fellowship of the Eighth Dispensation. A banned terrorist group, Journalists Without Beds, had written that the Fellowship was planning for the announcement of the Rapture of the First White Kernel, and they had distributed the story on the Internet; but mainstream interest was deflected by Gus's in-depth explication of the theology of the rapture, bolstered by extensive quotations from the Bible.

Late Wednesday afternoon, after a diplomatic marathon that involved the Exclusive Assembly and the Council of Seventeen, Boone had approved a contingency plan that presumed the finding of the firefighter alive: Boone would ascend the podium at the Stockman Hotel to rejoice in her safe return, attributing it to the prayers of the Fellowship faithful. He also approved a contingency plan in the event of a dead firefighter: a spontaneous outpouring of sympathy for the grieving family by ten thousand Christian Cadettes dressed in black crepe outfits—ordered late last night and promised for this morning, at the cost of extravagant special-order and rush charges.

But a still-missing firefighter was the worst scenario of all—and that was the one unfolding in front of him.

His thoughts were interrupted by a call from the director of communications.

"I just got in," Gus said. "I'm in my office. Should I come up?"

"No, I'll meet you there. I want to see the latest coverage."

* * *

"This is for real, huh?" Gus asked, half rhetorically, nodding at the rolling digits in the clock.

Dean Weed watched with palpable anxiety while Gus put the second count-down clock away in a credenza.

"Duane told me himself," Dean Weed answered. "Realistically, there are still three options—dead, alive, or missing—but we'll have to go to air with missing and the rapture."

Gus grimaced. "The membership is hot for the rapture, but our enemies are hoping the Fellowship will fall on its face. I hope Duane has called this one right."

Dean Weed did not look reassuring.

"What does Krator say about the Grazziella search?" Gus asked.

"They have no idea where she is."

The director of communications shook his head, his face a mixture of anxiety and determination.

"Gus, yesterday morning, there was a story floating in the media about the possibility that Kelly Grazziella might have been stalked by a serial killer. What do you know about that?"

"It was probably planted by Krator, as a contingency plan, in case she's found dead," Gus explained to the executive director. "That way they can claim they were on to the case all along but didn't want to tip the killer."

"So there's no truth to it?" Dean Weed asked.

"I don't know. Ask Krator."

"Can I use your secure phone?"

"Sure, there's a Krator-direct line in the control room," pointing to the glassed-in cubicle that looked like an oversized, twentieth-century telephone booth.

Dean Weed called Vaughn MacVain a second time.

"I never thought it would come down to the wire like this," he told the senior attorney in a conciliatory tone.

"Neither did I. Believe me, Krator is throwing all available resources at it."

"I know that, but now we need to assume that she'll continue missing past the deadline. And we both agree that after the rapture is announced, finding her dead *or* alive is to be avoided at all costs. We need Krator's help to ensure that it won't happen."

"You have it," the senior attorney assured him. "We'll keep the red alert in place at a reduced scale as well as checkpoints in the target zone, so if she ever shows up, we'll be able to intervene in a timely manner."

"Yesterday there was a news report that she was being stalked by a serial killer."

Vaughn MacVain waited to hear more.

"If there were any physical evidence of that, already in Krator's possession, it would be better if it were not released once the prefiguration of the rapture is announced," Dean Weed told him. "It might raise doubts in the public's mind."

"No one at Krator wants to spoil the Fellowship's prophecies."

"And what assurance do we have about the firefighter not turning up again after the announcement?"

"She'll never turn up again," the senior attorney assured him.

Dean Weed wished he could be so confident.

In the command center, Tammy Jo Boone was standing by the prophetic clock, watching it count down. "I've been watching One World News, and the search has hit a wall," she told the executive director solemnly. "Is that the real situation?"

"I'm afraid so."

"I guess we have to face the fact that Duane is going through with this," she said. "What if that firefighter shows up after the announcement?"

"Vaughn MacVain understands that the reputation of the Fellowship is at stake," he explained, lowering his voice to a whisper. "He indicated that if she does not show by eleven o'clock today, she will never show up again."

Tammy Jo Boone avoided his eyes. "Duane depends on us to do the right thing," she said.

***

MacVain received a call from G. Lyle Acre, commander of the Special Operations brigade in Matamoros.

"It was like old times the other night," the general enthused, turning up his country-boy charm.

"It's that bracing mountain air," MacVain said. "What's up?"

"You were right about the problem. All three of the pre-indites were involved in what we talked about. But Chad

258

Weed's first two assignments have been successfully carried out. Only one more to go."

"Let me confirm it before we go any further," the senior attorney said.

He queried the police reports database and learned that two of the women who had been subjects in Tweecus's experiment had been found dead in Davis, California, on Wednesday evening. One had died from a drug overdose, the other from a fatal cerebral hemorrhage.

"We confirm that two problems have been solved," MacVain told G. Lyle Acre. "That was very fast."

"The boy's real good," the general said in his down-home accent. "And he's operating on his home turf. But how realistic is a solution to problem three? I hear Duane is going ahead with the rapture."

"We're keeping the red alert in place until there's evidence she's dead or alive. There's a possibility that she's hiding until the hubbub dies down, and she'll reappear after the rapture to embarrass the Fellowship. But Krator is prepared for that possibility."

"And what do we do with the 'senior investigator'?" Acre asked.

MacVain's lips pursed at the thought of Chad Weed. "If he were my boy, I'd bring him in now to make sure he gets proper medical attention."

* * *

When the phone rang again, the senior attorney could almost see the heavy jowls and Brezhnev eyebrows of the gloomy, corpulent accountant.

"What are the chances that Grazziella will show up alive?" the Chairman asked MacVain.

"There's no evidence that she's dead, no evidence that she's been abducted, and no evidence that she's a conspirator. So maybe she's suffering psychological trauma and will reappear. Her pre-indite says she's a home body, so she will try to make contact with her loved ones once again."

"And Krator has a plan in place to deal with that?" the Chairman asked.

"Yes, we do. If Krator nabs her first, no one will ever know. If local law enforcement nabs her, we will claim federal jurisdiction, black out the news, and dismiss any leaks as terrorist disinformation. If there's no sign of her, the Wildfire task force will be kept active at reduced capacity indefinitely."

"Indefinitely is a long time," the Chairman said with a hint of skepticism.

"Well, she can't live in a goddamn hole—ask Saddam Hussein."

"No one wants her reappearing *after* Boone proclaims her," the Chairman emphasized.

"Once the rapture is announced, she might as well be in heaven."

"And what if she turns up between now and then?"

"We'll hold her for medical examination. That will give us time to weigh the alternatives and devise a permanent solution consistent with the Fellowship's response."

"It better work," the Chairman said.

Probable Cause

There are ten miles of dirt road between Dancing Coyote Ranch and the highway to Laredo. Often there are no cars at all, and today Deirdre saw only her neighbor going by in the opposite direction. Both raised a finger in reflexive greeting as they passed. As she turned onto the paved highway, Deirdre was singing along with a country-and-western vocalist, the flickering fence posts keeping the beat, when suddenly in front of her loomed a flashing digital billboard:

All vehicles must stop.

Beyond a wall of red tail lights she could make out the black and tan uniforms of the internal security police, a branch that Krator had formed from the most callous elements of the former federal Border Patrol. It had authority to launch impromptu roadblocks wherever illegal aliens might be in transit, which was anywhere in the United States and Canada.

Her heart best faster as the column of cars limped forward.

An officer pointed her towards a lane marked with orange cones. Suppressing the urge to floor the accelerator, she edged her king-cab pickup into the inspection zone and turned off the engine as instructed. Mentally, she scanned every corner of the truck. Was there a shred of anything that could connect her to Jack Adair?

The police were hovering over a silver Honda ahead of her, taking the biometrics of the driver and the passengers. To her right, a Ford sedan was parked under a sunshade on the roadside awaiting further inspection, its occupants, a family of four, guarded by two masked men with assault rifles. The suspects were White not Mexican.

Now it was Deirdre's turn.

"How do you, Ma'am," the officer said, chewing his consonants like a cud. He was in his early thirties, with a good physique tautened by regular visits to a gym, but his skin was pliable and pasty, as if he had been raised under lights like a fast-food chicken. He held up the touchpad for her handprint, then photographed her eyes.

"Is that you?" he asked, turning the tablet so she could see her name and photograph pulled from the Krator database.

"Yes, that's me."

"Where are you headin' today, Ma'am?"

Had they found an EarthRage communiqué in the camouflaged pipe at the ranch?

"Laredo," she replied with feigned sangfroid.

"Do you have business there?"

"Yes."

"What kind of business?"

She wanted to tell him that it was none of his, but she bit her lip and struggled to be pleasant. "I'm meeting a friend."

"I have to ask you to step out of the vehicle."

Deirdre opened the door and stepped tentatively to the ground.

In her tight blue jeans and bespoke *rebozo*, she looked like an ad for country living.

A second officer gave an appreciative glance at her red hair, then gestured for her to move behind the yellow line.

She smiled warmly, hoping to turn him into an ally.

"What's the problem, officer?"

"Just a random inspection. It just takes a few minutes," he explained.

Technicians in jump suits swarmed over her truck, pulling up the seats and the floor mats, while robotic creatures with probes moved to and fro under the chassis. They were like a detailing team from hell.

Finally, one of the technicians signalled to the others, and they all merged back into the shadows from which they had come.

"You can go now," the officer said.

She walked back to her truck, her fists clenched in anger. As she climbed into the cab she looked back at the second officer. He was still studying her long legs and red hair.

The Christian Cadette Corps

Deirdre parked in front of Amadeus's church and bounded up the handicap ramp to the office. Amadeus was in the parlor, setting out a tray with pastries and coffee.

"What's the matter?" he asked. "Car trouble?"

"You could call it that." She described the roadblock, giving full vent to her fury.

Amadeus listened until the storm had passed, then suggested they sit down for coffee.

She studied Amadeus's face. "You look depressed. Is it today's announcement?"

He nodded affirmatively.

"But you said the Rapture of the First White Kernel was not inevitable."

"When I said that, I thought they would find the firefighter. Now it's too late." He opened the doors of a wall unit and turned the television to One World News. It was still the pre-event coverage, and Boone had not yet appeared on stage.

"There hasn't been a thing on television about the Fellowship's intentions, except 'special programming' in that time slot," Deirdre noted.

"There's been a total news blackout in the United States, and the Europeans have no idea what the prefiguration of the rapture means."

"It makes you wonder if they disappeared her on purpose," Deirdre noted.

"That's been suggested on the Internet. One thing is for sure—once the Rapture of the First White Kernel is proclaimed, we'll never see her again."

The pre-event coverage cut to the football stadium where ten thousand teenage girls were practicing gymnastic routines. The camera zoomed down to the field where a boyish news reporter was standing next to a tall, middle-aged woman in a cowboy hat. The reporter addressed the audience:

> "Young women and girls have been arriving from all over the country this morning, in jets, in small planes, in cars, and buses to help provide the ceremonial decorum so important to such an historic moment.

"The head coach of the Christian Cadette Corps, Fanny Mae Mather, is with us here today to tell us about this exciting spiritual drill team. Fanny Mae, do these energetic young people come from every corner of this great country?"

"By all means, Bob. We have young people here from Tysons Corner, Virginia; Shepherds Corners, New York; and the Four Corners, to name just a few."

"And they are all good Christian girls?"

"Oh yes, the Christian Cadette Corps is very proud of the fact that we have taken orphan girls and found them good Christian homes and loving families. Every single one has taken the pledge of chastity until marriage. And as athletes, of course, smoking, coffee, drink, drugs, and staying up late are out of the question too."

"You must have a rigorous training program to harness this kind of young energy—not a single Cadette is out of step on these routines."

"You're right, Bob, it's prayer, practice, and probity. And lots of ice cream."

"I understand that many of these girls are identical twins."

"You're right, Bob, more than fifty percent are identical twins, a good many of them identical triplets too."

"More than fifty percent! The Cadettes must be very proud of what they have accomplished."

"We are proud, Bob, very proud—but we could not have done it without the Lord."

"I am sure that very many in our audience will say 'Amen' to that, Fanny Mae, and I wish every one of you out there in our viewing audience could be right here on the field with me and feel the *energy* that I feel standing here next to these wonderful examples of American Christian youth. Thank you, Fanny Mae Mather, head coach of the Christian Cadette Corps, for talking with us today."

"It makes me so mad!" Deirdre fumed. "All those helpless orphans being indoctrinated into a cult of right-wing fanatics! Did you notice? Those girls even *look* the same, like they've been cloned."

She grimaced as animated stages of history marched across the television screen, each historically significant event paired with the passages from Scripture that purportedly predicted it.

"How can people believe this prophecy nonsense?" she asked, her eyes narrowing.

"Prophetic history is not Christian prophecy," Amadeus said firmly. "Prophetic history denies the indeterminacy of free will and repentance."

"What about the seven seals and all that—isn't that a prediction?" Deirdre asked.

"No, it's an expression of faith—that in the fulness of time, goodness will triumph over evil, but not at any specific time," Amadeus emphasized.

"Duane Boone III says that 'prophecy is just history that hasn't happened yet,'" she chided.

Amadeus looked scornful. "When the disciples ask Jesus if he is going to restore the kingdom of Israel, he says 'It is not for you to know the times or seasons that the Father has established by his own authority.' What could be plainer?"

Deirdre looked thoughtful. "I never asked you—what does your church teach about prophecy?"

"It teaches that God sends messengers to warn us and console us."

"Why hasn't God sent anyone to warn us about Krator?"

"God has, but we've chosen not to listen."

Behind them, talking heads mouthed words on the screen.

"Isn't it interesting how religion keeps popping up again just when you think you've gotten rid of it forever?" she observed.

"Every generation, rationalists announce its imminent death. But religion's not the superstructure—it *is* the structure."

Deirdre gave Amadeus a knowing glance. "It's also the blind spot of the intelligentsia. They never take it seriously until it's too late."

The Finale

In the communications command center in Lone Star Christian Tower, Gus stood up and gestured for everyone's attention.

"Duane is leaving his office now," he announced. "Lift-off is set at eleven minutes after eleven. The rapture is go."

"Take it away, Bankers Stadium!" a co-producer barked into his head set.

"Roger that, stadium on-site control activated," the speaker phone barked back.

"We're moving out," Gus shouted to the people around him, moving toward the elevators.

On the ground floor, a cordon of Krator security police had roped off the lobby, forcing pedestrians into a narrow path leading from the front door to the elevators. Any assassin would have to run a gauntlet of assault rifles to get into the building.

Duane Boone III, carrying his prize Bible pressed to his chest like a baby, walked briskly toward his royal blue Cadillac. Its distinctive hood ornament—an American eagle of solid gold with a lamb clasped in its talons—gleamed like a tiny sun. The televangelist slid into the back seat where Tammy Jo was already waiting. He gave her hand a reassuring squeeze. The door clicked shut, the column began to move, the cars full of bodyguards leading the way.

As requested by the security staff, Duane and Dean never traveled in the same vehicle. The executive director got into a VIP car at the end of column, while the co-producers joined the video crew in the mobile communications van. Behind the Foundation's staff vehicles, there was a rear guard of Homeland Security troops, enough to fight a holding action with a platoon of well-armed guerrillas. Police sharpshooters were stationed on the overpasses, and traffic was stopped on the cross streets. They reached the Stockman Hotel in a matter of minutes.

At the hotel, there were even more uniformed police, and Duane Boone III and Tammy Jo entered the main lobby to spontaneous applause. Dean and Gus were some distance behind them.

When Dean Weed arrived, Duane had already disappeared into the ballroom, but the lobby was still thick with people. Dean hated crowds, and he felt relieved when his assigned security team cut a swath through the milling gawkers.

The main ballroom bristled with camera crews from all the major media. Gus must have been busting his balls to get such a great turnout on so little notice.

"Is it true that Dr. Boone will announce the Rapture of the First White Kernel?" an Internet anchorman asked the executive director.

"Wait and see," Dean Weed said. There was still hope— maybe God would intervene.

Dean Weed found a spot to stand in the doorway of Gus's control booth, where technicians had to squeeze past him. He needed to be close to the breaking news.

There were several reporters from the TV news networks standing nearby swapping opinions of the event.

"Well, Boone also prophesied that his shit-kicking church in Laredo would become the most powerful religion in the United States," one newsman said to another. "Who would have thought that would happen?"

The house lights dimmed, the spot lights came on, and the murmur began to die down. There was enthusiastic applause from the Fellowship members in the front ranks.

The master of ceremonies gestured for quiet, and a hush descended over the ballroom as the leader of the Fellowship ascended to the stage.

Duane Boone III opened his prize Bible as if it were a talisman. In a sonorous voice, he began quoting from memory the biblical passages that foretell the Rapture of the First White Kernel.

* * *

In Amadeus's parlor, Deirdre leaned forward in her chair, her fists clenched, as if ready to do battle with the television.

"He makes me so mad!" Deirdre fumed. "All those zombies he surrounds himself with. And the politicians who suck up to him—they're even worse! I would like to see that creep fall right on his face. I would love to see the firefighter appear on TV right after he announces that she's been taken into heaven!"

Rubicon Point

The walk had been all down hill, and Kelly made good time in the cool morning air. She had seen no sign of human life since yesterday afternoon, when helicopters swooped overhead, forcing her to hide in the crevice of rock. Now at the entrance to the trailhead, cars hummed past at sixty miles an hour, taking no notice of the hiker on the roadside.

Kelly emerged from the pine trees and headed for the one public telephone remaining in California. It was maintained in working order by the Historical Society to preserve the Old West ambience that tourists loved. She was wearing a T-shirt, shorts, and firefighter shoes, with her blond hair bunched under a "Modesto Wines" cap, the brim pulled down over her eyes. She was sun-tanned and healthy.

At the Krator Remote Surveillance Center, deep inside Cheyenne Mountain, Wyoming, monitoring software tripped an audio alarm that signified a face on the watch list.

"Camera output from a public phone on highway 89 in California," a young trainee announced to her assigned mentor, the assistant telecom watch officer.

Even though the Cheyenne Mountain facility had never been instrumental in the capture of a single Muslim terrorist, its director was confident he could catch an American firefighter. That morning he had given his officers a pep talk: "Krator is fourth down and goal to go on this. We can't afford any more dropped passes."

"It looks like a match to that missing firefighter," the trainee announced excitedly. On the screen was a blond-haired young woman, her eyes obscured by a baseball cap, her mouth half-hidden behind a telephone.

The watch officer, a former U.S. Customs agent, bent down to look at the screen. He resented his transfer to the underground bunker far from the flow of drug money and was counting the days to retirement.

"It could be her, but remember the procedure," he told the trainee in a methodical tone of voice. "Always look at the confidence score first. In this case it's low because the subject's mouth and nose are covered by the phone, the eyes in shadow. The confidence level is point five."

"Shouldn't we transfer this to the Wildfire task force anyway?"

"Let's wait a second—when she puts that phone down we'll get a more reliable confidence score."

Kelly Grazziella pressed the reverse-the-charges button. She dialed her father's home number.

A phone company computer in Uzbekistan rang the Grazziella family home in Oscuridad, California.

Kelly's father heard the telephone ring and turned down the volume on the broadcast from the Stockman Hotel.

"A collect call from Kelly Grazziella in Olivado County, California," a computer-generated voice asked him: "Will you accept the charges?"

"Thank God, yes."

"Don't worry, I'm all right," Kelly told him. "I had a kind of memory loss. I'm sorry if I worried you."

"I never doubted you were alive."

"Somehow I knew you knew."

"Are you injured?" her father asked.

"Oh, no, I'm fine," she replied in a normal voice.

"Where are you?"

"In the Sierra—Lake Tahoe. But I need some money to get home. I lost my purse and cell phone."

"Just stay right there," Kelly's father told her. "I'm going to call the deputy in Missing Persons and see what he can do. I'll call you right back."

Cole Kincaid was in the security bunker getting a Dr Pepper when he heard the klaxon from the FANTOM trace sounding in the control room. He rushed back down the hall and gulped with excitement: it was Kelly Grazziella! He rang Cato Magruder as instructed but was told that the MacVain's henchman already knew.

Several minutes later Tricia Culhane learned of Kelly Grazziella's phone call from the director of the Cheyenne Mountain facility. "We've got a confirmed sighting," he announced proudly. "She's on highway 89 near Rubicon Point in the Sierra Nevada." The screen showed a map of Olivado County with a blinking icon.

The special assistant activated the Wildfire command post, and the participants' pictures arranged themselves on her computer screen like tiles on a floor, spinning One World News into one corner. "Grazziella's just called her father from a pay phone in the Sierra," she informed the assembled faces. "Remember, Senior Attorney MacVain wants Krator to take her into custody first."

She shouted for her secretary. "Rose!"

No answer. Rose Underwood must be in the lounge watching the rapture. She rang Rose's beeper.

A young man she had never seen before popped into the window for Apprehension and Detention. "Deputy bureau chief Magruder asked me to sit in for him," the aide explained.

Tricia Culhane's eyes narrowed—task force Wildfire had become a dumping ground for interns.

"How long to intercept?" she asked Magruder's aide in the voice of a woman scorned.

"Krator units are reforming in Placerville," he explained.

"You've got to be kidding?" she said.

"It's true."

Tricia Culhane realized that the redeployment of Krator units that she had approved could not have come at a worse time. "Alternatives?" she asked calmly.

"California Highway Patrol and Olivado County Sheriff are a lot closer, five minutes tops," Cheyenne Mountain told her.

"Nix that," she said. "Krator-only. What about air?"

"Olivado County Sheriff has a chopper on standby," Cheyenne Mountain reported.

"Only MacVain can authorize pickup by another agency," the special assistant said.

"Someone's bound to spot her and notify local law enforcement to get the reward," the bureau chief of Domestic

Surveillance worried. "Then we'll be following the sheriff's parade horses."

Rose Underwood rushed in.

"Vaughn's not answering his phone," Tricia Culhane told her. "Ask Charlene if she knows where he is."

"Right away!" Rose said.

"Shouldn't we alert the Fellowship?" the bureau chief of Domestic Surveillance asked her.

"No. The directive is clear—Krator-only."

Rose Underwood came back a minute later. "Charlene says he's on his plane at Freedom Field and incommunicado."

Tricia Culhane noticed the blank space where MacVain's personal security officer should be. He had not even bothered to log in.

She called Cole Kincaid on his personal line.

"Kincaid here."

"Task force Wildfire is in emergency session," Culhane said in a voice like a hanging judge.

"I've been ordered to report to Magruder," he replied.

She hung up without a word, then sat staring into space.

"The Fellowship has a need to know," the bureau chief of Domestic Surveillance insisted. "How about I make a confidential call to Dean Weed?"

"MacVain said Magruder would contact Dean Weed himself," she explained.

With an audible sigh she repeated MacVain's standing order to what was left of the task force: "This is a Krator-only search and rescue."

She felt humiliated even as she said it.

* * *

At the field command center in the Sierra Nevada, Cato Magruder studied the FANTOM trace of Kelly's phone call to her father.

"The voice print might be counterfeit and her picture inserted digitally," he told his staff. "What better way to rain on Boone's parade? We need physical confirmation before we call the party off."

"The closest units are local law enforcement," an aide informed him.

"What's the status of the airborne command center?" Magruder asked.

"It's out back, fueled and ready."

The signals intelligence officer gestured for attention. "We've got another intercept of the firefighter's father. He's calling the office of Missing Persons in Oscuridad." He put the call on the speaker:

> "Kelly just called me," Joe Grazziella told the deputy. "She's at a pay phone at Lake Tahoe. She says she's unhurt."
>
> "That's great news!"
>
> "What do we do now?"
>
> "Just wait. Krator will have intercepted her audio by now."
>
> "But I haven't heard from them."
>
> "Well, give them a few minutes."
>
> "I told Kelly that I'd call her right back. And I'd like to be able to tell her that someone is coming to get her. Isn't there something you can do?"
>
> "Well, maybe Olivado County Sheriff can help," the deputy wondered aloud. "I'll talk to them and call you right back."

"We're going to Tahoe!" Magruder shouted.

Immediately, members of his team grabbed their laptops and backpacks, then sprinted for the aircraft, no one wanting to be last. As the rotors began to turn, a hail of twigs and tan bark clattered on the aluminum roof of the now empty field command center.

Magruder caught the eye of his signals intelligence officer. "When the sheriff takes a leak I want to hear the tinkle."

* * *

In Olivado County, the dispatcher escalated the incoming call to the sheriff himself.

"An officer from Missing Persons in Almaden County is on the line," she told him. "He says that Kelly Grazziella's father just told him that his daughter telephoned from a pay phone near Rubicon Point on highway 89. He wants to know if we know about it. I'm connecting you."

The officer from Missing Persons came on the line. "Kelly's father is concerned that she has no money and no way to get home," he explained.

"We'll pick her up," the sheriff assured him. "Tell her dad that she'll be in good hands."

How far is our closest unit to Rubicon Point?" he asked the dispatcher.

"Five minutes max."

"Tell them to take Grazziella into protective custody and proceed to Eagle Falls Lodge. Tell them I'll meet them there by helicopter. And tell them to double-check the firefighter's identity. We don't want any false positives."

"Should I notify Krator?"

"No, they're reforming in Placerville. We can get there ahead of them."

The sheriff dialed the telephone number of the editor of the Tahoe *Ponderosa*, a newspaper best known for its in-depth coverage of snow. "Eddie," he said to the editor in a dramatic voice, "have I got a story for you."

The editor listened, his eyes widening. "We'll send a photographer there right away," he assured the sheriff. "Sure, you can be standing next to her—but you'll have to take me to lunch!"

The editor of the *Ponderosa* dialed one of his stringers who lived off highway 89 in a week-end tourist cottage that had been converted to permanent occupancy. "Grab your gear and get the hell over to Eagle Falls Lodge. The sheriff found Kelly Grazziella. Be sure to take a picture of her and the sheriff together."

At One World News in Los Angeles, the producer of disaster coverage was at his desk for the first time in several days, having just returned from a get-away to the wine country. The first call of the day was from a freelance news photographer he knew in Olivado County, a man he had worked with on a number of wildfires in the Sierra Nevada. The freelancer was selling him exclusive footage of the finding of the missing firefighter, Kelly Grazziella.

"Is this a joke?"

"No. The sheriff called my editor. I'm on my way there now."

"Sure, we'll buy it—at twice the usual price."

"Ten times the usual price, plus ten times our usual finder's fee. Or I call a Sacramento station."

The producer initiated GPS tracking of the call. "We'll meet that price," he said. "But on the condition that you give us the location now."

"You'll get the location the second I upload."

"Tell me your terms once again so I can write them down," the producer said, stalling for time.

"Ten times the usual per second, plus ten times our usual finder's fee," the free-lancer repeated.

The computer locked on the photographer's cell phone and projected his destination based on the trajectory. It was an easy computation in an area with only one highway.

"You got it," the producer said. "I can't wait to see that footage."

The producer of disaster coverage dialed his boss. "The missing firefighter's been found. She's near Eagle Falls Lodge on highway 89, near Tahoe. We have a freelancer heading there now. I'm copying you with the GPS coordinates. Expect an Internet upload pronto."

"You are hot!" the manager of disaster coverage enthused.

The manager called the news director. "The producer of disaster coverage says Grazziella's been found! There's freelance footage coming in too."

"We can't afford to be wrong on this," the news director told his staff. "Confirm with the sheriff's office in Olivado County and with Eagle Falls Lodge on highway 89. Make sure it's really her. I want eye-witness confirmation. Do *not* confirm with Krator—they'll just shut us out until they're ready."

* * *

In the Krator airborne command center, Cato Magruder listened to Joe Grazziella calling his daughter.

> "The local sheriff is sending a patrol car to pick you up. Just stay where you are. They'll be there in a couple of minutes."

> "They're here now," Kelly said. "Thanks, dad, see you soon."

At Rubicon Point on Lake Tahoe, the patrol car came to a stop in front of California's only pay phone.

"Are you Kelly Grazziella?" the deputy asked the young woman in the baseball cap.

"I am," Kelly said.

He photographed her retina with his tablet and asked for her thumb on the touchpad.

"Can I see some hard identification too?"

She showed him her firefighter's badge.

"A lot of people have been looking for you. I've been asked to take you into protective custody."

In the approaching helicopter Magruder listened intently to the patrol car's radio traffic.

"Live retina print and thumb print confirmed, plus her badge—it's her all right," the signals intelligence officer said.

Magruder turned to the two aides who were standing by waiting for confirmation of the firefighter's status: "Notify Dean Weed and Skipper Van Squint that Grazziella's alive."

Magruder clicked the intercom and announced the situation to his staff: "Attention! Olivado Sheriff confirms a visual ID of Grazziella, her firefighter's badge, retina, and a thumb print."

There was a murmur of disappointment in the aircraft as Magruder's staff realized that Krator had failed to nab the missing firefighter first.

"We're going to intercept that patrol car!" he said, galvanizing his troops.

The signals intelligence officer gestured to Magruder. "There's more coming in. The sheriff's informed the local press. And he plans to grand-stand at the Eagle Falls Lodge. The news about Grazziella has gone downstream. To One World News in Los Angeles."

"Send the intercepts to Van Squint. Tell him he's got work to do."

* * *

At Eagle Falls Lodge, the helicopter carrying the sheriff of Olivado County touched down on the helipad. As he opened the hatch, the photographer from the Tahoe *Ponderosa* shouted to him.

"Hold it there, sheriff. Let me get some shots of you getting out of the chopper. That way we can segue to the arriving patrol car."

"Good idea," the sheriff agreed, squinting like Clint Eastwood and thrusting out his jaw. He was already savoring his fifteen minutes of fame.

***

In the grand ballroom of the Stockman Hotel, Dean Weed was reading along with the script when two Krator agents appeared in the doorway of the control room. One of them bent down and whispered in the executive director's ear.

"Cato Magruder told me to tell you that Kelly Grazziella is alive," the agent said.

"Grazziella's alive!" Dean Weed shouted to Gus.

"Oh, my God," Gus said, pressing a button that activated a warning light on the podium. "Script Rejoice?"

"Yes," Dean Weed affirmed.

"Grazziella's alive!" Gus told Boone through the televangelist's wireless earpiece. "Go to script Rejoice!"

Duane Boone III, trouper that he was, accommodated to the new timetable without giving any indication that the Almighty had changed His mind. He shortened his preamble without appearing to rush, then closed his prized Bible with a dramatic flourish. As he made eye contact with the audience a hush of anticipation descended over the crowd. Then in a voice tremulous with awe and humility, he advanced to the Joyous Moment:

> Over the past three days, members of the Fellowship of the Eighth Dispensation have prayed for the safe return of Kelly Grazziella. In every military base, in every major shopping mall, and at her father's home in Oscuridad, California, we have prayed for her delivery...

***

Magruder's helicopter, painted white with a huge red cross on the fuselage, landed on highway 89, blocking traffic. A half dozen officers poured out of the aircraft and set up an impromptu roadblock with flares and cones. A moment later, the sheriff's patrol car carrying Kelly Grazziella rolled slowly

278

to a stop in front of Magruder. The tall, skin-headed officer with the handlebar mustache peered into the back seat and into the eyes of the startled firefighter.

Cato Magruder gave the two deputies a contemptuous look. "Can't you see that this poor girl needs medical attention?"

He turned again to Kelly Grazziella: "Miss, I have to ask you to get out of the car and into that helicopter over there," he said in a solicitous voice. "We can get you home a lot faster."

Cato Magruder telephoned Skipper Van Squint.

"Grazziella's in Krator custody," he announced.

"You're certain?" Van Squint asked.

"Take a look at the video feed."

* * *

In the control room at the Stockman Hotel, Gus activated the alert on the podium a second time. "One World News is going with the Happy Camper script," he announced to the televangelist. "Advance to the Joyous Moment."

Boone skipped ahead two paragraphs without losing a beat, then looked into the camera, his eyes conveying deep sincerity:

> Today, on behalf of the Fellowship of the Eighth Dispensation and to all the people of the Free World, I say 'Welcome home, Kelly Grazziella!'

At a nod from Gus, the missing firefighter's face, telecast in the pink of unraptured health, filled the wall behind the stage. A shout went up from the video crews, followed by an outburst of spontaneous applause by the audience. The televangelist beamed, accepting the approbation with a simple affirmative nod, his face flushed with piety and pride.

On half a billion television sets, the helicopter carrying Kelly Grazziella burst through a stratum of cloud to reveal the distant, snow-capped peaks, enhanced by the theme from "The Sound of Music."

279

An actress wearing an over-sized red-cross armband put her hand tenderly on Kelly's arm and looked at the firefighter with a grateful and compassionate gaze. Behind her, a second video camera focused on Grazziella's face. "You're safe now, firefighter," the make-believe nurse said. "How does it feel to be going home?"

"I owe my life to the Goddess," Kelly said humbly.

At One World News, the vice-president of news management could not believe his ears. Thank God for the seven-second delay, he thought, and nudged the audio producer.

"I heard her," the producer said, already positioning his cursor over the last syllable displayed by the digital syllabary. He gave the mouse a decisive click. As the segment disappeared from the screen, he selected and clicked again.

Kelly Grazziella's voice went out to a grateful nation: "I owe my life to... God," she said.

Then the network cut to the stadium in Dallas where ten thousand Christian Cadettes gave leaps of jubilation in their white-fringed miniskirts.

* * *

On the tarmac at Freedom Field, Vaughn MacVain finished his interview with a tall, blonde woman in her early twenties and escorted her through the softly-lit foyer of his executive jet. He took her hands in his and wished her a successful career. Then he returned to his on-board office and lifted the communications blackout.

"There is something you should see," his telecom officer told him in an urgent voice, turning on the video screen.

MacVain watched impassively as Kelly Grazziella waved from the open door of a medevac helicopter while music filled the room.

The senior attorney reflected that the strategic situation had rotated 180 degrees. An hour ago all that was needed was a simple snuff of the firefighter by a Mexican stalker. But now Krator would have to keep her alive while keeping her quiet—a scenario that he had not adequately considered.

* * *

In Laredo, Celestine had been so captivated by the televised rapture that she had not heard the summons to the meeting of task force Wildfire. When Kelly's face filled the television screen, she raced to her computer and saw the Wildfire alarm blinking silently, the audio turned too low to hear. Her stomach churned with guilt and disappointment, and she telephoned Tricia Culhane to explain.

"Yes," the special assistant answered in a voice so cold that Celestine trembled.

"I'm sorry," Celestine blurted out. "But I didn't see the alert in time. And that's why I wasn't at the meeting."

The special assistant did not realize until then that Celestine had not been present in the virtual command center. "You didn't need to be there," she said reassuringly. "In fact, I didn't need to be there either," she added in a voice edged with bitterness.

"Oh, I was so worried," Celestine responded with obvious relief.

"Well, don't worry. It's nothing to worry about."

"Also, am I still on special assignment? I'm not sure what to tell my supervisor."

"You're on special assignment until 5 p.m tomorrow. Take the day off," she added, without her usual enthusiasm.

"I'd like to, but I'm meeting with Senior Attorney MacVain tomorrow morning."

The special assistant thought of the surveillance that MacVain had ordered for Celestine's bedroom—it made her furious. Not even an innocent like Celestine was safe from Vaughn's predatory attacks.

"What time are you meeting him?" the special assistant asked.

"Ten thirty."

"On his executive jet in Laredo?"

"Yes."

"I will put a favorable evaluation in your personnel file for your excellent work on Wildfire."

"Thank you very much," Celestine said, her anxiety dissipating. "And I really enjoyed having had a chance to work for you."

"You have no idea how much that means to me right now."

* * *

Rose Underwood studied Tricia Culhane's demeanor like a physician on rounds.

"You look a little unwell," she told her boss.

"Just tired," the special assistant lied. She wanted to tell her secretary that MacVain had used Kincaid to torpedo task force Wildfire and that Magruder had cut her off at the knees, but she fought back the impulse. Was it because she wasn't a tall blonde?

Rose Underwood hovered sympathetically. "Is there anything I can do?"

"Just hold my calls. I am going shopping until I calm down."

Tricia Culhane drove into downtown Colorado Springs and parked two blocks from a copy shop that rented computer work stations by the hour. Several times before, she had hidden there while working to a deadline, and no one had been able to find her. This time she wore sunglasses and a big hat to disguise her appearance.

Donning disposable gloves, she printed out three sheets of paper. The first contained Celestine Brittle's home address in large letters to serve as an address label. The second sheet was the requisition authorizing the surveillance of Celestine Brittle, a document printed on Krator letterhead and signed by "Cole Kincaid, Security Officer to U.S. Senior Attorney Vaughn MacVain." The last page was an anonymous explanatory note to include with it:

> MacVain likes to meet young women alone on his airplane. The camera is in the mirror frame of your vanity. Burn these documents immediately after reading. Yours Truly, A Friend.

Cash transactions were illegal, so Tricia Culhane paid the copy shop with a debit card: one that she had acquired while working as legal counsel to the federal agency that had become Krator's covert operations division. The debit card had been issued posthumously to a woman who had died in federal prison some years before. And to ensure its continued purchasing power, it was linked to counter-biometric technology, replacing the thumbprint and retina scan of anyone who used it with the thumbprint and retina scan of the dead woman. It was the ultimate platinum card—it could make any commercial transaction completely anonymous and charge it to someone else.

Tricia Culhane carried the documents back to her office in a paper folder she purchased at the copy shop. It was no longer possible for an ordinary citizen to send a letter anonymously, since all physical transactions required biometric scans of the sender. But Krator headquarters still had drop boxes for its courier service in the lobby, just as its lending library had physical books that circulated. Envelopes delivered by courier were billed to an internal account number, but for security reasons no one but the sender and recipient saw their contents.

Still, Tricia Culhane did not want her own office's account number associated with a letter that betrayed the senior attorney. She returned to headquarters, went into her inner office, and locked the door. Behind her desk was a bland, earth-tone painting of a Southwestern Indian pueblo that she had bought at a gift shop in Sedona, Arizona. She moved the painting sideways on its track to reveal the wall safe hidden behind it. Inside was a small sheaf of papers. She removed a sheet of gummed bar codes, and, using tweezers, she affixed one of the bar-coded strips to a cardboard courier envelope. When scanned by the courier service, it would bill an account in covert operations, while blanking out the name of the sender. Then she slipped Celestine's address into the transparent sleeve, put the security requisition and the warning note inside the envelope, and sealed it with the attached adhesive strip. She hid the envelope in the top drawer of her desk and buzzed her secretary.

"Call Celestine Brittle and tell her to be at home between eight and nine tomorrow morning in case I need her help with anything."

A little while later, when Rose left the office on an errand, Tricia Culhane slipped the courier envelope into the stack of out-going physical mail.

13

ON THE TARMAC
AT LAREDO

Genetic engineering will raise the IQ of the
economically less fortunate to the point where
they will be intellectually equal to tenured
faculty.

Wassily Tweecus, M.D., Ph.D.,
on accepting the President's Medal
of Freedom

At eight o'clock on Friday morning, Celestine Brittle was
standing in front of the mirror on her vanity, assessing the
silk blouse she planned to wear to the meeting on the senior
attorney's plane. To her surprise, the doorbell rang, and it was
a uniformed courier from a package delivery service. When
she attempted to sign with her thumbprint, he refused, asking

only her name, which he compared to the one on the shipping label. Then he handed her the parcel and disappeared.

The envelope was unlike any that Celestine had ever seen before, as it had no information about the sender at all, not even a city of origin. Inside it were two sheets of paper: one a requisition on Krator letterhead, the other a short note printed out by a computer. She put the sheets side by side on the kitchen counter and examined them with apprehension. There was no doubt about the conclusion: she was under surveillance by order of Vaughn MacVain. The note confirmed it.

She tiptoed into the bedroom and examined the vanity. It was made of oak veneer, with a large elliptical mirror framed by the same material. The frame was decorated with brass studs, symmetrically spaced around the perimeter of the mirror. She examined each one of them, tapping it with her fingernail. One had a pinhole bored in the center. As she pried out the stud, she noticed that it was connected by a thin wire that disappeared inside the wooden frame. She pushed the vanity away from the wall, and found the corresponding spot in back, which was covered by a wooden insert made of the same wood as the vanity. A casual observer would never even see it, and a suspicious observer would judge it to be a knot hole. Using a nail file, she pried it out and recognized the glint of a wristwatch battery embedded inside the mirror frame. She yanked the wires until they pulled away from the tiny chip hidden inside the wood.

Then Celestine remembered to destroy the documents that the mysterious benefactor had sent her. She burned them on a piece of aluminum foil in the kitchen sink, forgetting to disconnect the smoke alarm. In the ear-splitting noise, she stood on a chair, struggling with the reset button.

Slumping down at the kitchen table, Celestine wanted to cry. More modest than most women her age, she thought of all the times she had stood naked in front of the mirror, as well as all of the occasions when she sat at the vanity plucking her eyebrows and picking her teeth. Who knows who reviewed her surveillance photos? Only yesterday she had run naked from the shower to the telephone wrapped only in a towel. The recollections turned her red with humiliation.

When Celestine thought of Vaughn MacVain she saw him pacing like a tiger in virtual space, a sour, serious man in no way attractive. How could she possibly meet with him knowing that he had seen her naked?—the thought sickened her. Her first impulse was to run away, but that was out of the question—one did not cancel appointments with the senior attorney.

She logged onto her Krator account and confirmed that her high-level clearance had expired along with the Wildfire task force, but technically she was still under special assignment to Tricia Culhane. In some respects that was better than a clearance.

She called the data processing manager who had been assigned to task force Wildfire. "I have a question about Krator surveillance devices," she asked.

"Shoot."

"Suppose a camera were planted in someone's home, say in a bedroom, would it provide audio as well as visual?"

"It depends on the device, but the standard kit provides both."

"What about range? Could it pick up a person's conversation in the next room?"

"It depends on the distance, the thickness of the walls, and so on. I would really need to see some numbers."

"Well, suppose it was a normal one-bedroom apartment, with a door between the bedroom and the living room. And the door was normally kept closed?"

"In that case, I would recommend putting one in the living room too."

"The device I saw didn't have an on-and-off button. How is it activated?"

"Normally, they are programmed by a hand-held computer. It is also voice-activated, so it is not drawing current when no one's there, and at night when they're asleep."

"And where's the data stored?"

"Usually, there is a small amount of local storage on the device, at the recording site, but the data are transmitted wirelessly as soon as possible to the nearest permanent communications channel, like a laptop or a telephone, and are sent to Krator from there."

"Can the recording device be used by itself, without the telecommunications module?"

"The old spy-camera-in-the-lapel sort of thing? Absolutely. It will zip right through airport security too."

"It's so amazing what the standard kit can do!"

"To really see what it can do, you should take a look at the manual," he said, giving her the URL of a Krator internal Web page.

Celestine learned that the device planted in her bedroom had a voice-recognition capability, and that the recording feature could be programmed to activate to a specific word or phrase. It also had counter-detection technology that hid it from common sweeping devices.

She examined the device that she had removed from her vanity. She programmed it with her laptop, using a driver downloaded from the Web page.

"That's close enough!" she said, repeating the phrase several times, to ensure that the activation switch of the audio recorder was working.

"Excuse me, excuse me," she said, programming the shut-off switch.

She rigged it so it fit comfortably on the underside of the lapel of her jacket, behind the white security badge, then confirmed the audio sensitivity through the fabric by speaking the commands in a normal voice.

"That's close enough!" she said firmly, turning it on.

288

She began to hum to her lapel: "Amazing grace, how sweet the sound…"

"Excuse me, excuse me," shutting it off.

"That's close enough!" she said, turning it back on.

She hummed again. "Raise us up on eagle's wings…"

"Excuse me, excuse me."

She played it back and heard herself singing two hymns— it worked perfectly.

She would not be boarding the senior attorney's airplane unprepared.

*   *   *

Alone on his executive jet, all communications blacked out, Vaughn MacVain retrieved the genetic prospectus provided by the Institute for Genetic Assessment and Profiling and read it for the first time. He nodded approvingly at Brittle's family history. There was no evidence of ex-slaves or Jews trying to pass for White, and the count of her deleterious recessives was well within normal limits. From the pre-indite he learned there was nothing remotely suspicious in Celestine Brittle's life. Her father was a cofounder of the Fellowship church in Midland, and her mother was a teacher in a private religious school. Celestine attended church every Sunday and had taken a vow of celibacy until marriage. The surveillance report prepared by Cole Kincaid was not incriminating either. The security officer had found nothing worth noting in the videos that had been taken in Brittle's home.

MacVain swallowed hard—the lack of a prophylactic pre-indite gave the impending liaison an even sharper edge.

*   *   *

When Celestine Brittle approached the entrance of the government terminal at Laredo airport, the guards already had her risk assessment profile displayed on the screen. Since mandatory pat-downs had been instituted at airports, the

Council of Seventeen had determined that its functionaries were far too important to stand in the same lines as ordinary citizens. Now, almost every airport in the country had special facilities where military officers, high-ranking government officials, and executives of major corporations could be speeded through security checks and given preferential seating on airliners.

Celestine was asked to leave her purse, key ring, and cell phone with the guard at the gate. Then a uniformed officer escorted her to the priority lounge, where he handed her off to a ground steward, who led her through a hangar to a white, windowless jetliner with a blindfolded Athena painted on its tail.

Before she reached the airplane, a muscular security guard in a blue Krator warm-up suit and ball cap appeared out of nowhere and checked her biometrics again with a hand-held device. "Celestine Brittle, senior attorney MacVain is expecting you. This way please." He led her over to the gangway, gesturing to the forward hatch.

When she reached the top of the ramp, the hatch hissed open, then closed behind her automatically.

Celestine entered a softly lit reception area with honey-colored paneling and upholstered maroon side chairs.

"Welcome, Celestine," a voice rang out from a hidden speaker. "Just come through the next door to my office."

As she looked around, one of the wooden panels slid back, revealing a spacious office paneled in dark wood and furnished with antiques. The senior attorney was sitting behind a narrow Louis XVI desk, his legs obscured by a tapestry that spilled over the side in a triangular fold and ended in a tassel. Under the recessed ceiling lamps, his bald spot was as conspicuous as a tonsure, and his hair appeared more blond than brown. "Please be seated," he said, gesturing to one of the two soft leather armchairs set diagonally in front of his desk.

As Celestine sat down, the soft foam compressed under her weight, causing her torso to sink into the cushions and her skirt to ride up above her knees, leaving her legs prominently displayed. She clamped her knees together and held them there, afraid that from the senior attorney's vantage point he could see up her skirt. The senior attorney peered down at her, then smiled as if amused by her discomfiture.

MacVain swiveled in his chair and began reading from a document conspicuously labeled "Celestine Brittle Security Profile."

Celestine thought of the surveillance video, and a wave of anger and indignation surged through her. Before MacVain could lift his eyes from the report, she spoke up in a voice that was calm and non-judgmental. "You're married, aren't you?"

"Yes," MacVain admitted, not wishing to explain away his wedding ring.

"What does your wife look like?" she asked on impulse.

MacVain put down his document and studied her with curiosity. "She looks a lot like you. Blond, with fine bones and long-limbs." Even though he was looking at her directly his eyes were focused somewhere inside his head.

Celestine tried to hold them there. "What is your wife's favorite color?"

"Metallic green."

"How do you know that?"

"When we were first married I gave her a present wrapped in metallic green ribbon and she was thrilled. The store chose the wrapping, but I noticed the effect."

"Noticing is good. Does she like flowers?"

"Not really. Artificial flowers, maybe."

"What about jewelry?"

"Oh, yes. Insatiable. She always wants more."

"What about her birthstone?"

"Not interested. She wants diamonds."

"Do you buy her cars too?"

291

"Of course."

"Like what?"

"The latest is a Land Rover. She fancies herself on safari."

"Do you have a picture of her?"

"No."

"Not even on your desk?"

Celestine's forehead glowed with perspiration, and she felt trickles of water running down her neck. The airplane appeared to not be air-conditioned.

"You must be warm. Let me help you with your coat." He stood up and moved towards her chair until he was on the edge of her personal space, where he hovered almost menacing. Her usual protections, her cell phone and key chain, had been checked with the guard at the gate.

"May I take your coat?" he asked.

She activated the microphone. "That's close enough!" she said.

"Excuse me?" he asked, thinking perhaps he misheard her.

With a back stroke as practiced as a tennis champ, he opened a closet door next to him, exposing a full-length mirror, similar to the mirror on Celestine's closet door at home.

"Your coat," he said, almost politely. "Please stand up."

Celestine was happy to be free of the compromising chair. Once on her feet, she abruptly turned to face MacVain. Now she was the taller of the two, even taller than she expected. As she calculated the distance to the cabin door, he seemed to read her thoughts.

"The hatch only opens to my voice command," he said matter-of-factly. "And I've given orders that we be left strictly alone."

"Isn't a married man supposed to have sex with his wife instead of with strangers?" she blurted out. Celestine was startled by her own words—she had never before mentioned sex while alone with a man.

MacVain was surprised too. From his years on the tarmac he knew that some women initiate sex while others dance around the subject until encouraged to do otherwise. For some, intimate personal conversation is as arousing as foreplay. But he was surprised that Brittle did not try to play the innocent longer. He wondered if perhaps her Christian virginity was a pose.

"As much as I enjoy this subject, would you mind if we discussed your transfer to Dallas?"

Without waiting for an answer, MacVain stepped behind her, grasped her lapels and pulled down her suit jacket. Her suit coat dropped away, exposing a blouse of cream-colored silk designed to be worn under a jacket. In the mirror, MacVain was staring at the brassiere visible through the thin fabric. Then he hung the coat in the closet and closed the door.

Celestine realized that the closet door was made of metal and that the audio recorder in her jacket was useless. If played back now, it would show her to be the sexual aggressor. Her career in field operations had ended before it had even begun.

"I am going to activate the virtual reality system," MacVain told her. "Have a seat." He sat down at his desk and swiveled toward the side wall.

The cabin filled with Wagnerian music, fading to a voice-over that sounded like Charlton Heston, perhaps created on a digital synthesizer:

> "For millennia, human progress limped along with a body developed through an animal level of existence—hunger, thirst, fear, anger. Only today, with the advent of biotechnology can human beings transcend animal nature to take rational control of their bodies."

> The scene shifted to a modern medical center rising from a cultivated plain, with snow-capped mountains on the horizon.

"Now scientists can create an embryo by combining sperm from a donor father with an egg from a donor mother."

The film showed an interior shot of a laboratory, then a wall lined with blinking high-tech equipment. In the foreground, a white-coated scientist was deep in conversation with a graduate student, both of them studying a pipette in the senior scientist's hand.

The older scientist had an aura of white hair like Wassily Tweecus.

My God, Celestine realized—it *is* Wassily Tweecus!

"Once created, the embryo can be implanted in the womb of any healthy woman, where nine months later it emerges as a happy, healthy baby."

The montage cut to a perfect White baby with its perfect White mother.

"In the pre-conscious history of life, the genes available to each embryo are a hit-or-miss process, but now human beings can bring intelligent choice to genetic selection. Nothing is more important than choosing the best possible sperm and ovum for the creation of the embryo."

The visuals showed a veterinarian impregnating a mare with a catheter while the happy owners in cowboy hats looked on. Then the scene cut to the winner's circle of the Kentucky Derby, then to a fast and powerful cheetah pulling down a speeding gazelle.

"Conscious selection is even more important with human beings. And that is why the Institute for Genetic Assessment and Profiling has developed the egg-donor program."

The visuals showed a slim blonde in her mid-twenties working at her computer terminal. She looked at her watch, then stood up to put on a beautifully tailored jacket.

She headed for the elevator, re-emerging at the door of a fertility clinic. She paused so the audience could read the sign, then smiled with satisfaction and went inside.

In a comfortable treatment room, a doctor reviewed the procedure for egg extraction. He had an earnest but reassuring voice:

"It is a painless process that begins with the controlled release of gonadotrophic hormones in order to synchronize the donor's menstrual cycle with that of the embryo recipient. This also stimulates the ovaries to release multiple eggs, or oocytes. The control is achieved by means of a hormone stimulating agent administered daily over a two-week period. The removal of the eggs is done under sedation using a needle guided by ultrasound. This is followed by a course of antibiotics, just to be on the safe side. That's all there is to it."

The doctor smiled, radiating confidence, then left the room while the egg donor undressed in a diffuse glow like a perfume commercial, suggesting a perfect body with long curvaceous legs, the breasts well-shaped and firm.

When the lights came up, MacVain was leaning over the top of his desk assessing Celestine's reaction. "What you have just seen is top secret, known only by a few Krator personnel. The existence of this program is not to go beyond this room."

"Tricia Culhane didn't brief me about this program."

"Only women who have been chosen to be egg donors know about it."

"So that's why I'm here."

"Yes. To get your consent. If you choose to participate in the program, your transfer to Dallas will be effective today. Should you choose not to do it, you would no longer have the leg up on your career path that you now enjoy."

Nordic beauty was a prerequisite, but loyalty and obedience were the traits MacVain wanted most in his egg donors.

"Do I have to decide immediately?"

MacVain could see no reason why a loyal American would not be eager to move the nation forward to its genetically engineered future. But Brittle was a fundamentalist—that could be a problem.

"The egg donors are the shock troops in the war against genetic diseases," he told her in a caring voice. "It is an act of Christian charity, like giving blood to the wounded. And your transfer to Dallas can be done today," he added with feigned cordiality.

"Am I free to go?"

"Unless you have something else in mind," he said slyly. Some of the prospective egg donors threw themselves at him to secure a desired promotion, while the few who objected to sex with the senior attorney were soon persuaded by a look at their security profiles.

Celestine stood up and turned abruptly toward the closet.

"Let me know your decision before five tomorrow," MacVain said.

She did not look or respond.

The closet door snapped open to his voice command.

As he watched her put on her jacket, he reflected that virginity is not a strong selling point in a woman her age, and he was not about to chase her around the desk. The silly bitch even prayed on her knees like a child.

"Hatch open!" he ordered, and the wood panel slid back, revealing the honey-colored foyer and the open hatchway beyond.

Without saying good-bye, Celestine turned, walked into the foyer, and stopped at the top of the ramp, just far enough to break the beam and hold the door ajar. She looked back at Vaughn MacVain.

He studied her with immobile, reptilian eyes.

"I know about the surveillance camera," Celestine said sharply. Then, without another word, she ran down the gangway, the door hissing closed behind her.

MacVain sat watching the closed hatch in disbelief, as if thinking that it might open again. Then he called his secretary.

"That predictive criminality analyst who is serving on task force Wildfire, Celestine Brittle. Put an evaluation in her file," he told her. "Mark her performance 'unsatisfactory.' Also, she's requested a transfer to Dallas—call Personnel and tell them it's been denied."

Then he telephoned Tricia Culhane but was put on hold because the line was busy. As he drummed his fingers impatiently, the past few days scudded by like a hundred-year storm: L-RetroBan disclosures, goddess worshippers, aborted raptures, miraculous reappearances—and now a born-again bitch who didn't appreciate all he had done for her.

"How's the weather in Texas?" Tricia Culhane inquired in her cheerful voice.

"There's a problem with Celestine Brittle," MacVain snarled. "Someone tipped her about some surveillance I ordered—and there's only one person it could have been."

Tricia Culhane saw the guillotine blade rise in its wooden tracks and heard the squeak of steel against wood.

"The surveillance specialist in Laredo," MacVain told her. "I want the place sifted—a complete security evaluation report."

"Yes, sir! I'll do it right away."

Reflections

Vaughn MacVain never gave much thought to the past, except in rare cases when it needed to be revised. For him, the future beckoned, as alluring and seductive as a beautiful woman. And for him, beautiful women were mile posts marking his line of march. Yet the meeting with Celestine Brittle continued to occupy his mind in a new and disturbing way. There was something about her that he did not understand, a problem so undefined as to defy a choice of solution.

He called his personal security officer in the basement bunker.

"Do we keep the surveillance on candidates for Tall Blondes?" MacVain asked.

"Yes, sir," Kincaid gulped.

"On Celestine Brittle?"

"Yes, sir," he gulped again.

"Is there a portfolio?"

"Yes, sir."

For the first time, MacVain opened the file of surveillance videos selected by Cole Kincaid.

Brittle was tall, slim, and blond, just as he liked, but she was not exceptionally attractive. He would not call her beautiful, just conventionally pretty in a cattle country kind of way. There were thousands of women in Texas just like her.

As he watched, a nearly naked Celestine, wet from the shower and wrapped in a towel, ran past the camera and stood in the kitchen talking on the telephone, water running down her limbs and puddling on the tile floor, her buttocks framed in the doorway as if in a painting. She turned and walked slowly through the bedroom, full frontal to the lens, her tiny, pink nipples peeking out over the top of the towel.

In the next scene, Celestine was sitting topless in front of the vanity, her shoulders narrow, her arms even thinner, her firm breasts perfectly shaped, almost too big for her delicate torso. But she was not looking at herself in the mirror. Her eyes were focused on infinity, her mind totally absorbed by something besides her body and its reflection.

MacVain's face hardened in anger and disgust. The surveillance confirmed how right he had been to deny her transfer and downgrade her performance review. Brittle answered to some higher power: such people are unpredictable—and often traitors.

BOOK III

EXTRAORDINARY RENDITION

14

A FINAL SOLUTION

Few people ever see the Chairman. Only cnce, early in his career, did he ever appear on television, and then as a subpoenaed witness in a Congressional incuiry into the Charleston Banking Group. Viewers still remember the arrogant cast of his hairless head, the flippar.t, half-hostile smile, and a paunch with the girth of a truck tire. Since that day he has attended only virtual meetings, and those only in audio mode.

The Chairman called the meeting to order in a disembodied voice as deep as a kettle drum. The virtual images of Vaughn MacVain, Dean Weed, and G. Lyle Acre turned to look at the empty seat in cyberspace.

"We're here to find a solution to the Grazziella problem," the Chairman announced. "Skipper will be joining us shortly. Vaughn, you have the most up-to-date information on the case. Bring us up to speed on this."

The impassive senior attorney morphed into a grim and confident prosecutor.

"Krator took Grazziella into custody before she could talk to the media. But there's no doubt she can compromise our project. She has no memory of the wildfire, but she told the intake officer that she was abducted from a fraternity party and used as a guinea pig in a scientific experiment. So she probably remembers a lot more than she is telling. She is *not* pregnant, by the way. The medical observation ploy is only good for a couple of days—then the public will wonder why she hasn't been reunited with her family."

"Did Krator ever find out how she got two hundred miles from the fire?" Acre asked.

"No. She says she doesn't remember. Krator talked to every winery in Deep Creek valley, but no one reported a vehicle. No Good Samaritan has ever come forward either. But it's a moot point now."

The Chairman cut in: "One World News is proposing a seven-figure advance for her biography—both a book and a miniseries. It would set her up for life."

"I agree that we need to have disinformation out there, but it is not a complete solution in the Grazziella case," MacVain cautioned. "She is already blaming Krator for holding her for medical observation, so I can see her going public with her own version of events, advance or no advance."

"I agree with Vaughn," Acre said. "She's headstrong and resourceful. She won't stay bottled up."

"OK, so we don't buy her story; what is step one?"

"First, I want to bring this group up to date on the situation in California," MacVain announced. "Almaden County Sheriff concluded that there was no crime involved in Grazziella's disappearance, so they closed the case. Somehow, a group of Goddess worshippers obtained the plastic impression of the firefighter's body from the crime lab and are claiming it as proof of her miraculous deliverance from the fire by the Goddess."

General Acre snorted.

Dean Weed looked grave. "Since Duane's speech at the Stockman Hotel, the public sees the Fellowship as rescuing the firefighter. And now she turns out to be a Goddess worshipper. This is a problem."

"How did the public learn that Grazziella is a Goddess worshipper in the first place?" the Chairman asked.

"Her father mentioned the Goddess in a statement on social media," MacVain explained.

"That plastic impression could revitalize the entire Goddess movement in California," the Chairman growled. "We need to nip it in the bud."

"I know," MacVain agreed. "But now that Grazziella is a household name, it greatly limits our choices. Let me review the options."

MacVain tapped an icon, and words appeared as bullets on the virtual desktops of the other participants.

"A short history lesson, gentlemen."

- Raoul Wallenberg
- The Dead Kennedys
- Jack Ruby
- Patty Hearst
- Flight 800
- The Ophelia scenario

"The Soviets didn't kill Raoul Wallenberg—they just disappeared him into the gulag. But if that scenario were applied to Grazziella, it would fuel the rapture speculation all over again. As for the Dead Kennedys, killing her outright would make God's deliverance of the firefighter look flawed. The Jack Ruby solution (crazed member of the public kills her while she's in police custody) would make Krator look incompetent, so that is unacceptable too. The Patty Hearst scenario (brainwashed by her captors until she becomes a willing terrorist)—that would have been a good option if there

305

had been time to paint Grazziella as an eco-terrorist, but now it's too late.

The second-to-last scenario, Flight 800 (putative short circuit ignites explosive vapor, killing all on board)—that's about as convincing as an Elvis sighting. So we're left with the Ophelia scenario."

"Who the hell is Ophelia?" the Chairman asked.

"A woman who goes mad because of her moody lover," MacVain explained. "But post-traumatic stress syndrome will work just as well."

General Acre looked intrigued.

"We announce that Grazziella is traumatized by the fire and has a history of mental illness," MacVain told them. "We let her talk to TV in a controlled interview, letting the public see that she has forgotten all knowledge of the wildfire. They see that all she wants to talk about is a secret government laboratory. Her official biography is released at the same time, hitting the themes of bravery, struggle, determination—and her progressive mental deterioration. That way, if she ever mentions prior events of a controversial nature, people are already predisposed to discount them."

"But if she imagines being made pregnant at a secret government laboratory, then the secret is already out," the Chairman objected.

"Not if she is already perceived by the public as delusional," MacVain countered.

"I still don't see how we get her to sound crazy on TV," Dean Weed wondered.

"Self-revelatory interviews are not a problem. The questions are edited in after the answers we want are recorded in response to other questions. And the live broadcast is simulated," MacVain explained.

"Vaughn, is there video footage of Grazziella's intake process?" the Chairman asked.

"Yes, Krator has got 24/7 from the moment the helicopter picked her up."

"Is there any footage where she talks about the laboratory instead of the fire?" the Chairman prodded.

"I don't think she talks about the fire at all. Just about the laboratory."

"That material could be used to document her confusion and amnesia in the way you suggest," the Chairman said. "But it doesn't address the Goddess problem. Also, there's another factor that's just come up. I've asked Skipper to explain it—he's here now."

The nattily-dressed spin doctor popped up in virtual space. "Gentlemen. Over the past twenty-four hours, One World News has done extensive polling in North America of attitudes towards the missing firefighter. And the results are a little surprising. A majority of the public, sixty-four percent, doubt that Grazziella is being held for medical attention. They think she must have been burned to death in the fire and that Krator faked the rescue."

"*Was* she burned in the fire?" Acre asked.

"No, not a mark on her, except for a few scratches on her arms and legs," MacVain answered.

"I can't believe that God Almighty would allow a Goddess worshipper to pass through the fire untouched," Acre said.

"I agree with Lyle," Dean Weed affirmed.

Van Squint continued: "Among the Fellowship faithful an overwhelming majority (ninety-seven percent) agree with you. They believe that God would not let a Goddess worshipper escape from a fire unscathed."

"Amen," Acre said.

"But most Americans (sixty-eight percent) have no problem with a Goddess worshipper being rescued by God."

Dean Weed looked grave. "You mean to say that more than two thirds of the American people think that God would rescue a Goddess worshipper? What a sad commentary on the spiritual health of the nation."

"Is Krator certain that there are no burns on the firefighter?" the Chairman asked.

"Burns are hard to miss," MacVain said.

"Well, we need to be sure about this, because if she had some burns, it would solve the problem of miraculous deliverance by the Goddess."

MacVain looked skeptical. "It would also compromise miraculous deliverance by the Fellowship."

Van Squint cut in. "Not exactly. Ninety-eight percent of Fellowship members believe that Goddess worshippers will be left behind when the rapture occurs. But some Christian blogs are suggesting that the firefighter was spared by God so she could warn other Goddess worshippers about what is in store for them unless they repent."

"Like a foretaste of hell," Dean Weed clarified.

"Exactly," Van Squint said. "We went back and addressed the hell issue in the polls. We found that ninety-two percent of Fellowship members believe that a foretaste of hell implies some burns. So a burned firefighter would explain why God rescued a Goddess worshipper while explaining why she's being held for medical attention in a burn treatment facility."

Dean Weed brightened: "In the old days, they used to burn witches."

MacVain's steel gray eyes betrayed a glimmer of amused contempt. "Grazziella waved from the helicopter on national TV," he reminded them. "She told her father over the telephone that she was unhurt. Maybe there are other witnesses we don't even know about."

"Perhaps she was burned in areas covered by her clothes?" the Chairman suggested. "Lyle, is that possible?"

"In a state of shock, wearing fire-resistant clothes—burns from radiant heat, leaving the clothing intact? It's been known to happen," Acre replied.

"Remember," MacVain said, "that Krator plans to release her to her family, and she'll be examined by her own doctors, maybe even by terrorist sympathizers. The burns would have to be consistent with being caught in a wildfire."

"A good point," the Chairman noted. "Lyle, how hard would it be to produce burns that could pass the scrutiny of outside examiners?"

"The 888th has the capability. But it would take time to set up."

"Could it be done by Monday?"

"How burned does she have to be?" Acre asked the Chairman.

"She was lying on her stomach, and she had gloves and boots on too. So her face and front look normal. But suppose her legs and backside had been burned real bad?"

"It will be a challenge, but we'll give it our best shot."

"But we still haven't solved the problem of how to keep her quiet," MacVain said. "Suppose she tells her family that she got the burns *after* she was rescued?"

"There's another possibility," Van Squint interjected. "Neuroscience is on the verge of making human memory more like computer memory, so we can erase it or write over it. It can produce a witness who remembers all or only what we want him to, whether it happened or not." He looked at the general. "Can't we use this technology on the firefighter?"

"Like Skipper says there's been real progress in this area," Acre answered. "But the drugs have some reliability problems. It would be better to just speed-up the standard psy-op protocol."

"How long would that take?" the Chairman asked him.

"I think three days is possible."

Van Squint looked around the table summoning support. "A burned Goddess worshipper gives the Fellowship membership exactly what it wants—and what it expects."

"I agree," Dean Weed said.

"The clock is ticking on this medical examination ploy," the Chairman warned. "A burned Grazziella would explain why she was taken to a burn hospital instead of released to her family."

"And it squashes the 'saved-by-the-Goddess' claim once and for all," Van Squint noted.

"A burned, crazy firefighter who rambles on about being taken to a secret government laboratory—who's going believe that?" The Chairman asked rhetorically.

"Why not just announce that she was hospitalized because she was delusional?" MacVain asked.

"Because we want her crazy in three days," Acre explained. "We need real burns to accelerate the psy-op protocol."

"So the burns are essential to making her delusional?" Van Squint asked.

"That's right," Acre said.

"And what about the problem of *keeping* her crazy," the Chairman asked. "Vaughn, does your plan address that issue?"

"Yes, that's already in place. Krator will boost her flashbacks by doctoring her medication after she returns home. Then, once she's out of the news, we gently end her suffering with an overdose of pain killers."

"Trauma from the fire, pain from the burns, lung damage from smoke inhalation," the Chairman summarized. "Why she'll thank us for the overdose," he laughed.

The general and the spin doctor turned to MacVain, who was sitting in silence, alone with his thoughts.

"Well, what do you think?" Van Squint asked.

"It's risky," MacVain said. "But it's probably the best that can be done within the time available."

"Then we have closure on this," the Chairman announced. "Skipper, what do you need?"

"One World News can create the media buzz about the firefighter's condition, both mental and physical. But the Fellowship needs to tell its members about Goddess worshippers getting a foretaste of hell."

"We'll get on it right away," Dean Weed said.

"We don't want Krator's intake records to be a problem down the road," General Acre said.

"The intake photos will be changed retroactively to show she was burned in the wildfire," MacVain assured him. "But Krator will need to be copied with the burn photos from Special Ops."

"You'll get them," the general said.

"So we have a plan," the Chairman said with enthusiasm. "Special Ops will teach the tree hugger the danger of her line of work, the Fellowship will emphasize a foretaste of hell to the rank and file, and One World News will hammer the public about the firefighter's burns and delusions. Any other issues?"

No one responded.

"Krator will transfer the firefighter into the custody of Special Ops immediately."

15

MORAL COURAGE

Celestine went straight from the airport to her apartment. Then, with a furtive glance at the vanity, she stripped off her clothes and packed them in a plastic bag to take to the dry cleaners. She jumped into the shower, lathering herself several times and letting the hot water flow into every pore.

She dressed in newly laundered clothes and turned on the television, but there was still no word that Kelly had been re-united with her family, only a video reprise of yesterday's dramatic rescue by helicopter, followed by the announcement that the firefighter was being held for medical observation in a Krator medevac facility near Sacramento, California.

Until the encounter on MacVain's airplane, Celestine Brittle had wondered whether the firefighter's baby was the result of drunkenness at a fraternity party or the progeny of a serial rapist—but now there was a third explanation that accounted for the cover-up of a date-rape case and an adoption agency that did not exist. As much as the conclusion frightened her, its logic was inescapable: Kelly Grazziella had been an incubator for one of MacVain's babies.

She thought of the questions she wished she had asked MacVain on his executive jet—questions that a short time ago would have been interpreted as natural curiosity but now would be unlawful investigation of a classified project. Where does the sperm come from? What happens to the babies? Do the birth mothers get to keep them? Are some adopted out?

She called Agent Profumo, the former narcotics cop in the Sacramento office. He picked up right away.

"Yeah," a gruff voice answered.

"This is Celestine Brittle again. I am trying to learn something off the record."

There was a pregnant pause.

"I am worried about Kelly Grazziella. There has been no word from her since she was picked up by the medevac helicopter yesterday afternoon. I am trying to find out where she is."

"Is she a friend of yours?" he asked.

"No, but I don't like it when they mess with our firefighters."

"I can't help you. The Air Rescue Wing reports direct to Colorado Springs."

"Nothing classified, of course, but anything, anything at all would help," she pleaded.

"I've got nothing," he insisted. "But say hello to Angelina for me," he told her, hanging up.

She wondered if Profumo had confused her with somebody else.

As she worried about Kelly, the events of the past replayed in her mind, but they always returned to the acrimonious meeting with MacVain on his executive jet. She remembered holding the door open, then the stare of his sinister, reptilian eyes. Her stomach churned at the thought of returning to her cubicle at the Predictive Criminality Center—she never wanted to see it again. Fortunately, Tricia had told her supervisor not to her expect her back at work until Monday.

Celestine decided to re-examine the entire Grazziella case from the beginning, thinking there might be facts she had overlooked in her innocence.

She typed a search string into her browser:

+oscuridad +"West Ridge Road"

She got hundreds of pages, most of them related to the recent fire, and scrolled through them absentmindedly, hoping for something she did not know. Suddenly, a name leaped out at her, a name she recognized from the pre-indite she had prepared for the Wildfire task force: "Ridgeline Castles, L.L.C." She recalled that it was one of the two buyers of the Grazziella farm, the other being Indian Springs Winery. The link was to an old article from the *Oscuridad Tribune*:

> Gallery owner adds French hill town look to gated community

Celestine read that Ridgeline Castles had gone into partnership with The Glass Nativity Gallery to make its condo clusters look more like the medieval hill towns of France. The architectural ambience would be designed by Titania Troy, the founder of the well-known art gallery chain, while Ridgeline Castles would translate her concepts into stucco and steel. There was also a photograph of Titania Troy, a tall, blond woman standing on the slope above the road where Kelly had disappeared, at one of the projected building sites for the fortified condos. As the gallery owner told the Oscuridad Optimists over lunch:

> The architecture of southern France is adapted to a sunny, Mediterranean climate like we have in California; like us it evolved under the cloud of constant Islamic threat.

Judging from the architect's rendering published by the *Oscuridad Tribune*, evolution in that epoch had selected for crenallated half-round towers that were as aesthetically indefensible as they were physically impregnable.

Although Titania Troy and Kelly Grazziella had apparently never met, they seemed to have bobbed along in the same river, separated in time but swept in the same direction by the current. Both had drifted into the Nathan Whyte Laboratory, and both had stood on the same hillside in Oscuridad within a quarter of a mile of each other.

As she tried to put the pieces together, her attention was disrupted by the ringing of the telephone. She flashed on that morning's anonymous letter warning her about the hidden surveillance. She picked up the phone as if it might bite.

"Is Angelina there?" a gravelly voice asked, a commingling of cigarette smoke and bad attitude that reminded her of Agent Profumo. He had used the name Angelina.

Celestine played along, affecting a convincing calm. "No, I don't know where she is or when she'll be back."

"I heard she went to Matamoros," the man said.

"Matamoros," Celestine repeated. "Would you like to leave a message?"

"Forget it," the man snarled. "She won't be coming home."

Celestine knew that Matamoros was situated across the Rio Grande from Brownsville, Texas, not far from the Gulf of Mexico. From the Internet she learned that many factories had relocated there in order to circumvent environmental laws and labor unions in the United States. Now, it was a city of over half a million people, most living in shanty towns without clean water or sewage treatment. From the Krator database she learned that Matamoros is also the location of an extraordinary rendition site—a secret prison where American citizens are held indefinitely without charges.

Celestine realized she was in a race against time.

* * *

315

Celestine phoned her colleague Ziggy, the senior analyst in the tax investigation section. "I need some quick information on a company," she told the affable number cruncher.

"What company?"

"Ridgeline Castles, L.L.C., in California."

"I've got it on screen." There was a pause of thirty seconds that seemed like as many minutes. "Boy, this company is dynamite!" he exclaimed. "What have they got?—a money machine?"

"Better. They build fortified condos in California," she informed him.

"Last year, before-tax revenues of three billion and change, all in California."

"All in California?"

"No foreign income at all," he told her.

"You're sure there's no connection to Mexico?"

"No business at all in Mexico," he confirmed.

"Darn, I was looking for a thread to pull on," she said. "I was so sure that they had some connections outside the country."

"Hang on." He did some more exploring. "Will a tax credit do? They gave money to a charity for the past three years, Universal Medicine Foundation. It's a medical organization in Switzerland.

"How much was the donation?"

"A half a million each year."

"Is that a lot or a little?"

"You gotta be kidding! On revenues of three billion dollars plus a year? And it's their *only* charitable contribution!" he laughed. "Mother Teresa they're not."

"Really?" Celestine was intrigued by a charity that could get such scrooges to give anything at all.

From the charity's Web page, she learned that Universal Medicine Foundation is a respected practitioner of scientific population control. From its headquarters in Switzerland, it sponsors projects in Africa and Latin America, where it distributes free contraceptives to the poor. In Mexico these charitable projects are handled by a Latin American subsidiary, MEDUSA. The subsidiary has its headquarters in Mexico's industrial north, in the city of Monterrey, where it opened free clinics that provide maternity care for unwed mothers.

Celestine called the toll-free telephone number for information, and the call was answered by a pleasant woman in Bangalore, India.

"I see you are calling from the United States," the representative told Celestine. "May I ask what state?"

"Texas."

"Ah, Texas. Since Universal Medicine began opening free contraceptive clinics in Mexico, we have had phenomenal support among Texans. A supporting membership costs only fifty dollars a year," the woman told Celestine.

"I am interested especially in corporate contributions, say a company that wants to offset income with a contribution to charity."

"Yes. Universal Medicine is registered with the IRS for tax-exempt donations in the United States. But you will need to talk to the corporate donations officer. He is in Switzerland. It is after closing time in Europe, but it is possible he is still there. Let me transfer you."

The corporate donations officer spoke perfect English with a slight German inflection. Celestine told him that her uncle had a construction business in Texas and that he had long advocated distributing free contraceptives to Mexicans. She wondered if it would be possible to obtain a corporate charitable contribution by making a donation to Medicina Universal South America.

"Certainly," he assured her. "We do it all the time for American businesses."

"Is there a minimum level of support?" Celestine asked.

"Ten thousand dollars is the minimum donation—there is the expense of accounting, tax forms, and such," he explained. "Most of our donors are professional corporations—doctors, lawyers, and the like. May I ask what amount your uncle has in mind?"

"Would five hundred thousand dollars be considered large?"

"Yes, it would be very generous. May I have your uncle's name?"

"My uncle would not want his name given as a potential donor before he has had a chance to study the prospectus."

"Oh, yes, I understand perfectly. May I ask how you learned about our organization?"

"Through one of your donors—Ridgeline Castles, L.L.C., in California."

"Did they contribute recently?"

"For the last three years.

"As a corporate contributor?" he sounded perplexed. "I am not familiar with that one." There was a hint of suspicion in his voice.

"Perhaps it is under another name?" Celestine suggested. "Titania Troy?"

"Oh! Why of course," he exclaimed, his voice resuming its sycophantic smoothness. "Please tell your uncle that when he is ready to make his donation, he should call me directly. I will give him a bank account number where he can wire the money and a PIN he can use to obtain any tax credit verification. Also—very important—tell him to be sure to mention Titania's name when he calls me so the money gets properly credited."

"I certainly will."

"Also, inform your uncle that his donation will be earmarked for the Mexican program and that the minimum donation at this level is for a half a million dollars a year."

"Thank you. That answers my question."

Celestine sat back and reflected on what she had learned. Even though Titania Troy's first husband Nathan Whyte was long dead, she was still interested in reproductive issues and had probably assembled a substantial group of anonymous backers for Medicina Universal's free contraceptive program in Mexico, each contributing half a million dollars a year. The Swiss charity also confirmed the connection between Mexico and Titania Troy—but not the connection Celestine had expected. Not the central highlands of Mexico with its colonial architecture and pre-Columbian monuments but the squalid shantytowns and *maquiladoras* of the northern desert and borderland, a world as far from French castles and Californian wineries as it is possible to get.

The telephone rang again—she thought it might be Profumo calling back.

"Celestine Brittle?" a deep baritone voice asked. It was not anyone she recognized.

"Who is calling, please?" she inquired.

"Am I speaking with Celestine Brittle?"

"Yes."

"This is Krator counter-espionage. Could you call me on a secure line so I can confirm your identity." He gave her his phone number.

She steeled herself, then returned the call by computer in audio-only.

"This is a routine inquiry," the agent explained. "I need to confirm that it was you, Celestine Brittle, who asked the department of tax investigation to search a target. The target's name is Ridgeline Castles, L.L.C."

"Yes, that was me," Celestine admitted.

"Were you asked to do that by a superior?"

"I was asked to investigate a classified matter by Tricia Culhane, special assistant to senior attorney Vaughn MacVain. I am on special assignment."

"Special assignment to Tricia Culhane. I see." His tone of voice confirmed that he had all that he needed to know. "Will the special assistant confirm that?"

"She's taken a long weekend. I don't know if she will be responding to routine inquires before next week," Celestine replied with an airy self-confidence that she did not know she had.

"I will leave her a voice mail," the agent said, his mind already onto the next tripwire. "Thank you for your cooperation. Enjoy your weekend."

Celestine sat for a moment in stunned silence. The call from counter-espionage confirmed that Ridgeline Castles was more than a condominium developer—it was also deeply connected to Krator.

* * *

Celestine logged on to the national medical database and searched on the name "Wassily Tweecus." She had been thinking of him in terms of civil genetics and resonant DNA, but when she read his bibliography she learned that he had also done basic research on implanted embryos. She followed the links and learned about blastocysts and fertility drugs, about the increased incidence of multiple births, and the special problems of identical siblings. She learned how Christian fundamentalists had adopted the hundreds of thousands of surplus embryos produced by fertility laboratories, keeping them alive in cryogenic facilities until that future time when God found them welcoming wombs.

She thought of her uncle in Midland with his obsession with racial purity. That explained everything about him— his hatred of Blacks, his outspoken opposition to Mexican immigration, and even his religious conviction that God had bifurcated the human race into the chosen few and the multitude of the damned. She decided to call him—they had not spoken in a couple of months. She made herself comfortable in the one upholstered chair and telephoned her deceased father's brother.

He was delighted to hear from his niece. They talked about family for awhile, then the diminishing prosperity of Texas and the uncertainties of the construction business and the interminable war in the Middle East. He asked Celestine about her job, and she told him of her dashed hopes of getting transferred to Dallas. Then she asked him the question for which she had called him.

"Maybe you have a suggestion," she said. "Suppose a friend wanted to adopt a White baby, and only a White baby. Is there an adoption agency that could get them what they want?"

"Why, Celestine," her uncle said, in a tone that accorded her new respect. "Your friend wants Three Kids Christian Adoption Agency in St. Petersburg, Florida. They do good work."

Celestine looked up the agency on the Web. The 3Kids agency found homes for orphans from the former Soviet Union, and all of the pictures showed fair-haired, blue-eyed children, many of them identical twins and triplets. The company had branch offices in Denver, Dallas, and Sacramento. The Sacramento office was located in the business park at Krieger Field, not far from the Krator Air Rescue Wing. Celestine clicked the "getting there" page, which provided a road map and a photograph of the medical-dental building that housed the adoption agency. It was decorated with faux half-round towers with crenellated tops—Titania Troy's unmistakable aesthetic.

But she needed to confirm it. Any children coming into the United States from Russia would have been issued digital identities, and it was a simple matter to search the immigration database for Russian immigrants less than one year old and to spew out a list of the legal entities involved in their adoption. But suppose there was a tripwire? She decided to formulate a generic query that left out the name "3Kids." Carefully, she asked for a list of children from Europe adopted during the past year, under one year of age, sorted by adoption agency.

Instantly, the system displayed a long list of adoptions, headed by the only agency whose name begins with a numeral. Last year, a mere half dozen Russian babies were handled by 3Kids, barely enough to justify the claim made on their Web site.

"A *real* phony adoption agency in Sacramento!" she whispered to herself.

* * *

Celestine spent all afternoon consolidating her research findings. She recorded whatever information she remembered from the meetings of task force Wildfire and combined it with facts gleaned from the Krator databases. The more she worked, the more she appreciated the magnitude of the evidence she had acquired, much of it until now a collection of unrelated facts: Titania Troy's first marriage to the founder of the Nathan Whyte Laboratory; Chad Weed's date-rape case; the censoring of Agent Profumo's report about that case; the fact that Kelly's tenure at Davis overlapped with that of Wassily Tweecus and Chad Weed; the phony adoption agency and the sudden death of the other two mothers; Profumo's off-the-cuff statement that Kelly had been sent to Matamoros; Titania's connection to Ridgeline Castles and Medicina Universal Sudamerica; the mysterious 3Kids adoption agency with its de facto White-supremacist policies; and Domestic Surveillance's own confirmation that Ridgeline Castles was a Krator front company—these interconnections were beyond coincidence. And they clearly showed why Vaughn MacVain wanted Kelly Grazziella dead.

* * *

322

Celestine needed to talk with someone about her experience with the senior attorney, but to do so would be treason. She decided to call Amadeus, the minister she had never met—but not on her own telephone.

She went to the manager's office on the ground floor of her building.

"I'm having trouble with my telephone," she explained., making an excuse for stopping by. "Would you mind if I made a private call on your phone?"

"Go right ahead." He got up and busied himself in back on some pretext.

Celestine summoned her courage and dialed the office of Amadeus's church. Until now, they had communicated only by e-mail, primarily about prophecy and the book of Revelation.

A man answered.

"Is this Amadeus?" she asked in an anxious voice.

There was a startled silence—she did not know that no one at the church knew him by that name, as he kept his pastoral and Internet personalities distinct.

"Who is inquiring?" the man asked cautiously.

"This is Celestine Brittle."

"Why, Celestine, what a pleasure!"

"Something happened that is very disturbing," she told Amadeus. "I need spiritual counseling, and I don't want to go to the Fellowship for that."

"You can come by now if you'd like," he said. "To the church office."

Amadeus's office was in a rambling, pre-World War II house next door to a steepled church that dated from the mid-twentieth century. It was located in a racially-mixed neighborhood in an old part of town. As she climbed the well-worn steps to a weathered but spacious verandah, a heavy-set, middle-aged man opened the faded front door, now protected by a heavy, iron grate, and unlocked the deadbolt.

He did not look like a clergyman.

A figure appeared behind him. "You must be Celestine!"

Amadeus was much younger than Celestine imagined. On the Internet, she thought of him as an elderly college professor with silver hair and a rumpled sweater. In real life, he was a dark-eyed, handsome man, perhaps in his late twenties, with the soft-spoken courtesy of the Old South. Celestine could not help but notice his sensual fingers and the absence of a wedding band. A pianist's fingers, she thought.

Amadeus turned to the volunteer who was helping him lay out the Sunday bulletin. "My unscheduled consultation has arrived."

"Take your time," the middle-aged man said.

Amadeus led Celestine into the adjacent parlor. Some years ago, when half the church's congregation had left to join the Fellowship of the Eighth Dispensation, the administrative offices were moved to the ground floor of the pastor's house and the parlor was converted to an informal meeting room. It was comfortably furnished with upholstered armchairs and a built-in bookcase that filled an entire wall. He closed the sliding glass doors to ensure privacy.

Celestine Brittle sat down in one of the arm chairs. She was conservatively dressed in a tailored jacket, minimal jewelry, and a dark skirt that showed her slim but shapely legs. Her glossy blond hair reflected highlights from the ceiling lamp. Her face was angular and serious.

Amadeus sat down opposite her, separated by a narrow coffee table.

"I work for Krator as a research analyst," she began. "This gives me access to classified information, some of it at a very high level. I know what my legal responsibilities are. I need clarification of my Christian duty."

She looked carefully at Amadeus—he had kind and sympathetic eyes that made her want to tell him everything.

"When I went to work for Krator, I signed a non-disclosure agreement, under penalty of treason, that clamped a lid on virtually anything that happens at work. I thought nothing of it at the time, but now I realize that what holds the system together is that it has stolen everyone's stories. The most important experiences of your life are locked in a database, never to be read by anyone," she said sadly.

She felt betrayed by the organization that had taken almost four years of her life, but that feeling was still too new to put into words. In the peacefulness of the ecclesiastical setting, she was able to compose her thoughts for the first time.

Amadeus waited patiently.

"Then, this morning, something happened."

She wanted to tell him about MacVain's secret breeding program and the police report on a serial rapist that had been deleted from the Wildfire database. She also wanted to confide her concern about Kelly Grazziella. Especially her fears about Kelly—but she dared not.

Amadeus noted her anxious, far-away look and thought she was concerned about nondisclosure. "Tell me as much as possible about the situation without any details that might compromise you legally. Were you asked to lie?"

"Never. But I provide information that is used by others to create a false impression."

"Did you know it would be used that way?"

"Four years ago, no, but now I know what is done with what I do. I feel guilty for not having done something before now."

"Awareness takes a while. Certainly, there must be occasions when the information you provide contributes to justice?"

"Sometimes it probably does—but only because it is more expedient to do it that way."

Amadeus smiled at her cynicism. "And today you were asked to provide information that would run counter to justice?" he wondered.

"No, the main problem is not what I have been asked to do—but what I *ought* to do, given what I know now." She stiffened like a deer in the headlights, her face turning away from him, blank with fear.

Amadeus waited a moment, then moved the conversation in a new direction. "How did you happen to go to work for Krator?"

"In college, I was approached by a recruiter. It was a small, conservative, Christian college. He urged me to take the Krator exam, so I did, and got the highest grade in the school. The highest in Texas, actually." She was not bragging, just recounting the facts.

"I went to work for Krator because I wanted to serve justice. Now I realize that what I'm doing is a sham. That's why I wanted to talk to you."

Her words sounded logical and articulate, but inside she felt incoherent and tongue-tied.

"You want to know what God wants you to do?"

"Yes," relieved that he asked the question for her.

"Today you learned something that frightened you?"

She nodded yes, wanting to tell him what it was—though she did not dare.

"Something you can't tell anyone legally?"

"I am afraid of what I know!" she blurted out. "Does God give courage?" she asked plaintively, meeting his eyes. "I feel like the cowardly lion."

"There's natural courage and God-given courage," he told her. "Natural courage is a lioness defending her cubs. God's courage is the courage of conviction. The courage needed to do the right thing even if everyone calls you a fool."

"That's the courage that I lack," she said forcefully, fending off the emptiness that threatened to swallow her up.

"The gifts of moral courage and discernment are on God's timetable, not ours," Amadeus said.

She noticed the glint of his opalescent eyes in the light of the reading lamp. She felt his kindness and acceptance.

"What if someone's life were in danger because of my cowardice?"

"God does not ask us to act through fear and anxiety but through courage and conviction."

"When I joined Krator, I swore an oath to uphold the government of the United States and to enforce its laws. Now, I feel that Krator has betrayed my trust, but I'm stuck because I swore an oath of loyalty."

Amadeus's eyes met hers. "In taking an oath, we ask God to be a witness to the truth of what we say. Did you swear to uphold the Constitution of the United States?"

"I did."

"Did you swear to oppose all enemies both foreign and domestic?"

"I did."

"In an oath, we ask God to witness our commitment to ideals. Did you swear to uphold lies, false imprisonment, and torture?"

Celestine made no reply for no reply was needed.

"For Krator, oaths are just another way of silencing its critics," Amadeus added "They think oaths are for suckers."

Celestine felt like the weight of the world had just been lifted from her shoulders.

"You have more to tell me," he said in a calm yet professional voice.

Her words came out in a torrent. "I know where the missing firefighter is—Kelly Grazziella. They are sending her to a rendition base in Matamoros. I know why she is being silenced too." She paused, wondering if it was safe to go on. His eyes were deep pools drawing her in. "Kelly knows about a secret breeding program to make a race of geniuses through genetic engineering. If I don't do something right away, they will kill her."

"My God," Amadeus said.

"You said that God does not ask us to act out of fear and anxiety but from courage and conviction."

"That's true."

"I feel that conviction now," she said in a calm but resolute voice. "Can you help me?"

"To do what?"

"I am going to tell the world what I know. I have written it up and put it on a server, where it will be automatically distributed over the Internet with a single command."

"My God," Amadeus said. "You are serious."

"I am," Celestine assured him.

"Before you do this, you need to make sure it is the right thing to do," Amadeus said with concern. "You need to pray like you've never prayed before."

"Believe me, I have prayed."

"As a spiritual advisor, I cannot counsel a course of action that will almost certainly result in your death."

"I am willing to take that risk."

"If you sacrifice yourself and they kill Grazziella anyway, what have you actually accomplished? They will torture you to find out who else you told this to and execute you as a traitor."

Celestine looked away, her face stark white, her body stiff with fear. She felt the hope and self-confidence draining out of her.

"When I talked to God about telling the world the truth, that's when I felt the sense of confidence and commitment," she said in an anguished voice. She looked again at Amadeus. "Surely those feelings come from God."

"Surely they do. My concern is that you think that telling the truth is something that you can do as a lone voice on the Internet. Those days are past—and Krator will silence you before anyone hears your words.

"To save Kelly you will need the help of others—people with access to the worldwide media, people who can authenticate what you say, people who can protect you from Krator's wrath."

Her terrified eyes searched his. "But where do I find them?"

I will introduce you to them," he said.

"You can do that?"

"Yes. I have a direct link to people who can help you save Kelly. But right now you can help Kelly best by being her eyes and ears inside of Krator."

Celestine leaned across the table and took Amadeus's hands in hers.

Her fingers were as fragile as sparrow wings.

She held him for a long moment, then released him and sat upright, suddenly calm.

"Let's take a moment to pray for guidance," Amadeus said.

Celestine bowed her head.

"Lord God, our creator and our strength. Your daughter Celestine asks the gift of moral courage. Give her strength. Give her hope. Give her faith and self-confidence. Give her the wisdom to make good choices. God of justice, hear our prayer."

In the succeeding moment of silence, Celestine felt the presence of Jesus, so palpable she could almost touch him.

Coyote III

Sometime after midnight, Celestine fell into a deep sleep and dreamed again of the coyote. This time, the animal was a tour guide, wearing a blue and white baseball cap, and Celestine was following him through the streets of Laredo in a red double-decker bus, like they have in London. The tour started at the Krator Predictive Criminality Center in North Laredo, then led through a maze of streets in the old town to the bridges across the Rio Grande, where Celestine had never been. Then, the tour bus vanished, and she was walking in a grassy field somewhere with Amadeus. It was spring time and the field was filled with white blossoms, but it was on the edge of a steep river bank, which made her afraid. Then Amadeus took her hand in his and led her to the edge of the precipice so she could look down at the raging river below. To her surprise, what she thought was a torrent of white water were two shallow ponds where children were playing.

16

THE BURNING

It is time to hold disaffected minorities accountable to the will of the majority. For those of us who have devoted our lives to preserving freedom at great personal sacrifice to ourselves, that means curtailing the irresponsible accusations of those who would undermine our American way of life. We do it reluctantly, but do it we must.

Vaughn MacVain, Graduation address, Academy of Criminal Justice, Quantico, Virginia

Kelly Grazziella pretended to be asleep when the rendition team came to get her. She had been meditating for perhaps hours, reducing her heart rate as well as the flow of blood to her wrists.

"She ought to be awake by now," a woman said.

The man took Kelly's arm and felt her pulse.

"She's not. But she's scheduled for another sedation."

"That's your call," the woman said.

Without injecting her again, several pairs of hands lifted her onto a gurney, looped restraints around her wrists, and rolled her away. Whenever she thought that no one was looking, she opened one eye to catch a glimpse of her surroundings. She was moving through a windowless corridor, like the transport ramps that connect buildings in medical centers.

The movement stopped. Two orderlies, dressed in baggy hospital garb, were standing together at the front of the gurney waiting for something. Kelly stole a look around. She was in an aircraft hangar. A white executive jet waited nearby, its doors open and a mobile ramp wheeled into position. It had no identifying marks that she could see except for its fleet number, 289.

Kelly heard the sound of shuffling feet. Only a few meters away, a dozen people, of both sexes and all races, chained together at the waist and wearing orange smocks and black, eyeless hoods that covered their heads completely, were being pulled by a single guard with a leash. Their wrists were clamped together behind them with shackles, while chains between their ankles forced them to walk in tiny doll-like steps. It looked like a scene from Dante's *Inferno*.

"All set," a man shouted, and Kelly closed her eyes. She felt herself being pushed up the ramp and onto the plane. She felt the gurney being latched into place. She heard the whoosh of a curtain being closed around her. She heard the footfalls of the orderlies vanish. She opened her eyes.

She was aware of something swirling above her head, and she had to concentrate to determine what it was. It was the sort of mobile that mothers hang above children's cribs—a pink plastic angel on a spring.

* * *

After a flight that seemed like days, Kelly felt the plane descend. She heard the wheels go down and was jolted by the tell-tale bump of the touchdown. Only when they taxied on the tarmac did she feel the full force of her predicament. Her stomach began to churn and her mind began to race. Were they going to torture her to find out what she knew about the Nathan Whyte Laboratory?

Someone put a sack over her head, then unlatched the gurney and pushed her down the ramp. The air was hotter than California and much more humid. Her hospital gown stuck to her skin.

"Is this the firefighter?" a man's voice asked.

Kelly thought it sounded familiar. A voice from the past that she had wanted to forget.

"That's her," the orderly confirmed.

The familiar voice spoke again. "Let me see her face."

Kelly turned clammy with fear—it was Chad Weed!

"No," the orderly said. "It's against regulations."

"This way," a third man said.

Kelly was bumped over an uneven pavement as a plane was taking off nearby. Suddenly it turned cooler and darker—an air-conditioned building. Kelly felt chilled in her flimsy hospital gown. She desperately wanted to urinate but had refused to go in the diaper they had put on her at the hospital.

Suddenly, she felt the jab of a needle.

When she awoke, her hood and shackles had been removed; she was lying on a built-in bunk in a small, windowless cell with an exposed toilet.

Chad Weed was nowhere to be seen.

* * *

Through the tinted windows of his office overlooking the main runway, general G. Lyle Acre and his adjutant watched the aircraft carrying Kelly Grazziella taxi across the apron and disappear into the intake hangar.

The adjutant was a taut, physically-fit man in his mid-thirties with cold blue eyes and a rigid bearing. He washed his hands at least two times an hour, and he emanated an aromatic fragrance from frequent applications of after-shave lotion. He was wearing starched, camouflage fatigues with the inconspicuous lapel pin that conveyed rank to the brigade's inner circle. Unlike the regular military, no one wore name tags in the no-name brigades.

The general told his adjutant how One World News had to alter the interview with the firefighter when she was rescued by the Krator helicopter, changing "Goddess" to "God" in the interest of public decency.

"It's disgusting," his adjutant agreed, "claiming the Goddess saved her."

"She really is a Goddess worshipper," Acre said contemptuously.

"But with God's help, we can fix that," the adjutant assured him. "The plans are almost finalized. But I still need to make a personal assessment of the firefighter and evaluate the results of the burn tests."

"I'll see you here at one o'clock," Acre told him.

As the adjutant left, the general's administrative assistant appeared in the doorway. "Chad Weed, senior Krator investigator, is here to see you," the soldier informed him.

"*Senior* investigator. An older man, is he?" the general asked wryly.

"No, sir, very young for his position."

"I am sure he is highly qualified. Send him in."

"What a pleasure to see you again, general," Chad Weed said enthusiastically, extending his hand.

"Likewise," G. Lyle Acre said cordially, his hands remaining at his sides.

Chad Weed was just like the general remembered him, with the same supercilious smile and look-at-me swagger.

"I heard that you successfully engaged targets one and two. Good work," Acre told him.

Chad Weed looked at him as if no other outcome were possible to contemplate.

"Target three is going to be the subject in a simulated wildfire this afternoon, and I want your help with that," the general told him.

"Krator is happy to assist the 888th."

"Also, your senior investigator status has been terminated. I'll take your Krator ID and have it destroyed."

Chad Weed handed him the badge.

"My adjutant will contact you when everything is ready," the general said, dismissing him.

As soon as Chad Weed had left, the general called MacVain in Colorado Springs.

"I've got good news," he told the senior attorney. "Your package arrived. And Chad Weed has volunteered to assist this afternoon. But it's a dangerous exercise. He could suffer fatal injuries from smoke inhalation and burns."

"I am sure his father will be proud if his son dies in the service of his country," MacVain replied.

* * *

"Where are we in the plan?" Acre asked the adjutant.

"I've had a radiant heat generator flown in from the Afghan proving grounds, along with the technicians to operate it. It arrived early this morning. It's powered by an array of propane torches, with a metal reflector that allows the heat to be directed onto a target area with great precision. First and second degree burns can be produced by only few seconds of exposure while leaving flame-resistant clothing intact (though in some cases with a little discoloration of the fabric). Radiant burns look different depending on the fabric used, so the subject will have to be wearing her own uniform. I had some extra firefighter suits flown in to fine-tune the parameters."

He showed Acre photos of a dozen women prisoners who had been serving as guinea pigs. They were wearing firefighter uniforms and were lying face-down in a row with their hands shackled behind them. Their pants and undergarments had been pulled down to reveal naked buttocks disfigured by prominent burns.

"Look at the detail in that burn pattern!" the adjutant said with enthusiasm, pointing to red and pink stripes of different intensity. "In the tests, we used a sharp-edged test pattern to highlight differences due to the fabric. But when we run the firefighter, we'll program the machine with a statistical mean from real wildfires, so the burns will look natural."

Acre nodded in satisfaction. "And when will it be tested on the star witness?"

"As soon as we get her firefighter's uniform. It's being flown in from Krieger Field and should arrive in about an hour."

"Have you made a personal evaluation of her?"

"She's a hard nut," the adjutant noted. "A runner. A rock climber. A firefighter. But her pre-indite says she's lived most of her life within five miles of where she was born. That's the key that unlocks her door: destroy that safe haven in her mind and everything else is up for grabs."

"What's your plan to do that?"

"First, make her believe that her father and brother have betrayed her."

The adjutant paused, thinking back to his days in southern Mexico where such tasks were so much easier to do. "We don't have time to do the real thing. But PsyOps is preparing an audio simulation of their voices. Second, convince her she'll be burned to death in a wildfire."

"How do we do that?"

"On the artillery range we're building an exact replica of the wildfire site at Indian Springs. The idea is to make her relive the experience, then ratchet up the trauma with real burns."

"So she'll think she's back in the real wildfire."

"Yes, to break the boundary between memory and reality."

"Can we get lasting results in such a short time?" the general worried.

"PsyOps thinks it's possible by combining the brush fire, the betrayal, and the burns. Then we follow up with the usual drugs."

"I hope PsyOps has called this one right," Acre confided. "If there are any glitches let me know right away."

* * *

Chad Weed took a swig from a Dr Pepper that he had filched from the general's personal refrigerator. It is all too pat, he said to himself—Acre flying me to this godforsaken place just to help burn Grazziella! The simulated wildfire site is off-limits to all personnel without the permission of the commanding officer. Nobody will be happening by. Once the firefighter's out of the way, then only Tweecus and I will know what happened in the laboratory that night. And then there will be only one.

As he watched, two bulldozers shaped a mound of earth into a replica of the hillside above Indian Springs Winery while a gang of laborers with hand tools scoured out a ravine that exactly matched the one above the Italian-Swiss Monument where Kelly had been caught by the blaze. Trucks brought in thick bundles of dried brush, while ground crews arranged them in two rows that converged at the top like an inverted letter "V."

The general's adjutant was consulting with the pyrotechnic engineer when G. Lyle Acre drove up in his Hummer.

"Walk me through the setup," Acre told the adjutant, jumping out of the vehicle.

"We've re-created the physical conditions of the wildfire," the adjutant replied. "The engineers worked from photographs and diagrams from the arson report from the California Department of Disaster Response. The height and slope are the same as the embankment on the fire road at the site of Monday's wildfire." He pointed to some massive industrial fans. "We've replicated the wind conditions too."

The general's face showed a glint of enthusiasm.

"What will be the extent of her injuries?"

"First and second degree burns, backside only, from boot tops to waistline."

"There can't be any burns on her face and hands," the general said, reminding him that she had already appeared on TV.

"She'll be wearing insulated gloves and a breathing hood," the adjutant assured him. "To get maximal precision, the burns will be produced by the radiant heat generator, not by the fire. The fire is just for believability in the psy-war phase."

"But suppose the fire gets too hot. Is there a way of getting her out in a hurry? She needs to be able to stand, maybe walk off a plane."

"She'll be surrounded with thermal sensors." the adjutant assured him. "If any one of them reaches a critical safety value, sprinklers will douse the flames. With this arrangement, Krator can announce with confidence that the firefighter was burned in a brushfire."

The general chuckled to himself. For once, Vaughn MacVain will be telling the truth.

* * *

There were no windows in Kelly's cell, and the lights were kept on continuously, so she had no way of knowing how much time had elapsed since she had been taken off the airplane. An active, outdoors person, she felt like a laboratory rat when cut off from the wind and weather.

Suddenly, the cell door opened, and a man wearing a black ski mask brought in the rucksack that Kelly had carried on her visit to the Goddess. Two other guards were standing in the doorway ready to intercede. At the sight of something so familiar, the week's events came surging back, reminding her that there was still a world outside. She remembered being taken off the bus by the sheriff's deputies, being seized by the policeman with the handlebar mustache, and waking up in a hospital gown with her limbs fastened to the bed. She wondered where she was now.

"Get dressed!" the soldier ordered, opening the rucksack and pulling out her firefighter's uniform. He slammed the cell door behind him.

Kelly leaped at the familiar clothes, shedding the baggy prison smock. She was delighted to be back in her cargo pants and sturdy boots. Her badge and name tag were still in the flap pocket. If they planned to torture her, she told herself, they would not have given her back her firefighting uniform.

The Search

Giovanni usually slept late on Saturday mornings, but he had agreed to meet Joe Grazziella at the CDDR station where Kelly worked. When the alarm went off, the morning sun was already pouring through the venetian blinds, illuminating a photo of Kelly waving from the rescue helicopter. He liked to think that she was waving to him.

At the fire station, Joe Grazziella was talking with a steely, gray-haired man with the posture of a marine.

"Giovanni, this is Kelly's boss."

"Call me Jim," the fire captain said, crushing Giovanni's hand. "Joe told me how much you helped with the search."

"Jim has been a great help too," Joe Grazziella said, gesturing at a canary-yellow pickup truck parked in front of the office. "I told him that Krator bugged our conversation, so he suggested we use his truck today."

It was a 1958 Chevrolet Apache step-side pickup; its engine had been built before "smog" became a household word.

"Is that thing legal?" Giovanni asked.

"It's registered as a vintage car, and I've had it declared an alternate fire-fighting vehicle by CDDR so it can go anywhere. I rebuilt the engine myself. Go ahead, take a look inside."

Giovanni opened the door to a formidable array of electronics.

"It has police-band radio, military-grade GPS, encrypted satellite phone—the works," the fire captain said. "And there are no listening devices, and no transponder either—I made sure of that."

"What do you think?" Joe Grazziella asked proudly.

"It's a hell of a truck," Giovanni replied.

"Can you drive me on an errand this morning?"

"Sure, where to?"

"I'll tell you that when we're on the road," Joe said.

Giovanni climbed into the driver's seat as if he belonged there. He looked around for the starter button.

The firefighter handed Giovanni the key to the truck. It was made of solid metal, like the key to an old-fashioned padlock. It took Giovanni a moment to realize what it was.

"The key goes into the keyhole there," the fire captain told him, pointing to the slot. "Turn it to start the engine. Have you driven a stick shift before?"

"One of my buddies inherited a pickup truck like this. We took turns driving it around the property."

Giovanni pressed down the clutch pedal with his left foot and tried out the different positions of the gear shift. He put the gears in neutral and turned the key.

The truck gave a confident roar.

Joe Grazziella climbed into the passenger seat.

"Keep this baby for as long as it takes to get Kelly home," the fire captain said.

Giovanni slowly eased up the clutch while slipping the transmission into first gear. The vehicle lurched down the driveway.

"Now slip it into second," Joe Grazziella said. "Easy on the clutch."

As the canary-yellow pickup turned onto the toll road headed south, other drivers slowed to take a closer look. A car full of teenagers honked and waved. For a moment, Giovanni imagined that he was going to the beach with Kelly.

"I talked with the deputy in Missing Persons who's been keeping me posted," Joe Grazziella said. "He told me that the closest Krator medevac base to where she was found is Krieger Field, a former air force base near Sacramento. I suggest that we go there this morning and try to see her."

"That's a great idea!"

"But before that, I want to stop at Vitus Veritas Winery. Ever since you told me about the trucks dropping off grapes from the central valley, I've wondered if that's how Kelly got all the way from Oscuridad to the Sierra without being seen. Now it seems more important than ever."

"Why?"

"Because yesterday, I was sure Kelly was coming home." He hesitated. "But now I think," he paused, his eyes fixed on the road ahead. "I think she's been renditioned."

They turned off the highway onto Valley Road and pulled into the visitor parking lot at Vitus Veritas Winery.

"Do you think they'll tell you anything about the trucks?" Giovanni asked.

"Oh yes. Don't worry about that. I'm the father of the famous missing firefighter—and I made an appointment with the general manager."

"Should I wait here?"

"Hell no. I want a witness."

The executive office for Vitus Veritas was a three-story Victorian mansion originally built by a timber baron. The house had been meticulously restored in the style of the Gay Nineties, and the general manager's office was located in the former billiard room. The walls were dark with historic tobacco smoke, and the ceiling was supported by hand-hewn beams of local oak.

"Joe Grazziella! What a pleasure!" the general manager enthused, glad to make a celebrity's acquaintance. He was solidly built like a football player, and his dark hair was combed forward to cover a bald spot. He walked around his desk to shake their hands, gesturing for them to be seated. "How can I help?"

Behind him, the credenza was lined with framed photographs of a much younger man dressed in the football uniform of the University of Southern California Trojans.

"Well, Kelly is still not safely home yet," Joe Grazziella announced.

"Yes, I heard on the news that she is being held for medical observation, that she was injured in the fire," the general manager said.

"Yes, that's the story they told me too, but I think there's more to it than that," Joe Grazziella said.

The general manager placed his hands on his ample stomach.

"First of all, she was not injured in the fire. I spoke to her on the phone before she was picked up by the helicopter at Lake Tahoe. She told me she wasn't injured."

The general manager was hanging on every word.

"I think the official story, that Kelly is injured, is a cover-up so Krator can hold her for a period of time," Joe Grazziella said with concern. "I want to find out why."

He paused.

342

The only sound was the faint rumble of passing trucks on the highway a half mile away.

"So how does this relate to Vitus Veritas?" the general manager asked finally, a puzzled expression on his face.

"We are looking for a truck—the truck that picked up Kelly on the morning of the fire." Joe Grazziella told him. "What can Vitus Veritas tell us about that?"

"Nothing," the general manager said with a wave of his hands. "Krator interviewed all the winery staff, and no one saw anything at the time of the fire."

"Vitus Veritas had its first crush the morning of the fire. Did Krator interview the workers in the vineyard."

"I don't know for sure. But if Krator had found anything, I probably would have heard about it. So they probably drew a blank."

"Did Krator talk to the drivers of the trucks that delivered the grapes from the central valley?"

The general manager turned the color of zinfandel. "We don't get any grapes from the central valley!"

"We've been told that Vitus Veritas had deliveries of grapes from the central valley on the morning of the fire," Joe Grazziella said.

"Well, I don't know who told you that, but any grape purchases are made by corporate. You will have to talk to them." The general manager looked furious; he stood up to dismiss them.

Joe Grazziella and Giovanni remained seated.

"I don't care how you run your business," Joe Grazziella told him in a calm voice. "But if Krator learns that you lied about the truck Kelly got away in, you are going to have bigger problems than me."

The general manager sat down again.

"I want the name and phone number of whoever provides the trucks," Joe Grazziella told him. "And I want you to call him and set up an appointment with me—for this morning. Tell him you want him to give me his complete cooperation."

The general manager sat silently, his mouth working as if chewing invisible gum. "Why should I do that?" he asked finally.

"Because it's your only option. If you don't, I hold a press conference announcing that a truck carrying central valley grapes made a delivery to Vitus Veritas the morning of the fire and that's how Kelly got to the Sierra."

The general manager's face drained of color.

"Make the call now," Joe Grazziella told him. "We won't leave until you do."

* * *

Joe and Giovanni drove eastward through California's central valley, a flat, Midwestern landscape of rectilinear farm fields crisscrossed by power lines and dotted with bulbous water towers. Sprawling, treeless subdivisions marked the outskirts of Modesto. The sales manager of Modesto Wines agreed to meet them at his office adjacent to the highway exit.

"Call me when you're within five miles. You'll see my car in front—a silver Lexus with a 'Support Our Troops' bumper sticker," the sales manager instructed.

The Lexus was easy to spot in the nearly empty parking lot. Giovanni pulled in next to it.

"You should have told me you were driving a fifties pickup—those are classics," the sales manager said a little enviously. "Call me Wade."

He was a trim, clean-cut man in his late thirties, dressed in expensive sports clothes favored by collegians a score of years younger.

"Let me get one thing straight," Wade told them. "I am meeting you because I was asked to do it by my largest customer and because I want to help your daughter. It is not against the law to sell grapes to another winery. And if a client

344

asks me to keep a business relationship confidential, I do that too. It's just good business."

"Don't worry, I'm not interested in grapes," Joe Grazziella told him. "I am interested in finding out how my daughter got from the wildfire to the Sierra. And I want to express my appreciation to anyone who helped her."

Wade nodded sympathetically. "Vitus Veritas gave me a green light, so I'll tell you that Modesto Wines sent six truckloads of grapes to Oscuridad on Monday. But I don't know who the drivers are—we contract with another company for that. I don't know anything about my contractor's labor practices either." He took out his phone and dialed.

"José? this is Wade." He laughed. "Saturday off—me? Hah! Remember the wildfire near Vitus Veritas on Monday? I've got two people here—the father of the missing firefighter and her boyfriend. They heard that one of the trucks picked her up at the scene of the fire. They want to talk to the driver. No, they're not from Immigration. They were referred to me by the general manager of Vitus Veritas. Here, talk to them yourself."

Joe Grazziella told the story again, with special emphasis on reuniting with his daughter.

José reluctantly told them he would be at the truck yard all day.

The trucking company was in an area of decaying produce sheds near the main north-south railroad track. Many of the buildings had been cleared for redevelopment, and the trucking yard occupied one of the newly vacant lots. José's office was a trailer guarded by pit bulls.

When Giovanni drove the Apache pickup into the yard, a mechanic in grease-stained coveralls crawled out from under a produce truck to stare at the canary-yellow vehicle as if it had come from outer space. Even the dogs fell silent, and José emerged from the trailer, finally convinced that his visitors were not from Immigration. He was a short, dark man with biceps like a body builder and a flattened nose like a boxer. Prison tattoos climbed both arms.

Joe Grazziella explained the situation to José again.

"Took her to Davis you say?" José asked.

"Monday morning, six truckloads of grapes from Modesto Wines to Vitus Veritas," Giovanni reminded him.

José kept his roster of drivers in his head. "The guys you want are out on a job right now."

"Is there any way we can contact them?" Joe Grazziella asked. "We're only in Modesto for today."

José shrugged, unable to offer any helpful suggestions.

"Look, Wade's biggest customer wants this to happen," Giovanni told José.

"It's easy for them," José retorted. "What about my business? How do I get drivers after it gets around I turned a guy in?"

Joe Grazziella nodded sympathetically. "I don't need the driver's name. I don't need to know what he looks like. I just need to ask him a few questions—if he gave a ride to my daughter. If I get what I need, no one else will ever hear about it."

"He speaks only Spanish," José objected.

"You know, Krator will be really interested in how Kelly got out of Oscuridad," Giovanni said sharply. "And it's illegal to hire undocumented drivers."

José finally understood that he had no options. "Come with me," he growled.

The pit bulls lunged on their chains as the visitors followed José into the trailer. The small, dark interior was dominated by a wobbly table piled high with auto racing magazines and broken computers. An empty water cooler was in one corner, a battered coffee urn in the other. The walls were adorned with auto parts calendars showing scantily clad maidens in the arms of Aztec warriors.

Joe Grazziella and Giovanni sat down on the worn car seat that served as a bench.

"Monday, one truck came back late because of the wildfire," José explained. "I sent two men on that job, a regular driver and a new guy." He dialed a number and spoke to the man at the other end in Spanish, occasionally glancing at Joe Grazziella, as if including him in the conversation.

José looked at his visitors and translated the driver's words into English. "They *did* pick up a firefighter—the same girl that was on the news. He says that they took her to Davis because she ordered them to."

"I wish I could talk to him!" Joe Grazziella said, ruing that he did not know any Spanish. "Ask him if Kelly told them why she went to Davis."

José talked in Spanish for what seemed like several minutes, then turned to his visitors. "She said she needed to get home. She was afraid."

"Did she say why she was afraid?"

"He says she was being chased by a man in a silver BMW who worked for a government laboratory. She refused to go to the police. She wanted them to drop her at the university—so they did."

"Ask him if she had any burns or injuries."

"He says she was not injured, but confused and afraid," José said.

"Thank him for saving my daughter from the fire."

José relayed the message, then looked at Joe Grazziella. "He says he did nothing. It was Our Lady of Guadalupe who saved her."

* * *

"Now what?" Giovanni asked, as they climbed back into the pickup.

"Krieger Field near Sacramento."

The GPS showed a straight line north on the U.S. 99 toll road, estimated driving time one hour.

Krieger Field was a redevelopment triumph, a successful business park of three-story, Mission-style office blocks adjacent to the drab frame buildings of a former air force base. A glossy sign at the entrance pointed to the modern offices; another sign of weathered redwood announced the base to be on the nation's registry of historic places.

The Krator Air Rescue Hospital straddled the boundary between old and new. The hospital and heliport were accessible to the public through an entrance adjacent to the parking lot, while a windowless building behind it reached out to embrace the runways of the former air force base. The windowless building was protected by two rows of high, chain-link fence, like a prison, and appeared to be accessible only by air. A sign identified it as a commercial executive jet service.

"Is this where Kelly is?" Giovanni asked, visibly apprehensive.

"That's what the deputy in Missing Persons said."

They parked the pickup and walked through the automatic glass doors of the medevac hospital. A young woman in a Krator uniform was on duty at the counter.

"Can I help you, gentlemen?" she said.

"I hope so. I am Joe Grazziella, the father of the firefighter Kelly Grazziella. The sheriff told me my daughter is here, and I want to see her."

The woman blanched. "Who did you say you were?"

"Joe Grazziella, the father of the firefighter Kelly Grazziella. I am here to see my daughter."

"Just a minute, Mr. Grazziella." She checked her database. She looked in the log book. She called her supervisor.

"There is a gentleman here claiming to be the father of Kelly Grazziella the missing firefighter. He wants to see her. Oh."

The receptionist put down the phone. "May I have your thumb on the touchpad, please."

Joe Grazziella obediently put his thumb on the machine.

"Hmm…" she said. "You are Joseph Grazziella of Oscuridad, California."

"Yes, I am," he said.

She smiled wanly. "No one told me about this. Excuse me." She called her supervisor again.

A little while later, an angry woman of indeterminate age and frosted hair emerged from an inner office, her hips and buttocks demonstrating the impressive expandability of the regulation Krator uniform.

"Is this the gentleman?" she asked the receptionist.

"That's him."

"Mr. Grazziella," she said in the accent of southern Appalachia. "We have no record of an expected visit by you. I cannot approve a visit without a clearance from Krator HQ."

"So she *is* here." Joe Grazziella said.

The woman looked flustered. "I am not saying she is here and I am not saying she is not here. I cannot say whether she is or not."

"But you do *know*," he said, leaning closer to her. "Just between you and me—we both understand that she is here."

The supervisor looked away in confusion. "Don't just sit there," she snapped at the receptionist. "Call security!"

The security officer was a former military policeman who had left the navy to take a more lucrative position at the Krator Corporation. His previous experience was arresting drunken sailors in base-side bars in the Philippines.

"What's this all about?" he said.

"This gentleman is the father of Kelly Grazziella, and he wants to see his daughter. I told him that I cannot tell him whether she is here or not. But he won't listen."

"You heard the lady. Get a move on."

"I can't do that," Joe Grazziella told him. "I am here to see my daughter. I know she's in there, and I want to see her."

"Mouth off with me, Pop, and I'll haul your ass to the brig."

The supervisor tugged the security man's sleeve. "He *is* the missing firefighter's father," she warned him.

"I don't care whose father he is," he told her.

"I'm calling the CO," she whispered.

The commanding officer was a former US Army captain whose previous experience had been supervising the arrest of suspected insurgents in Iraq. He mentally scored Kelly's father on a checklist to determine if he should be sent to Syria to be tortured—then remembered that it was the government of the United States that was withholding information.

"How do you do, Mr. Grazziella?" he said politely. "I'm sorry about the misunderstanding. Kelly Grazziella is not here. She was transferred to another facility where she can get ongoing medical care. We are strictly an intake and triage facility."

"I was told this is where she was taken after she was found," Joe Grazziella reminded him.

"Yes, Thursday afternoon, she was here. But she is not here now."

"Do you know where she is?"

"I'm sorry, I don't."

"Can I see the record of her release to the other institution?"

"No, our records are strictly confidential for our patients' protection."

"When did she leave?"

"I am not at liberty to say."

"Where was she taken?"

"I don't know."

"But she is being well-cared for?"

"Certainly, I can assure you of that."

Joe Grazziella leaned forward and looked the officer in the eye. "Listen, soldier, since Krator took over this country, I feel a thousand times *less* secure than I did before. I plan to stay right here until I get some answers."

The officer looked amazed—no insurgent had ever talked back to him before.

Giovanni went outside to the pickup truck and retrieved the encrypted satellite phone. He called the producer at One World News whose name was on the mailing list for Indian Springs zinfandels.

"I met you in the Indian Springs tasting room on Monday morning before the fire," Giovanni told him.

"Sure I remember you—you're the guy who told me nothing ever happens in Oscuridad!" the producer laughed. "Don't tell me there's another wildfire."

"Sort of—Kelly Grazziella has disappeared again."

"You're kidding! Where are you?"

"Krieger Field, Sacramento."

The producer checked the airfield's coordinates on the GPS. "Don't move. We're dispatching a mobile unit there now."

MEDUSA II

In the safe house, Jack Adair read an urgent dispatch from Monterrey; then he sent for Ocampo and El Tigre.

"We all saw the video of Maria in Matamoros," he told the EarthRage staff. "Well, skeptics wondered if Maria had been raped and had repressed the memory of it. Others wondered if the prison hospital she remembered might really have been a home for unwed mothers. Well, the Hoosier's group has been checking out these possibilities. It turns out, women are regularly taken by van from MEDUSA clinics in Monterrey to homes for unwed mothers in Matamoros. The homes are high-security installations—from the outside, more like prisons than homes."

"That confirms Maria's story," Renato announced.

"Monterrey also confirms Maria's statement that the staff are all Brazilian."

"Why Brazilian?" Constanza signed.

Jack shrugged. "Maybe to avoid any connection with local people."

"How many homes?" Renato asked.

"Three so far. Each big enough to hold perhaps a thousand women at a time. Maria apparently saw only one ward. Anyway, people in the neighborhood speculate about what goes on there, and EarthRage has learned that two kinds of vehicles regularly come and go from the homes. Dark blue vans carry the staff, while white ambulances carry the mothers. Today, EarthRage followed one of these ambulances."

Both Constanza and Renato leaned forward as if trying to see where they went.

"The ambulance went to a private maternity hospital that is located on the outskirts of Matamoros—adjacent to the airfield that is the secret base of the 888th Special Operations Brigade," Jack told them.

"Wow!" Constanza gestured, speaking for them all.

Jack looked at Renato. "Is there a rational explanation for all this?"

"The simplest explanation is that the babies are loaded onto returning rendition planes," the Philosopher said. "If we make this assumption, we can hypothesize that the baby traffic goes primarily to three places. We know from Guloggers that most flights to and from Matamoros go to Dallas-Fort Worth airport. Smaller fractions go to Sacramento and Twentynine Palms, California. Maybe the babies are handed over to adoptive parents when they reach the other end. If so, we should look for a facility on the U.S. side analogous to the one in Matamoros—a hospital that doubles as an adoption agency."

"Focus on Mexico now," Constanza wrote. "Need to watch moms full time."

"You're right," Jack said. "Contact Lazarus in Monterrey and let him know that we need full-time video surveillance of that maternity hospital adjacent to the Special Ops airfield. And tell them I want the Hoosier leading the team."

Confrontation

MacVain was putting papers in his briefcase, preparing to spend the weekend at the ranch, when he received an urgent call from Cato Magruder, the deputy bureau chief of Apprehension and Detention.

"Have you seen the breaking news on Grazziella's father?" Magruder asked.

MacVain clicked the news icon on his console and watched grimly as a handsome, gray-haired man with the determination of a long-distance runner convincingly countered Krator's most slippery spokesperson before the close-up lenses of several live cameras.

"Goddamn it!" MacVain growled—silencing Grazziellas was like putting chains on Houdini.

"He refuses to leave without his daughter," Cato Magruder explained. "I just need a doctor and a syringe."

"We don't want any more medical mysteries. It will just fuel speculation."

"The American people love Kelly Grazziella," the nation's second-ranking cop insisted. "And they are gonna love her dad too."

"It's a Saturday afternoon, with a pro football game on," MacVain replied. "I'll ask Skipper to kill the coverage."

It was five minutes before Skipper Van Squint called back on his satellite phone—an eternity in the world of broadcast television.

"I am sailing off Catalina with my family," the spin doctor explained. "The northwesterlies picked up, and I had to trim the main."

The senior attorney was sympathetic—he was a sailor himself. "We've got a media problem," MacVain informed him. "Grazziella's father has holed himself up in the Krator medevac facility in Sacramento and refuses to leave until he's reunited with his daughter. And it's being covered live by One World News."

Van Squint's effervescence went audibly flat. "That son of a bitch."

* * *

In the lobby of the Krator Air Rescue hospital at Krieger Field, the producer of the mobile news unit received a call from Los Angeles. A moment later, he signaled his crew to turn off their microphones and cameras.

Soon a One World News helicopter landed in the fenced-in area behind the hospital, debouching a squad of dark-suited men led by an over-weight, crew-cut man who looked more like prison guard than a television executive.

"Party's over, boys," he told the newscasters assembled in the lobby. "From now on, *no* coverage of Joe Grazziella. You can keep a crew here to film the firefighter when she's released—but the old man's off limits. Understood?"

"When *is* Kelly going to be released?" one of the newscasters asked him.

The executive looked through the reporter as if he were not there, then abruptly turned back to the helicopter, leaving a few dark suits behind to make sure there was no more news.

* * *

The Chairman of the Council of Seventeen called Vaughn MacVain a short time later to complain.

"The Council counts on Krator to keep things out of the public eye, not to host a media circus every day. Your public relations guy was out-gunned," the corpulent accountant added, confirming the senior attorney's own assessment.

"One World News dropped the ball on this," MacVain said coldly. "But I can suggest a proactive response."

"I'm listening."

"I re-examined Grazziella's health report by the intake physician at the Krator Air Rescue facility in Sacramento," MacVain told him. "Just as I thought, there's not a mark on her except a few scratches on her arms and legs."

"Lyle is going to fix that."

"Right, but her old man's grand-standing has upped the sympathy quotient. The burns might backfire. It would be better to leave her untouched and claim that Krator took Grazziella into custody in order to spare the family's feelings—knowing what we now know about her precarious mental condition."

"How precarious?" the Chairman asked.

"Rambling, incoherent, unable to tell fact from fantasy. We'll get the video to prove it. I'll talk to Lyle about it."

"But it doesn't solve the problem of God rescuing a Goddess worshipper," the Chairman pointed out.

"No, but it shows that God rescues crazy people who believe in goddesses."

* * *

Jack Adair was in the living room watching One World News, fascinated by Joe Grazziella's moving plea for his daughter's life.

Suddenly the firefighter's father vanished from the screen, replaced by a documentary on pastry chefs.

Jack called together Constanza, Renato, and El Tigre for a meeting in the safe room. He pulled over a stenographer's chair and sat down on it backwards, his arms folded over the backrest. El Tigre made himself comfortable on the beige settee with the black metal arms. Constanza stood by her whiteboard, while Renato sat at the table with his notebook and Post-its.

Jack replayed the clip of Joe Grazziella at Krieger Field hospital, noting its sudden termination.

"What do you think?" he asked.

"I don't think it was staged," El Tigre said. "I think Krator got caught with its pants down."

"I agree," Renato said. "'Medical examination' is obviously a cover story, since her father announced on TV that his daughter said she was uninjured."

"Guloggers says that a plane left Krieger Field at midnight and went straight to Matamoros," El Tigre said. "And they think Grazziella was on it."

"What's the evidence for that?" Jack asked.

"If she were still at Krieger Field, Krator would have defused the stand-off by letting her father in to see her," he continued. "Do you know why she was taken into custody?"

"It's a mystery," Jack said.

"Anyway, if Krator planned on killing her, Matamoros would be a logical place to send her," El Tigre said. "Guloggers thinks there's a great opportunity here."

Jack looked at him, waiting for more.

"Our companions in arms are thinking of publicly announcing over the Internet that Grazziella is at Matamoros," El Tigre said. "They think that whatever publicity is generated will expose what is being done there."

Constanza nodded agreement.

"The downside is that she might *not* be there," Jack said.

"They are not concerned about that," El Tigre replied. "They want to force the Mexican government to act—to repudiate the safe haven for American rendition flights."

Constanza wrote on her whiteboard: "Mex gov claims to know *nada* [nothing]."

"You are saying that it plays into the seizure of the oil fields, just like the art thefts?" Jack asked.

"Yes," Constanza signed.

"Our companions in arms want to move fast before Krator kills the firefighter. That way, Krator will be forced to produce her," El Tigre said. "And they specifically asked if we could help them make the announcement more attention-getting. They want to get the message to the general public, not just to people in the resistance."

"What's EarthRage's exposure on this?" Jack wanted to know.

"We're out of range," El Tigre said.

"None," Constanza signed.

"It's a great plan," Renato agreed.

"Enough discussion!" Constanza signed emphatically. "Tell them to do it!"

Jack gave his signature grin. "Tell Guloggers to copy us with their communiqué and we'll get it on European TV."

Wildfire

Manacled and hooded, Kelly Grazziella was taken to the simulated wildfire site in an infantry transport vehicle. Two soldiers in combat fatigues helped her down the ramp and walked her to the top of the man-made hill between two converging rows of tinder-dry chaparral flown in from California. As the trio reached the top, one of the soldiers kicked Kelly's feet out from under her and pushed her face-down in the dirt.

"Do we burn her now?" one of the soldiers asked.

"They're still stacking the wood. It'll be a few more minutes."

G. Lyle Acre drove up in his Hummer and signaled to his adjutant.

Chad Weed slipped closer to the two officers so he could listen to the conversation. He was dressed like a Florida real estate agent in bright, tropical colors that looked out of place among the gray-green camo uniforms and drab earth tones of the arid brush.

"We've had a change of plan," the general told the adjutant. "No physical marks on the suspect."

"No burns?" the adjutant said, barely concealing his disappointment.

"That's right, no burns. Her dad is on TV pleading for his daughter's life; the bleeding hearts are having second thoughts. But her mental health—that's another matter. They still want her psycho."

The general turned toward Chad Weed as if noticing him for the first time. "They say the Krator senior investigator is an expert in psychology," he said. "Maybe you could lend my adjutant a hand?"

Chad Weed waited until the general's Hummer had sped away before expounding on his credentials. "I was in charge of the psychological warfare unit in the undeclared Pakistan war," he told the adjutant. "I also have a Ph.D. in interrogation from Hardwood." His face assumed an authoritative, clinical look. "Why don't you let me prep her first?" he suggested. "It will make it easier for your guys."

"How long will that take?"

"Five minutes. The first five minutes are critical in these operations."

"All right," the adjutant agreed.

Chad Weed slogged up the steep slope and gestured to the two soldiers.

"General Acre says to give me five minutes alone with her," he told them. They hurried back down the hill.

Chad Weed squatted down next to Kelly.

"Can you hear me?" he asked.

"Yes."

"I'm Chad Weed. You and I met at a fraternity party at Davis," he told her. "I was a pre-med student."

"I recognize your voice," she told him, her heart racing with terror.

"Do you remember the Nathan Whyte Laboratory?" he asked her.

"How can I ever forget it?"

"You and I are the only two people left alive who know what happened there that night, except Tweecus. You remember Dr. Tweecus?"

"Yes."

"They want to make you crazy so no one will believe what you say about the lab. They would have killed you already if you weren't the famous missing firefighter. Just like they killed the other two women who were made pregnant that night."

Kelly gulped. She had not known that there were other women. Then she remembered that Tweecus had a colleague, a stout, gray-haired scientist who was investing in Ridgeline Castles. How could she have forgotten that? She remembered the man's exact words when he walked into Tweecus's lab: "The one you used on the other two?" *Other two,* she thought— so there must be other women. Then she remembered that Tweecus had made notes about the experiment in a little green notebook that he put in the drawer of a stainless steel utility cart along with two other notebooks.

"Where am I?" she asked.

"You are in Matamoros, Mexico, on an American rendition base," Chad Weed informed her. "Do you know what a rendition base is?"

"I do now." She knew he was telling the truth about that.

"They think I am going to help make you crazy. But once you are crazy, they plan to kill me. So you and me—we walk out of here together. Is that a deal?"

She did not know if he was still telling the truth, but she was not in a position to bargain.

"Yes," she assured him. "It's a deal."

"I know you live in a cabin near Indian Springs Winery. I know your father lives on Brandywine Way. You will not tell anyone here that we are going to escape together?"

"I promise I will not tell anyone."

"The soldiers are coming back. They will tell you that you are going to be burned alive in a brushfire. But you won't be—Krator is afraid of bad publicity." He laughed. "They are under orders to not leave a mark on you. So act scared."

"I'll do my best," she assured him.

She heard him move away, heading down the hill.

A moment later the soldiers returned.

"Let's cook the bitch alive," one said to the other. He ignited a flame thrower, and incandescent vapors flared with a terrifying roar. The other soldier laughed.

Kelly thought of her grandfather—the day that she had driven him up the fire road to the Italian-Swiss Monument. The memory was so real that she felt his presence.

"Kelly, never be afraid to pass through the fire—it's your element," he told her.

She felt at peace and unafraid.

"Dallas Is Losing, Sir."

As Vaughn MacVain was preparing to leave again for the ranch, Cato Magruder called a second time.

"One World News has fucked up again," the nation's second-ranking cop informed him. "Look at European TV."

MacVain clicked on the news icon—and his bile rose into his throat. One of Europe's most-watched anchors was delivering a terrorist communiqué as if it were a papal encyclical:

> A world-wide organization that tracks American political prisoners, Guloggers, has announced today that the firefighter Kelly Grazziella is in an American concentration camp in Mexico.

> This camp is run by the United States 888th Special Operations brigade. It is disguised as a Mexican air force base. It is located near the town of Matamoros, across the border from Brownsville, Texas.

"Where the fuck is One World News on this?" MacVain exploded.

"I just called them and got a weekend warrior who didn't know shit," Cato Magruder complained. "He said everyone took off, and he's been trying to figure out who to call."

"Krator will handle it!" the senior attorney barked, grabbing the red telephone.

The phone rang and rang.

"Skipper doesn't answer," the senior attorney growled to his communications officer. "Find him!"

MacVain started to call Tricia Culhane, then remembered that his special assistant had gone to visit her mother for the weekend and had turned off her cell phone.

MacVain called Kincaid, his personal security officer. No one answered in the basement bunker.

He skewered his communications officer with cold gray eyes. "Find out where Kincaid is. I want to talk to him now!"

Kincaid was in the mountains with his varmint rifle, trying to find something small enough to kill with a .223. In three hours he had seen only a buck, a bear, and a mountain sheep.

The satellite telephone rang.

Cole Kincaid sat down on a rock, put his rifle on the ground, and activated the telephone.

"Let me see if I got this," he told MacVain. "A subversive organization, Guloggers, has ID'd a secret U.S. redition base on television?"

As he spoke, a ground squirrel came out of a burrow and stood on a rock ten feet away as if taunting him. The ground squirrel had pouty cheeks and a fluffy tail. The tail flicked like a metronome. The security officer could not concentrate on what the senior attorney was saying: he was trying to figure out how to pick up the rifle without putting down the phone.

"Are you listening to me?" MacVain growled.

"Yes, sir. You want me to launch an investigation?"

"Forget it," MacVain snorted, hanging up.

The ground squirrel darted back into its burrow.

* * *

In Matamoros, G. Lyle Acre received a call from the officer in charge of base security.

"I thought you were on leave," the general said.

"I am. I am calling from a hotel in Monterrey. There's something on television I think you ought to see."

"What is it?"

"The base, sir. The Mexican news channel is showing pictures of it."

"What the hell?"

"Now they are showing pictures of that missing firefighter. They are saying she is being held at the base against her will."

G. Lyle Acre's anger was palpable through the phone—he felt violated when terrorists tracked his rendition flights.

In the administration office, the single clerk on duty snapped to attention when the general materialized in front of him.

"At ease, soldier. Is there a television in the building?"

"I don't know, sir. There is one in the enlisted men's club."

"Call the officer's club and ask if they have a television."

The general waited impatiently while the clerk made the call.

"This is base administration. General Acre has asked me to ask you if there is a television in the officer's club. I don't know. It does? I will tell him."

The clerk looked at the general. "The officer's club says that if you want to watch the preseason game between the Dallas Bankers and the San Francisco Gold Diggers, the enlisted men's club has a much bigger screen."

"Call my Hummer."

When G. Lyle Acre stormed into the lobby of the enlisted men's club, a surprised master sergeant jumped to attention. Unlike the regular military, Special Operations facilities were not out-sourced to corporations, and soldiers were expected to pour their own beverages.

"Sergeant, this is a fire drill. Evacuate the building through the emergency exits."

The sergeant ducked into the lounge and shouted: "Fire Drill! Emergency exits only. Evacuate the building now!"

A grumbling, gray-green wave of fatigues surged out through the side doors, leaving behind a styrofoam army of half-finished cokes and milkshakes. There were no alcoholic beverages in the no-name brigades.

The general marched briskly through the empty lounge to the enormous television screen. He told the sergeant to find the Mexican news, then stared in disbelief at an animated map of northeastern Mexico that highlighted the location of his airfield, followed by a clip of white executive jets taking off and landing. Then the map morphed into the healthy, wholesome face of Kelly Grazziella. He did not know the language but he knew what they were saying.

A moment later, Vaughn MacVain telephoned G. Lyle Acre, but the call rolled over to intercept. The duty officer at base security picked it up.

"General Acre is not responding to his cell. I can patch you through to an insecure phone at the enlisted men's club," the officer told the senior attorney.

"The enlisted men's club? What the hell is he doing there?"

"Watching the Dallas Bankers preseason exhibition game, sir."

MacVain knew that Acre thought that tiger hunting and polo were the only sports worthy of an officer and a gentleman. Had the general gone funny in the head too?

"Patch me through."

At the club, the sergeant ran up to the general and handed him a cordless phone. "An urgent call for you, sir."

"Acre here."

"Base security, sir. Will you accept a call from senior attorney MacVain. It's not encrypted."

"Put him through."

There was the tell-tale chime in the background, indicating an insecure line.

"Where was Krator on this?" the general asked sharply.

"This is an insecure line," MacVain snapped.

"So what? They can watch us on TV. I am sending the package back where it came from. We'll talk later." Acre hung up without the usual shucks and by-golly.

"Anything else, sir?" the sergeant asked the general.

"No, sergeant. Tell the men they can resume watching the game. What's the score?" Acre asked.

"Dallas is losing, sir."

"Yes, it is," the general muttered. "It is, indeed."

* * *

At the wildfire simulation site, the adjutant instructed his troops in the requirements of psychological warfare. "This time, set some of the brush alight so she can feel the fire coming at her."

Grazziella was still lying in the inverted V of dry brush, shackled and unable to run.

Two of the soldiers climbed to the top of the hill and ignited some of the nearby brush so she could feel and hear the flame.

The adjutant's cell phone rang.

"Take Grazziella to the departure hangar right now," G. Lyle Acre barked.

"The departure hangar, right now?" the adjutant echoed. "We just started the second session."

"You heard right."

Kelly Grazziella, still hooded and shackled and with a soldier supporting her under each arm, stumbled down the steep hill. At the bottom, they guided the firefighter up the ramp of the personnel carrier and helped her onto a bench seat. The vehicle had the anomalous odor of after-shave.

The adjutant looked at the darkening sky and frowned, realizing they would have to protect the dry brush from the rain if Chad Weed was going to die by smoke inhalation as planned. He wondered if the base had any plastic tarpaulins.

"You come along with us," he told Chad Weed impatiently.

"It's going to rain in a minute," Chad Weed observed, pointing to the clouds gathering in the east.

"The doctor from Hardwood is a weatherman too," a Teutonic-looking soldier from Oklahoma sneered. The other men guffawed.

Chad Weed did not respond, but the phrase "the doctor from Hardwood" exploded inside his head with the force of a grenade. The former pre-medical student had been to three colleges but had never graduated. As the vehicle rolled along, Weed imagined a bayonet blade buried in the Okie's big belly, digging deeper with each bump of the gravel road.

* * *

The body language of General Acre's assistant conveyed the urgency of the call. "Sir, the head of the Mexican counter-insurgency command, General Julio César Somoza, is on the line. He says it's urgent."

Acre's face betrayed his sullen resignation.

"Juli, how you been?" Acre said cordially.

"I am well. How have you been?"

"Getting in shape. I run every day. I do pushups."

"I should exercise more like you. My son is a runner and urges me to take it up."

"I recommend it. Exercise keeps you young." Acre said.

"And your family? Is your family well?"

"The kids are doing great," Acre said proudly. "My oldest boy's been promoted to captain, and last week my daughter gave me my first grandchild."

"A grandchild. That is very good news. A boy or a girl?"

"A girl, looks just like her mother."

"And your son is regular army or special operations?"

"He takes after his old man —special ops."

"Your children are a credit to you." General Somoza said with feeling. Then he paused. "But unfortunately I must convey some news that is less good."

"You mean the exposure of the base?" Acre asked rhetorically.

"Yes. There are television trucks at the ends of the runways trying to get a picture of this missing firefighter. But the Mexican government will continue to insist that it is a Mexican air force base. So, you understand that it would be better if no American aircraft used the base until, well, the situation is more favorable."

"I understand," said Acre.

* * *

The troop carrier raced to the airfield a little ahead of the rain and pulled into the departure hangar, which was little more than a roofed portion of the apron adjacent to the runway. A white, unmarked executive jet, the same plane that had flown Grazziella to Matamoros, was fueled and waiting.

Chad Weed knew that his only chance was to board that plane with the firefighter. He touched his pocket, reassuring himself that he still had the real Krator badge with his biometrics, not the stolen one he gave to Acre. He jumped out of the vehicle and followed Kelly Grazziella, who was being escorted by soldiers to the airfield departure desk, where two burly military policemen were waiting to transfer the prisoner to the airplane.

The adjutant's cell phone rang: "Base security's been compromised," General Acre informed him. "All American aircraft have been grounded until further notice."

"What about the Brownsville shuttle?"

"Mexican aircraft are still flying, but it's too risky. Take her to the maternity hospital. There's an ambulance waiting. They'll drive her across the border as a medical emergency."

The adjutant motioned to Grazziella's escorts to return her to the vehicle.

He turned to the tall, Teutonic soldier with the Oklahoma accent. "Starbutz! Stay with the Krator investigator, and don't let him out of your sight."

Starbutz nodded with a look of malevolent satisfaction while Chad Weed watched in stunned silence as Kelly Grazziella was driven away, realizing that the lifeboat had left without him. He eyed the waiting airplane—there must be a way to slip on board.

The rain clouds that threatened a few minutes earlier passed by with only sprinkles, and the control tower revised the forecast to clear. A few minutes later, a small turboprop airliner with a Mexican logo taxied up to the departure hangar.

"The Brownsville shuttle's here!" the desk sergeant called out. "Outgoing passengers need to sign in!"

A half dozen soldiers carrying duffle bags filed down the gangway, while a ground crew unloaded boxes from the cargo bay. The pilot remained in the cockpit.

Then a pickup truck painted with medical insignia drove into the departure hangar and stopped next to the turboprop. Together, the driver and a medical corpsman removed a large portable cooler from the bed of the truck and carried it to a roped-off section of the tarmac where outgoing cargo was temporarily stored.

"I can see what you've been doing this week!" one of the military policemen joked.

"This week?" the corpsman shot back in mock indignation. "This is only this morning's!"

All the ground crew laughed.

"What's in the cooler?" Chad Weed asked his escort.

Starbutz blushed and pretended not to hear him.

Chad Weed approached the medical corpsman and showed him his Krator badge. "I'm Krator senior investigator Chad Weed, and I'd like to ask you a few questions about your program here."

The corpsman turned with a startled look. "No one told me about this."

"General Acre asked to keep this investigation hush-hush," Chad Weed confided. He lowered his voice in confidence. "The general asked that I talk with you here—away from the hospital—and that you give your full cooperation."

"Oh!" the corpsman said.

"Where does this cooler go when it leaves here?" the senior investigator asked.

"The specimens are shipped to the supply depot in Twentynine Palms, in California. I don't know where they go from there."

"But you're in charge of them here?"

"Yes, I consolidate the specimens into a shipment."

"What exactly is involved in that?"

"The soldiers come to the base hospital, and I give each one a sterile container—there's a bathroom so they have privacy. Then I log the sample and put it in the cooler. That's all there is to it."

"But each soldier takes his own specimen?"

The corpsman laughed nervously. "Nobody helps them, if that's what you mean."

"So any tampering has to happen after the specimens leave the base," Chad Weed concluded in a matter-of-fact voice. "In my report—what is the technical term I should use to describe the specimens?"

The corpsman looked thoughtful. "I guess 'sperm samples' is good enough."

Chad Weed suppressed his surprise—he had assumed the specimens were urine samples being sent to the States for drug testing. He sensed an opportunity to parley his new-found knowledge into a plane ticket out.

"Are all the soldiers required to give these specimens?" he asked the corpsman in a voice devoid of personal interest.

"Oh no, only those with a high IQ and demonstrated bravery in battle."

"Do you make that assessment?" Chad Weed asked.

"No, I get a list from the base commander's office."

"Do you know who puts together that list?"

"Yes, the general's adjutant."

"Thank you for your cooperation," Chad Weed told him. "And remember, keep this conversation between you and me."

Chad Weed approached the departure counter. The sergeant on duty remembered him as the Krator senior investigator whose visitor's authorization had been signed by General Acre himself.

"Someone's been tampering with the medical specimens after they leave the base, and Krator is trying to find out who," Chad Weed told him, flashing his badge. "General Acre wants me to accompany the shipment to Twentynine Palms."

369

"It's going out on the Brownsville shuttle," the sergeant informed him, nodding at the turboprop. He retrieved a touchpad from under the counter and pointed to a square on the form. "Your fingerprint right here."

"Also, the general has assigned one of his men to assist me," Weed told him, nodding towards Starbutz, who was standing a short distance away, his hands planted aggressively on his hips. "Will there be room on the flight for him too?"

"There's plenty of room," the sergeant said.

"Does he need to sign in too?" Chad Weed asked

"Everybody needs to sign."

Weed gestured to Starbutz to come up to the counter.

"What's goin' on?" Starbutz stammered.

The sergeant handed him the touchpad. "Put your fingerprint right there."

Starbutz did as he was told.

"I don't know about this," the soldier worried aloud, trying to get Chad Weed's attention, but the Krator investigator was making small talk with the sergeant about the Dallas Bankers game.

The ground crew closed the cargo bay.

"Passengers can board now," the sergeant announced.

"Let's get going," Chad Weed said.

Starbutz hesitated. "We're supposed to wait here," he said without conviction.

"You were ordered to stay with me and not let me out of your sight," Chad Weed reminded him, turning his back on Starbutz and walking boldly up the gangway.

* * *

In the ambulance bay of the maternity hospital, the adjutant gave instructions to the doctor who would accompany Grazziella on her trip to Brownsville. He was a portly, Cuban-American man in his forties, with a double chin and nervous eyes. He had been fired from a hospital for self-medicating with controlled substances and had started over in the gulag. Although he was not licensed to practice in Mexico, the hospital was physically located on the U. S. airfield, and paramilitary lawyers argued that it was technically foreign territory and beyond the law of both countries. On his white coat he was wearing a badge with the name of the Mexican doctor who had signed the documents that would get the patient through Mexican immigration and onto a chartered plane at a commercial U.S. airport.

"Remember, this is a civilian mission, not a military one," the adjutant told the doctor in a no-nonsense voice. "She's a patient, not a prisoner, and you'll be traveling through Mexican jurisdiction—so no rough stuff. Remember, she's a vacationing Canadian college student named Mary Jones— that's important; one slip of her real name to an official could blow the whole operation."

The doctor nodded gravely, indicating that he fully understood the magnitude of his responsibility, but the adjutant was not so confident. The doctor had no field experience in covert operations, but he was all that was available on a Saturday afternoon with five minutes lead time.

While they spoke, a white ambulance, one of the vehicles used to haul women in labor from the homes for unwed mothers, backed into the loading dock. The ambulance bay was more a cargo depot than a medical facility, with room for a half-dozen ambulances to unload simultaneously. Motorized transport carts, each carrying twenty Plexiglas bassinets, were lined up against one wall.

A paramilitary, disguised in the green garb of a hospital attendant, helped Kelly Grazziella into the ambulance. He undid her shackles and slowly removed her hood, while a woman in a white nurse's uniform, her features hidden by a surgical mask, hovered over the firefighter, holding a white, rectangular bandage. The nurse was a veteran of special operations in the Middle East, where she kept prisoners alive during interrogation; now she worked in the same capacity with rendered Americans but at much higher pay. As the hood slipped away, the nurse slapped the bandage over Kelly's eyes and taped it down, making it impossible for her to see.

"Your eyes were injured while you were vacationing in Mexico," the nurse told her. "If you say otherwise to anyone, I will kill you by injection."

The nurse opened Kelly's rucksack and took out the T-shirt and shorts she had worn in the Sierra Nevada.

"Put these on, and quick," the nurse barked. "And don't touch your eye bandage."

The nurse helped Kelly dress, then produced a pair of flip-flops to replace the firefighter boots. She packed the uniform into the rucksack for shipment back to the United States.

As the nurse inspected the prisoner, she spied the thin, dark ribbon that held the Lady of Guadalupe medallion that the Mexican truck driver had given her. With a brisk snap, she pulled it out from under the T-shirt and examined it.

"You won't be needing this," the nurse informed Kelly, ripping it off the firefighter's neck with a savage pull.

"Give it back," Kelly snapped, speaking for the first time since Chad Weed had whispered in her ear while she waited to be burned. Her memory of recent events was improving, and she treasured the moment when the Mexican trucker had given her the medallion on the edge of the Davis campus.

"You're supposed to be Canadian," the nurse snapped. "And it can be used as a weapon."

"Give it back!"

The adjutant appeared in the doorway of the ambulance and scowled at the nurse for creating an incident. "Give it back to her," he ordered.

The nurse returned the medallion to Kelly, her red-faced fury magnified by the contrasting white of the surgical mask.

The paramilitary closed the double doors of the ambulance from the inside with a definitive click.

Kelly Grazziella, made blind by the bandages, was sitting on the gurney, repairing by feel the broken ribbon of the medallion and giving it the meticulous care that rock climbers give to knots.

The Cuban-American doctor got into the front seat next to the driver.

"Get going," the adjutant ordered.

The ambulance headed down the access road and passed through the gate into Mexican territory. As it turned in the direction of Matamoros, the adjutant telephoned General Acre.

"The package just left the base."

* * *

"Help her lie down so we can strap her in," the paramilitary said, filling a syringe with a tranquilizing drug.

The special operations nurse, still smarting from the tongue-lashing by the adjutant, pushed Kelly on to her back and tried to grab the medallion a second time.

"Give it back!" Kelly shouted, clawing at the eye bandages until they fell away.

The nurse recoiled from the exposure.

"Our orders are to sedate her," the paramilitary snarled. "The goddamn medal can wait."

Kelly lunged forward and grabbed the nurse's wrists, summoning the strength that had once hauled her own weight up the vertical face of El Capitan.

"You little shit!" the nurse screamed. Unable to bite Kelly through the mask, she writhed helplessly like a skewered snake.

The paramilitary hovered over them, trying to bring the syringe into range.

The doctor heard the shouting in back and yelled at the driver: "Stop the car! Stop the car!"

As the ambulance screeched to a halt, the soldier fell backwards against the front wall, banging his head on the oxygen tank, the needle jabbing into his thigh. As he collapsed on the bench, Kelly used the nurse's tightly-clamped fists as a battering ram and with one blow broke the woman's jaw.

Following behind the ambulance in an open dune buggy, the EarthRage fact-finding team trained the video camera on the rear doors. The team leader, a hefty American wearing a Chicago baseball cap, the man they called the Hoosier, narrated in English into a hand-held microphone as the camera rolled:

> We are following the ambulance that emerged, only seconds ago, from the hospital at the airfield of the U.S. Special Operations Brigade in Matamoros, Mexico. The ambulance that is believed to be carrying Kelly Grazziella. As you can see, there is a person, dressed in a white doctor's coat, trying to open the rear doors. Did you hear that? Screams from inside the ambulance. Terrifying shouts and screams.

Kelly Grazziella pulled her medallion from the nurse's injured fists, then turned her attention to the door. Outside, the doctor was fiddling with the latch. As Kelly pushed the doors open with all her strength, they hit the doctor in the face and sent him sprawling into the mud-filled gutter, his nose spurting blood on his starched white coat.

"There she is!" the Hoosier exclaimed into the microphone with the enthusiasm of a sportscaster. "Kelly Grazziella has beaten up her guards, she has broken open the doors..."

Framed by the white of the ambulance, an athletic blond woman, unmistakably the missing firefighter, kicked off the flip-flops, jumped to the pavement, and streaked down the highway like a track star.

* * *

In the lobby of the Krator hospital at Krieger Field, Joe Grazziella confided to Giovanni: "Now they've even locked the bathrooms, but I plan to stay right here until I get Kelly back." In spite of the brave words, he sounded tired and demoralized.

"Don't worry," Giovanni said, gesturing to the supportive crowd assembling behind the yellow police tape. "They know they're being added to the watch list, but they're still coming anyway. And thousands more watched you on TV in other countries. At this point, Krator will have to release Kelly."

"I couldn't have done this without you," he told Giovanni.

One of the spectators, apparently drunk, came up to them and loudly asked for Joe Grazziella's autograph.

"Maybe later," Giovanni said, blocking the man's path.

"Ah, come on, be a sport," the man said.

"It's OK," Joe Grazziella said, gesturing for the man to come closer.

"Jus' sign t'is right here," the drunk said, pushing into Joe's personal space and handing him a beer mat and a pen. As Kelly's father signed, the man surreptitiously slipped a cell phone into his pocket.

"You're a real gen'elman," the drunk announced.

As the phone started to vibrate, Joe Grazziella put it to his ear and heard a flat, recorded message:

> Kelly Grazziella has escaped from an American rendition base in Matamoros, Mexico. She is safe in friendly hands. She is telling her story live on Mexican television. This is a message from Guloggers.

"Thank God," Joe Grazziella said, his body language shifting into an attitude of excitement, gratitude, and hope.

The bored newspeople on the scene noticed the change immediately.

"What can you tell us?" a newscaster shouted.

"Who was the call from?" a reporter asked from across the room.

Joe Grazziella signaled to the news crew, who could still listen though they could not repeat it. "I have an announcement to make. Kelly has escaped from an American rendition base in Matamoros, Mexico. She is safe in friendly hands."

The newspeople grinned, and a murmur passed through the crowd.

"You know we can't mention the rendition base. Or even that she's been held against her will," a reporter told him.

"I know, but she's being broadcast live on Mexican television."

"Come on!" the reporter said excitedly, grabbing Joe Grazziella by the arm. "We can watch it on satellite in the mobile unit!"

* * *

On a roadside in Matamoros, Kelly Grazziella told her story to an English-speaking reporter in a satellite up-link truck, her words going out instantly to the news rooms beyond the Free World. In a calm and convincing voice, she told about her abduction by Chad Weed; how the President's-Medal-of-Freedom winner Wassily Tweecus forcibly implanted her with an embryo at the Nathan Whyte Laboratory; that at least two other American women had been implanted; that two of them had probably been murdered to keep them quiet; and that she believed that the baby she had given up for adoption had been killed so its brain could be extracted for an autopsy.

The reporter asked her about her breath-taking escape from the US gulag.

"I owe my life to the Goddess, the Black Madonna, and the Virgin of Guadalupe," she told him.

As Kelly emerged from the improvised studio, she found the Hoosier waiting in the electric dune buggy.

"Thank you for the offer of safe haven in Mexico, but the TV station is sending a plane to take me to Monterrey," she told him. "And I have been offered safe passage by the

Mexican government and a free flight to San Francisco on a Mexican airline."

"Are you sure you want to return to the United States?" he asked her. "It's not safe, and we could use you here."

"Thank you, but didn't you tell me that regime change begins at home? The Mexican government is arranging for my father to meet my plane. And the foreign ministry has told me that the U.S. government has agreed to not interfere with Mexican news coverage of my arrival. I don't think Krator will dare kidnap me again," she said with a mischievous smile.

"Well, remember, you've got friends here," he assured her.

"I hope I won't have to accept your offer, but thank you."

"You've got that phone number and code word I gave you in case you need to reach EarthRage in a hurry?"

"Yes, safely memorized," Kelly assured him.

"OK, well, then, have a safe trip, *buen viaje,*" the Hoosier said with forced cheerfulness, patting her arm.

* * *

At Tranquility Base, Jack Adair watched the interview with Kelly Grazziella, torn between elation at her bravery and fear of how Krator would respond.

"The firefighter's speech is a game changer!" he told Renato. "But Krator will claim that she was made delusional by the wildfire. So we've got to confirm her story fast!"

"How about we release the video of Maria?" Renato suggested. "Maria confirms the forced pregnancy, as well as the breeding facility and the amnesia. It proves the Matamoros connection too."

"That's a great idea. Let's do it."

In the safe room Constanza was already preparing the video for the couriers.

* * *

Vaughn MacVain abandoned his plans to spend the weekend at the ranch and returned to Krator headquarters. The security staff was not expecting him, and the virtual reality projectors had been turned off. The Doge's Palace had disappeared, replaced by a forlorn, rectangular room, sparsely furnished with a Renaissance side chair, an Empire desk, and a clunky, red telephone dating from the time of the Cold War.

The red telephone rang the moment the door closed. MacVain hesitated, then picked it up.

"Yes," he answered without enthusiasm. He felt the Chairman's ponderous presence.

"Do you know that Grazziella was on Mexican TV talking about Wassily Tweecus, Chad Weed, and the Nathan Whyte Laboratory?" the Chairman growled.

"The problem was getting a White woman mixed up in this in the first place," MacVain snapped. "That was Tweecus's brainstorm. Krator never approved it."

"But the fact remains that the story's been shown everywhere outside the Free World."

"Talk to Acre about that."

The Chairman adopted a more conciliatory tone. "Skipper assures me that once she's back in the Free World anything she says will be completely blacked out by the media. And when Tall Blondes is just Mexican women again, no one will care."

"He's right."

The Chairman paused, as if shifting gears.

"You and I know the demographic projections," he said in a worried voice that MacVain had never heard before. "It's getting hard to find a mall where the clerks speak English."

"I know," MacVain agreed.

"And the abortion ban has not had the effect we had hoped for."

MacVain suppressed the urge to say "I told you so." Since the fundamentalists added the anti-abortion amendment to

378

the Constitution, abortions had become so expensive that only White women could afford to have them.

"The future of the West is in our hands," the Chairman continued. "History will judge us harshly if we lose our grip now. I've sounded out the other members on this, and they're all agreed. We think that Krator should occupy the high moral ground and re-unite the firefighter with her family as soon as possible."

"Is she crazy yet?"

"No."

"That's risky," MacVain said.

"Even sane people need corroborating evidence. There's video of her running away from an ambulance in Mexico and delivering a delirious rant to a known terrorist. Skipper recommends that tomorrow we hold an open house in the Nathan Whyte Laboratory so the foreign media can see that there's nothing there but a boring science facility producing genetic therapies."

"How about a museum documenting its medical history?" MacVain suggested. "That way they can see that Grazziella's story is a tale told by an idiot."

"Can a museum be built in a day?"

"Tweecus built a museum at Nathan Whyte years ago, but we wouldn't let him open it for security reasons. But now it proves that the laboratory has nothing to hide."

"Do it!" the Chairman said.

* * *

El Tigre came into the safe room at Tranquility Base.

"Monterrey's received an urgent communiqué that you need to see," he announced. "Laredo's developed a source within Krator itself—and it confirms the firefighter's story."

He unfolded a sheet of computer paper and read it aloud:

EarthRageLaredo to EarthRage Monterrey:

We've developed a source within Krator. The source reports the existence of a project to breed a race of geniuses by means of genetically-engineered embryos. The embryos are implanted in women abducted by means of a secret date-rape drug called L-RetroBan.

Kelly Grazziella was one of the experimental subjects. Details to follow.

"Wow!" Jack exclaimed. "If they think the firefighter's speech was a bombshell, wait until they hear this—and straight from the belly of the beast!"

* * *

When the plane carrying Kelly Grazziella landed in San Francisco, an official boarded the aircraft and informed the pilot that SFO airport had been evacuated due to a terrorist bomb threat. Kelly Grazziella could disembark as planned, but all the other passengers and crew would be diverted to an airfield across the bay.

The missing firefighter walked down the ramp into the lenses of the Mexican television cameras, as the State Department had agreed. But the welcoming crowd was an assembly of professional actors, whose cheers and signs had been carefully scripted by One World News.

Joe and Giovanni were waiting behind a yellow cordon of police tape outside the range of the microphones. Kelly embraced them both, for a moment unconscious of the camera lenses bearing down on them. She was bursting with things to tell them, but officials hovered within earshot, so all three of them walked silently down the empty corridors toward the exit, not daring to speak. In the main concourse, a big-screen TV was tuned to One World News. Kelly stopped to watch a nearly-live picture of herself embracing her father at the airport. An anchorman read from Van Squint's script:

> "Kelly Grazziella, the firefighter captured by the Mexican terrorist ring, Guloggers, returned home safely this evening, after the Mexican authorities negotiated her release. Grazziella had disappeared from the site of a wildfire on Monday morning under mysterious circumstances. On Thursday, she was located by a search-and rescue team and taken to a hospital in Sacramento, California, for medical observation. A short time later, she was abducted from her hospital room by the Guloggers terrorist ring and taken to Mexico."

> The video showed an unflattering, close-up of the Cuban-American doctor who had been in the ambulance with Kelly, his white coat smeared with blood and dirt. The newscaster identified him as the ringleader of the kidnapping plot.

> "The authorities refrained from reporting this event to the public until the safe release of the firefighter was assured. Senior attorney Vaughn MacVain of the Krator Corporation said in a rare public statement today that 'The government of the Free World categorically does not negotiate with terrorists, but it does encourage friendly governments to assist in situations where the life of the hostage is in imminent danger. Our sole concern was to reunite Kelly Grazziella with her family as soon as possible.'"

"Isn't that the doctor you beat up in the ambulance on Mexican TV?" Giovanni asked.

Kelly did not hear him—she was still transfixed by the television:

> The words "Nathan Whyte Laboratory" were scrolling behind the anchor desk.

> "Today, Wassily Tweecus, winner of the President's Medal of Freedom, announced the opening of a new museum in Davis, California."

Kelly watched in amazement as the white-maned scientist gestured through a glass wall to the laboratory where she had been taken by Chad Weed years earlier. The scientist's face glowed as he announced his museum to the world:

> This laboratory is where I made my most fundamental scientific discoveries. And it's been preserved exactly as it was, as proof of my priority in this important area of research. It is a monument to the discovery of remote diagnosis, a process for identifying genetic diseases *in utero*, making their treatment so much easier. Beginning tomorrow, the public will be able to look through this window into one of the great moments in the history of science.

Kelly remembered with vivid clarity the time she had spent in that room. She saw Tweecus transcribing the readouts of the instruments into a small green notebook, then pulling a wheeled, stainless steel cart closer to him. The cart had several open shelves holding medical supplies needed for the experiment. She recalled that the sturdy frame of the cart was dented in one place, as if it had once collided with another. She remembered Tweecus rotating the cart to reveal a small drawer at the opposite end—inside were two experimental log books of the same size and color as the one in his hand. He had added Kelly's notebook to the stack and closed the drawer again.

The television camera panned Tweecus's laboratory through the window of the exhibit. Everything was exactly as Kelly remembered it. And there, in one corner, the steel utility table on wheels with the little drawer where Tweecus had stored his hand-written logs of experiments. Kelly's heart raced as she wondered if the little green notebooks were still inside, documenting, in Tweecus's own fastidious script, exactly what he had done to her and the other two women.

He was so obsessive, they must be there—Tweecus himself had just said that his shrine was preserved exactly as it was at the time of the experiments. And now the secret laboratory was open to viewing by the public—and penetrable by EarthRage!

Kelly and her father, led by Giovanni, quickly exited the terminal and walked to the vintage yellow pickup truck parked in the VIP lot. "Your boss told us to use his truck to drive down here to meet your plane," Joe Grazziella said. "And I've fallen in love with it."

"The engine's not computerized, so it's real hard to bug," Giovanni explained. "And it's got no transponder."

Kelly slipped onto the bench seat next to Giovanni.

Suddenly she saw a man hovering outside the car—and a wave of terror swept over her as it had on the hillside in Matamoros.

Kelly's father wrapped his arms around her, holding her tight like his little girl.

"He's a friend of mine," he assured her. "He was watching the truck while we were in the airport—in case Krator got any ideas."

He held her until her breathing returned to normal.

They looked at one another with a closeness that they had not shared in years.

"I love you," she said, burying her head in her father's shoulder.

"I love you too," he told her.

For several minutes they sat motionless, entwined like vines.

"When your mother died..." Joe Grazziella hesitated, watching Kelly's reaction.

She was listening but did not stir.

"The farm. I'm sorry that it came between us."

"I'm sorry too," she said.

"I didn't know what else to do, and the Clydesdales promised to keep the oaks."

Kelly's eyes met his. "That's all behind us now," she said.

Giovanni turned the ignition, and the truck started with a menacing growl. He merged it onto U.S. 101. Because it had no transponder, it was invisible to the vehicle-tracking system mounted on the cell towers.

"There's a phone number that I have to call, but it needs to be done by someone not on the watch list," Kelly told them. "A person not connected electronically to any one of us. And it should be done before we get home."

"I know just the person," her father assured her.

"I thought you'd want to rest a bit after all you've been through," Giovanni said.

Kelly placed her hand on Giovanni's muscular thigh—until now she had only touched his hand.

"There's not a moment to lose," she said. "We've got to be in Davis tomorrow. For the museum opening!"

17

COYOTE DANCES

How does one respond to such fantastic allegations—that the government of the Free World kidnapped an innocent person, held her without access to a lawyer, and tortured her in a Mexican prison? This is the standard refrain of known terrorists. But this latest claim—that Krator is hiding a secret biotech breeding program that uses genetic engineering to manufacture a master race—such charges would be monstrous, and monstrously offensive, if they came from someone who is not delusional.

Spokesperson, Krator Inc., London Office

When Amadeus arrived at the Hungry Coyote Restaurant, Deirdre was already waiting in the parking lot, her somber mood caught by the glare of the security lights.

"What's the matter?" Amadeus asked her. "I thought you'd be glad that our source's story is on its way to you-know-who."

"I am, but working in a media blackout wears me down. I mean, will her information ever see the light of day? Maybe someday we'll hear we've done great. But sometimes I wonder if it's worth it—all this risk while the big shots are beyond the reach of justice."

Amadeus gave her arm a sympathetic squeeze.

Above the door, a neon sculpture of a coyote pulsed with a palette of vivid colors, welcoming customers with repetitive sweeps of its tail.

"And then the other day," Deirdre continued, oblivious of the neon, "when Boone was about to announce the Rapture of the First White Kernel, what happens?—the firefighter shows up in the nick of time!"

Amadeus held the door open.

"God, that made me mad!" she fumed. "Only thirty seconds more, and the Fellowship would have been history. Couldn't she have stopped to tie her shoelaces?"

There was a party of seven ahead of them, talking loudly with one another while they stood waiting for a table.

Amadeus signalled the hostess, holding two fingers aloft.

Just a short wait, she signalled back.

"You've said that Boone is a false prophet," Deirdre continued. "You've said that he's made the Bible into a golden calf."

"Yes, I did say that."

"You've said that Boone is not even a real Christian."

"He thinks that loving thy enemy is a sign of weakness."

Deirdre's sea green eyes locked onto his. "So why didn't God take Boone down when he had the chance?"

Amadeus paused, caught in the crosshairs.

The party of seven moved into the dining room, making the foyer as quiet as a church.

"The conventional answer is to refer you to the Book of Job," he said:

> "Were you there when I placed the planets in their orbits? Was it you who shaped Leviathan and gave him dominion of the deep?"

He could see in her eyes that it was not the answer that she wanted.

"Will we ever see big shots like Boone brought to justice?" she asked pointedly.

"See it? Maybe not. Justice happens in the fulness of time—and not always in the way we expect it."

The hostess led them to the table and handed them copies of the over-sized, glossy menu.

On the cover, a cartoon coyote sprawled across the letters of the restaurant's name.

Underneath was an explanatory caption:

> The American Indians see the mischievous Coyote as a trickster with creative powers. Coyote's amazing adventures delight audiences while explaining the inexplicable.

Coyote Waits

The Boones were in their Dallas town house watching Kelly Grazziella walk down the jetway at the San Francisco airport.

"She connived in her own disappearance," Boone said. "Cato Magruder told me it was a failed attempt to destroy the Fellowship. It would've been better for everybody if she'd died and stayed missing."

Boone raised himself slowly from the rose-colored sofa and reached for a coffee-table book on Japanese kamikazes—one of the signs of impending depression.

"We need to get away," Tammy Jo told him, taking the book from Duane's hands and replacing it on the table. "Let's spend a few days at the ranch."

She called Orville Fuller, the Fellowship's liaison to Krator, and asked him to accompany them. Fuller had been at the televangelist's side since Boone was a penniless pastor at a cinder-block church in Laredo, and the presence of old cronies made Duane feel less anxious and depressed.

Boone went into the study to retrieve his prize Bible, the book that had once belonged to Silas Garvey, the fundamentalist theologian. It had been bound in rust-red deerskin and given to Duane Boone III in honor of his achievement as television's top-grossing evangelist.

Boone reverently took the book in his hands, awed anew by the inscription embossed in gold upon the cover:

Dr. Duane Boone III, Christian, Leader, Prophet

It made him feel like the book's author.

He opened a manila folder thick with his transcriptions for the *Book of Voo* and inserted each sheet of paper written in longhand after the chapter and verse of Scripture that it replaced. When he had finished, the closed Bible bristled with squared-off spines like a mutant stegosaurus.

"Let's take it back to the office before we leave," his wife suggested.

"No, I'm taking it with me."

"We could leave it here in the fire-proof safe."

Boone did not answer but went outside to the huge RV containing his mobile office. He locked the Bible into its glass-fronted, temperature-controlled cabinet, then nodded to the driver to take off. As the slowest vehicle, it left ahead of the column.

Boone, Tammy Jo, and Orville Fuller took the royal blue Cadillac with its distinctive hood ornament, an eagle of gold with a lamb in its talons. As the Cadillac turned out of the driveway, black SUVs full of bodyguards slipped in ahead and behind, forming a phalanx of vehicles.

The convoy took the main highways to the margin of the Dallas metropolitan area, then traveled on back roads as it got closer to the ranch. It was a clear, moonless night, and the vehicles were traveling at a steady speed down a two-lane road of rippled blacktop between parallel barbed-wire fences, starkly lit by cones of headlights. As they neared the ranch, they saw the tail lights of the office RV, and the column slowed to keep pace with it.

Suddenly, there was a coyote standing in the middle of the road, brazenly staring at the on-coming vehicles.

The driver of Boone's mobile office swerved to avoid it. Already top-heavy from the satellite transmission equipment on its roof, the big RV wobbled in a series of S-shaped skids, ran onto the soft shoulder, toppled onto its side, and then plowed noisily through the brush for a considerable distance, its left wheels spinning in the air. When it reached a depression eroded by rain, it tipped onto its roof and came to a stop.

Boone's Cadillac slowed evenly, stopping near the damaged RV. Miraculously, the driver was not hurt. His seat belt was fastened, and the air bag had inflated, locking him into place. Boone's staff found him hanging upside down in the turned-over truck, dazed and a little embarrassed but otherwise uninjured.

The mobile office was a dented hulk. The side door had popped open on impact, and almost everything inside the truck had piled up behind it. As the truck bounced from one hummock to the next, its contents were pushed out the opening as if from a dispenser, then pulverized under the careening side of the vehicle.

The furrow made by the disabled truck was paved with papers, office supplies, smashed mementos, pieces of furniture, and circuit boards from several dismembered computers. But Boone was most disturbed by the condition of his prize Bible.

A piece of metal, perhaps the sharp edge of a broken computer case or a panel from the twisted wall, had shattered the glass door of the Bible case, then sliced the book open along its spine, parting the deerskin like a surgeon. The book had exploded into separately bound folios that marked the track of the damaged truck as clearly as a dotted line.

Orville Fuller and Duane Boone III emerged from the car and surveyed the scene under the clinical glare of the headlights. Without a word, Fuller began moving methodically from one folio of Bible pages to the next, gathering them up and returning them to the car, until the text was fully restored. But he never found the inscribed cover.

Meanwhile, Boone was crashing through the scrub like an angry bull, searching for the looseleaf pages that comprised the *Book of Voo.* With the help of his chauffeur and bodyguards, Boone finally collected a fistful of remnants. But as the chauffeur opened the door of the Cadillac to place the stack of pages safely inside, a sudden, chill wind, like a foretaste of winter, swept the pages from his hands and tossed them about like snowflakes.

The driver pulled himself from the damaged truck and stood watching the frenetic quest. A moment later he began to laugh. The laughter made Boone furious, and the driver laughed even louder—howls of laughter, his eyes tearing over—as the only copy of Boone's revelations lifted into the air and disappeared into the darkness.

EPILOG

On the West Coast of Mexico

The Pacific Ocean was as blue as Jack Adair remembered it. In the distance, a white line of high-rise hotels marked the shoreline, but the surfing beach was almost deserted. Swells rolled in from the open ocean in long, semicircular arcs. A half-dozen young men balanced like acrobats on the moving curl of the waves, then swerved aside at the last moment as the emerald walls collapsed in a fury of foam.

Renato was waiting at the rendezvous guarded by two of El Tigre's men. He had come from Mexico City in a separate car so that he and the founder of EarthRage would not be traveling together.

"There's some gentler surf on the other side of the point," Jack said. "Easy waves, good for learning."

They rounded a small headland, and in front of them was a sprawling colonial villa of hand-hewn stone standing where the vista point had been.

Jack stopped in his tracks. "It's amazing! I know it wasn't here two years ago, but it looks like it's been here for centuries."

"It's an almost perfect replica of a sixteenth-century Spanish colonial monastery," Renato observed. "They've obviously spent a lot of money on authenticity, but it's still not right. Those half-round, crenellated turrets—they look like they've been air-dropped from medieval France!"

They edged closer, seeking a way around the edifice when they ran into two sun-tanned young men who stopped to admire Jack Adair's board.

"There used to be a path down to the beach here?" Jack Adair asked.

"Yes, when the rich *gringa* built her castle, she tried to wall off the beach entirely. But the tourist industry has money too."

"It's a lot of 'castle' for one person," the Philosopher noted.

"Well, they say she plans to turn it into an art museum."

The second surfer pointed to where the corner turret cast a shadow on the bluff. "Just beyond the wall there, the surfers carved out some steps down to the beach. The guards don't care if you don't make noise."

Jack hurried down the path and waded straight into the water, embracing the sea. Renato was right behind him, jumping up to let the waves pass under him. Ahead of them, in the cove, a fishing launch was anchored just beyond the surf, bobbing in a gentle swell.

The guerrilla journalist waved to the men in the boat, who waved back. "They're local guys who took over the poacher watch after EarthRage went underground," he explained. "Let's paddle over and say hello."

They paddled seaward in the lee of the headland, where the frothy backwash from the breakers helped to propel them further out. The azure water turned to emerald green, while the sandy bottom shaded from white to indigo. The white hull of the fishing boat slowly rose and fell in the gentle undulations.

Jack hauled himself over the gunwale and began bantering with the two crew members, while Renato circled the craft, looking for a place to board. He was able to get a handhold on the rail with the help of a mooring line tied to a cleat. When he joined the others a party was already underway, lubricated by beer from the ice chest.

The beer was refreshing, the stories convivial, but Renato's spirits were weighed down by the conversation that he had had the night before. He gestured for Jack to follow him to the bow of the boat, where the hull had been partially decked to create a small cabin below.

Jack stood on the point of the prow, his body moving slowly in synch with the swell, his restless eyes searching the sea.

"I've been waiting for a chance to tell you," Renato said quietly. "Fernando has returned to Mexico City."

"Is he OK?"

"Oh yes, he's the same as ever. For the past two years he's been working for a consulting firm in Europe, some data-analysis think tank. He's told me a lot, and he knows a lot more than he's told me."

"And what did he tell you?"

Renato lowered his voice to a whisper. "He says that Krator has launched a worldwide inquiry into the escape of the firefighter—and that the name 'EarthRage' keeps popping up."

Jack laughed. "Well, it's about time we got some credit!"

"Fernando says they plan to make an example of anyone who helped her."

"That means we're doing our job."

Renato's eyes narrowed. "The last time Fernando warned us it saved both of our lives. Have you forgotten so quickly?"

Jack unzipped the pocket of his swimsuit and removed the twenty peso coin to show that he still remembered. The coin was dull and discolored by seawater, but the Aztec god of the sun still danced the cycle of earthly years inside the eight-pointed compass rose.

"I remember when you gave this to me—that day when we first met on the beach. It's my lucky charm," he said, polishing the surface with his thumb as if summoning its power.

A sleeper wave jostled the boat.

Jack lurched forward, struggling to keep his balance. As he reached for the rail, the coin fell to the deck, then rolled on its rim towards the sea.

Renato lunged to intercept it, hitting the deck with a body block. As he pulled himself to his feet, rubbing a bruised arm, the coin was lying flat, a few inches from the edge.

He carefully picked it up, rubbing it between thumb and forefinger as if restoring its luster, then handed it to Jack.

"We make our own luck," Renato said.

ABOUT THE AUTHOR

Peter Reynolds is a native New Yorker who has lived and worked in six foreign countries—seven, if you count California. He has published three nonfiction books. This is his first novel.

You can purchase copies of this book directly from our web site.

http://www.borderlandnorth.com/greatdivide/